Falconcrest City.

What a shithole.

I mean, a lot of superheroes have a kind of reverent, nearly lover relationship with their hometowns, but I grew up on the streets of "The Worst City in America" and it wasn't until I was thirty that it moved up into just being one of the bottom twenty. That was a significant improvement by the way, too, thanks to me becoming one of the city's resident protectors. Props to other heroes like Gary, Mandy, and Amanda. Otherwise known as Merciless, Nighthuntress, and the second Nightwalker. I'm dating two of the three.

Don't judge.

Falconcrest City was a mixture of art deco buildings, modern skyscrapers, industrial hellscapes, and endless slums. It put the rust in Rust Belt with the bonus of being on the equivalent of a hellmouth, drawing every sort of supernatural baddy you could want to the place. The only businesses which remained in the city were arms manufacturing, a car factory that suspiciously made parts needed by billionaire superheroes for their vehicles, and three environmentally unsafe croc shoe factories.

Despite this, the city was not lacking for rich people. Quite the contrary, we had an extraordinarily large number of one-percenters in our ugly stepsister to the Cinderella City of New Amsterdam three states over. Tech bros, old money douchebags, and hedge fund managers were drawn to the city despite its nastiness, and I wondered if that was part of the hellmouth's charm. Either way, it made for a delightful target rich environment when you were a part-time supervillainess.

by C. T. Phipps

ISBN 978-1-63789-666-2
Mystique Press is an imprint of Crossroad Press Publishing

For information address Crossroad Press at 141 Brayden Dr., Hertford, NC 27944
www.crossroadpress.com

First Crossroad Press Edition - 2023

Foreword

Cindy showed up at my house one day. It was a surreal experience, seeing one of my creations coming to visit me in the real world. She was wearing her corset, short dress, and Red Riding Hood cape. Cindy batted her eyelashes, leaned in, and said, "So, who do I have to seduce to get my own book?"

No wait, that was a dream.

Instead, I conceived of the eighth Supervillainy Saga book when I realized that my universe had grown beyond Gary Karkofsky AKA Merciless: The Supervillain without Mercy™. Part of the writing bible for the Supervillainy Saga was that Gary was just a small part of a much larger comic book-esque universe that would have an implied history equal to Marvel or DC.

In the Garyverse, superheroes have been around since the 1930s and I've tried to keep a consistent list of all the ones I've referenced as well as the things they've done. Things like Ultragod capturing Hitler and Stalin or the Second Vietnam War where the US military fought PHANTOM. I created an entire host of superheroes like the second Nightwalker (Amanda Douglas), Mr. Inventor (Galahad Warren), the Black Witch (Selena Darkchylde), and Human Tank (Clarissa

Montehaven) who all competed for screen time when they showed up.

Part of the fun was the fact that Gary had interactions with a bunch of heroes close enough to other ones we know (but legally distinct according to my lawyers). All of these characters cried out for more attention to be paid to them.

Originally, I was considering doing a collection of tales starring the other heroes of the Supervillainy Saga. However, it occurred to me that even that wasn't quite enough to get the kind of stories I wanted to tell out of my head. No, I wanted to do entire novels (but not series) of other heroes in the Garyverse to see what happened. Cindy was the perfect (anti)heroine to start with.

Cindy Wakowski AKA Red Riding Hood has always been my second favorite creation after Gary, rivaled only by Jane Doe of the Bright Falls Mysteries. She was wicked, snarky, and even more of a selfish jerkass than our lead. However, Cindy was also loyal to her friends and willing to walk through fire for them (while complaining about it the entire way). I based Cindy on equal parts Harley Quinn, Kristen Bell's various irreverent characters, and Faith from *Buffy: The Vampire Slayer*.

It is my hope that I will do more stories of other Supervillainy Saga characters after this volume, but I got to give the spotlight to a lot of characters I felt deserved it in this volume. While Gary is correct that his universe literally does revolve around him, that doesn't mean there's not a lot going on beyond his activities. Here, it's the obvious plot for the world's sixth greatest thief: a heist.

And no, Cindy, I'm not telling you who the top five are.

No, Gary's not one of them. He's thirty-seventh.

And don't worry, Gary isn't going anywhere. He'll be back for *The Fall of Supervillainy*, the next volume.

Cast of Characters

Lead

Cindy Wakowski AKA Red Riding Hood: Werewolf and former henchwoman. Now ready to take it to the big time. Gary Karkofsky AKA Merciless' long-term partner but *not* wife.

Supporting Cast

Achilles: The legendary Greek hero and badass. He is kind of a jerk. Getting married to Adonis.

Adonis: The legendary Greek narcissist and sorcerer. Occasional supervillain and jackass. Getting married to Achilles.

Gabrielle Anders AKA Ultragoddess: The most powerful woman in the universe and daughter of Ultragod. Gary's ex-fiancé. The mother of Mimi Karkofsky. Cindy's not so secret crush.

Colt Colton: Agent of the Foundation for World Harmony. Mandy's father. Real jerk.

Jerry Dabrowski AKA Cthulhuoid: One of Cindy's old boyfriends who now is a psychic squid monster. Real jerk.

Selena Darkchylde AKA The Black Witch: Mandy's ex-girlfriend and a reformed supervillain. Sorceress and eco-terrorist who also has a killer singing voice.

Jane Doe AKA Weredeer: An immigrant from the United States of Monsters books (specifically, *I was a Teenage Weredeer*). Gary and Cindy's babysitter for his children and a shifter druid. As snarky as both.

Amanda Douglas AKA The Nightwalker (II): A billionaire hotel magnate's daughter, she found out her family made its fortune through a deal with the Devil. Married to Mr. Inventor.

Case Gordon AKA Agent G: An immigrant from the Agent G series, Case Gordon is a bioroid master assassin and likes it in a silly superhero world more than his cyberpunk dystopia home universe.

John Holmes AKA Juggernuke: A former Foundation for World Harmony agent who received indestructibility and super-strength from a nuclear bomb going off on his face. He's since become a supervillain.

Gary Karkofsky AKA Merciless: The Supervillain without Mercy™: The world's worst (best?) supervillain. Cindy's longtime lover and father of her children. Incredibly dorky yet dangerous. Also, in a relationship with Mandy and Gabby.

Leia Karkfosky AKA Gizmo: Cindy's teenage daughter with Gary. Teen genius and telepath. She is far, far more mature than her mother.

Mandy Karkofsky AKA Nighthuntress AKA Calico: Gary's vampire wife. She is the daughter of Colt Colton and a Korean mother. Raised in Londonium. She struggles to maintain her humanity.

Mindy "Mimi" Karkofsky AKA Ms. Terri: The teenage daughter of Gary and Ultragoddess. She has super-strength and a genius IQ that gets somewhat overlooked compared to her sister's.

Liam Mancuso AKA Crowbar King: A Falconcrest City thug unimpressed with the Karkofsky family. He has a magic crowbar and super-strength.

Clarissa Montehaven AKA the Human Tank: Former villain turned heroine. A trans gadgeteer genius who wears a suit of armor that incorporates alien technology. Briefly involved with Gary's brother when she was part of the Nefarious Nine.

Red Sindi: Red-headed barbarian warrior from the Hyborian Age. Possibly an ancestor to Cindy alongside all other ass-kicking flame-haired warrior women of the past ten thousand years.

Red Splotch: Steve Otkid is the clone/brother of Stanley Otkid AKA Splotch. He has the same power set but is significantly younger.

Revolutionary Girl AKA Gabby: Most certainly not Gabrielle Anders AKA Ultragoddess. She has a ponytail. Ultragoddess does not.

Smog AKA Dragon King: An alien dragon the size of a skyscraper and one of Earth's richest beings. Smog is also a chief financier of terrorism and predatory business practices. Because she's a predator.

Nikki Tesla AKA Doctor Scientist: The new CTO of Omega Corp and Gary's ex-henchwoman. Nikki has no time for this "a rising tide lifts all boats" nonsense. Every villainess for herself.

Dana Vandergast AKA Damselfly: A woman with the power of shrinking and becoming a damselfly. She isn't really very good at this villainy stuff.

World Emperor: A former archvillain from the nineteenth century with steampunk super tech and magic.

[illegible] Montbarron AKA [illegible] Tango [illegible] [illegible] [illegible] [illegible] [illegible] [illegible] [illegible] mor that incorporated electric [illegible] [illegible] revolution [illegible] part of [illegible] [illegible] [illegible] [illegible] [illegible] from the [illegible] and [illegible] [illegible] [illegible] alongside all other [illegible] [illegible] of the [illegible] [illegible] [illegible]

Red [illegible] [illegible] [illegible] [illegible] [illegible]

Revolutionary Girl AKA [illegible] [illegible] [illegible] [illegible] [illegible]

[illegible] Dragon King: An [illegible] dragon, the [illegible] [illegible] [illegible] [illegible] [illegible] [illegible] [illegible] [illegible]

[illegible] Tesla AKA [illegible] [illegible] [illegible] [illegible] [illegible] [illegible] [illegible] [illegible]

[illegible] AKA [illegible] a woman with the power [illegible] [illegible]

[illegible] [illegible] [illegible] the [illegible] [illegible] [illegible]

Chapter One

I Am Not a Henchwench

Falconcrest City.

What a shithole.

I mean, a lot of superheroes have a kind of reverent, nearly lover relationship with their hometowns, but I grew up on the streets of "The Worst City in America" and it wasn't until I was thirty that it moved up into just being one of the bottom twenty. That was a significant improvement by the way, too, thanks to me becoming one of the city's resident protectors. Props to other heroes like Gary, Mandy, and Amanda. Otherwise known as Merciless, Nighthuntress, and the second Nightwalker. I'm dating two of the three.

Don't judge.

Falconcrest City was a mixture of art deco buildings, modern skyscrapers, industrial hellscapes, and endless slums. It put the rust in Rust Belt with the bonus of being on the equivalent of a hellmouth, drawing every sort of supernatural baddy you could want to the place. The only businesses which remained in the city were arms manufacturing, a car factory that suspiciously made parts needed by billionaire superheroes for their vehicles, and three environmentally unsafe croc shoe factories.

Despite this, the city was not lacking for rich people. Quite the contrary, we had an extraordinarily large number of one-percenters in our ugly stepsister to the Cinderella City of New Amsterdam three states over. Tech bros, old money douchebags, and hedge fund managers were drawn to the city despite its nastiness, and I wondered if that was part of the hellmouth's charm. Either way, it made for a delightful target rich environment when you were a part-time supervillainess.

Today my target was Klaus' Jewelry store on Bill Finger Street. It was a big stone building nestled between two brokerage firms and focused on getting cheating douchebags to buy sparkly apologies for their trophy wives. That or buying presents for their mistresses. I think they had a special on getting gifts for both. Which meant they had both good business sense and were sexist assholes. It was well-guarded by some low-level Supers who worked as henchmen for the various gangs but didn't want to go full supervillain, as well as a state-of-the-art lethal security system that was manufactured by Omega Corp (for all your generic evil corporation needs).

I was presently dressed in a trench coat and sunglasses with a wide-brimmed hat and a scarf, and stood to the side of the building with my picnic basket. A low-level glamour spell was over me, preventing anyone from recognizing me until I removed the coat to reveal my costume underneath. Secret identities weren't much of a thing among supervillains since we were often identified as soon as we were captured and then were in the system. However, I did maintain a life outside of being Red Riding Hood as Doctor Cindy Wakowski, M.D. Which, yes, I know is redundant title-wise, but I worked hard for that doctorate.

I pulled out my Omegaphone and slowly started disabling all surrounding security cameras, alarms, and lethal traps in the vicinity. I'd spent weeks scoping out the area and getting the right equipment. Klaus was getting a shipment of blood diamonds in from the Red Slaver and I intended to go fifty-fifty on my profits with Supers without Borders. With any luck, the prize would be mine and I'd be gone before anyone knew I was there.

"Come to mama my little sparklies," I said, rubbing my hands together.

That was when the front of Klaus' Jewelry exploded like someone had set off a bomb inside. Seconds later, customers and staff running out indicated it was something else, especially when energy blasts shot randomly above their heads and between them. Yes, another supervillain had beaten me to the punch.

"Goddammit," I muttered. "I thought this only happened to Gary."

The original Nightwalker had fought a losing battle against evil in the town for a century before dying of old age but the only actual improvements in the city had happened because of a frigging zombie apocalypse finally getting rid of the cult that had made everything so terrible. That and the fact Gary and I had poured billions into the city's infrastructure. Mind you, we'd stolen all that, but it turned out that you could do the Robin Hood thing while making a tidy profit in the process. Besides, everyone from Al Capone to drug lords knew that getting the public on your side was a good thing for a criminal mastermind to do.

"Run! It's probably Merciless and his henchmen!" one of the nearby bystanders shouted. "The Diabloman or the girl who looks like Snow White!"

"Red Riding Hood!" I shouted at her as she ran past me.

"Sorry!"

"Fine," I said. "I'll just have to rob the robbers."

Other supervillains had not been so accommodating to rebuilding Falconcrest City and while zombies, gang wars, and a vampire I occasionally struggled with the fact he had eliminated three-fourths of the city's supervillains, but there were still more than twice the number of superpowered baddies in your average major metropolitan hellhole's. Clicking my magic shoes that turned from high heels to combat boots, I threw off my trench coat and became Red Riding Hood. I ran as quickly as possible to make sure my score wasn't getting stolen from me before I could steal it.

"Murder! Pillage! Plunder!" A deep gravelly voice shouted from inside. It was like a tuba put through a megaphone. "Oh, I love being a bandit!"

Cursing under my breath, I said, "I swear, there's just no professional courtesy in this town."

Klaus' Jewelry's interior was an open two-story central chamber with a balcony for the really, really rich customers to peruse their gemstones in private. Right now, the first level was trashed and a seven-foot-tall mountain of muscle in a turtleneck and men's XXXL jeans, sporting an ordinary ski mask over his face was swinging around his magic crowbar. The guards were dead at his feet as was an innocent counter girl who looked like he'd stepped on her neck after knocking her down.

"Crowbar King," I muttered, reaching into my picnic basket and pulling out my Aeon Ray. "Just when I thought this town's caliber of villain couldn't get any lower. Back away from the goodies, Liam, this is my score."

Crowbar King AKA Liam Mancuso was one of those Supers who compensated for a lack of brains with hitting the jackpot in terms of superpowers. He was indestructible, super-strong, immortal, could fire energy blasts, and even capable of sharing a lesser version of his powers with thugs who swore to him. That was because his crowbar contained the spirit of a demon king that had been imprisoned under a building by Queen Isis during the 1930s. Crowbar King had somehow managed to get it sucked into his crowbar when breaking into the place and could wield it because he was a pure soul: pure evil that is. Yeah, I didn't get it either, but the Sixties were full of stupid villain origins.

A bald spectacled man on the ground seemed to brighten up at my presence before frowning. I recognized him from my research as Klaus Junior. "Oh, it's you, Cindy. I was hoping it was one of the *real* superheroes or villains in town."

"Wait, what?" I asked, looking down at the man. Realizing he was spoiling my entrance, I fired an energy blast in the air above my head. "Halt evil doer! I was here to rob the jewelry store first and I call dibs! I am Red Riding Hood! Reddest of the Hoods!"

Okay, yeah, as catch phrases went it wasn't great but there were worse. Believe me. Besides, I had red hair, so it worked.

Crowbar King turned to me and smiled. I could see his face under his ski mask, which meant he hadn't spent much on a very effective disguise. It looked like something he'd bought at a gas station. "Ah, it looks like Merciless has arrived! Come out and face me, dog!"

I narrowed my eyes. "Uh, just me, chief. Red Riding Hood. Werewolf and medical doctor."

"Bah!" Crowbar King said, disgusted. "I was hoping to have a thrown down with the king of this city! Instead, he sends his sidekick."

My eyes widened and I felt the rise of the beast within me. "Sidekick? *Sidekick*?"

Crowbar King laughed. "Not even that. Henchwench."

Oh, now he'd done it. It wasn't like I was surprised. I'd been a professional criminal for over a decade, and it wasn't like I hadn't dealt with sexist pigs the entire way through. Here's a news flash, they didn't tend to be politically correct as a general rule. Being a hot, bi, Jewish woman was not something that tended to encourage respect. Which was, of course, the reason you had to take it by force.

Powering up my Aeon Ray, I aimed it. "I've moved on from being a henchperson. I'm now headlining my own shows."

With that I unleashed a powerful blast of crimson energy that sailed across the jewelry store and struck Crowbar King in the chest. I had charged it to maximum and it was a blast capable of disintegrating a small building. Much to my irritation, the blast crackled against him as little bolts of red lighting before dissipating. His crowbar's glow became a bit brighter for a second before returning to normal.

"Was that supposed to hurt?" Crowbar King asked.

"Yes, unfortunately," I said, disappointed. "It would have been much more badass if it'd blasted you out the wall. I suppose that would require it to be generating a hard light construct as opposed to a pure ray blast, though."

"I don't know what any of that means!" Crowbar King shouted before charging at me with his weapon.

I ducked and dodged underneath his massive, telegraphed blows while trying to figure out my strategy for dealing with tall, dark, and stupid. Crowbar King was considered a perpetual jobber—wrestling-speak for someone real stars beat up to look good—among the superhero world. Everyone had beaten him from Ultragoddess to Maid Marian but that didn't mean he still wasn't a human wrecking ball.

The reason you didn't hear about the people he'd killed was because they were the people who couldn't think around someone who dramatically overpowered them. I was determined to avoid becoming one of those.

"Missed me!" I said, figuring some good old-fashioned taunting would make him act stupider than he already was.

"I will kill you!" Crowbar King shouted.

"I get that a lot!" I snapped, watching him swing around his crowbar and smash up numerous counters.

"Once I kill you, Merciless will have to come face me!" Crowbar King said, turning toward me.

"What?" I asked, even more offended. "I'm the one fighting you, dumbass!"

"Killing the hero's girlfriend is the perfect way to establish a superhero-supervillain relationship!" Crowbar King said, rubbing his foot on the ground like he was a bull about to charge.

I stared at him. "Where the hell did you learn how to be a bad guy? Misogynists U?"

I was getting genuinely pissed now. Gary and I had a relationship. Hell, we even had a child together and that was nine months of my life I wasn't getting back, but I was an accomplished supervillain myself. I'd been there from the very start and had been instrumental in every one of the gang's successes. It wasn't even a case of being the woman behind the man, it was being the woman *beside* him.

"Once I have defeated Merciless, all will acknowledge me as the ruler of Falconcrest City! I will be the man who broke the King of Fools!" Crowbar King charged at me, going through every barrier in the jewelry store like they weren't even there.

"Well, I agree with your assessment of Gary," I muttered, doing a leapfrog over him as he smashed through the wall behind me. Being as he was a super-strong indestructible moron, he continued through the next wall and into the alley behind it.

That gave me a second to rummage through my picnic basket for more toys: magic fire ax, miniature atomic bomb, indestructible marbles, gas pellets, rocket launcher, and bad luck horseshoe were all options available. Supervillains often limited themselves to one gimmick and that was just stupid in my opinion. You could get an amazing combination of gadgets just by bribing the police to look through their evidence locker. Not that I didn't have powers of my own, but I tried to hold them back for a rainy day. I wasn't quite there yet with bull-in-a-jewelry store here.

That was when Klaus Junior grabbed me by the leg. "You have to call the real heroes! He's already killed three people and my android counter girl."

"Gynoid," I corrected him. "Wait, she was a robot?"

"Yes, you don't have to pay them," Klaus Junior said. "I'll pay you. You can have anything you want in the store!"

"You jerk, intelligent machines are people too!" I snapped, putting away my Aeon Ray and scooping up one of the diamond necklaces on the floor before looking at it intensely. It was amazing what you could see with lycanthropy enhanced eyes. "Wait a goddamned minute, these are all cultured diamonds! You bastard!"

Klaus Junior faked offense. "What? That's ridiculous."

I threw the diamonds back at him. He let go of my leg and caught them. "Do not argue with me about diamonds!"

"Because you're a Jewish woman?" Klaus Junior asked, making me somehow even madder than Crowbar King.

I narrowed my eyes. "Because I'm a supervillain! Where are the blood diamonds?"

The thing about diamonds is that, chemically speaking, they're simple to make and just lumps of carbon. The entirety of their demand depends on them being rare as well as pretty. Cultured diamonds or synthetic diamonds were the great antithesis of this as they had the potential to utterly bottom out the market. It was why the diamond cartels enforced an artificial rarity and insisted that the ones that came out of the ground were the only truly valuable ones. It was why wars were being fought over what really amounted to an especially clear lump of rock. And people called me a villain. Still, you robbed what people wanted.

Klaus' eyes widened at my statement. "How did you know about those? I mean, it doesn't matter! No one can tell the difference among our clients and they're higher quality anyway."

"I can tell!" I snapped. "Now I want my damn products of evil!"

"Here's Johnny!" Crowbar King said, returning to the monster-sized hole in the wall he'd made on his way out.

I stared at Crowbar King. "Your name is not Johnny and forget it, you can keep this loser."

"Wait, what?" Klaus Junior said, terrified.

"I kind of just do what I want. Sometimes I protect the city, sometimes I rob things. Gary prefers antivillain over antihero. I really don't care," I said. "Either works for me."

"You're not going anywhere until I've had my way with you!" Crowbar King snarled.

I blinked. "Really? We're going there now? That escalated quickly. Now I have to kill you. Make me an offer, Fritz."

"What?" Klaus Junior asked, offended.

"I'll take the blood diamonds to kill this guy. Otherwise, I'm bolting. Also, you need to repair your gynoid because she deserves better. A raise too. I also accept Nazi gold. Don't think I don't know what your family did during the war."

"That was never proven!" Klaus Junior said, indignant.

I pulled out my Aeon Ray from my picnic basket and aimed it at his head, not even bothering to look at him.

"They're upstairs in the safe," Klaus Junior said, dryly, putting his hands up. "The combination is 4-20-1889."

"Hitler's birthday?" I asked, turning and staring in horror.

"I had no idea!" Fritz said, looking genuinely appalled. "It was my father's safe!"

"Ahhhhhh!" Crowbar King charged again, lifting his crowbar above his head and charging at me.

"We're going to have words," I said, tossing the gun back in the picnic basket before throwing it to one side.

It was time to be a bitch. My face shifted along with the rest of my body, gaining massive amounts of body hair and mass as I turned into a nine-foot-tall lupine killing machine with claws like steak knives. I even developed a tail as I felt a savage bloodlust erupt in the heart of my stomach. Tonight, was a full moon so the change was almost effortless.

Crowbar King stopped in his tracks, stunned at my new appearance. That gave me a moment to knock his weapon from his hands. I then bit into his throat, betting my magic would trump his since it came from one of the Primal Orbs of the Universe. The satisfying taste of blood, muscle, and bone told me I was right. So did the satisfying crunch that followed as I snapped his neck between my jaws. Behind me, I could hear Fritz screaming his lungs out, which only added to my amusement.

I can't believe he called me a henchwench!

Ooo!

Chapter Two

Where I Conceive My Evil Plan

Well, I successfully got my bag of blood diamonds and was carrying it from the back of my fire engine red Ferrari into stately Warren Manor. The place had briefly been a school for gifted youngers, but we'd managed to buy it back. I was covered in blood but that was hardly going to draw any attention in this neighborhood since my home was in the kind of gated community where you needed a telescope to see your neighbors.

Honestly, the experience of robbing Klaus' Jewelry had turned out to be far less satisfying than I expected. Even though I'd killed the Crowbar King and acquired my target, I'd already heard the news reporting it as an "unidentified supervillain's work." Fritz had either thought he was doing me a favor by not identifying me or he was embarrassed that he'd been rescued/robbed by me, which was even worse.

Passing by my teenage daughter, Leia, and Mindy (who was going by "Mimi" these days) playing video games in the front room, I mentally cursed myself. This was my fault, really. I'd devoted myself to making "clean" heists where I very often never had to shoot up the place and often got away without any fights. I'd forgotten that reputation was everything in this business and if you wanted respect then you had to seize it.

"Are you okay, Mom? You're covered in blood," Leia said, looking up from her sofa chair. She honestly looked a lot like a white-haired teenage version of me and that just made me feel old even if I had stopped aging. Still, I loved her and was glad that I only had to interact with her at mealtimes and holidays. I wasn't about to screw her up the way my mom did me. Gary and his posse were doing a much better job raising her than I ever could.

"It's not mine, sweetie," I said. "Go back to playing *Fortnite*."

"Pfft!" Leia said. "Like anyone is still playing that."

"Where's your father?" I asked, realizing I could wander around the building for hours before finding him.

"By the pool, mom," Mimi said. She was Gary's daughter with Ultragoddess, the world's greatest superhero and thus Leia's half-sister. Mimi already looking like a young Jurnee Smollett. It was nice for my biological daughter to have friends her own age and I happily considered Mimi to be my kid too. The fact Mimi could leap vast distances and lift buildings also made sure that both were safer than most Super children their age.

"Thanks!" I waved back, not correcting her it was Ms. Wakowski. "Have fun at your party. The weed is in the leftmost cabinet. You know where the alcohol is."

Mimi and Leia exchanged a glance.

"Uh, neither of us drink or do drugs, We're fifteen," Mimi said.

"And?" I asked, wondering why she thought that was an inappropriate age to start either.

"We're also not throwing any parties," Leia said.

I tried not to roll my eyes. These kids are such disappointments.

"I heard that," Leia said, reminding me she was telepathic. I blamed that on Gary's side of the family. His brother had been a supervillain and probably stored a bunch of radioactive isotopes under his siblings' beds.

"Right-right," I said, walking over and rubbing Leia's head. I accidentally got blood all over her hair. "Remember, there's nothing either of you could do to disappoint me unless you became cops or started hooking before the age of eighteen. Be sure to keep up on your birth control and cans of Hatchet body spray because boys your age stink. Wait, are you two straight? It's okay either way. I mean—"

"Please go bother Dad," Leia said. "I'm feeling compelled to make robot versions of us to deal with you. Again."

"It wouldn't work," Mimi said. "The last ones we made ran away."

"Ah," Leia said.

"No respect," I said, heading out the side door of the lounge to the backyard pool. "At least I know I'm not screwing up parenting. You can't do that if you're never there."

"We love you too, Mom!" Mimi called back.

I didn't flip them the bird, which I considered to be a sign of growth. Like I said, I loved my kids, but I wasn't meant to be a wife or a mother. My mother, Lindsay Wakowski, had been a drug addicted junkie who sold me to Shoot-Em-Up when I was fourteen. I'll let your mind fill in what that entailed but it was only by a miracle that I ended up escaping and putting myself through school. I owe that to Gary's family who, supervillain sons or not, were the first genuinely nice people I'd ever met in my life.

Opening the glass door to the outside, I hissed as bright sunlight poured down on my face. The Warren Estate had an

Olympic sized swimming pool and its own miniature country club around it, complete with tiki bar staffed by robots. Lancel Warren had barely kept up the place and we'd had to decontaminate the pool because he'd been using it to cool the building's nuclear reactor. I still wasn't willing to take a swim without giving it a once over with a Geiger counter.

Gary was sitting on a deck chair beside the pool, wearing a pair of black swim trunks, and showing off the Hollywood physique that came from equal parts hard work mixed with the fact he'd been blessed by Death as her chosen. Rather than make him a skeletal monster, Death decided to make my lover a pale-skinned white-haired pretty boy as a form of advertising. As solid and dependable as he was as a partner, he wouldn't have had nearly as much luck with me or others if he didn't look like the actor hired to play him in a movie.

"Whoever said it's what's on the inside that counted was ugly as sin," I said, taking him in appreciatively.

Sitting beside him on a beach towel sporting the House Baratheon logo in a green bikini was Jane Doe AKA the only straight(ish) woman in the world I trusted never to sleep with Gary. She had black hair, pale copper skin, and a short but curvy build. Jane was the kind of girl you thought of in novels where the heroine thinks she's plain looking but all the guys fall over themselves to date her. It was incredibly annoying, and her personality arguably made it worse. She was every bit as geeky as Gary and if I didn't miss my guess, they were probably discussing something incredibly inane.

"So, I'm halfway through the comics you sent me," Gary said. "The ones from your world that doesn't have superheroes."

"I know about my world, Gary, I'm from there," Jane said, putting on her sunglasses. It made her look even more cute yet approachable.

"So, the Cyclops guy has eye beams, but they don't incinerate people," Gary said. "They just knock them around."

"Yes, because they're kinetic," Jane replied. "I guess you'd call them hard light constructs."

"See that makes sense," Gary said, coincidentally coming up with an explanation for why the Aeon Ray didn't work. "But he married the clone of his girlfriend, had a child with her, and then abandoned said wife and child to go be with his resurrected girlfriend. So, his wife turned evil and became possessed by Satan yet she's the one treated as the bad guy?"

"Yeah, Madelyne Pryor," Jane said. "I know this is confusing but it's Chris Claremont and—"

"What's confusing?" Gary asked, completely sincere. "This is pretty straightforward superhero dating. I'm just saying he's a deadbeat dad and a crappy husband. His telepathic girlfriends should date Wolverine instead."

I kicked Gary's deck chair into the pool, my lover going with it. The Chosen of Death was promptly soaked.

"Gah!" Gary said, thrashing about. "I have to take radiation pills every time I use this pool."

Jane helped him out. "I only sit around it because it's Illinois in the winter and the pool is like a warm fireplace."

I looked between them both, crossing my arms. "Listen up, you primitive screwheads, we have a problem."

Gary spat out some water. "Did it require you knocking me into the pool? Also, you do realize you look like you just went on a killing spree, right? I'd suggest taking a dip in the pool yourself but I'm afraid you'll attract sharks."

"Oh right," I said, looking down at my blood-soaked outfit. "I do kind of look like a slasher movie victim."

"More like villain," Jane said. "Did you eat someone?"

"Cindy doesn't eat people," Gary said. "I think."

"You keep telling yourself that," I replied, spitting up some Crowbar King that got stuck in my teeth. "Anyway, we have something important to discuss, something that benefits me."

Jane rolled her eyes.

Gary stood up, turned intangible, and passed through me before floating over to the tiki bar where Murderbot was serving drinks. I hated when he pulled his powers on me. Then again, it was a full moon tonight, so it was possible I was just being overly aggressive. It was also possible I had every right to be pissed.

"What's the issue?" Gary said, pouring himself an alcoholic lemonade. It was about five o'clock and the perfect time for one. Walking over, I grabbed his and drank it down in front of him. That was when I realized, to my disappointment, it wasn't alcoholic lemonade but just lemonade. Seriously, what the hell was wrong with my family?

"People don't take me seriously as a supervillain!" I said, practically spitting with pent up venom. No, wait, that was slobber. Damn full moons! How did Jane deal with this? Why wasn't she eating leaves or frolicking in the woods somewhere with Bambi?

Jane looked at me funny. "Are we *supposed* to take you seriously as a supervillain?"

I stared at her. "What the hell does that mean?"

Jane cocked her head to one side. "You call yourself Red Riding Hood, carry a picnic basket full of weapons, and dress in a sexy version of a children's fairy tale character costume."

"And?" I asked, confused. It seemed a perfectly normal supervillain identity to me.

"You are also a bit old to be playing dress up," Murderbot said, behind the bar.

I gave him a sideways look with eyes that I swore turned yellow with predatory rage. "How old do you think I am?"

I wasn't about to bring up the fact Gary and I were about to hit the big forty. Not counting time travel and parallel universes.

"You're, uh, what, twenty-two?" Murderbot said, looking away in terror.

"Better," I muttered. "Anyway, I was humiliated during my heist today."

"I will never understand this world," Jane muttered. "So, what happened, my second favorite werewolf?"

"I kind of ate the Crowbar King today," I said, feeling like I needed to throw up. The guy hadn't bathed in like a month.

"I'm so sorry," Gary said, bringing me a pink lemonade.

I drank it down. "Wait, is this sugar free? Must all things be lacking in enjoyment now that I am a parent?"

"You're not a parent by most standards, Cindy," Jane said.

"Thank you," I said, taking her zing as a compliment. "That's why we hired you as a babysitter."

"Nanny," Gary said. "They're nannies when they live with you."

"Only weekends and Thursdays," Jane said. "The rest of the time I'm back in my home dimension."

"The thing is he called me your sidekick!" I snapped. "Your sidekick, Gary! That's worse than henchwoman!"

Gary kept his expression inscrutable, but I could smell he didn't take me seriously. "That's terrible. The incel, steroid-abusing moron didn't recognize your worth before you killed him."

I blinked. "Gary, how the hell would you feel if no one took you seriously?"

"No one does take me seriously!" Gary said. "How do you think I've gotten away with ninety percent of what I've done? People thinking I'm a fool. Which I'm not."

Jane and I both stared at him.

"Uh-huh," I said.

"Yeah, we totally think you're pretending," Jane said acidly.

"I remind you the Fool card of the Tarot deck is a very important card," Gary replied. "He's a risk-taker and someone who is capable of bringing about great change."

I knew magic was objectively real and thought Tarot was stupid. "Gary, we need to focus. He called you the *King* of Fools."

"Yeah, which is better. Almost a compliment," Jane said.

"Focus!" I snapped. "I'm going to need to borrow one million dollars in cash, the Nightmobile, one of the Omega Corporation's private jets, and complete access to the vault of villain gear we store in the basement."

Gary sighed as if I was asking to borrow the car for a weekend. "Alright, if you want my help then I'm happy to give it. It's your fortune too."

Gary had asked me to marry him on two occasions and if I'd accepted then I would have had access to the legal part of his fortune, which was mostly owned by his sister but that was just to keep the government from seizing it. The truth was that I didn't want to bog down Gary in my drama and I didn't want to link my finances to his either.

It was stupid because I was happy to rob my way to glory, but I had my pride and my own, much smaller fortune. I also knew that, as much as I loved Gary and vice versa, I'd never be more than second or third in his affections and probably was closer to fifth since I knew how much he loved his daughters. Gary loved his (un)dead wife Mandy and probably Gabrielle more than me. He was my best friend and vice versa plus the sex was great but his feelings for them were just different.

"Cindy?" Gary asked, looking into my eyes.

"Oh sorry," I said, blinking. "I was just lost in my own thoughts for a second."

It was a good thing that Leia couldn't read my mind just then. Then again, I had no idea what the range of her powers was and was scared to ask. I also had a fairly good idea she knew what sort of disaster my relationships and feelings were.

"Okay," Gary said, not really understanding. That was another factor in our relationship. He was supportive, kind, and didn't understand a damned thing about me most days.

"You can't help directly," I said, wishing I could make things different between us. "This is something I must do for myself. I need to do something that will cement myself as a supervillain that everyone has heard of, and everyone fears."

"Speaking as someone who spent the better part of his adult life trying to become an infamous supervillain, I think it's important to note that being one isn't all it's cracked up to be," Gary replied. "We've managed to find the happy medium of killing most of our enemies, staying useful to the heroes, and taking advantage of the power vacuum in the city. Becoming a big name may mean putting a target on our family's backs."

"Are you going to try to stop me?" I asked.

"I wouldn't dream of it," Gary said, showing that bright warm smile that made me want to headbutt him. "Just tell me if there's anything I can do for you."

"I'll keep it in mind," I said, and then I looked at Jane. "You think you can protect the kids while I'm gone?"

Jane had pulled out an Omega DS and was playing the *I was a Teenage Weredeer* video game. "Yeah, because I haven't been doing that for most of their lives."

I stared at Jane. "If I return from this mission deciding that the real supervillainy was the friends I made along the way or that my real focus should have been my family, I give you permission to shoot me."

Jane made a finger gun at me without looking up. "I will too."

"Good," I said, meaning it.

"Have you decided what crime you're going to do in order to make your mark?" Gary asked.

I nodded. "Yes, I'm going to rob a dragon."

Chapter Three

Robbing the Dragon King

Jane put down her Omega DS. "Okay, you had my curiosity, now you have my attention. You have dragons here on your world, too?"

"Yeah, we also have Mariah Carey," Gary said, looking at her. "I don't see why dragons would surprise you."

"Mariah Carey is a dragon on this world?" Jane asked, hopefully.

"No," Gary said.

"Oh," Jane said, disappointed.

As I understood it, Jane was dating a dragon back on her own world named Lucien Lyons. Which was confusing since with a name like that, you'd think he'd be a werelion. Jane was guarded about the details of her life back on Earth Urban Fantasy or whatever Gary called her home planet. I got the impression that nanny—or whatever her job was here—was something of a vacation from what she did on her world.

"I think she is referring to the great and powerful Smog," Gary said. "The richest being on our Earth."

"How has Tolkien's estate not sued you?" Jane asked.

"Smog as in pollution," I replied. "Albeit it's pronounced almost the same so you're not the first person to make that mistake. He's the last great dragon and I want to hit him. More precisely, I want to hit his casino."

"Way back in 1954, an unexploded American atomic bomb was detonated under the ocean by PHANTOM, and it woke up Smog," Gary explained. "Smog stomped across Tokyo multiple times and fought Mega-Gorilla as well. Later, a bunch of giant alien monsters started attacking Japan and Smog secured for himself a pardon by battling them instead. Eventually, the giant monster attacks stopped being a thing around the Eighties and he turned to investment banking. He built the Golden Hoard casino on his own private island and pretty much manages most of the world economy from the comfort of his underground lair."

Jane just stared. "Godzilla is not only real in your world but he's an investment banker. Now I've heard everything."

"I wouldn't really call him a dragon," Gary said. "He's more like an intelligent amphibious dinosaur. Like a giant crocodile or alligator with magic. That breathes fire."

"Yeah, we have a word for that," I said. "It's called dragon."

Gary continued his description of Smog, ignoring my correction. "The Machinist used to fight him a lot during the days when being a billionaire was its own superpower. Hey, remember those team ups that Smog had with the Iron Khan? Japanese Splotch and his giant robot joined in. Western Splotch doesn't have a giant robot and he still gets flack for it."

I rolled my eyes. "Gary, we're really going to need to get your ADHD looked at."

"I don't have ADHD," Gary said before pretending to see something on the ground. "Ooo, shiny!"

I had Murderbot prepare me another lemonade. Even when I didn't have my fur, I ran exceptionally hot in my blood. I also felt the blood crusting and decided I needed a shower. Whether I had any company would depend on how annoying I found Gary in the next few minutes. "Here's the thing, Smog possesses the biggest treasure trove of cash and valuables you're going to find outside of Fort Knox. Whichever supervillain manages to get in there and grab his fortune is going to go down in history as a legend. It'll be the heist of the millennia."

"You'll also be making an enemy of one of the most powerful beings on Earth," Gary said.

"Not if he's dead!" I said, cheerfully.

Gary grimaced and I rolled my eyes. My husband-in-all-but-name was a man who had serious issues with setting out to murder people during robbery. Which was ridiculous since he'd killed dozens of people. I, by contrast, was someone who didn't sweat the details when it came to felony murder. All my victims were bad anyway. Usually.

"Uh huh," Gary said, listening. "Keep going."

"Obviously, I'll need a team, making this up as I went along. "The thing is that I know plenty of supervillains and a few flexible superheroes that might be willing to rip off Smog."

"Why is that?" Jane asked. "I thought he was a good guy after beating the hell out of all those giant monsters."

"He got a pardon," Gary corrected. "Which is different from becoming a good guy. Smog has managed to make himself indispensable to the world's economic and political structure but he's very much not a good guy. He's believed to be the chief financial officer for groups like PHANTOM, the House of Serpents, and the Gene Nation."

"God, your world is such a rip off," Jane muttered. "How does your writer sleep at night?"

"Huh?" Gary asked.

"I said give me a lemonade," Jane said.

Gary handed her his, as opposed to what would be my answer to telling her to get off her fluffy white tail and get her own. Man, he was such a pushover.

"The thing is that Smog just uses those terrorist organizations to manipulate the market and keep Dragon Island from being absorbed by China or Japan," Gary said. "He's also been instrumental in things like negotiating the end of the Second Vietnam War and the reunification of Korea."

"He's a big deal," Jane said. "I get it. Wait, the home of the world's last dragon is Dragon Island? Real bucking original."

"Says the weredeer named Jane Doe," I corrected. "Imagine what we could do if we managed to make off with his hoard, Gary. We could buy the Amazon, the forest not the company, or maybe Greenland."

"President Omega already tried that," Gary said. "They weren't selling."

I narrowed my eyes, "We'll make them sell."

"Uh huh," Gary said.

"We could end world hunger or maybe make an enormously tacky space elevator out of pure gold! Fund research into curing space cancer or buy the *Star Wars* IP for ourselves! The possibilities are endless!" I said, less concerned about what I would do with the money than just taking it in the first place. This was a matter of pride which—as anyone who made stupid decisions based on it can attest—didn't have anything to do with logic.

"Alright," Gary said, nodding his head. "So, you want to assemble a team and go Ocean's Eleven on this."

"More like Thorin's Fourteen," I said, referencing *The Hobbit*.

Jane looked at me.

I looked back. "Let's face it, we've already made the Smaug reference, we might as well own it."

"Fourteen ways is a lot to split the money," Gary said.

"Good point," I said. "We'll pare it down a bit."

"Not what I meant," Gary said. "You should take as many allies as you can bring. This will be hard. I really would like to help."

"No, Gary," I said, taking a deep breath. "This isn't about you stealing my thunder."

"It isn't?" Gary asked.

It was but not entirely. "No. This is going to be my magnum opus of crime. I'm aware of the dangers, though. I need you to be there to take care of the kids in case I fall."

This was, of course, the easiest way to manipulate Gary. Having grown up with a family that loved him and was far more extended than I had ever experienced, he was always prone to thinking of putting them first. I didn't really buy it since if he was putting them first, he never would have become a supervillain in the first place. However, props to him, he was a much better parent than I ever was. Gary did his best to try to be the best boyfriend he could be and support me in my endeavors. If I didn't believe marriage was an inherently misogynist concept meant to rope women into financial dependence, I'd say he was the best husband I could have found. Still, I did feel the teensiest bit guilty about the fact that if you pointed out something would be him sacrificing for the family then he folded like a deck of cards. I kind of hoped he wouldn't fall for it, but he did every time.

Gary blinked then nodded. "I understand."

Case in point. "I do, of course, expect you to avenge me if I die even if it costs you your life."

"Uh huh," Gary said.

"Uh, doesn't that defeat the purpose of him not going along—" Jane started to say.

"One-two-three quiet mouse," I said, making a zip-it gesture with my fingers to Jane. "Or quiet deer in this case."

The quiet game was literally the only game I'd ever played with my mother growing up. Unfortunately, time travel shenanigans and altered reality meant I'd never gotten to take full advantage of the lesson with my own kids. On the plus side, that did mean that I didn't have to do the majority of parenting growing up. That was what sisters-in-law and Janes were for.

"Oh, for Deer Chrissakes," Jane said. I was pretty sure she meant Deer Christ as in the animal versus Dear Christ in addressing Rabbi Joshua ben Joseph. I guess Jane believed in the herbivore version of Aslan.

"I'll figure some way of poisoning the dragon like Saint George," Gary said. "I promise."

"Thank you," I said. "I know you have a phobia of dragons anyway due to something happening in your past."

"You mean, my wife being murdered?" Gary asked, looking like he was already getting sick of this conversation. "The one currently sleeping in a coffin in the basement?"

"Wine cellar," I corrected. "Only poor people have basements."

"For that we'd have to have wine down there," Gary pointed out. "Also, if you can afford a basement then you're probably middle class or above. At least in this city."

"Wine cellar in training," I said, giving him a kiss on the cheek and leaving a blood smear. "I appreciate you understanding all of this."

"I don't understand it in the slightest," Gary said. "However, I support you as a partner should."

I snorted. "Yeah, because that's what romance is all about."

"It kinda is," he replied. "Want to grab some lunch? I was going to do BBQ."

"No thanks, I already ate," I said.

Gary grimaced. "Right. I'll make the preparations you need. Are you starting immediately?"

"No time like the present," I replied. "I'll go wake up Mandy."

"You better shower first," Jane said. "Otherwise, she'll go into a blood frenzy, and it'll be *Fur vs. Fang III: Vampire vs. Werewolf Edition*."

"People would pay money to see that," Gary said. "Oh wait, the *Underworld* movies already exist."

Mandy was Gary's (un)dead wife who'd died fighting a dragon as mentioned before. She was one of the few people in the world I loved, a feeling she returned, and that certainly made both Gary and my lives easier. Oh, and she was a vampire. So, yeah, that was a thing.

I rolled my eyes. "Not everything is a movie, guys."

"I beg to differ," Gary said. "Just don't hesitate to call if you need help."

"I'll have all the help I need," I said, smiling. "Don't worry."

I was incredibly worried because there actually weren't that many supervillains and heroes, I could count on not to rat me out to Smog or who would be inclined to rob him in the first place versus some nebulous "bringing him to justice." I had my first recruit lined up, but I'd need more than her to pull this off. The problem was that my best option really was Gary but the moment he joined the crew, everyone would assume he was in charge, and I couldn't have that.

Either way, I turned into my giant wolf form and did a dog paddle around the swimming pool. I made the entire thing look like someone had slaughtered an army inside, because blood diffused well, but it managed to clean me off. My lycanthropy would also deal with any lingering radiation. I did a dog shake on the side of the pool and turned back into a human before heading on in. Bizarrely, my clothes were now soaking wet but completely clean. That was magic for you, though. Anyway, at least my first recruit was close by.

"Good luck!" Gary called as I trotted off.

"Try not to get killed!" Jane called back.

Heading into the mansion library, I tracked down a bust of William Shakespeare on a desk and opened it up to push the red button inside. That revealed a secret door that led to a pair of firemen poles. I had no idea why the Nightwalker had installed these versus just putting in an elevator, but I jumped on the pole and slid downward. That took me to one of the Nightwalker's two secret bases in Falconcrest City: The Night Den or—as most of us called it—Mandy's room.

"I swear," I muttered, looking around. "Who keeps their lair under their mansion? Talk about advertising your secret identity."

Lancel Warren had been a weird combination of gadgeteer hero and sorcerer, eventually favoring the latter as his health failed circa his hundredth birthday. As such, his base of operations resembled a combination laboratory, trophy room, and a library of much more interesting books than the ones in the official library upstairs. There were ionic columns holding the place up, glass cases containing magical artifacts, and an enormous bed for him to crash on when exhaustion took him. Mandy's occupancy meant the place now also had a bunch of framed punk posters, a coffin next to the bed, a Wiccan altar, and set of electric guitars to practice on. Lancel and she couldn't have been more different in many ways, but they were similar in many others.

To my complete lack of surprise, there were a pair of cosplaying groupies in Mandy's bed. They were dressed as Viking Lad and Valkyrie Girl, which was just wrong since they were brother and sister in real life. The heroes they were cosplaying as, not the groupies, I hoped. Mandy needed regular blood and had stopped killing criminals, so she needed a supplementary source of hemoglobin. It wasn't like any of us here could condemn her for it since Gabrielle still regularly showed up for booty calls. Hell, my little black book was an entire phone book.

Walking up to the groupies, I slapped my hands together and howl. Both jumped up in the air. "Out, out, out! Get some cookies and orange juice from the kitchen. If you need a transfusion, I'll call the hospital for you. If you're already dead, well, I'll know in a minute and have your body incinerated. That's much better than Gary raising you as intelligent zombies. We're not going through that again."

Both groupies moaned and looked disappointed.

"But we were hoping to see Merciless!" the Fake Valkyrie Girl said. "He's on our list."

The Fake Viking Boy nodded. "We have a hundred hottest superheroes list. We're blogging about sex with each of them. We're about halfway through."

I had to admire their brand of investigative journalism. "He has strict threesome rules, dear. Only people he has known a long time or elves. Believe me, I've tried to get him to loosen up on them. But like Chandler and Joey, you just can't jump into it."

The Fake Viking Boy frowned in disappointment or confusion. It occurred to me he was young enough to have been a kindergartener during *Friends'* original run yet was now somehow legal. God, I wished Gary hadn't fixed the time stream to function in a straightforward consistent manner. It made me feel old.

"Who? Are they superheroes?" Valkyrie Girl asked, depressing me further. "Listen, maybe you could get us the number of his sidekick? You know, the hot redhead with the fairy tale gimmick. Are you her mother?"

Somehow, they managed to make it out the room alive. I'm not sure how. I managed to scare them both up the firemen's pole There were objects thrown and bites. I'm like ninety percent sure my bite doesn't turn people into lycanthropes. They rarely lived long enough for me to see. Either way, these ones were not my concern right now.

Mandy was a trained spy from practically birth, her father being a Foundation for World Harmony agent who wanted her to follow in her footsteps. Add the fact she was a vampire with the power of an Elder and she was perfect for my plan. There was no one I could think of better to help me pull this off. So, I walked over to her coffin and knocked on it. "Wakey, eggs and Bloody Marys."

"Suck off!" Mandy muttered from within. "It's barely noon."

Okay, maybe this would take some convincing.

Chapter Four

Where I Get My First Recruit

One of the things about vampires in our universe versus, say, Jane's was the fact that while they didn't like sunlight, they didn't explode when they were put inside it either. At least the powerful or old ones didn't. Instead, it just made them irritable to wake up in the morning. Which wasn't that dissimilar to me after I had an all-nighter. Unfortunately, I wasn't going to wait until sundown to talk to her about this.

I knocked on her coffin some more. "Gary's been kidnapped by aliens! We must rescue him!"

The top of the coffin popped open, and Mandy sat up, wearing a white gown that made her look like she'd escaped from a Hammer Horror production. Her coffin was full of native soil but, somehow, it didn't stick to her. Hell, her hair was exceptionally well done and looked naturally curly too. Gary often compared her to a Eurasian Kate Beckinsale, but I personally didn't see the resemblance. She was just hot, pale, and dark haired. Oh, and a vampire. So, okay, maybe they had a few things in common, but she reminded me more of several other actresses.

"Where? What aliens?" Mandy asked.

"It was the princess of moon," I replied. "She and her sailor scouts intend to kill him by snu-snu."

Mandy sighed. "Of course, you were tricking me."

"Don't joke, I expect that's how Gary will ultimately die," I replied. "Well, at least that's how I think he'd want to."

"Don't rip off *Futurama*," Mandy said, turning to me. "What do you want, Cindy? Also, don't use Gary being in danger again as an excuse."

"Scouts honor," I said, crossing my fingers.

"That's not how you do the oath," Mandy said.

"I was never a very good Girl Scout," I said. "It's a great way to case people's houses to rob them. You drug the cookies and you're in."

Mandy stared at me with her cold dead eyes that resembled a feline's. It made me want to bark at her. Really, I needed to get some shots for this or something. "Cindy. Please."

"Fine, fine," I said. "I will never use Gary against you again, or the kids, or the world ending. Anyway, I wouldn't wake you up and chase out your snacklettes unless it was important."

"A shame as I could use a bit to eat if I was going to listen to this," Mandy said.

"I'm here," I said, offering my neck.

"You smell like blood and radioactive chlorine, which actually puts me off eating," Mandy said. "Did you eat someone today?"

"Crowbar King," I said.

"Ah, no great loss then," Mandy said, sliding her legs out of the coffin and getting up. "I guess I'll have to do with bagged blood unless one of Gary's hand-me-downs is still around the house."

I snorted. "Gary is actually pretty monogamous. There's only like four other women he sleeps with other than the two of us. Not counting alternate versions of ourselves and elves."

Mandy gave me a sideways look.

"What?" I asked.

Mandy headed to a nearby bookshelf where she pulled a copy of Dracula and revealed a secret compartment. This had originally been used by the Nightwalker to store evidence, but Mandy had converted it to a walk-in fridge. She emerged seconds later with a bag of O-positive and a bottled water that she tossed to me.

"Here ya go," Mandy said. "I'm sorry I don't have any dog bowls for you to lap it out of."

"Funny," I said, popping it open and drinking it down in a few gulps. Killing people made me thirsty. "In the words of Meredith Brooks, I'm a bitch, I'm a lover, and I do not feel ashamed."

Mandy stared at me and finished off her blood bag. "Okay, you got me up in the middle of the day. I'm energized for the next hour or so, horrifying ball of fire in the sky or not, so what exactly do you want? It better not be ear scratches."

I snorted. "How much of a dog do you think I am?"

Mandy raised an eyebrow.

"Fair enough," I said. "To be fair, ear scratches are awesome, but I want to become the world's greatest supervillain."

Mandy didn't react at all for a moment. "Okay. I'm going back to my coffin. Wake me up when the moon is in the sky unless you're chasing your tail."

Mandy turned to walk away.

"I want to hit Smog the Dragon," I said. "Hopefully we won't need a dozen dwarves, a Mage, and a landed gentryman to claim it all."

Mandy stopped mid-step. "You know Tolkien fans would say the two names are not actually similar. It's more Smowg than smog."

"And if it were Justin Timberlake explaining it, I still wouldn't give a shit," I replied, annoyed my Tolkien fandom was being questioned. "I still want to steal his fortune."

"Alright," Mandy said, spinning back around. "You want to hit the Dragon King's hoard. I am intrigued."

"The who?" I asked.

"The Dragon King," Mandy said. "Smog is his name. The Dragon King is his codename. You know like I'm Calico and you're Red Riding Hood."

"I preferred Nighthuntress," I said. "Why change it?"

"I wanted to be my own thing instead of a legacy," Mandy said. "Besides, people were always confusing me and Amanda. I figured she had enough problems living up to the Nightwalker's legacy without me complicating things."

"So, you decided to become Calico the Vampire Cat," I replied. "Even though you wear all black and can't become a cat as far as I can tell."

"I'm working on that," Mandy said. "Give me some time to master shape changing. It's harder than it looks."

"I don't think that's the issue," I said. "You're confusing your naming conventions. You need to stick—"

"Do you have any plans whatsoever?" Mandy interrupted.

I made a pair of finger guns and pointed them at her ample chest. I swear, they'd gotten bigger despite the fact she'd gone on an all-liquid diet. "Not in the slightest. I figured I would find some super-intelligent ne'er do well and have her plan it for me."

I'd had a plan for robbing Klaus' Jewelry today and we saw how that turned out. From now on, I was going to wing it.

Mandy raised one eyebrow. "Uh-huh."

"The Dark Lady of Mordor does not share power, but I do delegate," I replied.

Mandy pinched the ridge of her nose as if she was getting a headache, which I was pretty sure vampires didn't get. "So, why would I want to help you in this?"

I knew I had her. All that mattered now was going through the motions to let her be convinced. "Because the Dragon King is a financier of terrorism. Because you are just like me in wanting to establish your rep among the world's superheroes. Because it's the kind of intellectual challenge that you'd enjoy solving. Also, you hate dragons."

Mandy had once been an ordinary human woman, at least in terms of biology, before she'd decided to become a superhero and fight evil. I know, what a waste of her talents. She'd ended up getting herself killed saving my life from a dragon. A different one from Smog, strangely enough. Gary had brought her back with the *Book of Midnight* and now she was the wonderful bloodsucking creature of the night we knew and loved. Minus a couple of hundred years in the future and failed attempts to cure her (long story).

"I do not hate dragons!" Mandy said, offended.

"A dragon killed you!" I said. "Of course, you hate dragons."

"That would be speciesist!" Mandy replied.

"Oh my God," I muttered, disgusted. "Supernatural giant reptiles are not a race! They're a monster. Have you been hanging out with Jane?"

"Jane raises your children," Mandy said. "I don't think I have room to complain about monsters, being a vampire."

"Yes, so I don't have to!" I replied. "And of course, you do! Listen, if pigs had guns, then they'd shoot farmers. Being a monster isn't a bad thing, but they can't hold it against people when their prey shoots back. The real point of this is all is undeniable, anyway! Money!"

Mandy stared at me. "I have an IQ of one hundred and eighty, and I have no idea where this conversation went and how."

"I should point out I'm not far from that and am a medical doctor," I replied.

"You *were* a medical doctor," Mandy corrected. "You aren't allowed to legally practice medicine in the United States anymore."

"That case is still under review as long as I'm rich," I replied. "Funny thing, it's not because I'm a supervillain but because I deliberately killed a patient for money."

Mandy blinked.

"It's okay. He was bad. Probably. I think he was like a drug lord or something," I said, crumpling up my bottled water and throwing it into a wastepaper basket. "Score!"

Mandy shook her head. "Alright, well let's pretend you've persuaded me."

"Yes!" I said, wrapping my arms around her and giving her a kiss. "Money, money, money."

Mandy smiled. "We just have to assemble our team and equipment before Friday."

It was Sunday. "Uh, why?"

"You didn't do any research whatsoever, did you?" Mandy asked.

"I did research!" I said, pausing. "I know Smog is a rich dude! And a dragon! Also, he has an island! Somewhere! Probably in the ocean."

Mandy reached into her coffin and pulled out her cellphone. After a few seconds of typing, she handed it over. "You should probably read this article on Omega News."

"I never watch Omega News. It used to be Far Right nonsense and now it's just Gary's liberal social anarchist nonsense."

"Just read," Mandy said.

I reluctantly took the cell phone and read the headline: DRAGON KING SMOG PREPARES TO RELOCATE HIS ENTIRE FORTUNE TO THRAN STAR EMPIRE.

"Goddammit!" I snapped. "Why the hell is he moving his fortune into space?"

"He bought a moon," Mandy said. "Also, President Anders is trying to impose sanctions on Dragon Island for, you know, the financing of terrorism it's owner has been doing."

"Goddamn superhero politicians!" I said, smashing her phone between my hands. "Always trying to do the right thing and ruining my chance to become stupid-rich."

There was no way we'd be able to get to Smog's fortune if he managed to get into the Thran Republic. The Thran were basically lizard men Nazis but, oddly enough, not shape-shifters like the Tsavong who had colonized Venus. So, David Icke was still a frigging nutcase. The thing wasn't that it would be impossible to rob Smog in another part of the galaxy, harder certainly, but the fact that Thran money was impossible to get transferred back to Earth currency once exchanged. To quote *The Phantom Menace*: "Republic credits? They're no good here. I need something more real." And yes, I just stated that currency exchange was harder than planning an intergalactic heist. Besides, I wanted to be infamous on Earth not Thran Prime. That's like being a famous rocker but only in Japan. I leave that to Spinal Tap.

"You're already stupid rich," Mandy said. "What do you even want with a trillion dollars in cash?"

"A trillion dollars in cash is its own reward!" I snapped. "I'd swim around in it like Scrooge McDuck!"

"I don't think you can actually swim in piles of coins," Mandy said. "Because they're made of metal."

"I'll keep it in cash bills and roll around in it like a leaf pile," I replied, "and yes I've thought about this way too much."

"At least you admit it," Mandy replied. "Also, you're buying me a new phone."

"You can afford another one," I snapped. "Okay, we have to get started quickly. I've already got Gary to finance this shindig and some basics. However, we need to do this before Friday. Are you in or not?"

"I'm in," Mandy said. "I already know at least five or six candidates that might be willing to go along with this crazy scheme. We'll need to do some sub-heists, though, to get the equipment to rob Smog's casino."

"Good," I replied. "Just don't recruit more than five other people."

Mandy looked confused. "Why?"

"Because we're Cindy's Seven," I replied. "If it goes over seven then it doesn't sound right. Cindy's Eight isn't as cool."

Mandy replied. "Are you counting yourself among the seven?"

I paused. "That's a good question. Okay, maybe you can recruit six other people."

"Ocean's Eleven doesn't need to rhyme," Mandy replied.

"And Frank Sinatra didn't realize the best way to rob a casino was just to bribe the people guarding the vaults like they did in Robert De Niro's *Casino*," I replied. "That was before super-technology and magical spells were standard issue. Plus, you know, dragons guarding the treasure."

"Yes, we'll have to slay Smog," Mandy replied. "That will take a serious heavy-hitter."

"Thankfully, my years of playing *Dungeons and Dragons* will finally come in handy. I am a font of dragonslaying lore. Is Smog a Chromatic or Metallic dragon in your opinion? On a scale of one to fifteen Tiamats, how powerful is he?"

Mandy ignored my important stat crunching. "Thankfully, my first recruit for our team is in Falconcrest City."

"Who?" I asked, hoping she didn't mean Gary because that would just be embarrassing for us all.

"The Nightwalker," Mandy said. "We'll just have to deal with some ninjas first."

"I hate ninjas!" I said, grimacing and shaking a fist in the air. "See! Hatred is fun!"

Chapter Five

Night of a Million Billion Ninja

It wasn't until nightfall that we could recruit the Nightwalker, Amanda Douglas rather than Lancel Warren, so we just hung out until then. Well, after I took a shower and changed since the radioactive pool didn't do a great job of cleaning me off. Okay, *I* hung out since Mandy ended up retreating to her coffin when I tried to get her to hear my pitch for a *Game of Thrones* remake with me as Daenerys.

I had the sneaking suspicion that Mandy was the only one of us without any real geek interests but that she tolerated the rest of the house's because we were both sexy as well as delicious. Which, fair enough, was better than the basis for most of my other relationships.

Falconcrest City after dark pretty much became a whole different city. I'd already mentioned the place was a nexus for bad juju, but you never really felt that until after the sun had passed the horizon. After that happened, I swear the city became an entirely different place. It was a crime ridden hellhole in the daytime but during the evening, the place became the Transylvania of the Midwest. Well Transylvania meets film noir meets crime ridden industrial hellhole.

Really, it was hard to put into words, but the place was some sort of Gothic Punk nightmare with the shadows cast by the skyscrapers seeming even darker and the light seeming only to provide extra contrast. And it sure seemed that the full moon was also ten times its normal size and just existed to provide an eerie contrast to the slums below. It was oddly one of the most religious cities out of the Bible Belt but in the context of people nailing crosses, stars, and Buddha statues above their doors to keep out the monsters. There were honestly times I could hear a Danny Elfman score playing in the background as I ran across the rooftops with Mandy to our destination.

I huffed and I puffed as I ran, which I swear didn't start as a wolf pun. "Is there, huff, a reason, huff, that we aren't just taking a car!"

Mandy ran ahead of me, showing no sign of exhaustion. Probably because the undead didn't get tired. "It's good exercise."

"You are dead, and I don't need exercise!" I snapped at her. "I am the total package!"

"Cindy, not everything is about looking good."

"No, just most things!" I replied. "It's hard to say which is more important, looks or brains when you have both like me. That's why I'm determined never to lose either."

The only person who ever cared about me before Gary and Mandy was my grandmother, Hannah, who had adopted my mother in her old age like the saint she was. She was an ancient German-Jewish woman who occasionally woke up screaming, so I'll let you fill in the blanks of her past. Eventually, Grandmother Hannah lost her mind, and my mother stole everything she had before abandoning her in a home where she died alone. I was sold to Shoot-Em-Up a few days later. So, losing my mind was one of my few fears and it was also a reason I was happy to hang around a minor god of death and a vampire. Those who believed immortality was a sucker's game to pursue were quitters!

"You worry too much, Cindy," Mandy said. "Haven't you ever just stopped to revel in being a Super?"

"No," I replied. "Because I'm too busy enjoying being rich, smart, and beautiful. That's enough for me."

"Spoilsport," Mandy said.

"Says the woman who literally has already died and spent years either as an insane monster or possessed," I replied.

Mandy's sarcastic but can-do nature was a fairly new addition to her personality. After her transformation into a vampire, she'd spent years (not counting her time in the future that was who knows how long) as a marauding vigilante killing the worst of Falconcrest City's monsters. I didn't see much problem with that, but Gary had objected to his oh-so-perfect wife becoming mean. He'd thrown himself into finding a cure for vampirism and ended up driving himself halfway insane. Given that's when we initially started our present-day relationship, it perhaps said more about us than even I was comfortable admitting. Mandy had later gotten herself possessed by a dead witch and seemingly cooled off after she was exorcised.

Mandy paused. "That's in the past now."

"Do you want to talk about it?" I asked.

"No," Mandy said. "Freud would have a field day with my issues."

"Freud didn't believe in the female orgasm," I said, simplifying things. "He's not someone I would turn to for psychoanalysis."

Mandy snorted. "I'm just glad to be with you and Gary. It's been a long road getting from there to here."

"Yeah, I'm sure you got faith of the heart," I replied. "Really, *Star Trek: Enterprise*?"

"I thought that was Bryan Adams," Mandy said. "*Star Trek* is an instrumental piece. Doo-doo-doo."

I stared at her. "Philistine."

Mandy looked on clueless then shrugged. "In any case, Amanda said to be around here. She invited me to help deal with the Fist's plot."

I sniggered. "The Fist? Really?"

Mandy stared. "The Fist is what the ninja clan calls itself. It's a centuries-old secret society that practices martial arts, sabotage, murder, and magic."

I grinned. "Is their martial art called fisting?"

"Grow up, Cindy," Mandy said. "Peoples' lives are at stake."

"I've worked the ER, Mandy," I said, dryly. "Peoples' lives are always at stake. If you don't learn to laugh at death, then death laughs at you."

"That would be more profound if not for the fact we know Death and I'd be terrified of laughing at her," Mandy said.

"No, *Gary* knows Death," I said. "He lives in a funny cartoon world where he's pals with Satan. We live in the real world where our lives could end at any second. So, we should enjoy every moment of it."

"That explains a lot of your personality in a nutshell," Mandy said. "Unfortunately, I'm immortal and divorced from the natural cycle of the world."

I rolled my eyes. "Oh, boo hoo, you're pretty and eternal. You just must drink the life blood of the innocent. You and the rich both."

That was when a voice spoke behind me. "I try and be an Arthur Warren style billionaire. Donate to the poor while building up infrastructure."

I jumped in the air. "Gah!"

Mandy smirked. "We're where I was supposed to meet with Amanda."

"No real names, please," the voice spoke.

I turned around and saw the figure of Amanda Douglas AKA the second Nightwalker. Gary tended to call her either Nightgirl or Nightwoman, not realizing it was neither cute nor funny. She wore a long black cloak that was of the same substance as Gary's and provided her a pair of magical "moon-eyes" that looked deep in the soul. Her voice was also given a creepy reverb effect that disguised her identity. I always found it a bit funny that Gary got none of these elements, but he didn't bother with a secret identity anyway.

"Hi, Nightlady," I said, pausing. Wait, damn, I'm doing it too. It just seemed like she was trying way too hard about the whole thing, and it left you wanting to deflate her a bit.

"I am the darkness that moves with the wind," Amanda said. "I am the wrath of the victimized."

"I am Edgelord," I replied. "Yeah, I need your help against a big bad supermonster. To help the widows, orphans, and puppies of the world."

"I'm always happy to help Gary. No matter how much he protests, he's one of the good guys," Amanda said.

I grit my teeth. "Yeah, about that—"

"This is more a Cindy and me project," Mandy said.

I glared at Mandy. It was a 'we' project now? Then again, it occurred to me that I might need her help in all this. I didn't have the best reputation with the cape and cowl set. Even worse than my reputation with the villains of the world really. I mean, collateral damage was to be expected, wasn't it? No, I'm not going to elaborate further but the old lady had it coming. She was probably an agent of PHANTOM or something.

"Uh huh," Amanda said. "Well, I'm willing to hear you out but I have to deal with the Fist first."

I burst out laughing.

"Something funny?" Amanda asked.

"Cindy is mentally fourteen," Mandy replied.

"With a doctorate!" I replied, cheerfully. "Also, the body of a twenty-year-old."

Both Mandy and Amanda looked at me skeptically.

"Shut up," I replied, putting my hands on my hips. "Bio-sculpting aliens were paid for this. The same ones who do half the stars in Hollywood."

"Is that where you were when you disappeared for a month," Mandy said. "We literally thought you were kidnapped."

"Is that why Ultragodess attacked their office in Bel Air," I muttered. "I suppose all the bandages didn't help. Still, she could have used the door. They charged me extra for the replacement walls and roof."

Amanda rubbed her temples. "This is a pretty important mission guys and I could use your help but if you're going to natter on, I'll pass on both your mission and help."

"Natter?" I asked. "Are you my grandmother?"

"What's the sitrep?" Mandy asked.

"The Fist Clan has allied with the Brotherhood of Infamy to destroy Falconcrest City," Amanda said, like she was discussing the weather.

"The Brotherhood of Infamy is still around?" I asked. "Merciful Moses, you'd think we'd have killed enough of those guys to get the message across."

The Brotherhood of Infamy was one of the first groups Gary and I had fought as supervillains. They were kind of half-way between a Cthulhu cult, a hate group, Wolfram and Hart, and the Stonecutters. Their philosophy could basically be summarized as "Supers suck" and "worship demons to give us wealth and power." Which, say what you will about its particulars, was at least an ethos.

They were allegedly behind the decades of criminals regularly breaking out of prison and the general hellhole-ish nature of the city. The more suffering they created, the richer its members got, which allowed them to cause more suffering. Given the rest of the world was full of supervillains constantly escaping imprisonment, I wasn't sure how much I really blamed them for the world's state.

"It's an international cult," Amanda explained.

"Oh," I said, immediately contradicted in my assumption. "Well, that explains a few things."

"You also can't kill an idea," Amanda explained.

"I beg to differ," I replied. "You can kill everyone who holds an idea. I'm still working on that with Gary regarding the Nazis."

The only fight I'd ever had with Gary was when he'd revealed he'd been traveling to alternate timelines to murder their versions of Hitler. How dare he do that without me! That's like vacationing in France without your spouse or mistress!

Amanda opened her mouth then closed it. "Anyway, the Fist and the Brotherhood are planning to manufacture an enormous chemical weapon that they're going to use to kill most of the city."

I blinked. "Huh, that seems like a Society of Superheroes thing."

"Pfft," Amanda said. "They're already backlogged with the events in Ruritania, two alien wars, an invasion by their parallel universe counterparts, and an earthquake in South Asia. That's today by the way."

"I thought things would get better under President Anders," I muttered, noting that Gary had been convinced his tinkering with the timeline would fix everything.

"That *is* improvement," Mandy said with no small amount of bitterness. "The number of supervillains to superheroes has gone down from forty to one to more like ten to one. I attribute it to increased educational opportunities for Supers and less draconian laws. Still, there's a long way to go."

"Face it, every major city needs a superheroic protector and we flat out don't have any out-of-town backup when city-destroying crises like these are going to happen," Amanda said. "It's why I rely on Mandy, my husband, and Gary. Where is Gary anyway?"

Mandy lifted her cellphone. "I called his Superheroes for $$$ building. He can't make it. Apparently, Nyx the Goddess of Night from Greek Mythology has stolen the souls of two dozen children."

I muttered. "Frigging Greek Gods. Didn't we kick them out during Hannukah?"

"That's either an incredibly smart reference to the Maccabean Revolt or literally a reference to you and Gary beating up the Greek Gods on Hannukah," Mandy muttered.

I shrugged. "You screw Zeus a few times and Hera gets all uppity. Then he gets mad if you do his brother."

"Poseidon or Hades?" Mandy asked.

"Ahem," Amanda cleared her throat. "The thing is that we have a disaster to prevent and very little time to do it. This is the third attempt by the Brotherhood to destroy the city this year. Do I have your help or not?"

"Of course," I replied. "Falconcrest City is where I keep my stuff. There are schools named after me here."

"Which teach more than pole dancing," Amanda said. "Surprisingly."

I frowned. Did Amanda and I have a beef I didn't know about? I mean, not that I had anything against pole dancing, but I thought we were friends. Then again, I kind of felt like an asshole given they'd apparently been going around fighting evil while I'd just been robbing banks and jewelry stores. I was dangerously on the verge of an epiphany before I decided that since I donated large chunks of my fortune to charity, it didn't matter, and I should just focus on doing what I had to do to get Amanda to join my heist crew.

"Pole dancing requires an athleticism most women can't match," I replied. "So where are they manufacturing this chemical weapon anyway?"

"Acme Chemicals," Amanda said.

I blinked. "Is Wile E. Coyote helping them?"

"Acme comes from the Greek word *akme*, which means best," Amanda said. "You can't copyright it."

"Fun fact, that many products were named Acme back in the Thirties because that put it in the front of the yellow pages," Mandy said.

"Thank you for that useless bit of trivia, Mandy," I replied. "So, we just go inside and kill everybody. That work?"

"I'd prefer to take them all alive," Amanda said.

"Of course, you would," I replied, sighing.

"Dead cultists tell no tales," Amanda said. "Well, sometimes they do as I can talk to ghosts, but they tend to resent their killers. The more we can imprison, the more we can drain resources from the organization."

"Yes, because that's worked so well with other organized crime," I replied. "Anyway, I'm ready when you are."

"So are we!" Leia said, suddenly standing right beside me in a teenagers' version of a science hero's jumpsuit. Mimi was standing beside her, wearing what appeared to be Carmen Sandiego's outfit except in blue.

I did a double take. "When the hell did you get here?"

"I don't work with children," Amanda said, objecting. Mandy looked as stunned as I did.

"I have super-hearing. How the hell did you sneak up on us?" I asked.

That was when the ninjas attacked.

Chapter Six

Teenage Mutant Zombie Cyborg Ninjas

The ninjas were a purple-colored band of heavily wrapped up warriors that looked straight out of an anime. They were armed with swords, sais, bo staves, nunchucks, and the odd spear for variety. Apparently, no one had told the Fist (hehe) about the invention of guns. On the other hand, if you saw a guy wielding a sword walk toward a bunch of muggers in Falconcrest City, it was probably best to bet on the guy with the sword. It was basically the "Boy Named Sue" rule.

Natural Selection weeded out those poor bastards who couldn't survive wielding anachronistic weapons so that only the scary bastards who didn't need ranged munitions remained. That was when a bunch of flaming arrows held by ninjas wielding bows ignited on the rooftop of a building beside us, about two floors higher. That was just cheap! We were now surrounded by what looked like thirty or more ninjas and that was just excessive. Everyone knew ninjas were more effective when you were only fighting one!

"Cindy!" Mandy shouted in horror. "How the hell did you let the kids get involved in all this?"

"You can't blame me for this!" I snapped, horrified at the situation. "That would require me to do any parenting in the first place!"

"That's true," Mandy said, assuming a fighting position. "Do you want to blame Gary?"

"Sounds good," I said, turning my fingernails into claws as I grew about a foot in height and put on enough muscle that I became a female bodybuilding enthusiast's wet dream.

By the way, werewolves can do that. Well, I could do that. I wasn't sure about other werewolves. In addition to being able to assume wolf, human, and hybrid form, I could also change my body partially to just be "Cindy the Amazon." I hadn't perfected it since it tended to leave a copious amount of body hair I had to regularly remove—too much information I know—but it did give me a decided advantage if I wanted to do something other than savagely tear apart all my opponents.

"Dad thinks we're studying," Leia said, covering herself in an energy shield before shooting out a set of energy claws that I was pretty sure she'd gotten the idea of from one of Jane's other universe comics. Mimi just powered herself up with Ultra-Force energy and looked like she was surrounded by an aura of pure ass-kicking golden power.

"Ha!" Mimi said. "As if the Cindy Wakowski School for Superhumans has anything left to teach us."

I wondered if it qualified as child abuse if comments like that made you want to reintroduce corporal punishment. I didn't seriously entertain the idea anyway. My mom had beaten the shit out of me on a regular basis and it hadn't done anything other than make me want to murder her. My kids were smart enough to get away with it and, worse, Gary and Mandy would believe they didn't do it.

"You know I can hear you, Mom," Leia said, telepathically. *"You don't have to pretend to not care because you are terrified of*

emotionally and physically abusing us the way you were. We understand that your deep-seated phobia, linked with your issues regarding aging, don't actually impact your affection. Every day you work hard to provide for us and make the world a safer place is all the I love yous we need."

"Leia?" I said, aloud.

"Yeah, Mom?" Leia replied.

"Shut up and kill some ninjas," I said. If I wanted to be psychoanalyzed, I would have volunteered the family for a very special episode of Doctor Mindful, Super-Therapist and made a shit ton of money off it.

That was when the leader of the ninjas, I knew he was the leader because he was the only one wearing orange in a sea of purple, stepped forward. "Nightwalker, Nighthuntress, and Red Riding Hood. You were foolish to bring your children—"

"Hold on," Mandy said, holding out her hand. "Cindy, did you seriously just tell our daughter to kill people?"

"Yeah, and?" I asked. "I mean, is this a favoritism thing because she came out of me vs. Mimi?"

"Eww, Mom!" Leia said.

"It's not," I swiftly corrected. "Mimi, go kill people too."

"You got it!" Mimi said, giving two glowing thumbs up. Lightning crackled around her golden aura, showing her full power. Carmen Sandiego never looked like a thunder goddess but maybe that would keep the copyright lawyers off her.

"I mean don't have our teenage daughters kill people!" Mandy snapped.

"Why?" I asked. "My Russian grandfather used to snipe Nazis at their age."

"He didn't have a choice!" Mandy said.

"I'm pretty sure he would have chosen to do it," I replied. "Family tradition. Easiest way to get me in the mood with Gary."

Both my children looked disgusted.

The ninja leader coughed. "Really people? I've got a whole speech prepared here and you're kind of ruining it."

Amanda shook her head. "Sorry, I can't help it. They came with the city."

"I'd remind you that you were a kidnappee when we first met you," I replied.

"You were the one doing the kidnapping!" Amanda said.

"Screw it," the orange ninja said. "Kill them all."

"Including the kids, Overlord?" one of the ninjas asked.

Overlord aimed his hand at the ninja speaking to him and froze him until he exploded. "Yes, including the kids!"

"You're a ninja with ice powers?" I asked. "Oh God, you are just begging for a lawsuit. This is why I liked Multi-Ninja. If I have to choose—"

That was when a bunch of fire arrows were shot at me and I had to duck, dodge, roll, and maneuver out of the way of the enemy archers' attacks. Then the ninjas charged at us all at once, turning the rooftop into an enormous brawl. I used my picnic basket as a club against one of the ninja mooks, only to knock away his mask.

That exposed a hideously deformed desiccated corpse with a metal jaw and glowing electrical eyes. I also saw weird alien growths sticking out from its dead neck, like fungus combined with cancer. The thing smelled terrible, and I would have been able to detect what it was, whatever it was, if not for the fact the wrappings were sprayed down with some kind of industrial deodorant. Body spray! My one weakness aside from silver, fire, decapitation, explosives, magic, super-science, pain, and being hit really hard!

"Hey guys, they're dead so it's not murder!" I said. "Great news."

"Is it?" Mandy said, turning into a swarm of bats before appearing behind one of them to slash their backs with her claws. I questioned how a single person could become multiple animals before becoming one but decided the answer was probably just, 'magic.'

"You're the one with the murder problem!" I snapped, slaying cyborg zombie ninjas with my claws as I dodged under katana and around sais.

"I have a problem with murder!" Mandy said. "That is not a murder problem!"

"You used to be cool!" I said, taunting her about her former past as an antihero. Was it dickish of me? Yes. But I was having fun.

"Shut up and fight!" Amanda said, shooting lightning bolts out of her hands and throwing people around with telekinesis. Her powers were slightly different than Gary's, though both had grown significantly stronger than they'd been when they'd first acquired their Reapers' Cloaks. They were still far weaker than the Nightwalker, even with Gary's semi-godhood, due to Lancel Warren being the Archmage of Earth.

"I'm trying!" I shouted, assuming full dire wolf form and biting one of them in half. Bleah. Cyborg mutant ninja tasted terrible!

I decided to bother with superhero parenting for once and look back to make sure neither of my kids were dead. Much to my surprise, and perhaps annoyance, both were standing over a good fifteen slaughtered ninjas with Mimi jumping through the air to land on the rooftop where the archers were. Then she grabbed one of the ninjas by the leg and started using it to beat the others like he was an improvised club.

"Stop showing off!" I snapped, still able to speak in wolf form. "You're making us look bad!"

"They can show off all they want when we're saving the world!" Amanda called, struggling to battle Overlord as he punched through every spell she conjured. Apparently, he wasn't just a one-trick pony.

I got jabbed in the gut by a bo staff before promptly being smacked around a few more times with a final thwack sending me spinning onto the ground. That resulted in me returning to human form and feeling like crap. "See, that's why no one thinks you're better than the old Nightwalker! No sense of marketing!"

"Do you know how hard it is to be a legacy hero, Cindy?" Mandy asked, jump kicking the bo staff wielding ninja's head off. "You not only have to deal with people always comparing you to the hero who inspired you but there's also all the neckbeards that can't handle a woman in the role. Let alone an Asian woman."

"Then maybe she should do her own thing!" I replied, getting up and kicking the severed head of the ninja off the side of the building. "This is why I think Ultragoddess really needs to go back to being Lightbringer."

"She was named that for like a week!" Mandy said, taking position back to my back. There were only a few ninjas left but Overlord was kicking the crap out of Amanda. Leia and Mimi were also having difficulty with the last ninja that had grown shadow tentacles. What can I say? The less ninjas you fight, the tougher they are. It's a rule.

"I'm just saying, set your goals higher than honoring some dead old guy," I replied. Honestly, I was just being an asshole for the sake of being an asshole. I'd gotten to know Lancel Warren posthumously and he was a pretty decent fella. He'd since gone on to the Great Beyond—well even more so than he had when he died and became a ghost—and I missed him. Certainly, he made Gary more tolerable.

I mean, I loved Gary, and I never thought I'd say that about any of my boyfriends—or girlfriends—but we never forced Disney to redo the *Star Wars* sequels when Cloak was there to reign him in. The amount of stupid shit we've done has just grown since Cloak's final death. The least Gary could have done was force them to pay us a ransom for it. Ah well, with Smog's money, I would finally get the live action *The Hobbit* adaptation I deserved.

That was when I was frozen in an enormous block of ice by Overlord. He'd successfully beaten Amanda and frozen Mandy as well. Freezing someone normally kills them, unless you're a Super immune to cold or have developed life-suspension freezing like the Chillingsworths, but it still hurts like hell. In my case, I could feel the ice on my eyes, and it was pissing me off.

Overlord laughed and stared at me, ignoring that my daughters were beating the crap out of the final ninja behind him. "Insufferable fools! You never suspected that this day would come, did you? That I would spend years nursing my hatred and plotting my revenge! You may have destroyed my mutant zombie cyborg ninjas, but it was all worth it to get you in my clutches!"

I paused. Did I know him?

Overlord ripped off his mask and revealed…a generic looking white guy with brown hair that I didn't recognize. "Ta-dah!"

I was frozen so I couldn't respond. However, the ice around my eyes had melted enough due to my exceptionally high body heat that I could display a bit of emotion on my face. So much so that Overlord recognized I had no idea who the hell he was.

Overlord spoke into the lapel of his costume, to what I presumed was a microphone. "She doesn't recognize me, Jerry. You said she'd recognize me!"

Oh, hell no.

I struggled to break out of the ice, which was actually possible due to the fact I was a *frigging shapeshifter*, and the Overlord hadn't accounted for this little factoid. If he had, he might not have done it on the full moon when I was at my strongest. Turning into a nine-foot-tall wolf-human hybrid, I shattered out of the ice then shoved my clawed hand through his chest. It actually went out the other side before I clenched it.

Overlord looked at me before getting a poetic expression on his face, well as much as someone bleeding internally could. I could also smell him crapping himself, which happened a lot more upon the moment of death than even supervillains liked to admit. I mean, there's just no dignity.

"Live by the fist, die by the fist," Overlord whispered before passing.

I stared at him with my wolf eyes and said something surprisingly human despite having a muzzle. "I mean, it's not my thing but you do you."

That was when I was knocked over by an enormous green thing landing on the rooftop behind me, sending me flying and bouncing against the still-frozen Mandy and Amanda. Neither of them had escaped yet, which annoyed me because Mandy didn't have to breathe, and Amanda could turn insubstantial. Either they were incapacitated to the point of not being able to use their powers or they were letting me do the fighting because they thought I needed a lesson in humility. I had fifty-fifty odds either way.

Turning my attention to the newcomer, I saw a figure that would have made all but die-hard H.P. Lovecraft and D&D nerds puke with its monstrousness. It was an eight-hundred-pound green, blobby humanoid with an octopus head, dragon-like wings, four eyes, and tentacles sticking out of its back. It was naked with very human-like genitalia that also made the male creature the kind of supervillain that would never get on network television. Even the Behemoth wore nice stretchy purple pants to avoid this kind of situation.

"Cthulhuoid," I muttered, addressing him by his cheesy supervillain name despite recognizing him. Deciding he didn't deserve even that minor respect, I decided to switch gears and use his real name. "Also known as Jerry Dabrowski. Great, just great. How ya doing? Miss me?"

"Hello, Cindy," Jerry said. "Not at all."

I have a confession to make. This may shock you, but I don't always have good taste in the men and women I hook up with. I know, I've clearly just blown your mind. There are mistakes and there are mistakes, though. Jerry is probably the absolute worst one that I ever let get inside me, though. Into my heart, I mean! God, get your minds out of the gutter people. That's my place.

Jerry Dabrowski, before he looked like a creature from the mind of everyone's favorite racist Pulp writer (H.P. Lovecraft notably made an exception to his bigotry for Jewish girls like me—eww), was my rebound guy when Gary married Mandy after college graduation. I admit I like pretty nerds and he had the same David Tenant/Matt Smith quality I enjoyed while the two of us were in medical school together. Then he fell into an aquarium of radioactive sea creatures and became the horrifying thing now before me. No, I don't know where the wings came from either. Maybe Mother Nature thought the Lovecraft look wasn't complete without them.

I got up and assumed a fighting stance. "I've got to ask: who the hell was Overlord?"

"Timmy Wolnotz," Jerry said, stretching out his wings as his red but humanlike eyes glowed.

"Not ringing a bell," I said.

"You broke his heart," Jerry said. "Like you broke mine."

I stared blankly.

"2018," Jerry said. "He was shocked you were with other men. Also women."

The way he spoke the last two words was full of revulsion and mild intrigue. You know, how misogynists thought of two women together.

I had no idea who this Timmy guy was and was also offended at the fact he thought he was enough for me and that he dismissed my girlfriends. I had only been tempted by a couple people to be monogamous with and they were sleeping with each other. Which is one of like two lucky breaks I've ever had in my life. But the implications of Jerry's words were what were really bothering me.

I stared at him and looked at him sideways. "What, are you like assembling an army of evil exes? We're reduced to ripping off *Scott Pilgrim versus the World* now?"

"I don't know what that is," Jerry said, crackling with unnatural green bioelectricity.

"It's a movie where Michael Cera is the hottest man in Canada," I replied. "You know, science fiction. The manga at least makes him an adorable cartoon man."

Jerry snarled. "You abandoned me in my hour of need, Cindy! When I needed you most! You could not stand my monstrous new visage!"

"Well, I wasn't dating you for your personality," I replied.

You know, I really am the asshole in most of my relationships. I just realized that now.

"Now I will destroy this city to ruin you!" Jerry shouted. "Activate the bomb, my cultists!"

Wait, he had a cult now? That was when I noticed a bunch of robe-wearing jerks were coming out to fight my daughters and me. These were wielding magical staves and wands. I hoped they worked because, honestly, they were just embarrassing themselves otherwise. I think I saw a few of them even sporting House Slytherin scarves. If this was the best the Brotherhood of Infamy could muster these days, then I suspected the city was safe.

That was when, across town, I saw ACME Chemicals (or so I presumed) explode in a ball of green flame that sent a hideous cloud of gas into the air.

Ah hell. What a time to be wrong.

Chapter Seven

My Super-Ex-Boyfriend vs. My Team

Well, crap. One of the things to know about superheroes is the fact that people quickly forgot their accomplishments while never forgetting their failures. You could save the world a hundred and fifty times but if you didn't prevent a town from getting turned into gorillas then no one ever let you forget about it.

Seeing the poisonous cloud rising from ACME Chemicals, I had the sneaking suspicion this was going to be one of the latter. It also bothered me to no end that it was Cthulhoid that was responsible because him becoming the world's fifty-second worst terrorist was going to have some blowback on me. Let's face it, if you were known as the girl who used to bone the Unabomber that was all you were going to be known for. It had happened to one of my colleagues at the hospital who was permanently tarred as Psychoslinger's side piece.

Thankfully, I heard the Nightplane's engines in the air as the raven-shaped hover vehicle flew over our heads with the whine of a TIE Fighter. Did you know that they're named for their twin ion engines? I do, unfortunately, thanks to Gary. The super-plane went over the cloud and released some sort of white fluid before the poison gas started to dissipate into nothingness.

"What the hell?" Jerry said, staring at the sight and shaking a big tentacle-fingered fist.

"Mr. Inventor was making a counter-agent back at the Clock Tower," Amanda said, finally emerging from her icy prison by turning insubstantial and passing through it. "Your evil plan is thwarted, Cthulhuoid!"

"Quiet, I'm talking to my ex here," I said, giving her the hand.

"What now?" Amanda asked. "He's your what? He was my villain first!"

"Trust me, you don't want him," I said. "I used to find him cool geeky but that was before I realized he was the kind of geek who pens thirty-page essays about H.P. Lovecraft not being racist at all."

"He wasn't!" Jerry said, appalled. "He was a misunderstood genius!"

"Listen, I like the guy's monsters as much as the next girl, but Robert E. Howard of Conan the Barbarian fame threatened to beat the guy up in a letter if he didn't stop supporting fascism."

I'd always felt a weird connection to the writings of Robert E. Howard and his writings. I particularly loved stories about Red Sonja, who I'd been shocked to discover had been created by Roy Thomas in the Seventies. There was just something about barbarians, mighty thews, swords, serpents, and treasure hunting that appealed to a primal part of me that I couldn't put into words.

Amanda looked at me. "How do you even know that?"

"I'm a fantasy nerd," I said. "What?"

Jerry roared, which is something that sea life absolutely did not do. "You have not thwarted my plans, Red Riding Hood! I shall punish your city!"

"Finally, some goddamn respect," I said, crossing my arms. "Even if it does come from a guy who worships an eldritch god that has stuffed toys and fuzzy slippers."

"This is my city!" Amanda said, appalled. "I saved it."

That was when Mandy finally broke out of her ice prison. "Technically, it was Mr. Inventor."

"He's *my* sidekick," Amanda said. "Also, my husband but totally my sidekick."

"Like Gary and me!" I shouted.

Amanda looked at me sideways. "Gary's saved the entire multiverse. Twice."

"Silence!" Jerry shouted, a huge psychic wave washing over us. His enormous head began to crackle with bolts of yellow lightning.

Did I mention Cthulhuoid was also psychic? That was some strange radioactive seafood he'd fallen into, I gotta tell you. Unfortunately, that meant the overpowered squamous horror was more of a threat than all these undead cyborg ninja thingies combined.

"I'm sorry, Amanda, but you're going to have to give me this villain," I replied. "We have a personal connection. I was tied to his origin story. I also personally want to kick his ass."

Amanda sighed. "Fine, alright. It's not like I don't have plenty of other bad guys to replace him."

"Thanks," I said, turning to face Jerry. "Jerry, I'm sorry. It's not me, it's you. You're an ugly dumb son of a squid that looks like someone glued bat wings to a fat illithid. On the plus side, I want you to know that it's not just your looks that repulse me. I was already going to dump your ass for getting involved in all that fake conspiracy stuff regarding former President Omega."

"He was meant to win the election and trigger the Storm!" Jerry snarled. "President Omega was going to eliminate all Supers and establish an eternal dictatorship! The Informant says that a time-traveler using the Primal Orbs rewrote reality, so he lost the election against Moses Anders and never triggered a massive genocide of the world's peoples."

I blinked. "Actually, that's surprisingly accurate. But I suppose a stopped clock is right twice a day. The fact that you support genocide of all Supers is stupid, though. Because, you know, we are Supers."

I was also a bi Jewish woman so it's not like I was a big fan of President Omega's fanboys in the first place. Oh, and I had a brown kid too. Mimi might not be mine by blood, but I didn't mind the motherhood thing if it required nothing from me but cash and vague platitudes. God, I just realized Mimi was a black Jewish female Super. My sorta-adopted kid was gonna get screwed by society so bad. No wonder Gary wanted to take over the world to make it easier for her.

"There's too much competition," Jerry said. "I think the world could do with ninety percent less Supers. We can start with your kids."

I stared at him. "Weirdly, I'm feeling an even greater desire to kick your ass now."

"Bring it, whore," Jerry said, making a come get some gesture with his tentacled hands.

"You say it like it's a bad thing," I said, assuming my nine-foot-tall war form.

"I shall make you kill your own allies!" Jerry proclaimed, fully embracing his status as a stock supervillain.

That was when Mimi picked him up from behind by his legs, held them together and started smashing him around the roof like he was a rag doll being thrown about by a toddler. Jerry let out some confused and terrified screams as Mimi spun him around in the air prior to hurling him through the air toward the moon. I didn't know if he hit it or would fall before he broke the atmosphere because I lost sight of him after the first few thousand feet. Both Amanda and Mandy joined in watching the supervillain disappear into the horizon. It was certainly a display of the fact there was super-strength and then there was *super*-strength.

Mimi dusted off her hands and posed triumphantly. Leia was standing beside her, looking equally smug.

"Another victory for the Super-Science Sisters!" Leia said.

Oh God, they had a team name already picked out and it was adorable. I needed to put a stop to it, but I wasn't sure I could. It didn't help that both of them were geniuses in addition to being grossly overpowered little twinks. Why is it the kids of superheroes were always stronger than their parents? At least Mimi wasn't quite as powerful as her mom, yet.

"You didn't do anything!" Mimi said, turning to her sister. "I beat up Cthulhuoid all by myself!"

"I suppressed his psychic powers during your attack," Leia said, crossing her arms.

Mimi blinked. "Did you?"

"You'll never be able to prove otherwise," Leia said, smiling. It was the same look I gave Gary whenever I was pretending to be interested in the latest news about Star Wars sequels. Seriously, it's over, Gary. *Rise of the Skywalker* killed it.

I frowned at my daughters. "That's what's called kill-stealing, my lovelies. It is a breach of online MMORPG guild laws. Also, supervillain rules."

"Sorry, Mom," Mimi said. "However, I wanted to say I beat Cthulhu."

"He wasn't Cthulhu," I replied. "Cthulhu isn't real. At least in this reality. He's just the product of the fevered imagination of a prolific Rhode Islander that hated seafood and organized religion. Besides, Cthulhu is a mile tall. Cthulhuoid is more like one of his minions or cult leaders. Mommy and Daddy have beaten real Great Old Ones, or at least creatures legally distinct but effectively the same."

Amanda looked in the general direction that Jerry had been thrown. "Will that kill him?"

"Probably not," I replied. "Jerry is ridiculously overpowered for a guy with the combined abilities of a Red Lobster menu."

"Maybe he's cosmically possessed by the real Cthulhu!" Leia said. "Or a legally distinct—"

"Stop that," I replied. "Don't give the Primals ideas. The Powers that Be are a bunch of bored nerds writing our lives as amusement for their dull but omnipotent lives."

"Well, I'll ask the Society to pick him up if he reaches orbit," Amanda said, taking it in stride. "If not, let's hope he doesn't land on anyone."

"I calculated for landing in the middle of Lake Michigan," Mimi said, reminding me she was a genius. "I mean, I could have aimed for the Atlantic Ocean, but I figure that the Great Lakes are right here."

"Well, let's focus on the important thing: me," I replied. "I need your help, Amanda, and I helped you save the city. By which I mean I pretty much did all the work and you stood by."

"That's not remotely what happened," Amanda said.

"Whatever," I said, making the Jedi mind trick gesture. "I need you to help me and Mandy rob the Dragon King of his billions."

Amanda blinked. "Why would I help you rob a *kaiju* supervillain?"

"Because he finances terrorism," Mandy said. "The act of depriving him of his resources would seriously impact the flow of money to numerous illicit organizations. You also know that

Cindy, for all of her many, many flaws, will donate the money to charity."

"What I don't spend foolishly," I replied. "I might buy an island in Dubai, which requires buying a lake to put in the desert to make the island first. I'd then run around naked on it in defiance of local custom. Which yes, is probably legal as private property but Rome wasn't built in a day."

Both Amanda and Mandy stared at me.

"But there will be plenty leftover!" I reassured them. "I mean, he's also leaving the planet and won't be financing terrorism on our world after that in a week so the argument we're doing good-good doesn't hold weight but think of all the crimes he'll be getting away with! Do it for the anachronistic retributive justice system!"

"You are terrible at arguing," Mandy said.

"Eh, I figure she's coming no matter what," I replied. "Due to the ancient principle of 'you owe me.'"

"I told you that I didn't believe you actually helped that much," Amanda said. "Besides, saving the city helps you too."

I shook my head. "I mean for helping you avenge your mother and get superpowers in the first place. I may have kidnapped you at one point too but if not for me, then you never would have been inspired to become a superhero in the first place."

Amanda blinked. "Are you actually arguing that you were doing me a favor by kidnapping me?"

"Then you'd owe me twice but if you don't then you still owe me for that time I helped you out during the last zombie apocalypse," I replied. "Mandy died protecting you during that too, so you owe her too."

"I died saving you as I recall," Mandy replied.

"And I owe you for that," I said, unhesitatingly. "What do you want? Do we do this Solomon style? Because I have two kids. We don't have to divide them in two. You can just take one. Or both! I recommend both."

"You are a really terrible mother," Amanda said.

"She really isn't," Leia defended me. "For my eighth birthday, she got me my own T-Rex. We also can play in the morgue any time we want."

"Not many parents let you drive as soon as you can reach the pedals," Mimi said.

"Or have rocket launchers!" Leia added.

"Do I need to bring you in for child abuse?" Amanda asked.

"Honestly, probably," I said, not actually joking. "Children are incredibly fragile, and I have no idea how to deal with them."

"The kids are fine," Mandy said. "Cindy knows her limits and has devoted vast portions of her wealth to looking after Supers and getting mundane children out of abusive hones. Now do you want to help or not?"

"I do," Amanda said, sighing. "Though not for the reasons you think. The Dragon King is exiting planet Earth because he's staying ahead of the Foundation for World Harmony finally getting enough evidence to move against his corporate and criminal empire. He'll be out of Earth's jurisdiction but fully capable of continuing his activities through intermediaries as well as hypercomm communication."

"All he needs is Gary's cell service," I replied. "That thing reaches into other dimensions and the center of the Earth."

Did I sound jealous? Maybe a little.

"Everything I've found out about him says he's a credible threat to world security," Mandy said.

"It's worse than you know," Amanda replied. "The Dragon King is responsible for a massive number of the supervillains the Society has faced over the years. His high-interest loans and payments have outfitted hundreds of supervillains over the years. He pays for their lawyers, equipment, break outs, and medical bills. If you've ever wondered why so many seem to be a revolving door of justice, then it's at least partially on him. Plenty of supervillains rob banks and attack random buildings as part of his complicated payment plans. Businesses are intimidated into silence or heroes distracted while he makes his next chess move to up his stock."

"Ah, dragon loans," I said, nodding. "I always wondered why they were called that. All the experienced supervillains used to tell me never to take them out because they were worse than student debt. I was smart enough to pay off the latter by robbing banks."

Amanda lowered her head. "I hate my life."

"We need your magic for this operation," Mandy said. "Also, your help getting the other members of the team."

"Which we're a part of!" Leia said.

"The hell you are," I said. "No one is endangering my kids by using them in a heist. Not even me."

"Can you stop them if they press the issue?" Amanda asked.

I paused and thought that. "Crap."

That was when I heard a crack of thunder and Jerry descended from the sky, his wings spread out. He looked a bit worse for wear, though, from where Mimi had beat the crap out of him. "Fools! Did you think you could defeat the avatar of the Sleeping One? What is dead can never die!"

That was when Leia blasted him with a massive telepathic beam of mental power that knocked him out from the air. We spent the next twenty minutes beating on him.

Good stress relief.

Chapter Eight

Old Wounds Unhealed

Now, private jets are a luxury for the disgustingly wealthy. I don't like coach, any more than other people but that's why First-Class tickets exist. The ability to go anywhere anytime but also just relax with cocktails is something that should be reserved for people fighting terrorists or heads of state. Not corporate CEOS, movie stars, or televangelists. Maybe, if they're renting them. That's what I believe. Being that I am disgustingly wealthy, though, I very much am happy to make use of them if they are available.

Sipping my cocktail, I leaned back in my comfy chair. "Ah, the luxuries of embezzling from the Omega Corporation. This is what true evil is all about."

"What do you do at the Omega Corporation?" Amanda asked.

"No idea," I replied. "I am a representative of the executive board of stockholding vice president producers or something. Why?"

Amanda sighed. "Just saying we could have taken *my* jet. I don't like what it says about my image to be seen here."

"You afraid of being associated with a bunch of supervillains?" Mandy asked, her voice muffled because she was inside her coffin in the middle of the plane's lounge. The girls were currently both texting each other from two feet away and it was the weirdest thing I'd seen this week. Yes, that was including my ex-boyfriend the sea monster, a bunch of zombie ninjas, and a guy with a magic crowbar.

"No," Amanda said. "I just don't like being associated with a corporation that is still so dirty in its financial practices. Kerri hasn't managed to redeem it, just make it less evil."

Amanda was someone I really should have hated because she'd grown up with not so much a silver spoon as one made of platinum blessed by Ayn Rand. Somehow, against all odds, she'd turned out not to be a spoiled psychopath like most of her peers. Unfortunately, she did come with the same problem that Gary and I both suffered: rich people guilt.

That nagging sensation that you have it better and you should try to make it better for the poor. Having been poor, I should know that most of us wouldn't give a shit if our situations were reversed, but there was that weird desire among one percent of the one percent to do better. It never worked out but occasionally you got your Julius Caesars, Octavians, Art Carnegies, Bill Gates, and Arthur (not Lancel) Warrens.

I rolled my eyes. "Listen, unless you're Karl Marx, there's no reason you can't be rich and throw the money around. Capitalism is the worst system of government you can make except for all the others. You just need to reign in all the pigs that want to cheat the little guy even more than he already does. Kill maybe one out of ten of them as a lesson to the others. Eating the rich like Aerosmith says to just leaves you hungry in the end. Look at the French Revolution."

"Wonderful philosophy, Cindy," Amanda said.

"I want to be disgustingly rich," I replied, finishing my drink. "I just don't think anyone else has to be poor to make it happen. I call it the Franklin Roosevelt school of thought. Wealth redistribution the Cindy way: one for you, two for me."

"Is that how you plan to divide up the Dragon King's fortune?" Amanda asked.

"Yep," I said. "Bard should have gotten a portion of Thorin's hoard because he killed Smaug. There still would have been more than enough to go around, especially since Bilbo just wanted a pony's worth of gold coins."

"I never watched *The Hobbit*," Amanda said. "Is it any good? I understand there's a book version?"

I narrowed my eyes. "We are no longer friends."

Amanda raised an eyebrow. "We were friends?"

I had to acknowledge that burn. "Well played. So, where are we headed now?"

"Londonium," Amanda said. "The city of New Albion."

"Crap," I muttered. I hadn't really been paying attention when Amanda had made the arrangements and now, I wished I had been.

One thing I'd learned from my brief travels in the multiverse was that my Earth had a lot more nations controlled by supervillains and heroes than your typical parallel universe. Most of these were the size of postage stamps, the United States and Atlantis being the big exceptions, but Londonium was a particular oddball example of libertarian seasteading gone wild.

Basically, in the nineteenth century, a supervillain named the World Emperor arranged for a rocky outcropping off the Isle of Man to secede from the British Empire. The OG steampunk mad scientist, the World Emperor managed to successfully negotiate it when he helped save the country from the Martians or something. Personally, I think it boiled down to

Queen Victoria's advisors realizing he was building an enormous science city on their doorstep that would be a great source of weapons to help dominate brown people.

Which it was.

Londonium had its own personal connection to our family, though, or more specifically Mandy. Way back when she was just a spy's daughter, she'd grown up in this tax shelter excuse of a country and gotten knocked up at sixteen by a tourist. For reasons that are hers and hers alone, she went the full nine months and gave up the child for adoption. The process left her traumatized and never wanting to have kids again, which had proven an issue with Gary during their marriage. Sort of the thing you should have worked out before you made a holy commitment (bleah), but they'd coasted on until her death.

"Uh, Mandy, are you okay with us going there?" I asked, not sure what her mood was since she was in a frigging coffin.

"It's where the next piece of our puzzle is," Mandy said, calmly. "The Spear of Saint George, Dragonslayer."

I blinked. "The Spear of Saint George? Not a sword?"

"Yes, Saint George was a Byzantine knight rather than an English one," Amanda said. "The original story had him stab it while it was asleep but the magic of killing one of the Great Dragons plus his status as a canonized figure resulted in it gaining vast powers for the slaying of wyrms. It's since slain dozens and is possibly the only weapon that can kill Smog."

I looked at her. "And you don't think Smog will have tried to deal with it?"

"He has," Amanda said. "The spear is indestructible, and his every attempt has only brought it closer to killing him. Self-fulfilling prophecies and all that. He's the one who arranged for the World Emperor Museum to acquire the weapon. He can't carry out his purpose while being locked away among the Londonium Crown Jewels and the first atomic submarine."

Yeah, the World Emperor was the inspiration for Jules Verne's Nemo and Robur the Conqueror. The big difference being that Nemo hated the British Empire while the World Emperor had been a fetishist. Kind of disappointing, really.

"And you don't think the Spear of Saint George is going to object to being wielded by a vampire, a Jewess, and a necromancer?"

"A Jewess?" Leia asked, looking up from her cellphone.

"I'm using the word a Christian fanatic would use," I replied. "Also, Rebekah from *Ivanhoe* was called one and she rocked. All the literary world thinks Ivanhoe made the wrong choice."

Oh God, I'd developed the same habit of drifting into literary non sequitur as my boyfriend. Goddammit.

"It's just a tool," Amanda replied.

I rolled my eyes. "And you call yourself the Supreme Mistress of the Dark Arts!"

"I don't actually," Amanda said, confirming she didn't have the theatricality needed to be a proper superhero wizard.

"All I'm saying is that in my limited experience with the occult, mystical objects develop a life of their own," I replied. "*The Book of Midnight* gets a bowl of kibble a week since wandering back to us."

"She's not wrong," Mandy said, finally opening the coffin as the sun crested beneath the horizon outside the plane. This time she was in full pleather armor and looked like a horny geek's idea of a superspy. Because nothing said low profile more than immensely hot woman with every curve outlined by her uniform. But hey, you got it, flaunt it. "You have no idea how much it pains me to say that."

"Hold on!" I said. "I'm usually right when it comes to cynical commentary, and anything related to modern medicine."

"You can also name Captain Kirk's best friend," Leia said, returning to texting.

"Spock?" Mandy asked, as if it wasn't a difficult question.

"Gary Mitchell," I snapped. "The answer of a true Trekkie!"

"You say that as if it's something to be proud of," Mandy said, getting out of the coffin. "We may have to find a pure-hearted warrior to wield the spear for us."

"Great, because those are going to be down with robbing a casino," I muttered. "It also will throw our numbers way off. It might as well be Cindy's Three Hundred. We can get Gerard Butler and kick some Persians for good measure."

"That would be a better number for a heist of this size," Amanda said. "Even divided by three hundred shares."

"Nope," I interrupted. "We are still Cindy's Seven even if it has to be Cindy's Seven Plus One."

"You mean eight?" Amanda asked. "You are a very strange woman."

"No kidding," I said. "I'm entitled to my secrets."

"Like what?" Leia asked. "Literally, you're an open book. I say that as a telepath."

"You're kind of prone to oversharing in fact," Mimi said.

"That is a horrible but true thing to say," I replied. "But how was I to know talking about your sex life, murder, and medical emergencies was inappropriate?"

"Common sense?" Amanda suggested.

"If I had that, I wouldn't be a supervillain," I replied, crossing my arms. "Or awesome!"

Amanda pulled out a small computer with the Nightwalker symbol on it. "Either way, we're going to have to rob the New Albion Royal Museum of London to get the Spear of Saint George. I don't think the government is going to lend it out. The World Emperor may be dead but it's the most crooked Parliament you'll find, heavily in debt to the Dragon King. They supported Edward the Fourth for King during WWII and still have ties to his branch of PHANTOM."

"Who?" I asked.

"The Nazi King of England," Mimi said. "You should watch *The Crown*. It's my fifth favorite historical drama."

"Girls your age should be watching cheesy romances with horrible life lessons instead," I said. "*Kissing Booth, My Boyfriend is a Supervillain,* and *To All the Henchmen I've Loved Before.*"

"That's more an Aunt Jane thing," Leia said. "Mimi loves watching historically inaccurate shows about dead rich white people and the Great Wambariland Bake-Off hosted by the Golden Lion."

"Mostly because he's hot," Mimi said.

"I, being a neuroatypical ace romantic, prefer pure science programming or CrimeTube shows about rescue animals," Leia said. "Especially reptiles."

I blinked and made finger guns at my daughters. "I'm ninety percent sure I knew you were on the spectrum."

Unfortunately, Leia chose the absolute worst way of changing topics. "Do you plan on trying to look up your daughter in Londonium?"

Goddammit, Leia, how does someone who can read everyone's innermost thoughts not know when to keep one's mouth shut? Oh right, sort of a self-explanatory statement there.

Mandy's gaze narrowed and became like ice. "No. My daughter is dead. Worse than dead."

She wasn't kidding. Mandy's first daughter, I'd never learned her name or if she'd even been given one before Mandy's parents had whisked her away, had been Ret-Goned. Which was a term only superheroes really used because it was so staggeringly terrifying a concept. Basically, it was when due to time-travel or the actions of evil gods that someone was completely erased from existence. A Primal known as Destruction had been mucking around with reality for decades, subtlety and not-so-subtlety altering time to keep the melodrama of superheroes going forever. Superheroes would live, marry, have children, die, and then come back only to find out their families were robots or erased from continuity. Time would march on, but the heroes would be eternal—as would their enemies. Mandy had been a teen mom at one point but, apparently, her kid had been one of those casualties. It just was that she remembered having her anyway, which was the worst of both worlds.

"She could be back," Leia said, either not reading the room or badly misreading it. "Gary and Other Gary rebooted reality since then."

Yeah, that was another reason I needed to get out of my boyfriend's shadow. Dude helped rewrite reality once. The least he could have done was make us rulers of the galaxy. I mean, yes, we were billionaires with immortality but—wait, hold on, I needed to stop complaining.

"She's gone, Leia," Mandy said, keeping her opinion neutral. "Please don't bring her up again."

Leia opened her mouth and closed it. "Sure."

Wow, that was a buzzkill.

"So, are you two sure I can't introduce you to underage drinking?" I asked. "Remember, all the cool kids are doing it!"

That was when Mimi's cellphone started beeping. "Actually, we should all hold hands with Amanda and form a chain."

"Why?" I asked. "Are we going to sing Kumbaya? I'm going to tell you, we're the wrong religion for that."

"Now!" Mimi said.

Survival in my line of work was trusting your instincts and not questioning the weird or impossible. When someone shouted fire you needed to act like there was a raging inferno right next to you or you were toast. Jumping up, I grabbed Amanda's hand and grabbed her sister's. Mandy then grabbed onto my waist.

That was when the plane exploded.

Chapter Nine

Relationships and Plane Wrecks

Amanda turned us insubstantial literally a second before the plane went up in a fiery ball of fuel and fusion matter. Omega jets were designed to be able to take superheroes across the planet in a matter of hours and tended to go up spectacularly. Unfortunately, turning insubstantial wasn't exactly a cure for falling a thousand feet in the air to the ocean below and we weren't wearing parachutes.

"Great plan, Mimi!" I shouted as my possibly last words on Earth.

"It is, actually!" Mimi shouted back.

Enormous pieces of metal flew through our bodies, and it tickled a little as Mimi's aura moved up and down our bodies, eventually covering us in Ultra-Force. That was the weird energy that powered her mother, grandfather, and the Ultranian race that inspired all the myths of the gods that the actual gods didn't. Mimi hadn't gotten the full dose of the power that her maternal ancestor had but still had abilities far beyond those of any ordinary teenager.

"Stay still!" Leia said. "This is gonna be weird!"

"What?" I shouted.

That was when Amanda, Mandy, Leia, and me were all shoved together into a dogpile held up by Mimi with two hands despite the fact there was no way she could get leverage on it. That was when she slowed down our fall to a crawl. It was bizarre but she stopped our descent right as her toes hit the water. Thankfully, she slowed down our movement before that happened or we would have kept going through the water until Amanda's power gave out, surviving a plane wreck only to drown at the bottom of the ocean. Super-physics makes my head hurt and I'm a frigging genius.

"Everybody alive?" Mimi called up to us.

"No," Mandy said. "The others appear to be breathing, though."

"Ha-ha," Mimi said. "Okay, guys, I'm going to carry you to the shore."

Mimi rested her feet on top of the sloshing waves as I noticed there was a storm going on around us. I hadn't seen it before due to the whole, you know, exploding plane thing. Mimi then just started jumping across the waves with every leap covering a football field. Mimi, to make the experience even more irritating, sang Eddie Money's "If I Could Walk on Water" the entire way through.

Rhianna my daughter was not.

I'm not going to lie, I was about ready to throw up by the time Mimi managed to set us down on the barren rocky shore of Londonium's coast. Amanda actually did vomit, and Mandy looked queasy despite the fact she had no functioning organs. I supposed all the blood sloshing around inside her was still unpleasant. Leia was the only one who looked excited.

"Touchdown!" Mimi said, triumphantly.

"That was awesome!" Leia said. "Let's do it again!"

"The hell we will!" I snapped. "What the hell was that?"

"The plane was shot down by a laser-guided surface to air missile," Leia said. "Me and Mimi were monitoring potential threats on our phones."

"We wrote an app for it," Mimi said.

I stared at the pair. "You didn't think to tell us about this?"

"We did tell you about it," Leia said. "Hence why we're alive."

Amanda finished throwing up on the ground. "Who the hell knew we were coming?"

"Pilot, maintenance crew, stewards and stewardesses—" I started to name various potential sources.

"You mean flight attendants," Mandy said.

"Given the extra services I hired them for," I replied. "They were stewards and stewardesses."

Mandy looked disgusted.

"I mean so you can feed on them!" I snapped. "Also, sex on demand. But for the adults in the room! Anyway, they're all dead so I don't think they made a wise decision. Regular people don't come back from the dead even after the Reboot. Just cool and sexy people like us."

"But why is someone shooting us down?" Amanda asked.

"The Dragon King posted a ten-million-dollar reward for Mom's head," Leia said. "Well, Cindy Mom, not Mandy Mom. It went online an hour ago."

"And this didn't warrant mentioning?" I asked.

Leia shrugged. "I figured I'd tell you when we hit the ground."

"How the hell does he even know?" I asked.

"You've mentioned you were going after him one hundred and twenty-three times in the car ride over, the airport, and the flight," Leia said. "He has eyes everywhere."

"That's meant to be figurative!" I snapped. "Not actually mean he has warning I'm coming to kill him and take his stuff!"

"Ugh," Amanda said. "We should cancel this entire plot."

"Like hell we are!" I snapped. "We've come too far!"

"We've barely started," Amanda pointed out.

"Too far!" I snapped. "We have to kill the Dragon King in order to protect the children!"

"You mean, the children we threatened by introducing them into this battle?" Amanda asked, clearly not happy about my kids' presence.

"You mean the children who saved us from certain death?" I asked.

Amanda glared.

"How did you do that, anyway? I wasn't aware you could walk on water?" Mandy asked, looking unhappy to be in the rain. Maybe it was because vampires hated running water or maybe it was just, she didn't like being rained on. I could just shake it off. Literally.

"I have tactile telekinesis," Mimi replied. "The Ultra-Force allows me to move my aura around objects, so they don't break up when I hold them. I could lift the Eiffel Tower without destroying it, which I plan to eventually do when I steal it!"

I rolled my eyes. "You're not Carmen Sandiego, Mimi. Edutainment has poisoned your mind. What's next, a plot to help the Count von Count take over Sesame Street?"

"Maybe," Mimi muttered.

"Fine," Amanda asked. "We'll carry on our mission, but we need to find out who is hunting us."

"How far are we from the Tower of We're Robbing This Place?" I asked.

"About twenty miles," Amanda said. "We should get going and hopefully not by teenage girl. I take it you can't fly?"

Mimi shook her head. "I can leap from any surface, no matter how unsteady but actual flight? Not so much."

"Still useful," Amanda said. "Keep that in your strategies, Mandy."

"Already have," Mandy said.

"I'm going to go arrange for a distraction," I replied, walking away from the group and pulling out my cellphone. "You call us an Uber."

I, reluctantly, called Gary. I didn't need help, but I wasn't about to completely write him out if doing so endangered my kids. There was a difference between wanting to do something for pride, which this absolutely was all about, and being stupid. The phone initially went to voice mail but I waited a few seconds and "Sympathy for the Devil" started playing. I clicked the call button and got a video chat image of Gary lying in his bed, looking hung over. He was covered in bruises but there was a sign of a sleeping body in the bed beside him.

"Hi Cindy, how ya doing?" Gary asked, clearly looking like he'd had a night.

"Not well," I said, pausing. "Wait, is that Revolutionary Girl?"

The body in the bed raised a feminine hand and waved. "Hey, Cindy."

Revolutionary Girl was one of Gary's latest flings and annoyingly had become a regular. She had no powers but had managed to survive the worst that authoritarian communist and fascist governments had thrown at her. I had that itch in the back of my mind that I was missing something about the biracial anarchist carrying the fight to all the Post-PHANTOM block nations as well as other dictatorships around the world.

Part of this was undoubtedly due to the magic that I could smell on her that was designed to prevent people from knowing her secret identity. The *Secret Identity* spell had been created by Isis the Incredible in the Thirties and was one of the more common tools in the Society of Superheroes arsenal. It could be tied to a pair of glasses, wedding ring, headband, or whatever. Some superheroes even used it to maintain multiple superheroes identities—which I felt was cheating. It wasn't that it provided a disguise, per se, but you literally could not recognize a person as who your mind would normally put together. Even if you had it pointed out to you, your mind would just dismiss it.

I debated asking Ultragoddess about it since Revolutionary Girl looked exactly like Gabrielle Anders' civilian identity but since she obviously *wasn't* then there had to be some connection. I mean, it would just be silly for Ultragoddess to create an entirely new superhero identity to hook up with her old college boyfriend turned married supervillain. I mean, what was she afraid of? That it would taint her brand and get people she arrested freed from prison? Huh. No wait, that's ridiculous. Also, why did I feel like I'd just been neuralyzed by the men in black. What was I thinking about?

"Cindy?" Gary asked.

"Oh right," I said. "Gary, I need you to kill some people."

"I didn't hear that," Revolutionary Girl said.

"I'm trying not to kill people as a superhero," Gary said.

I rolled my eyes. "Are you still on that nonsense? Listen, they fired a missile at Leia and Mimi."

Gary blinked then immediately changed his attitude to one of cold simmering rage. "They're dead."

"Good to know. See ya soon, hun!" I hung up. "Wow, Gary works fast."

Much to my surprise, Mandy was right beside me. She'd turned to mist and floated over before coming up behind me to read over my shoulder. "Someone should create a new type of sorcery for him: pornomancy. The art of making female superheroes drop their tights for him."

"Gary is a god," I replied. "I mean that in the Greek sense. His sugar momma, Death, gave him an upgrade after the Eternity Tournament. It comes with plenty of fringe benefits like immortality, beauty, and the ability to never fuck up in the bedroom. Even before then he knew the key to repeat business was to show his partner a good time first.

Mandy grimaced. "Yeah. He does that have talent, doesn't he."

"You don't sound happy about that," I said, surprised. "Is there trouble in paradise?"

Honestly, I didn't see what the problem was. Vampires weren't exactly known for their problems in the bedroom themselves. If you had the sexy version of the Bite, you could make orgasmic bliss part of the experience of having your fluids drained away. Even more so than the other way. Ba-da-ching.

"Cindy, I don't like sharing my *lipstick*," Mandy admitted. "I couldn't imagine sharing a lover until I was forced to. Being a vampire doesn't help matters since we're all insanely jealous psychopaths."

I raised an eyebrow. "There's a lot to unpack there. I thought everything was fine in our little extended love decahedron. Also, you're not a psychopath. Now."

Mandy gave a pained smile. "I've been through a lot since being a superhero. Brainwashing, possession, forcibly fusing a soul to my body like someone had watched too much Buffy, and having a Primal Orb. Every vampire gets their best qualities removed when they become a vampire, leaving only a shadow of who they were. They're free to develop into someone else afterward, though."

"Ah," I said, not sure how to follow that. "Well, I like the person you are. So much so that I now feel guilty."

Mandy sighed, always a voluntary action for vampires. "I know, that's what makes it so hard. I overlook Gary with other lovers because I need to have more of them to feed safely. The male ego is a fragile thing that needs constant validation. It's just a little surprising he's quite so successful at it. Also, he stays friends with his hook ups, which ticks me off."

"Feed safely?" I asked, ignoring the rest of it as just self-obvious.

"It turns out you're less likely to kill whoever you're feeding on if you're screwing them at the time," Mandy said. "Playing with your food is literally a matter of life and death for vampires interested in ethical consumption."

I blinked. "That is an interesting and horrifying revelation. Puts a whole new spin on vampire romance. So, you'd rather be monogamous? I mean, the real way and not the joking way I put it."

Mandy shrugged. "I dunno. When I got married to Gary, one of the conditions I made was that he break off his friendship with you."

I blinked. "You did what now?"

Mandy crossed her arms across her considerable bosom, a fact I only noted because the spy outfit really brought it out. Seriously, I'd ask how Mandy could breathe in that thing, but I knew she didn't need to.

"Listen, how would you react to the fact your husband's best friend is the girl he lost his virginity to and had intermittent hook-ups with for a decade long friendship?"

"Ask for her number?" I asked. "I mean Gary is an acquired taste. It's always feelings, emotions, and support. It'd be nice if he could just shut up and enjoy the meaningless sex."

Mandy stared.

"Oh right, I can see how that would be threatening to your marriage," I said, putting my pinkie to my mouth like Doctor Evil.

"It was also a bit off-putting to finally regain my ability to feel again and find out you'd had his child," Mandy said. "You know, the one thing I could never do with him again and he desperately wanted."

I paused. "He was in a really dark place. I figured a kid would cheer him up."

It hadn't quite worked out like that because he'd not found out about my pregnancy or birth until after he'd got out of Merciful's underground prison. The double irony was that Mandy had gotten her soul back in the meantime and spent that time with him. Well sort of gotten her soul back. It was complicated.

"You hate kids," Mandy said.

"I don't hate kids," I said. "I hate raising them. Big difference. I love Leia and Mimi. It's why I introduce them as my little sisters wherever I go."

Mandy tried—and failed—not to smile. "Gary loves you and you love Gary. I also have a deep and abiding affection for you. I don't mind you being part of our lives and I don't think Gary could exist without you. He was diminished without you when we were trying to live normal, mundane lives in the first years of our marriage. To be fair, I felt the same way about myself. Neither of us was meant to be normal. Still, I wouldn't mind if there were a few less people in this twenty-sided dice we call a group marriage."

"Ixnay on the M-word," I replied. "Gary and I are not married. We just live together, share a child, and have legal documents regarding the joint ownership of half our assets."

"Of course," Mandy said. "Vampires are also legally barred from marriage due to the recent legislation that defines it as a union only between the living."

"You poor thing," I said, half-kidding. "So, by people you'd like gone from this I assume you mean Gabrielle."

Mandy grimaced then said, "Is it that obvious?"

"Yes?" I asked. "I mean, on a scale of one to ten, you do seem to hate her to an eight and a half."

"Of all the superheroes who I thought would want a normal relationship, I was hoping she'd be one," Mandy said. "Instead, she put her child with Gary to raise and just regularly shows up to assert her dominance."

"She's not that bad," I said, feeling put out because Gabrielle was my friend. I had a handful of those compared to lovers. I'd wanted her to be one of the latter as well, but it turned out some heroes were a zero on the Kinsey Scale. It was like finding a unicorn given the number of boundaries most pushed.

"She threatened to throw me in the sun once," Mandy deadpanned. "I honestly hate her self-righteous hypocritical public Pollyanna attitude compared to the scheming—and don't take this wrong as a werewolf—manipulative bitchy self in private. Hell, I'm pretty sure she considers herself broken up with Gary ninety percent of the time. She just uses him when it's convenient."

"To be fair, that's like all of my relationships with men," I replied. "It's like Pavlov's dogs with sex. You reward them enough and they come when you ring a bell. It works on women too. Gary once got a whistle for that reason, and I bit him for it."

Mandy responded by reaching around and scratching behind my ears.

"Ah-ah-ah," I said, panting. "Oh, don't stop. Oooo."

Mandy, unfortunately, didn't.

I gave her a big sloppy kiss for it.

"Eww, Cindy lick!" Mandy said in her most Lucy-like voice.

Chapter Ten

Welcome to World Emperor World

"You have got to be kidding me," I said, staring at the sight that greeted me.

The enormous statue of the hooded, metal-masked figure of the World Emperor wielding his scepter over the world had been altered as much as possible to look as nonthreatening as it could be made. They'd added little cartoon birds held up by wires around him and bunch of adorable animals as they played an annoyingly cheerful song about how the world would be fine once everyone was the same.

We were at the gates to World Emperor World, which turned out to be where the museum was located and was either something stolen directly from Walt Disney or vice versa. We had caught a cab from the coast of Londonium and ended up doing doughnuts around the island for a couple of hours before getting our own transport. The people of Londonium were notoriously tight-lipped without being paid in the local pounds or Euros—Brexit not affecting supervillain-run Commonwealth nations—but had eventually directed us to the Cheer-Cheer-Cheeriest Place on Earth.

"Remember, kids, we're at Steam Lass' parking zone," Mandy said to our daughters. "It's next to the Baron Death and Merciless' ones."

"Why the hell does Gary have his own parking lot here?" I asked, snapping. "This better not be a time travel thing."

"It's probably a time travel thing," Mandy said. "The only people who abuse it more are you and President Omega."

"Hey, going back in time to meet the Bronte Sisters is not an abuse!" I snapped.

Mandy stared at me, seemingly waiting for more to be said.

"What?" I asked.

"I was just expecting something dirty or self-serving," Mandy replied.

"I can do things other than both," I replied. "Mind you I may have given them some suggestions about sexing up the books. That deserves a parking spot here. What has Gary ever done?"

"Saved the world multiple times?" Mimi pointed out.

"Tore down PHANTOM?" Leia suggested.

"Got a movie for Daenerys after the awful *Game of Thrones* ending?" Mandy asked.

"Okay, I'll give you the last one," I replied. "So, we just need to investigate this cheesy theme park for the Spear of Saint George and make it off Londonium before whoever is hunting us finds us again?"

"Pretty much," Amanda said. "We should get a map from the gift shop and see where the museum is. We also need to avoid becoming noticed by WEW Security. This place may just be a theme park, but it's still guarded by an army of animatronics and has its own division of Foundation agents stationed here."

I stared at her. "Why?"

Amanda blinked and looked at Mandy. "I actually have no idea."

Mandy grimaced. "World Emperor World is built over the headquarters of the Foundation for World Harmony's European branch."

"You are kidding me," I said, staring in horror. "How? Why? Why in the world would they build it under a theme park?"

"Deniability," Mandy replied. "Virtually every Foundation for World Harmony base in the world is underneath an amusement park of one sort or another. They're perfect for disguising operations."

"I sincerely doubt that," I said, wondering if they were the people who'd shot us down.

The Foundation for World Harmony, or FWH, was kind of a necessary evil in our world that existed as a bridge between regular law enforcement and superheroes. Generally, if a giant monster was stomping down main street and you didn't have a local superhero then they would be the guys who made the call to the heroes needed to deal with it. They also tracked terrorism, cleaned up in the aftermath of Supers fights, protected VIPs, and handled much of the grunt work of figuring out how to incarcerate a man who could turn into mist.

The thing was, like the IRS, no one liked the Foundation for World Harmony. They were too public for an organization of super-spies and too clandestine for superheroes. Countries frequently believed the United Nations-adjacent group infringed on their sovereignty, were too harsh on Supers, and too soft, or plain useless against real threats. They were kind of like UNIT or Torchwood in *Doctor Who*. The organization existed to make the real protagonists look good. Really, the only time they ever did anything good was during alien invasions when they coordinated evacuation operations and what pitiful responses the militaries of the world could deliver.

"I thought this was a PHANTOM-allied nation," Amanda said.

"It was," Mandy said. "Which is why the base is here."

That wasn't a bad point. "Okay, well, let's go into the theme park and get some funnel cake and overpriced drinks at the adult's portion. We can then plot how we're going to rob the museum."

That was when Leia and Mimi walked over, both dressed up like steampunk cosplayers. Leia was wearing a bowler hat with gears glued to it, goggles, and had an exoskeleton arm designed to make laser noises. In her right hand was a vanilla ice cream cone she was licking. Mimi was dressed like Eliza Doolittle pre-Henry Higgins and was carrying a bunch of reproduced Victorian classic novels.

"What the hell happened to you?" I asked.

Mimi shrugged. "You guys were being boring, so we went to enjoy the amusement park."

I opened my mouth. "We've been here for like five minutes."

"Time Cube," Leia said, referring to a prototype scientific device that Gary had stolen for her. Leia and Mimi had already made numerous improvements to it. "We used it to go have an entire day's worth of fun without you. Also, to skip lines."

Obviously, I next asked the most pertinent question. "How the hell did you pay for it?"

"Really?" Amanda asked, looking at me like I was a terrible parent. Which I was.

"We own the patents on time travel and power suppressing cells," Mimi said. "Among other things like fluorescent pogs."

"Those made us most of our money," Leia said.

I pointed at both. "Grow up to be someone worth admiring like Ada Lovelace or Madame Currie. Don't grow up to be colonialist imperialists like King Leopold or Alan Quartermain. Wait was he real? Also, try not to die of radiation sickness or syphilis."

My children looked at me with the kind of gaze that hovered somewhere between confusion and pity.

"Sorry, I'm trying to do the parent thing!" I snapped. "It's harder than it looks."

Mandy, thankfully, rescued me from my own ineptitude. "What did you two find out in your journey?"

"We're using children as scouts now?" Amanda asked.

"The Nightwalker used teenagers as his Sunlights," Mandy replied.

"It was a different time," Amanda said.

"Age is no defense against being targeted," Mandy said. "I'd rather have them by our side than defenseless."

"They really don't get that we're stronger and smarter, do they?" Mimi asked Leia.

"Let them have this," Leia said.

I swiped Leia's ice cream cone.

"Hey!" Leia said.

"Consider it a life lesson in the value of experience," I said, licking it. "Wait, what the hell kind of flavor is this?"

"Organic vegan creme," Leia said.

"That doesn't even make any sense!" I said, handing back the ice cream cone.

Leia frowned. "I don't want it now; it's got dog lick on it."

Wow, my own daughter was speciest against my kind. Shame. I mean, all I did was turn into a horrifying cannibal monster whenever I got angry. You'd think she'd be able to appreciate the diversity to our family that brought. "Dog mouths are cleaner than human mouths, my disgusting but adorable little primate spawn. But if you don't want it—"

"I'll take it," Mimi said, snatching it with an Ultra-Force beam.

"You should probably avoid using your powers," Mandy said. "We don't know who fired that missile at us and you're pretty identifiable as is. It's not like you have been keeping a secret identity."

"Secret identities are pointless in the era of facial recognition and cell phone cameras," I replied. "It's why I finance my Super schools."

The Wakowski Academies were my primary charity outside of free medical care for as many citizens as possible. They were an alternative to the Society of Superheroes sponsored Guardian academies that were pretty much designed to teach Supers how to become superheroes. Which, among other things, meant they turned away people whose powers weren't good at heroics and pretty much left the majority of Supers without any alternatives to learn how to control their powers or a higher education.

My schools were designed around providing an alternative track for teaching kids with powers. In addition to providing a safe environment where you didn't have to worry about eye beams or being kidnapped to work for PHANTOM, it was primarily focused on getting people licensed for work in the civilian sector. Superheroics being the only viable job for people other than crime kind of created a polemic for your career paths that contributed to the hatred they received. You were either a famous demigod lording over humanity and saving the day or you were the monster under the bed.

Mind you, I generally thought this was ninety-nine percent the fault of the Muggles (Rowling can sue me for using the word) rather than the Supers themselves. Only about one percent of Supers had powers that were useful in combat situations, and they were more inclined to be victims of violence rather than the alternative. Much like the mentally ill, Hollywood had done a damn good job of making the empowered look like dangerous monsters rather than people who needed help. There was also the "crab bucket effect" to quote Sir Terry Pratchett (RIP). A lot of people just loathed Supers because of envy and were determined to make their lives suck to make up for whatever perceived advantage making your eyes change color or scissor hands gave you.

"Wow, Mom, that was a surprisingly eloquent set of thoughts," Leia said. "Who knew you had an altruistic side."

"You should," I replied. "But mostly I was thinking you should hide your powers because otherwise we'll get kicked out of the park."

"Huh?" Leia asked.

I pointed over to a nearby red sign that read, "Please note that all enhanced individuals must have Guardian accreditation before entry."

Mimi blinked. "What the hell does that mean?"

"It means that unless you're trained in superpowers and over eighteen, you don't get to enter," I replied.

"So, kids with powers can't enter," Leia said. "Suddenly, this place sucks."

"'Fraid so," I replied. "Look on the bright side, though. According to the website, it does allow Jewish and colored people now. The World Emperor wasn't a fan of either. It happened a long time ago too: 1994!"

"Yay," Mimi said, sarcastically. "I feel so included now."

"Wait, why *does* Dad have a parking lot then?" Leia asked.

"Probably helped kill the World Emperor with Steam Lass," Mandy said, giving both the kids a hug. "Never meet your idols, dear."

"If we can bring an end to this very special episode of Super Family Ties, we really do need to get our intelligence," Amanda said. "We can't rely on children—"

"We're not the only people wanting to steal the Spear of Saint George," Leia interrupted.

Amanda glared at Leia. "Excuse me?"

"We did do a once around the Tower of Londonium Museum," Mimi replied. "Being two teenage girls, no one questioned our presence."

"The Black Witch and Human Tank are there," Leia spoke, following her sister's introduction like they were sharing thoughts. "I picked up that they're here to steal the artifact we're here to steal."

"Goddammit," I muttered. "This is a complication I don't need."

Shocking as it may sound, I wasn't the only pseudo-villain/hero out there. Instead, there was the Shadow Seven that frequently didn't have seven members. They were a group of bad but not evil people assembled by Ultragoddess to do wetwork against various dictatorships or other important people that it would be politically sensitive to oppose. It was pretty much an open secret under President Anders but wasn't quite as effective at reformation as had been initially hoped. Plenty of crooks went right back to their criminal habits as soon as they'd worked off their sentences.

The Black Witch and Human Tank were special cases as well as people I'd consider acquaintances, if not friends. We'd teamed up on multiple occasions and they had a special relationship to both Mandy and Gary. The fact I didn't have a frenemy like them sort of bothered me.

"Is this going to be an issue?" Amanda asked Mandy.

"No," Mandy replied.

"Are you sure?" Amanda repeated.

"I'm sure," Mandy said, her voice lowering dangerously.

The Black Witch AKA Selena Darkchylde was Mandy's ex-girlfriend and the person who'd unwittingly wrecked Mandy's chance of being a Foundation agent. An early-blooming supervillainess, Selena had made Mandy her henchwoman and gotten the felony on her record that prevented her from ever becoming certified for government service. Strangely, at least among our extended love decahedron, they'd never spoken since despite our subsequent encounters. Apparently, the rift between them was less like an amicable breakup than love having turned to hate. Either that or the wound was still raw since I knew Mandy felt for her—had felt for her?—roughly the same as Gary.

"I like Aunt Clarissa," Leia said. "Why don't we recruit them?"

The Human Tank AKA Clarissa Montehaven was a former associate of Gary's brother, Keith, and apparently his lover if rumors were to be believed. She was a heroine who looked like a really ripped Alison Brie. Clarissa was a tech hero who could build her own suit of power armor—not quite as impressive as it was in the Nineties due to CrimeTube now sharing videos on how to make power gauntlets—and was probably the more heroic of the two. Unfortunately, she had a problem with me, and our last encounter had been a typical magic vs. science throwdown that nerds liked to bet on. I lost. I carried a grudge.

"That sounds like a good idea," Amanda said. "They're both career criminals who—"

"Nope," I interrupted. "We already have a tech guy."

"Thank you," Leia said.

"I mean Nicki Tesla," I replied. "She's on my list of recruits. What we must do is, instead, have some wacky hijinks-filled adventures to steal the Spear of Saint George first."

"Why does it have to be wacky?" Mimi asked, exasperated.

"Do you even know me, dear daughter?" I asked, appalled.

"I'm afraid I do," Mimi muttered.

"Why are we following her?" Amanda asked Mandy.

"It'll shut her up for a couple of years if we pull this off," Mandy replied.

Amanda nodded. "I suppose that *is* worth it."

"Oh, one more thing," Leia said, pulling out her cellphone. "My scanner says that the missile that shot us down was fired from here."

Well, crap.

Chapter Eleven

It's a Small(er) World After All

Oh my God, Cindy, is this really the best plan you could come up with?" Amanda asked, wearing the enormous Pinkie the Panda suit that I'd stolen from one of the poor World Emperor World employees taking a smoke break.

"It's my strategy," Mandy replied, wearing a Betsy Bunny costume. "World Emperor World is one of the most monitored locations on Earth and has massive numbers of cameras equipped with facial recognition software. There's no way we could get in without being spotted."

"Except our kids have already gone and done the tilt-a-whirl and rode the *Starcrash* ride," I said, wearing the Big Bad Wolf costume. "By the way, does anyone find it strange they have an homage ride to a crappy 1978 Italian science fiction film?"

"I find it strange that the country is called Londonium, but the capital city is called New Albion," Mimi said, still wearing her cosplay. "Shouldn't it be reversed?"

"Don't worry, Mom," Leia said. "Both Mimi and I brought holographic sequencer VPNs to disrupt any recording of our facial features. They make it so that the government can't track your face. You can buy them on the Dark Web."

"I don't suppose you brought enough for everyone?" I asked, knowing the answer.

"Nope!" Leia said. "We just sort of figured that you were tech savvy enough to have your own."

"You know there's a lot of things on the Dark Web you shouldn't be exposed to," Mandy said, speaking out of concern. "I worry about you kids."

"You mean like the ring of pedophile human traffickers and child pornographers we found and sent to Dad to murder?" Leia asked.

"Leia!" Mandy said, appalled. "How could you?"

I admit I was speechless as well.

Mandy, however, went a different way with that. "I could have eaten those people! They're just going to waste with your father!"

"Sorry!" Leia said. "You were out of town!"

"I feel like I should object," Amanda said, sounding bored. "So, I object. It is wrong to make teenagers accessories to murder. Shame."

"Consider us chastened," Leia said. "Does this mean we have to stop dealing in Bitcoin?"

"Yes!" I snapped. "I don't mind you setting up child abusers for horrid death, but I will not have you dealing in crypto currency! Money should be backed up by nation-states or precious metals! Plus, it's terrible for the environment. Am I clear?"

"Yes, Mom," Leia said. "We'll sell it for drugs and trade that."

"Good job," I said, hoping they were but not caring too much whether they were kidding.

The five of us proceeded past the huge number of gift shops, restaurants, and line-filled rides to get to the center of World Emperor World. There was the Tower of Londonium, which was the renamed Castle Deathpeak and the former lair of the Victorian Age's greatest archvillain. It was the actual castle and I had to wonder how the criminal mastermind would have felt about having hundreds of snot-nosed children wandering through his torture chambers and labs while begging to go to the bathroom.

"How did the World Emperor die anyway?" I asked. "I'm not looking forward to activating an ancient steampunk mecha or giant robot when we rob this place."

"Cancer," Mandy replied. "The Mysterious Island sank into the ocean as his tomb."

"I thought this was his mysterious island," I said.

"No," Mandy replied. "This was just his island-island. The Mysterious Island is also different from the island where he made the animal people."

"I used to think Victorian science fiction writers were incredibly imaginative," I replied. "Now I just think they paid attention to the news."

"Dude was a plagiarist," Leia said. "We went to visit him once and he totally copied our time machine. He was so mean to our Morlock friends."

Mimi growled and balled up a pair of glowing fists. "Stupid Eloi and their white privilege."

God, my kids were nerds. This was the result of my complete lack of parenting. They'd become dutiful, kind, studious young intellectuals rather than the little hellraisers they were meant to be. At least I could take comfort in the fact they'd broken like fifty laws in the past twenty-four hours alone. I wasn't a complete failure in raising them.

"You're weird, Mom," Leia said, undoubtedly referring to my thoughts.

"And proud of it, my dear," I said. "Anyway, let's get ready to smash into this place and grab everything inside."

"Or we could buy tickets," Mandy said, already returning with some in hand, err, paw. "Then we could grab the spear."

"Which involves more explosions?" I asked.

"Ugh," Mandy said, walking forward. "Mimi, Leia, Amanda, come on."

"No real names in public!" Amanda growled.

"You know, we need to talk about your codename, Mimi," I said, following.

"What?" Amanda asked.

"Mystery is an incredibly lame codename," I replied.

"First of all, it's Ms. Terri," Mimi corrected. "Two words."

"Which just sounds like your real name," I said. "Mystery is how you should have said it from the beginning, but you should have added something else to distinguish it. Lady Mystery, Doctor Mystery, Professor Mystery, Mystery Woman, etcetera. The masses are a lowest common denominator. They don't get subtlety or in-jokes. Believe me, it's why I wear this outfit. People don't buy my poster because of my ungodly intellect."

I could literally feel how grossed out my children were. It amused me to no end. I was still way too young to be their mother but appreciated the warm fuzzy feeling of torturing my kids. They were like the little sisters I never got to noogie.

"Ugh, Mom," Leia said.

"I'm just saying maybe we can get her a nickname before we rebrand her," I replied. "If Mandy can be Vampire Cat—"

"I am not Vampire Cat, goddammit," Mandy said.

"—then we can get you a better codename," I said. "Maybe something to advertise your powers like Punchy Girl or Strong Female Protagonist."

"I think that's taken," Mandy said. "Also, *Mimi* is her nickname."

"Yes, if I wanted her to grow up to be a stripper working her way through med school," I said. "You know, like I did."

"My legal name is Margaret Cinderella Anders," Mimi said. "Dad gave me the Mimi nickname. I used to go by Mindy, but it got weird when Mom returned from the dead and people kept getting us confused. *Wait, you don't know my actual name*?"

"Your middle name is *Cinderella*?" I asked in horror. "What child abuse is this?"

"This is actually a new low for you, Cindy," Amanda said, showing no respect for her own real names rule. "You don't know your own kids' names?"

"No way is that originally her name," I replied. "This is totally a retcon."

"Uh, Mom, she was named after you," Leia said.

"Is that why Gary did it? Merciful Moses, I suppose it's better than admitting my full name is Cindy Lauper Wakowski," I muttered, shaking my head. "I need to adjust to this first. Is there anything else I need to know about you two? I mean important stuff, not international conspiracy or murder-related stuff."

"We're members of a future superhero team that regularly take us into the thirty-second century," Mimi said. "I lost my virginity this summer to Kid Splotch."

"That bastard!" I said, faking outrage. "We'll have to discuss protection as well as other medical issues."

"Please don't," Maggie said.

"Sex is literally the only thing I am qualified to discuss as your mother," I replied. "I mean, unless you want to learn how to do heart surgery and I'm pretty sure Leia can build a machine that does that better than any human."

"You're right, I can," Leia said. "As for sex, I'm a gray ace. I want to marry a robot."

"I'm holding out for a god or alien monarch," Mimi said. "Definitely man-shaped, though."

"I stand corrected," I replied. "I am clearly unqualified to talk to you about sex."

The five of us went into the Tower of Londonium and didn't have to worry too much about lines. Apparently, visiting a real-life archvillain's old lair didn't have the same level of luster as going on the Dead Man's Drop or Splash Cliffs. Indeed, once we entered, I was kind of appalled as to what they'd done to the World Emperor's digs. The guy had been an antisemitic, pro-imperialism despot but even he hadn't deserved to have his great hall turned into a food court. On the other hand, I saw they were selling giant turkey legs and I hadn't eaten since I'd stolen Leia's ice cream cone.

"Mmm, turkey," I said.

"You know those are made from emu, right?" Mandy said.

"That's just an urban legend, like the World Emperor's head being preserved underneath the castle," I paused. "That is an urban legend, right?"

"Absolutely," Mandy said. "The Foundation for World Harmony's agents had to defeat the robot body his brain was inside to claim the underground complex. Last I heard, he's a paperweight in the director's office."

"I meant the emu," I said.

"No, it's emu," Mimi said. "They clone them here."

That was when Amanda tapped me on the shoulder with her big, costumed paw before pointing at a nearby stall. "Gary's here."

"Wait, what?" I asked.

I removed my wolf's head, regardless of the danger, and looked. Sure enough, Gary was standing at the front of a line with a beautiful but tomboyish Afro Latina woman with a ponytail in a headband. Her costume, if you could call it that, was a yellow and white runner's top that displayed her midriff with jeans. I hoped that was just an illusion over body armor because that was in no way practical as a superheroine's outfit. It was Revolutionary Girl alright.

"What do I want?" Gary asked, talking to the poor fast-food attendant. "I'll tell you what I want: world peace and equality. Is it something that people want, though? No, they must have it forced upon them. They will call whoever does this a tyrant, a killer, and a monster but maybe that person is just a liberator. But if liberty is forced upon people, is it truly liberty at all or another cage?"

"Sir, this is an Ultraburger," the attendant said. "I meant what did you want to order?"

"Oh, just some curly fries and a water please," Gary said.

"You stole that entire rant," the attendant said. "It was a popular meme and dad joke for a while."

"Memes are a good source for a cheap laugh," Gary said.

"They're really not," the attendant said.

"Gary!" I snapped, walking up to him. "You're supposed to be on a mission of vengeance."

Gary took his curly fries and put them under the horseradish dispenser. "I *am* on a mission of vengeance. A rampage if you will."

"Hi," the purple-haired woman said. "Nice to see ya, Cindy."

"Revolutionary Girl? Is that a new costume?" I asked. "Where do you hide your bow? Also, Gary, *did you bring your hook up on your rampage?*"

"Well, I promised to give her a ride to San Judas and figured we'd pick up lunch," Gary said, eating his now extra-spicy fries. "It turns out Gabby knows some arms dealers and hackers around here. She's been very helpful. We tracked down the people who fired the missile to World Emperor World."

"Wow, your name is Gabby?" Mimi asked. "That's my mom's name, too."

"That's because she's your mom is disguise," Leia said, looking at her sister.

Mimi glared at Leia. "That's stupid. Don't you think I'd recognize my own mom? Gabby has a ponytail. Mom doesn't."

Leia stared. "I hate magic so much. At least when it is not combined with science."

"Hi unrelated daughter person!" Gabby said, waving to her. "I am most definitely not Gabrielle Anders."

"See!" Mimi said.

I opened my mouth to object to Gary intervening before closing it. Gary managing to track down who'd attacked us within a few hours was impressive for a B-grade magician whose education in the Dark Arts consisted primarily of tabletop roleplaying games. Unfortunately, since this was a Foundation for World Harmony base, it didn't take a super-genius to figure out who had probably tried to take us out.

"Yeah, I'm going to have to ask you not to kill everyone involved," I said, feeling sick just contemplating it.

"What?" Gary asked, horrified. "But they're right here!"

"They're cops, Gary!" I replied. "Sort of! Killing cops is off limits unless they're dirty cops! Which is, yes, all cops in Falconcrest City but when in Londonium do as the Londonians do."

"You mean dress in silly costumes and speak with fake British accents?" Revolutionary Girl asked, speaking in a very real one.

"You stay out of this, Chick Guevara," I replied.

"They fired a rocket at our kids," Gary said, his voice low and dangerous.

"And me!" I replied then turned back to Mandy and Amanda. "Oh, and you guys too."

"Gee, thanks, Cindy," Mandy said.

"Finding out who is dirty and on the Dragon King's payroll is why I'm here," Revolutionary Girl said. "Also, to keep your husband from getting killed."

"He's not my husband," I snapped. "We just live together and have kids as well as share finances."

Revolutionary Girl stared.

"Totally different!" I said.

"I could take this entire base," Gary said. "I am an omnipotent *Dungeons and Dragons* wizard. My power has grown from the petty hedge mage I used to be, and I am eager to wreak some vengeance!"

"Gary—" I felt like I was already becoming his den mother. Again. Gary was referring to the fact he'd briefly had a group of omnipotent magical objects called the Primal Orbs. Before rebooting the universe, he'd given himself a power upgrade but instead of getting something useful like rulership of the world, he'd given himself powers akin to a roleplaying game wizard. I longed for the day when I could point out the idiocy of this and today seemed as good a time as any.

"Vengeance!" Gary repeated.

"Gary," I said, already regretting inviting him on this trip. "Before you gave yourself wizard powers, all your powers came from a magic cloak, right?"

"You know it."

"What did that cloak give you?" I asked.

"Fire, lightning, ice, and the power to turn insubstantial," Gary replied.

"And what does D&D magic give you?" I asked, wanting to throttle him.

"Fire, lightning, ice, mostly," Gary said, pausing as if he hadn't thought that through before. "I see your point. However, I can also shoot *Web*!"

"I'm sure that would mean a lot against their army of people with guns," I said, pausing. "Also, B-Grade Supers."

"I can handle people with guns," Gary said. "God, you know."

"Demigod," I replied. "With no worshipers. Like the angel of dryer lint. Oh, and Foundation laser guns can hit insubstantial beings like ghosts and star vampires."

"Star vampires are insubstantial?" Gary asked.

"According to the History Channel, yeah," I replied. "Well, before they started showing nothing but conspiracy theories and shows about how awesome the Vikings were compared to the Christian kingdoms, they raped and plundered."

Revolutionary Girl shook her head. "It's like the Super version of *Seinfeld*. I could stand here listening to you people all day."

I pointed at her then Gary. "Neither of you are on my team. There're not enough spaces in Cindy's Seven. So, go home and let us sort this out."

"Uh huh," Gary said. "Cindy, if you need—"

"I do not need help!" I snapped, perhaps too forcibly. "Sorry, this is already proving stressful."

That was when the ceiling above us collapsed as the Human Tank, Black Witch, a rain of magical relics, and a bunch of Foundation KNIGHTS agents fell through.

Chapter Twelve

No Plan Survives First Contact with the Enemy

Superheroes cause things to explode.

This is just something you must accept when you're someone who is involved in punching people for a living in colorful, often form-fitting attire. Seriously, it's been three days and I've already been involved in three explosions and a plane crash. Is it me? Yes, probably. It could also be my associates who stupidly choose to hang around me.

Either way, I was pleased to say that it made our attempts to rob the place better. In addition to supervillains and superheroes raining down on us, I saw several glass cases of extremely rare artifacts fall through the destroyed ground. There was the World Emperor's steam-powered magical armor, the severed arm of Marduk, Jack the Ripper's knife, a handheld time-machine, and the Spear of Saint George that glowed with an unearthly aura visible only to my enhanced werewolf senses.

Obviously, all the Muggles panicked and screamed like they were wont to do in the middle of superhuman fights. The Ultraburger guy notably teleported away in a puff of purple smoke, which marked him as a civilian Super. Revolutionary Girl pulled out a pen and tapped the end before it transformed into a bow that she drew a bolt of glowing Ultra-Force energy, taking aim at the Foundation KNIGHTS without hesitation.

Mandy tore apart her costume, letting her claws grow and her eyes turn a demonic shade of red. Amanda burned away her costume and revealed her hooded superhero self underneath. Leia tapped her cellphone and a glowing energy shield covered her as before. Mimi, of course, just glowed like a Super Saiyin and I hoped she didn't accidentally bring down the castle on our heads, well, more than already was happening. Mimi and Leia pulled behind and seemed unsure whether to attack or not.

The Human Tank was wearing a smaller version of her usual armor, one that had probably been able to be hidden underneath a trench coat and wasn't covering her head. Clarissa was a very lovely woman with long golden hair and probably could have been on the cover of *Sports Illustrated's Super Edition*. Really, I needed to get the number of her flesh-crafter Super. She was blasting away at the Foundation agents, only to be stunned at Gary and my presence. That got her blasted in the chest.

The Black Witch, by contrast, was already summoning hideous shadow demons that were rising from the ground and launching themselves at the Foundation agents. Selena was one of the most beautiful women in the world and even though my tastes varied from Gary's, we both agreed on it. She had that Angelina Jolie and Eva Green thing both that was accompanied by being a Goth witch. I mean that with pointy hat and everything.

We were in a Mexican stand-off or the beginning of one at least with the Black Witch and Human Tank on one side, us on the other, and a third side with the KNIGHTS. I hated Foundation KNIGHTS. They were the epitome of the second rate heroes that couldn't make it on their own.

"Hey Cindy!" One of the KNIGHTS said, waving to me. It was a supermodel good-looking man with midnight black hair and striking but difficult-to-place-the-origins-of features. He was wearing a business suit in contrast to the other black bodysuit wearing KNIGHTS. It was Case AKA Agent G AKA Jane's boyfriend.

What the hell?

"You! Abomination!" a blond-haired white guy pushing sixty and looking a bit like Sean Connery in his *The Rock* years shouted at Mandy. He was apparently the leader, and it took me a second to recognize him as Colonel Colt Colton, Agent of the Foundation. The world's most famous secret agent, which should tell you how much he sucked at his job.

"Oh, hi, Dad," Mandy said, sighing. "How are you?"

I did a double take. "Time out, what now?"

"No one says time out anymore, Mom," Leia said, sighing.

"Colt Colton is our grandfather?" Mimi asked.

"He doesn't consider me his daughter anymore," Mandy said. "To him, vampires are just their soulless reanimated corpses that should all be destroyed."

Which they normally were in our dimension, but I wasn't going to argue the point with Mandy. It had required an elaborate and bizarre series of events to turn Mandy in our version of Angel (the David Boreanaz version).

Colonel Colten pointed at Mandy and me. "There are the criminals we identified approaching the base this morning! They clearly survived. Shoot to kill! Ignore the others."

"I feel offended," Gary replied.

"Oh, and kill him too!" Colonel Colten said. "He got my daughter killed then took up with a bunch of murderous skanks."

"That is a half-truth!" I shouted, appalled.

Clearly, the issues of the family Karkofsky (and my semi-related part) were larger than I expected but I was mostly focused on making a run for the Spear of Saint George on the ground. Unfortunately, I could already see the Human Tank and Black Witch staring at it.

The KNIGHTS, who were all conventionally attractive-looking humans started conjuring fire and suits of armor among other superpowers to follow their leader's command. None of them had any codenames or distinguishing characteristics but seemed ready to follow Colonel Colten's orders out of hand. Well, all save for one.

"I'm sorry, but I'm going to have to pass," Case said. "I'm not here to kill associates."

"Kill him too," Colonel Colten said.

Wow, what a boss.

"Get the spear!" The Black Witch shouted, pulling out a wand. "We need it to stop Smog!"

"Oh, hell no!" I shouted. "That spear is mine!"

"Why are you here?" Clarissa asked, blasting away at the KNIGHTS. It was stun blasts, which I found to be lame.

"To steal the spear!" I said, turning into my warg form and rushing to grab the Spear of Saint George in my mouth, only for the Black Witch to blast me with green energy that sent me tumbling across the ground. Damn that hurt!

A group of shadow demons ran up to grab the spear in my mouth then tried pulling it out while I resisted with every fiber of my werewolfy being. I chipped a couple of teeth in the process before Revolutionary Girl fired an Ultra-Force arrow that caused them all to explode in a shower of light. Dammit, I hated owing her.

One of the KNIGHTS was a duplicator and immediately started turning into dozens of identical versions of himself before charging at Gary. My live-in partner threw non-lethal blasts of ice and electricity at them, which I felt was pulling one's punches when duplicates were not traditionally considered people.

Case didn't hesitate to pull out his guns and start shooting, probably because they didn't hesitate to turn on him. Our cyborg friend was dodging fireballs and lightning from another pair. He didn't kill any of his fellow agents, though because a third was conjuring glowing force fields around them all.

I had to give the KNIGHTS a hand—believe me, the only one I wanted to give them would be ripped from their limbs—but they fought well. A lot better than the bunch of amateur hour rent-a-heroes that I thought they were. Colonel Colton, in particular, drew a pair of katanas and attacked his own daughter like a whirling dervish that required every bit of her vampire speed to keep up with.

Apparently, those bodysuits weren't just decorative and designed to highlight every curve in those muscular All-American (err Londonium) good-looking agents. No, they were also nano-weave enhancement suits that provided every one of them superhuman strength and speed. That was in addition to whatever superpowers they had from birth or freakish lab experiment.

"Leave this alone!" Clarissa shouted, speaking with a booming voice through her suit of armor as she fired energy blasts from her arm cannon like Samus Aran. "We have to get the Spear of Saint George to slay Smog!"

"Dat's whad we'red doing!" I said, ducking under one of the blasts as I tried to figure out what to do with the spear in my mouth.

"You're trying to stop the Dragon King from invading the planet by bribing the Thran Empire?" Clarissa asked.

"Whad?" I said, still slurring my speech. "No! Ids for da money!"

That was when Colonel Colton threw Mandy through the air by her leg, sending her smashing into the World Emperor's armor case. The case shattered and the armor fell over before it landed on Jack the Ripper's knife and Marduk's arm, all of them starting to glow. The armor's eye slits turned red before it levitated.

"At last, after a century of paralyzed slumber, my spirit is free once more!" The World Emperor's voice sounded like a discount James Earl Jones. "The power of the gods and sorcery around me shall allow me to rise to my full power and conquer Earth!"

Huh, I would have thought the World Emperor would have sounded more like Christopher Lee's Dracula and less like Rita Repulsa. Either way, that gave me an idea. "Leia, gid da time machine on da fleur!"

"What?" Leia asked, standing there looking bored as a KNIGHTS agent unloaded a machine gun on her force-field protected body.

The fact he was trying to kill a teenage girl, let alone my daughter, made me inclined to rip the guy's head clean off. I generally avoided killing cops, even dirty ones, and checked my rage. Then I ignored that feeling and leapt on the agent's back, breaking several of his bones before dropping the spear out of my mouth. "I said, get me the time machine on the floor! We're out of here!"

"What?" Amanda asked, throwing lightning bolts at the World Emperor as he absorbed her attacks and grew stronger. His steampunk armor was powered by the forces of magic and she didn't seem to realize that. "We can't abandon the fight here! The World Emperor is a threat to all living beings!"

"Supervillain!" I shouted. "Not our problem!"

Mimi chose to enter the fight at this point, knocking KNIGHTS agents around like bowling pins before rescuing a downed Case that had burns on the side of his face that I wondered if he'd have to visit a body shop to fix. She prepared to throw-down with the World Emperor and I gave her even odds.

Colonel Colton jumped in front of her with his katanas swinging, only for Mimi to grab him in the middle of his attack by the wrists. "Don't make me hurt you, Grandpa."

"You are not any family of mine," Colonel Colton hissed. "Just a child of that goddamn asshole that killed my daughter."

"Mimi, you have permission to kill Mandy's father," I replied.

"You do not!" Mandy said, climbing to her feet. "Maybe just rough him up a little."

That was when the World Emperor shot forth a metal rubber tentacle from the back of his armor to grab the Spear of Saint George. "Fools! Do you not know that death when you see it?"

"Hey, that's mine!" I snapped. "I stole it fair and square!"

"Yes, from me!" The World Emperor chortled. "With this spear in hand, my armies will march across the globe and... AHH!"

The World Emperor was interrupted by Leia pulling out what appeared to be a proton pack from the 1982 *Ghostbusters* movie—not any of the sequels—don't ask how I can tell the difference—before pulling the World Emperor's disembodied spirit from the body then shoving a trap underneath it. The World Emperor screamed out in agony before he was sucked into the square device and vanished, his armor collapsing on the ground.

"Leia, where the hell did you get that?" I asked.

"What? You think I'd make a basket for all your goodies and not one for me?" Leia asked. "My favorite hobby is also bringing to life popular super-science. I've given Dad like twelve functioning lightsabers."

I rolled my eyes. "Like your father needs to play with his lightsaber anymore. Mind you, he seems to have a lot more partners than I'm comfortable with."

"Oh, that is rich!" Gary snapped, looking exhausted and soot covered.

"Just saying!" I said, looking at Revolutionary Girl. "Good lord knows where she's been!"

"Excuse me?" Revolutionary Girl said.

"She's Gabrielle Anders, Mimi's mom," Leia said. "Why am the only person who gets this?"

"You are so weird," Mimi said, throwing Colonel Colton on a pile of a hundred or so defeated KNIGHTS agents. Not all of them were the duplicated agent or the original team. It seemed that my children's suspicions about the park being a Foundation base were correct. I could hear helicopters moving into position outside the castle as well as the tell-tale sound of tank treads.

It was at that time I noticed that the spear had fallen to the ground and saw the Black Witch's shadow demons were mostly destroyed but a trio of them were rushing for it. I made a running leap for it, only to find myself once more grappling with them over it. The object again in my teeth.

"No! Gimme!" I growled, pulling on the shaft while the shadows tugged their way.

"We're trying to save the world!" Selena shouted. "I can't believe you're putting the welfare of the planet after your own selfish interests."

"Clearly, ya don't know me vary vell!" I said, through my clenched teeth. "Gawddammit Leia, ged da frigging time machine vorking!"

"Maybe we should listen to them," Amanda said, surveying the scene and seeing dozens of armed troopers entering with laser guns drawn. Perhaps it was only now hitting her she was in open revolt against the United Governments of Earth.

That was when Mimi walked over to the time machine that looked like an early 1950s television monitor combined with a typewriter that you held with two handles. It also had a rotary dial phone. Mimi started fiddling with it as more KNIGHTS agents rappelled down through holes in the ceiling to make us outnumbered, conservatively, a hundred to one.

"Mimi, whad arr ya doing?" I asked, trying to figure a way out of this that didn't involve us escaping from Super-Max Super-Prison. That would take weeks and probably would force us to miss our deadline for the Dragon King leaving Earth with his fortune. We could steal in space, but no one would care about a heist there.

That was when a glowing bright light washed over us, and I felt myself vanish from where I stood before going someplace else. Seconds later, maybe longer, I found myself in the middle of a corporate waiting room. There were leather couches, a secretary sitting behind a desk, and beige walls surrounding us. There were also those little tables full of magazines that I think everyone on the planet was sick of. Mimi, Mandy, Amanda, Case, Leia, and I were the only people there. We must have looked like quite the sight, especially since I was in giant wolf form and with a spear in my mouth. Leia was also holding a full ghost trap, still reeking of brimstone and ectoplasm (that smells like rotted meat).

I dropped the spear out of my mouth again then turned back into my human form. "Okay, Mimi, what the hell was that?"

"People keep forgetting I'm as smart as Leia," Mimi muttered and handed over the time machine to her sister. "I teleported us to the Omega Corporation headquarters in Falconcrest City. It's where Nikki Telsa was located and she's next on your list. More importantly, it was also away from the Foundation for World Harmony's mercenaries."

"So, you just abandoned Dad?" Leia asked, appalled. She nevertheless put away her trap and proton pack into an invisible space that made video game power up noises when she used it. She still took the time machine, though.

Mimi rolled her eyes. "No, I teleported Dad and his newest girlfriend back to the mansion with the Black Witch and Aunt Clarissa."

"She's not your aunt and you should have let them die," I replied.

"Cindy!" Amanda said, appalled.

"They tried to heist my heist!" I snapped. "It violates the sacred art of dibs."

Mandy shook her head. "Thank you, Mimi. You did well. You also probably saved the world, Leia."

"Oh, like the Society of Superheroes wouldn't have stopped the World Emperor anyway!" I snapped. "He's been a ghost in a suit of armor the entire time. It's worse than being the frozen head on someone's desk."

Leia stared at me.

"Not to take away from your accomplishment!" I said, raising my hands.

Case sighed. "I guess I'm no longer a Foundation agent."

I gave a dismissive wave. "You're too good for them anyway. Want to join me on a heist?"

"Sure," Case said.

That was when the secretary spoke. "I'm sorry. Do any of you have an appointment?"

Chapter Thirteen

Making an Offer They Can Refuse

"So, just so we're clear, you want to do what now?" Case asked after I asked the secretary to inform Nikki Tesla I was coming.

"Rob a dragon's hoard," I replied. "It's a pretty classic endeavor. There're no virgin maidens this time around but I'm not sure what those ancient Medieval storytellers thought a dragon needed with one anyway."

"I assumed to eat it," Mandy replied. "Really, I'd question what a dragon needed with a hoard of gold."

"Well, Smog invests it," I replied. "Can't build those giant lairs without a 401K and there aren't so many elaborate cave systems these days. At least ones outside of national parks, and who wants tourists in your home?"

"I dunno, that seems like a meal delivery service," Mandy said. "Speaking as an immortal predator, I think that would rapidly cut down on feeding issues."

"Yeah, but Americans are full of cholesterol," I said, pausing. "Okay, I feel we've wandered off topic."

"You think?" Case asked. "I'm still dealing with the fact dragons are real on your world."

"Dragons aren't on yours?" I asked, surprised. "Your world is so weird."

"He's a space dragon if that makes a difference, Uncle Case," Leia said.

"It does," Case said. "But we don't have those on my world either."

"Why were you working with the Foundation for World Harmony anyway?" I asked, confused. "You're like a cyborg assassin. Why would you want to work for a second-rate superhero-adjacent spy agency?"

"I wanted to have a steady job in this dimension," Case replied. "One that would hopefully not get me on the kill list of the government."

I made a dismissive wave. "There's like three names on the kill list and one of them is still Tom Terror. They refuse to believe he's dead."

"There's three names on the kill list because they keep killing them," Amanda pointed out.

Kill orders were the nuclear option of superhuman politics. Well, aside from actual nukes that were often authorized in the event of alien invasions or against the Behemoth going on a rampage. Something of which I have many opinions on, and we were lucky to have superheroes who could throw missiles in the sun and clean up radiation after to avoid triggering Armageddon.

Kill orders were when the Foundation for World Harmony's Director signed off on assassination of supervillains that had crossed lines that rendered them unfit for trial. They'd been very popular during the Dark Age of Superheroes and extended into the War on Terror before falling out of favor because, shock of shocks, the governments of the world abused them. It was all fun and games to take out a kill order on the Prismatic Commando for supporting democratic elections in

Taiwan or whatever, but that became something of a problem when you needed him to fight Tiamat or Gozer.

Generally, the government dialed back on kill orders due to pressures from the Society of Superheroes and the fact the Foundation took shots at supervillains meant they no longer felt inclined to hold back against them. A few crashed hellicarriers later and the only people still on the list were "real" terrorists, serial killers, and habitual anti-government types. If you restricted to killing people in the "business" like other criminals and gang members, then you almost never were associated with the so-called kill list.

"My father kept trying to get my name added to it," Mandy said, sighing. She conjured a pair of sunglasses from a pair of shadows and put them on. It was a cool little trick.

"He really hates vampires, doesn't he?" I asked, genuinely feeling bad for her. Mind you, I probably should have clued into the fact Mandy wasn't fond of her family since we'd been living together for years, and she hadn't mentioned them.

"He wasn't fond of me when I was bisexual, a criminal's henchwoman, married to a supervillain's brother, and a teen mother. I've never run out of ways to disappoint the Colonel," Mandy said.

"Damn," I said, unsure how to react to that. "Well, fuck that guy."

Mandy smiled. "Gary said the same thing. Either way, becoming a supervillain and thief is another way to spite him."

"You're a hero, Mandy," Amanda said. "Don't ever believe otherwise."

"You shut your mouth," I snapped. "She's my friend and I'm not going to let you badmouth her."

Amanda rolled her eyes.

"So, you want my help in this?" Case asked.

I frowned. "Well, you weren't initially on the list, but I think we can squeeze you in. We need something for ninety percent of the ladies and ten percent of the men in our audience."

"Please tell me you're not filming this," Amanda said.

I pulled out my cellphone and took a photo of me and Case standing together for my Omegagram account. "Hashtag New Teammate!"

Case snatched it back. "You realize I actually am trying to stay under the radar, right?"

"Then you shouldn't have joined Big Brother," I said, snatching my phone back. "You don't think you're now in a hundred thousand government databases now?"

"No, because in the event of my defection a specialized worm moves through the entirety of their files and removes all references to me," Case replied.

I blinked. "Okay, if I wasn't going to hire you before, I certainly am now. I should have had you do that for me."

Case shrugged. "Who'd want to kill you?"

It was cute he meant that. Unfortunately, Amanda couldn't leave it alone and started counting off candidates on her fingers. "Jealous wives, jealous husbands, the families of her victims, her still-living victims, vaccine deniers—"

"I think my strategy of saying that anyone who doesn't get a vaccine gets eaten was a good one," I replied.

Mimi shook her head. "Can we cut down on the cannibalism, Mom?"

"It's not cannibalism unless they're a werewolf," I said.

Mimi stared. "Promise you're not going to eat anyone else, Mom."

"Okay, sure," I lied.

Mimi sighed.

The secretary from earlier walked back in, having apparently gone to her higher ups to deal with the sudden influx of supervillains in her office. She was a blue-haired Hispanic woman with an immaculate set of nails and carrying a folder that I could see photos of me sticking out of. "I'm sorry, Ms. Wakowski, but I don't believe the CTO is willing to see you right now. Can you schedule an appointment for next week?"

I paused and slowly counted to three before responding. "What?"

"The CTO—" The secretary started to say.

"I feel like 'do you know who I am' is an appropriate response here," I said, taking a deep breath and avoiding releasing my inner Karen.

"You are the supervillain known as—" The secretary started to speak.

"I own the goddamn company!" I snapped. "Or my sister-in-law does if Gary and I were married, which we aren't, but she's a pushover so don't make me get her on the phone."

"You actually are one of the primary stockholders, Mom," Leia said.

"I am?" I asked.

"You own twelve percent of the company and Gary owns fifteen percent," Leia said. "Aunt Kerri is CEO primarily due to your votes that get cast by an autonomous bot that handles your finances."

I stared. "Who made that?"

Leia stared.

"Right," I said, sighing. "Of course."

The secretary blinked. "Err, that wasn't listed—"

"And yet you hired a supervillain to be your chief technology officer," Amanda said, sarcastically. "Or the bot did."

"Technically, she was chosen by the board—" the secretary started to say.

"Which is selected by me and Gary," I replied, remembering we actually had guaranteed Nikki Telsa a job for helping us out in the Hollow Earth. It was one of the few decisions I'd actually been involved in. "Keep up, Ms.—"

"Ms. Secretary," the secretary said.

I blinked. "Wow, your parents really had your life planned out, didn't they?"

"I'm an android," Ms. Secretary said.

"Oh," I replied, reaching over and patting Case on the back. "We have one of those too. You two want to have some hot robot sex? I can watch!"

"Please don't," Case said, stepping away.

"Sorry. Forgot you were in a monogamous relationship in this reality," I replied. "In any case, Nikki Tesla is the CTO of Omega Corp because I put her there. We all know that the sciences inherently inclined one to evil."

"Wait, what now?" Leia asked, looking up from the time machine in her hands.

"I don't think that's right, Mom," Mimi said.

"It's simple, good is dumb and full of punchy indestructible people. Evil is smart and full of mad scientists as well as wizards," I replied. "Plus, you know, sexy ass bitches like me who have PHDs."

"Cindy, that is not remotely true," Amanda said, sighing.

"She *is* a sexy ass bitch," Mandy said. "She also has a PHD."

"Thank you, Vampirella," I replied. "Besides, I know you want to defend your husband, Amanda, but we know Mr. Inventor will eventually flip out and kill everyone. It's inevitable due to having that IQ in four digits my daughters have."

"I am a super punchy indestructible person and super smart," Mimi replied.

"I know, or as we call in online gaming, a broken build," I said, shaking my head. "Save some for the rest of the gamers online. We may have to nerf you in our next update. Have you considered becoming vulnerable to aluminum? Losing your powers three days a month? That's a werewolf reference by the way. Not the other thing."

"I'm starting to regret coming on this adventure," Amanda said, sighing.

"Starting to?" Mandy asked.

"Point taken," Amanda said. "Listen, if Nikki Tesla doesn't want to see us then we should move on. I'm uncomfortable enough knowing you've involved with this arms-trafficking polluting hellhole of a company."

"It does twenty percent less arms trafficking and ninety percent less polluting under us," I replied. "Mind you, the arms trafficking section no longer sells to PHANTOM, SKULL, rogue nations, and crazy guys who think *Red Dawn* is an aspirational film, so I call my tenure as primary stockholder a win."

"Really, ninety percent less pollution?" Amanda asked.

"Yeah," I replied. "Leia built a portable hole on her tenth birthday, and we just dumped all the world's toxic waste into it."

"It led to a universe of radiation eating toxic slime monsters," Leia said. "They were very grateful. I'm now worshiped as the Goddess of Plenty on Grimeworld."

Mimi muttered something about it being her idea.

Case grinned from ear to ear. "And people wonder why I love this universe."

"I thought it was because it was full of sexually promiscuous professional fighters who all look like swimsuit models," I replied.

"No, my world has plenty of those too," Case said. "Besides, way more competition for me here."

Mimi rubbed her temples. "God, I wish my parents would stop talking about sex."

Leia gave her a sideways glance. "You think this is bad, imagine having their thoughts blasting in your head twenty-four seven."

Mimi blanched. "I will never envy your powers again."

"Did you know our parents once went on a sex tourism visit to Video Game Land?" Leia said.

Mimi stared in horror. "Who? No. I don't want to know. Wait, I do."

"Rhymes with Mara Soft," Leia said, sticking her tongue out in disgust.

"I'd be ashamed but that would require a sense of shame," I said.

"Your character in twelve words or less," Case said.

"Hush you," I said.

"In any case, I'm not going to stand around here and let Nikki Tesla tell me what to do. Who does she think she is?"

"One of the most feared and respected villains left?" Mimi suggested.

"One of the world's greatest scientists," Leia added.

"The person who actually has authority in this building," Mandy added.

"Yet another supervillain who is openly operating, further illustrating how broken our justice system is?" Amanda threw in.

"I don't know who that is," Case said. "Isn't she the Doctor Octopus rip-off from the comics in my world?"

I rolled my eyes. "She's a real person, Case. I swear, it's so weird that our stuff is fictional in your world."

"*That's* what you consider weird," Case said, positively brimming with sarcasm.

"Yes!" I replied before marching past Ms. Secretary.

"No, wait, you can't!" Ms. Secretary said.

"Watch me!" I replied.

It didn't take a PHD, which I had, to know where Nikki would be operating from. You didn't become a supervillain to work out of the penultimate floor. No, you always worked from the penthouse or an underground lair. Since Falconcrest City was built on a bunch of tunnels filled with mole people and dinosaurs, I decided it was best to simply head upward.

I decided not to take the elevator since if Nikki was going to be a pain in the ass about this, she'd probably drop it from thirty stories. I'd survive it—no werewolf ever died from a broken neck—but it would certainly hurt like hell. Instead, I loped up the stairs and waited for exploding mines or lasers to blast me. Much to my surprise, it didn't happen and it occurred to me that people used the stairwell for smoking and travel every day so murdering all your employees was probably a bad strategy. I didn't entertain the idea that Nikki hadn't rigged up the building like a Bond villain.

Either way, I reached the top floor in wolf form then smashed through the door before assuming my human form. "Nikki Tesla! I demand to speak with you in the name of the Supervillain's Code and the law of pissing me off!"

My entrance didn't have quite the same effect I'd expected. The top floor of Omega Corp had a huge skylight but, otherwise, seemed to be a perfectly normal super science lab with lots of computers and biological experiments running. Nikki Tesla, the black-haired German scientist, was dressed in civilian clothes except for her metal tentacles attached to her harness, and a lab coat. The only other person present was a petite blonde woman also in a lab coat that bore a passing resemblance to Anna Paquin.

"First of all," Nikki said, speaking with a slight German accent in place of her once comically exaggerated one, "there's no such thing as a Supervillain's Code. Next, I'm busy, Cindy. Go away."

"Blame Drew Hayes and I have a reason for you to interrupt whatever you're doing," I said, pointing at her. "I'm developing an all-female team (plus one hot cyborg spy dude) to go after the hoard of Smog the Dragon. That's S-M-O-G not the Tolkien monster. It'll be the biggest heist ever and we've already got most of the team. What do you say?"

Nikki fetched a cup of coffee from a nearby table that was the only non-science-y thing in the room. "I'm going to have to pass."

Chapter Fourteen

Meeting Our Latest Employee

"What do you mean you're going to have to pass?" I asked, appalled.

"I think it's pretty self-explanatory," Nikki said, finishing her coffee. A mechanical hand putting it over on the nearby coffee table. "I have no interest in helping you rob Smog the Dragon King."

"But this is a huge opportunity!" I said, genuinely surprised she didn't want in on this.

"Yes, to make an enemy of the world's richest being," Nikki said. "I'm also doing quite fine. As Chief Technology Officer of Omega Corporation, I have access to all of the resources I need to continue my research and plot my own supervillainous schemes."

"You actually used supervillainous schemes in a sentence non-ironically," I said, blinking. "Impressive."

"Thank you," Nikki said. "My assistant and I also cured cancer."

I stared. "Wait, what?"

The blonde woman beside her pulled up her Omegapad. "We're having impressive results shrinking the lumps of—"

"No one cares," Nikki said. "Cindy Wakowski isn't a real doctor anyway."

"The hell I'm not!" I snapped. "I'm qualified as both a general practitioner and surgeon!"

"And yet you're still running around in a miniskirt and corset," Nikki said. "There's a reason we female villains aren't taken as seriously as male ones."

"Do not blame my fashion sense for the patriarchy!" I shouted. "I look good in my costume and don't need to conform to societal expectations."

"Well—" the blonde started to speak.

"You can have Dana," Nikki interrupted, gesturing to her lab assistant. "I really don't have time to go gallivanting off for a casino heist, no matter how impressive the haul. I have henchmen of my own for that now. Dana here is still in the early stage of her career and I've gotten everything out of her that I'm likely to. She also needs the money."

"Wait, what?" Dana, presumably, asked. "I what? Huh?"

"Why the hell would I want your random flunky?" I asked, appalled.

"I am not a flunky!" Dana said. "I am a Doctor of Strange Physics and Engineering! Well, before the university revoked my degrees. Stupid Brigham Young University morality clause."

"She isn't," Nikki said. "She's Dana Vandergast AKA the Damselfly."

I knew of Dana Vandergast actually. She was most known for being a petty street level thief with shrinking powers and flight. Basic insect-themed hero stuff. Unfortunately, she had an incredibly toxic relationship in the supervillain community. Not only had she received her powers from Tom Terror, but she'd also been blamed for a bunch of ghastly human experiments that might not bother Nikki Tesla but certainly bothered me.

"I don't work with Nazis," I said, snapping.

"I am not a Nazi!" Dana said.

"You worked for PHANTOM," I said. "Despite the attempts to rebrand, their founder was a big ole one."

Nazis were one of the things most supervillains wouldn't deal with in the supervillain community, at least these days. Probably because Gary and I had both made a point of killing pretty much every member of the community who did. Supervillains, as a general rule, weren't the most progressive sort but could tell when the wind was blowing away from the "Revive the Third Reich" types. It was just eighty years too late.

"Not voluntarily," Dana said. "I was a slave!"

"Prove it!" I said, crossing my arms.

"I'm gay!" Dana said.

"Oh, like that gets you out of it," I replied.

"It should!" Dana said. "I hate Tom Terror! I never committed most of the crimes attributed to me! Leptonics Industries blamed me for all of their crimes when I tried to blow the whistle on the fact that they were conducting human experimentation for Tom Terror! Then they sold me to him!"

"She's telling the truth," Nikki replied.

Leptonics Industries was one of PHANTOM's cover companies and also the guys who outfitted two out of three war criminals since Omega Corp got out of the arms trafficking business.

"How do you know?" I asked, genuinely curious.

"I monitor all of my employees' personal computer search history," Nikki answered. "Her porn history is of a decidedly sapphic bent."

"Wait, you what?" Dana asked, horrified. Her face turned a bright shade of red. "That is a breach of personal ethics!"

"As for the rest," Nikki said, not bothering to defend herself, "Tom Terror has enslaved many supervillains over the years, myself included. I also note that she's the only employee of mine who complains about ethics violations."

"Hmmm," I said, not sure if I wanted to take a chance on her given her reputation. "I dunno."

"I don't want to be part of your heist anyway!" Dana said, putting her hands on her hips. "I have a job here, doing real important research."

"No, you don't," Nikki said, making a cup of coffee with her metal arms and bring it to her without looking in the machine's general direction.

"Wait, what?" Dana asked, shocked.

"Yeah, you're fired," Nikki replied. "I'm stealing all of your research and applying it to my plan for world domination."

"You can't do that!" Dana said, her mouth open like a lost puppy.

"Supervillain," Nikki said, amused. "In any case, I'll see $200,000 and the remainder of your apartment's lease paid as a transitional package. There's no need to be cruel when you backstab your employees."

Dana stared. "But, but, but, our research will be worth billions."

"Mmm hmm," Nikki said. "But believe me this is better than some reporter finding out you were involved and discrediting it. I mean could you imagine what would happen if people found out our one hundred percent effective cancer treatment was made by a supervillain?"

Dana shook with rage and if she wasn't already a supervillain, she probably would have had her origin story right in front of me. "You are a supervillain…."

"Not according to my incredibly high-priced lawyers," Nikki said, chuckling. She took a sip of her coffee. "I didn't do it, nobody saw me do it, if they did, they were lying, and if you have proof then I can always claim it was a clone or shapeshifter."

"Or guy from an alternate reality," I said, sighing. "I'm familiar with The People vs. The Wicked Queen."

Dana slumped in defeat then looked over at me. "I don't suppose that job with you is still open?"

"I don't recall offering it to you," I replied, dryly. "You know a lot of young women would love to be part of Cindy's Seven."

"Is that what we're called?" Dana asked. "You need to understand that even with that severance package, I have student loans."

I stared at her. "You're paying back your student loans despite being a supervillain."

"Yes?" Dana asked. "I mean, they may have revoked my degrees, but I still got my education."

"You're objectively terrible at this," I replied, shaking my head. "However, I need to get a mad scientist on this team who isn't my daughter. So, you're hired."

"Uh, good," Dana said, clearly not as enthusiastic about the prospect of being one of my partners in the greatest heist since Helios the Sun King stole the sun. I mean, yeah, we kind of needed that and I had no idea where he intended to sell it but props for effort.

"Yay," Dana said, clutching her pad and looking less like she'd gotten a new awesome job and more like she'd signed up for a suicide mission. Which, to be fair, she had done both.

"Now if we're done here with your attempt to recruit me into your faux-woke 'sisters before misters' sorority, I have work to get back to," Nikki replied.

I stared at her. "You know this bitchy girl boss routine isn't exactly the impressive display of feminist triumph you think it is. Especially since, I remind you, *Gary gave you this job*."

"Wait, really?" Dana asked, doing a double take.

"Yeah, she was a henchwench too!" I said, breaking my own aversion to the word. "Part of the same gang! Gary made her CTO as a retirement package for helping him beat PHANTOM!"

I felt like a little sidebar was appearing above my head with the words, "See *The Tournament of Supervillainy,* True Believers!" It was a weird feeling but hardly the first time I'd felt it.

Nikki narrowed her eyes. "No wonder he's cheating on you with a younger woman."

Dana looked like she wanted to hide behind her pad.

I snorted, her eyes turning yellow as my claws extended. "First of all, we have an open polyamorous relationship. Next, Revolutionary Girl is not younger than me. We're the exact same age according to *Anarchists Weekly*."

"Funny how I didn't mention who," Nikki replied, "And really? She looks like she's in her late twenties, tops."

Yeah, we really weren't friends anymore were we. "Well, then I guess I'll just leave you here alone to pretend you cured cancer instead of living off the accomplishments of others."

"Thomas Edison is widely known as the person who invented the light bulb despite the fact several other people had functioning ones before him," Nikki said. "If you want the respect this stupid plan is supposed to get you then I suggest you follow his example. Be less focused on who did what and more on making sure you get the credit. It will last longer."

"Bill Murray said that if you want to be rich and famous, try being rich first," I said. "I did and want to be famous now, too."

"Hopefully for more than your slutty Omegagram page," Nikki said. "You and Brittney are the only women your age who can pull that off."

Yeah, she had to die now.

Before I could carry out my mostly unprovoked overreaction, the skylight above us shattered and a figure who looked like a red ink blot in the shape of a person dropped down before landing in a standard superhero pose. It was Red Splotch, the brother or clone (I wasn't sure which) of Stanley Otkid AKA The Super-Duper Splotch Man.

The Splotch Family were something of a legacy of heroes dating back to 1962 when they'd swung on the scene wielding the Nega-Force to generate simple constructs and move rapidly through the city. They were working class heroes, parent to child, that never quite seemed to make much money from their efforts.

Gary had something of a mancrush on the one he'd grown up with, Stanley, and always spoke about them in glowing terms. Personally, I had a significantly less favorable opinion of the superhero dynasty. My opinion was that if you couldn't make money as a superhero then you were self-sabotaging, and your family was going to pay the price.

I also wasn't happy it was Red Splotch in the building. That was a bit like getting the B-team to come after you and as much as I held Stanley Otkid in disdain, he was at least an A-level superhero. Red Splotch was the B-Team, and I couldn't get myself in fights with lesser heroes if I wanted to be taken seriously as an archvillain.

Red Splotch pointed dramatically at Nikki Tesla. "I'm here to stop your nefarious plan, Doctor Scientist!"

I turned to Nikki Tesla. "Your codename is Doctor Scientist?"

"I'm not good with names!" Nikki said. "Your husband suggested Doctor Madness and Emperor Scientist."

"Both of which are objectively better!" I said. "He's also not my husband! Why does everyone keep saying that!"

"I'm just going to leave now," Dana said, slowly inching toward the door.

"Stop moving, kid," I said, dryly.

"You're like five years older than me," Dana said.

I growled.

Dana blinked and literally shrunk a few inches. Apparently, her powers weren't entirely voluntarily.

Nikki Tesla grabbed a huge metal table and threw it at Red Splotch before he grabbed it with his red tendrils of Nega-Force and threw it aside easily. "You will never take me alive, Steve Otkid! You should have accepted my offer to be my consort and rule by my side."

"Never, you beautiful sexy brain you!" Steve replied.

"What is happening?" Dana asked.

"Flirtatious banter," I said, sighing. "Apparently, we've stepped into one of *those* relationships: Gary and Ultragoddess, Nightwalker and Larceny Lass, Ultragod with that lady who wanted to breed superkids. It's a thing."

"It is?" Dana asked, confused. "Why would anyone want to sleep with someone who is trying to kill them."

"Ask James Bond," I said. "Well, since this doesn't involve us, we should probably—"

Red Splotch interrupted my statement by pointing again at Nikki Tesla. "I won't let you infect millions of people with the Blot Symbiote! Your phony cancer cure ends here today."

"What?" Dana said, her mouth hanging open. "Your what?"

"Eh, I was going to use the cancer cure as a vector to make millions of mind-controlled servants with the powers of

Splotch's archenemy," Nikki said, shrugging. "Well, other archenemy. Then I'd rule the world or ask for a trillion dollars. I'm not sure which."

Dana stared before degenerating into angrish. "You…what…I…huh. A cancer cure would already make billions!"

Nikki shrugged. "Yet it would also cure millions of people and make the world an objectively better place. Why would I want to do that?"

I gave a golf clap. "Okay, wow, you're going full in on the irredeemable bastard thing. Congratulations."

"Never go half-supervillain," Nikki replied. "No offense. Some offense."

"You monster!" Dana shouted, transforming into a foot-tall version of herself with webbed wings then flew at Nikki. I grabbed her in mid-flight and pulled her away. She still had the power of an adult woman of her larger size, but I was a frigging werewolf.

"Leave it for the superheroes, dear," I said, clutching her in my fist like I was King Kong, and she was Fay Wray. "We have more important things to do than deal with her evil plan of evil."

"There're more important things than the cure for cancer?" Dana asked, struggling against my fingers. It was kind of adorable really.

Beside us, Nikki Tesla summoned a horde of private military contractors wearing ski masks that made them look more anonymously evil. Oh, and cute little black berets too. They all had electrical prods and energy guns that couldn't kill someone like Splotch. Nikki, herself, stayed out of the main fight to watch and I felt dirty just being in the room. Merciful Moses, people, if you wanted to get it on that much then get a room or at least a rooftop.

The distraction did, however, provide an excellent opportunity to slip out the side door with my new partner—really a henchwoman—in tow. "Yes, Dana, like taking all of your research on how to cure cancer then open-source publishing it."

Dana blinked. "Oh, wow, that would be terrible."

"Yes," I replied. "Especially if we can patent it first with some lawyers from Omega Corp."

"You own Omega Corp," Dana said. "Well, you and a few other primary stockholders that are mostly your family."

"Which is why Nikki's plan has some flaws," I replied. "In any case, I need you to shrink a million tons of gold. It may not be a literal million but it's going to be a Smaug level hoard. Which is funny because it's Smog's hoard."

Dana looked confused. "I can't possibly shrink that much."

"Well, we need to move a crap ton of gold and other heavy metals," I replied. "You're my best option."

"I can try but I need a lot of equipment," Dana said.

"We can rob Omega Corp," I replied.

"You own Omega Corp, I repeat," Dana said. "It's not really stealing if you—"

"Do you want your old job back?" I asked.

"Yes!" Dana said.

"Well too bad," I replied. "You need to adjust to being a thief. Don't ruin it with logic."

Dana sighed audibly.

"Cheer up!" I said. "Which did you want to be anyway, an anonymous lab rat or a feared and hated master criminal!"

"A respected and loved scientist!" Dana squeaked.

I dropped her and she resumed to her normal size on the floor. "I can see you're going to need a lot of on-the-job training."

Chapter Fifteen

Integrating Our New Team

"Yo, bitches," I said, walking up to Mandy, my daughters, Case, and Amanda in the waiting room. Alarms were blaring and an order to evacuate the building was being repeated every few minutes. Pretty standard, "A superhero and supervillain are throwing down" emergency protocols.

"Please don't call us that," Mandy said, putting down a copy of TIME magazine with President Moses Anders on the front.

"I can say that word," I replied. "I'm a female werewolf."

"I don't think that's how it works," Mandy said.

"Mom, why do you have Tinkerbell in your hand?" Leia asked, looking up from her self-created cellphone that looked like it could hack the Pentagon. Probably because it could.

"Oh," I said, looking down at Dana in my vice-like grip. "I'd completely forgotten about you!"

"How?" Dana replied.

I'd pulled off a daring heist of the equipment we needed to rob the Dragon King by heading down to the laboratory storeroom then ordering it to be delivered via drone to the mansion. Okay, maybe referring to it as a "heist" was perhaps stretching definitions but just I wanted to keep my anti-corporate street cred.

"You don't have any anti-corporate street cred, Mom," Leia said, looking up.

"No reading minds, dear," I replied. "Gals, Guy, this is Dana Vandergast AKA Damselfly. She is the final member of Cindy's Seven."

"I don't work with Nazis," Mandy said, coldly.

"I am not a Nazi!" Dana said.

"She's not," I said. "Some of her best friends are Jewish. Specifically, me."

"Are we friends?" Dana asked.

"We will be if you help me steal a trillion dollars," I replied to Dana.

"Fair point," Dana said. "Can you let me go?"

"Oh right," I said, dropping the fairy-sized woman on the ground where she resumed her normal mass.

"Is this what being a supervillain is going to be like?" Dana muttered, slowly getting up.

"How green are you, Dragonfly?" I asked.

"Damselfly!" Dana corrected.

"Not caring," I replied.

"I've done things!" Dana replied. "Robberies, mostly. The occasional supervillain team up that mostly ended up with me beaten up and running away from masked vigilantes. I had an elaborate system for breaking and entering corporate facilities to retrieve high value scientific equipment then planned to resell them at a significant below market value. I never got to do that, though, because I was caught and ended up in Ironhyde supervillain prison. But I escaped! I am a wanted fugitive. Grr."

I stared down at her. "Uh huh."

"I'm not impressing you, am I?" Dana asked, now standing in front of me.

"If you stole scientific equipment, you should sell it for a higher price to other supervillains," I replied. "Plus, Ironhyde supervillain prison is the kiddy pool of Super prisons. It's not even on the moon, underground, or in another dimension."

Dana sighed and slowly got up. "I'm sorry, I guess I'm not used to working with a better class of villain."

"Not a villain," Amanda said, sighing. "Actually, I'm a superhero."

"Wait, the Nightwalker?" Dana asked, doing a double take as if she hadn't really seen Amanda until now. "What are you doing here?"

"That is a very good question," Amanda said. "But sometimes the line between good and evil is very thin."

"No," Dana said. "They're literally the opposite of one another."

I gave her a dope slap to the back of the head. "Listen, Dana, you're part of Cindy's Seven now. I'm letting you in because of your technical knowledge and this is your chance to shed any previous reputation you have."

"Yeah, Other Mom helped kill Tom Terror," Mimi said. "Think on that."

"Yeah, I suppose," Dana said, as if not quite believing that the supervillain was dead. Which was understandable since he'd managed to dodge death for almost a hundred years prior. It was just he'd met his final demise facing the Chosen of Death. I didn't mind giving Gary the credit there. He'd earned it.

"One question," Leia asked.

"*One* question?" Dana asked, as if she was dealing with hundreds.

"Yes, my biological daughter?" I asked. "Who will someday grow up to be almost as hot as me?"

Leia rolled her eyes. "Why is it Cindy's Seven?"

"What do you mean?" I asked. "I'm Cindy, you're my seven."

"Yes, and there's six of us," Leia pointed out. "If Dana is the last member, it should be Cindy's Six."

"By that logic, it should be Ocean's Ten," I pointed out.

"Are we discussing the Sinatra or Clooney versions?" Case asked, having mostly kept out of this conversation so far.

"I don't think it matters," I replied. "Listen, classic British sci-fi series *Blake's Seven* rarely had seven crew members unless they were counting the computers. We're going with Cindy's Seven and that's final."

"Fine," Leia asked, sighing. "I just still don't know why we need another mad scientist on the team. We should have gotten a magic user instead. Dad or the Black Witch. Diversity is the key to a successful operation."

"Do not lecture me on how to run a heist, young lady! Dana here cured cancer!" I pointed out, deciding that defending my latest recruit was important.

"Actually, Doctor Aeon cured cancer," Mandy said, handing over the copy of TIME. Inside was an article that he'd discovered a way to shrink tumors and safely remove them before restoring genetic equilibrium.

Dana snatched the magazine and stared in horror. "This was my idea!"

"Tough break," I said. "No one gives prizes for second place in science, I'm sorry to say. I guess making an army of Nega-Force goons out of dying cancer patients was a good use of your research after all."

Dana did a double take. "No, it wasn't!"

"Oh, look, Vince Gilligan is doing a remake of *Breaking Bad*," Case replied, picking up a copy of ENTERTAINMENT

WEEKLY. "Except it's going to be a superhero show called *Anti-Villain*. They're going to base it around Gary's life."

I glared at him. "Now you're just taunting me. Once this heist is through, I will be the one getting shows made about."

"That aren't unrated and only available on cable or the internet," Amanda muttered.

I smirked. "Okay, that's actually pretty funny."

That was when the entire building rocked.

"What the hell?" Case said, standing up.

I sighed. "Great, I recognize that sound."

"What?" Dana asked, clearly as unnerved as the rest of the group.

"Nikki Tesla is blowing up the top ten floors or so of the building," I said, sighing. "That was the top floor. It'll blow down one after the other."

A second one followed.

"That's insane!" Dana asked.

"Eh, the building is evacuated now but for us," I said, pulling out my cellphone. "Leia, you got the time machine still?"

"Yes?" Leia said, questioningly.

"Probably a good time to punch it," I replied. "Or we'll die."

"Yes!" Dana said. "Not dying is good!"

"This is a misuse of teleportation and time travel," Leia said, the third explosion happening right above us. She quickly entered the codes, though, and we once more disappeared in a flash of alien light.

The seven of us reappeared below the mansion in Mandy's crib, where I'd set up a large table that was covered in maps and print-out pictures of Dragon Island. I had a big six-foot-cardboard cutout of the Dragon King as well as action figures of myself, Mandy, and Amanda at the base to provide scale. I didn't have any of G, Dana, Leia, or Mimi so I substituted GI Joes I'd found in the attic.

"Shouldn't we have attempted to stop the explosion of the tower?" Dana asked.

"My connection to the police bands indicate that the area around the tower was evacuated," Amanda said. "I have every confidence in the Red Splotch stopping Doctor Scientist but I'm going to head back to make sure any survivors are protected."

"You do that, Amanda," I replied.

Buildings exploding in superhero fights was something that superheroes and villains had gotten down to an exact science since the Tragedy of 1941 when Antaeus had battled Count Reich. Any accredited superhero always made sure to evacuate civilians from the area as swiftly as possible while attempting to move the fighting into a more secure location. Gary had also made his one and only decent business decision for Omega Corp by creating a construction company that specialized in using Supers to rebuild locations destroyed by such battles.

We Can Fix It, Inc. had done a measurable job of reducing superhuman prejudice or at least stopping it from getting worse. It turned out Muggles hated Supers in large part because of fear of getting squished during battles or losing their house. Finding out it could be rebuilt in an hour thanks to a guy with super-speed or magical fixing powers took out a lot of the sting. Well, not the loss of possessions and almost dying but it had gone from "Supers should all be strung up" to "Supers should all be sued to oblivion."

"Please stop using my real name," Amanda said. "Especially in front of supervillains."

"What? You think Dana is going to reveal you're Amanda Douglas?" I asked, dryly.

Amanda narrowed her eyes.

"The heiress?" Dana asked, stunned.

I looked at Dana. "Dana, if you reveal Amanda's secret identity to anyone, I will hunt you down and kill you. See? There. Problem fixed."

"I can always wipe her mind," Mandy said. "I'm actually quite good at the vampire mesmerism thing."

"No mind wiping, please!" Dana said, squeaking. "Also, where are we?"

"Stately Warren Manor," I replied. "Former home of the Nightwalker and now home to the swingiest supervillains of them all!"

"Please don't describe us like that," Mandy said.

"Some of us are serial monogamists," Case replied.

I snorted. "Does Jane know that? I remember one night when—"

Case glared. "Can we stick to the plan?"

Leia began programming the time machine to transport Amanda away when she looked up. "This may take a bit. Precision jumps are hard, and its tachyon supply is running out. We may need to rob a particle accelerator."

"It's okay, we'll just hook it up to Lancel Warren's old-time machine," I replied. "Gary keeps it next to the treadmill."

"Lancel Warren was the Nightwalker?" Dana asked, stunned. "Wait, are you *Doctor* Cindy Wakowski the woman who owns all the free hospitals?"

I blinked. "Wait, you didn't know that?"

"Mom doesn't keep a secret identity," Mimi replied. "It's just she's so utterly blatant about it that no prosecutor is willing to bring a case against her."

"You said bribes in a very strange way," I corrected my daughter. "In any case, we're running out of time to get to Dragon Island to rob him of his hoard. The Incredible Shrinking Woman here is going to have all of our wacky equipment delivered from Omega Corp's warehouses and get us a way to transfer the stuff."

"That is a lot to ask…" Dana trailed off.

"I'll help," Leia said, cheerfully.

"No offense kid but you don't look old enough to have a doctorate in unusual physics," Dana replied.

Leia frowned. "I invented time travel and sent the first-time machine back to the Nightwalker."

Dana stared.

"Yeah, I regret showing her anime since that's when all the Gundams and robot maids started appearing around the house," I muttered. "Oh, Leia, why couldn't you have become a fan of Sailor Moon like your dear young mother?"

Dana looked like she was rocking on her feet, a very common response from her I expected. "Great, I'm not even the smartest person on the supervillain team. A team which includes two teenage girls. Which seems very irresponsible to bring on a dangerous mission to rob a space dragon if I may bring that up."

"You may not," I replied. "In any case, we have to work quickly. We have the Spear of Saint George and the time travel doohickey that works as a teleporter in a pinch. Add in our current crop of recruits and I think we have a not insignificant chance of pulling this off."

"I think our chances are actually pretty terrible," Mandy said. "However, I'm pretty sure I'll make it through it alive. Unalive. I can probably save both our children too."

Amanda, who hadn't teleported yet, looked at her. "You have an amazing way of reassuring people."

"Sorry," Mandy said. "I will mourn you. Also, Cindy. I mean, I don't know the Nazi."

Dana balled her fists and looked ready to attack Mandy. I suspected that would go very badly.

"At least you were mentioned," Case replied.

"I'm surprised we're letting guys on the team," Mandy said. "I thought this was going to be a girl's only team."

"There are places a male secret agent can go that supervillain women can't," I said. "Also, he's hot. Don't worry, Data, if you die, we'll have you rebuilt. Better, stronger, faster."

"Yeah, I don't think that's how it works," Case replied. "But I appreciate the sentiment."

That was when "Sympathy for the Devil", the Guns and Roses version, started playing and I turned toward the elevator and saw it ping open. Gary stepped out with Revolutionary Girl, the Black Witch, and the Human Tank. Jane followed up behind him, carrying a clipboard.

"And this is Mandy's secret lair!" Gary said, throwing his hands out as his theme music played from what I presumed was his cellphone.

"We've been here before, Gary," Selena said.

"Is that a coffin? I thought that was just a stereotype!" Clarissa said, holding up her cellphone and taking a picture.

"*Madre de dios,*" Gabby muttered under her breath. "Can we get back to the planning?"

"Gary, what are they doing here?" I asked, wondering how they'd arrived.

"Hi Jane," Case said, waving.

Jane ran up and embraced Case. "Where the hell have you been?"

"Fighting terrorists," Case said.

"Oh hi, Cindy!" Gary said. "I was just giving my new crew a tour of the place."

"Your new what now?" I asked, blinking.

Dana hid behind me.

I looked over my shoulder. "Dana this is Merciless. Merciless, Dana."

"I know who Merciless is," Dana replied, looking deeply uncomfortable. "He's the guy who acts like the Hamburglar and has killed more people than some wars."

Wait, was she scared of Gary? Oh, for God's sake. "Answer the question, Gary."

"Oh, Selena and Clarissa have decided to help me rob the Dragon King!" Gary said, cheerfully.

I stared daggers at him. "What?"

Chapter Sixteen

I Now Have a Set of Rivals

"What the hell, Gary?" I asked, staring at him. "You're trying to swipe my robbery?"

"Not at all," Gary said, cheerfully. "But yes."

"Okay, now I kind of want to stay," Amanda said, looking over at Leia. "But duty calls."

"It's okay," Mimi said, looking at her cellphone. "Hourglass showed up and reversed the destruction of the building."

"Oh, good," Amanda muttered. "I guess."

Hourglass was one of the new superheroines in town that I'd sponsored through my superhero summer camp last year. Well, the past few years really. A place where disadvantaged girls and boys got to train as heroes away from their crappy parents. Tina Time could turn back the physical damage and fatalities from an event an hour. She was useless in combat, but you didn't need to be when you had the power of resurrection. Her only downside, if you could call it that, was she preferred social media posting over heroing. A pretty good example of what could be accomplished with We Can Fix It, Inc.

"Gary and I had a conversation with Black Witch and the Human Tank while we were on our way to a Foundation for

World Harmony black site," Revolutionary Girl said. "It turned out they were planning on robbing Smog the Dragon King and were forming a crew. We offered our services and are now going to loot his treasure."

I glared at him. "Benedict Arnold! Traitor! Sneakthief!"

"A little healthy competition never hurt anyone!" Gary said, rubbing his hands together and looking pleased with himself.

"Yes, it does!" I said, putting my hands on my hips. "It hurts the losers!"

"We could do a team up!" Mimi said, a little too enthusiastically. "Cindy's eleven."

"With Jane it would be twelve," Case pointed out.

"Enough with the goddamn numbers!" I snapped. "This is supposed to be my heist"

"Actually, it's my heist," Selena said. "Clarissa and I were going to rob the Dragon King from the beginning."

"He's about to move his fortune off world," Clarissa said. "There's never going to be a better time to hit him."

"Imagine what that kind of money could do for poor countries suffering from capitalist oppression," Revolutionary Girl said.

"Down Che Girlverra," I said, pointing at her. "No one is spending my fortune on any charity but mine."

"Wait, you give your money to charity?" Dana asked, doing a double take.

"Well, I long since made more money than I could ever spend," I replied. "What did you think I did with it?"

Dana spluttered. "But…why? Why would you keep stealing?"

Wow, she just did not understand what being a supervillain was all about, did she? Oh well, she had plenty of time to learn. Supervillainy was feast or famine, and you eventually hit rock bottom or reached the heights of success, sometimes one after the other or multiple times.

"It's kind of a *Breaking Bad* thing," Gary said. "If you're good at something, why stop?"

"Do you know that Vince Gilligan is making a series about Gary?" Jane asked.

"I heard!" I snapped, about ready to wolf out and tear up the place. "Gary, I know you're used to people finding your antics amusing—"

"Has anyone ever found Gary amusing?" Selena asked. "I'm genuinely surprised if that's the case."

Oh yeah, there was no love lost between those two.

"I did," Mandy said. "Still do. Mostly when he's annoying other people."

"I also find Gary amusing," Revolutionary Girl said. "He is a true hero of the revolution when he's not being an annoying dork."

"So never," Gary replied.

Revolutionary Girl smiled.

"Mimi, why is your mom pretending to be a communist guerilla?" Leia asked her sister. "I mean, it's really weirding me out. Also, is she like twenty percent more Spanish now?"

Mimi looked confused. "What are you talking about? Ultragoddess is currently building a new space station for the Foundation for Celestial Harmony. She's been gone for weeks and won't be back for another month."

"*Si*," Revolutionary Girl said. "I am most certainly not Ultragoddess. Also, I am not a communist. I support democratic free elections with social reform."

"Yeah, not a fan of the Red Menace," Gary said, referring to the ironically named supervillain/hero of the Soviet Union. "I'm an *anarchist*, goddammit."

"Uh huh," Leia muttered, crossing her arms. "I'm not fooled here."

I decided I would take Leia to see a specialist after this. She was clearly clinging to this delusion of Gabrielle Anders being Revolutionary Girl a little too tightly. "Where was I? Oh yes, clearly, you're used to people finding your antics amusing Gary, but I do not. There's also nothing that you can provide me that I won't be able to do on my own."

"Oh, I disagree about that," Gary said, cheerfully.

"Is it a Y chromosome?" Jane asked. "I just noticed this is like the only superhero team other than *Birds of Prey* that has more women than men. No offense, Case."

"Some taken," Case said. "My genes are entirely synthetic."

Wow, she was right. It was ten to two gender ratio here. It was like a *Twilight* or *Supernatural* convention.

Dana looked around the room. "Huh, I did not notice that."

"I did notice that," Amanda said, looking around. "Maybe we can call it the Sorority of Supervillains plus one Superheroine."

"Yes, that was part of the point!" I snapped. "Sistervillains doing it for themselves!"

"What you don't have is an invitation!" Gary said, conjuring an invitation with common sleight of hand. It was ivory and emblazoned with gold lettering.

"An invitation to Dragon Island?" I asked, blinking. "How the hell did you score that?"

"It's actually an invitation to a wedding that is being held on Dragon Island," Gary replied. "Adonis and Achilles are getting married. It's the supervillain event of the decade."

"Achilles is a supervillain?" Dana asked. "I thought he was an ancient Greek hero."

"Clearly you've not met many actual ancient Greeks," I replied. "Changing values makes yesterday's heroes into tomorrow's baddies. I'm surprised these guys invited women to their shindig."

Gary looked to the side guiltily.

"Oh, come on! I wasn't invited!" I said. "What the hell?"

"Have you met Adonis?" Selena asked. "If you're not sleeping with him, you might as well not exist as a woman and even then."

"Yes, I have," I said. "Stupid sexy son of incestuous royalty blessed by Aphrodite."

"Eh, he wasn't that hot," Mandy said.

"He's insanely hot," the Human Tank said. "It's just his personality that is terrible."

"This is why I like Sparta over Athens," I replied. "They were much more respectful to women. I mean, sure the infanticide and being a slaving culture that other slaving cultures went 'woah nelly' about is bad but—"

We were getting way-way off track.

"I don't suppose I could defect to being a superhero?" Dana asked. "I understand that's a thing some supervillains have done. Like Robin Hood, Bloodscream the Retributive, the Human Tank, and Black Witch."

This is something I should have seen coming since I could tell Dana hadn't so much fallen into supervillainy as saunter vaguely downwards (to paraphrase Terry Pratchett and Neil Gaiman). Plenty of supervillains had the idea you could just defect to the other team like a Cold War spy or NFL draft pick.

"First of all, that never sticks," I said, gesturing to the last two. "Case in point."

"We rob bad people!" Clarissa said. "That's barely a crime."

"Agreed," I replied. "However, you don't get to defect because I called dibs on you."

"Wait, what?" Dana asked.

"The ancient law of dibs is to be respected," Gary replied. "Also, the Society of Superheroes is a bunch of yutzes."

"They are not," Amanda said. "Admittedly, the tenor of the place has gone downhill since Ultragod retired to be President of the United States. Captain Ultra is a complete dick for example and keeps acting like he's in charge instead of Guinevere. However, I believe you when you say you were framed, Dana."

"Thank you," Dana said, breathing a sigh of relief.

"It's just all the other crimes you've committed since then that matter," Amanda said. "Your best bet is to get someone like Gary to vouch for you."

"Wait, what?" Dana said.

"You're getting a lot of versatility out of those two words," I replied.

"I swear, it's like this entire planet is composed of snarky asshats," Jane said, leaning into Case's arms and snuggling him. They made a cute couple. It was too bad Jane was in a long-term relationship on her home planet and Case, for all his protestations of monogamy, had like a dozen cyber-Bond girls waiting for him on his. But hey, what happens in superheroland stays in superheroland.

"Gary's word carries a lot of weight with reformed supervillains," Amanda said.

"*Why*?" Dana asked, throwing her hands out.

"It's a man's world, dear," Amanda said. "By which I mean he literally rewrote reality, so he had the cheat codes to it."

"Whatever the case is, Dragon Island will be full of hundreds of supervillains in the next few days," Gary explained. "It's the perfect set up to take the dragon's hoard."

"It's also undoubtedly filled with other people who have the exact same plan as us," I said, cursing.

"It gets worse," Gary said, putting his hands up his sleeves like a Jedi or Sith Lord.

"How can it get worse?" I asked.

Gary pulled out his cellphone and showed me a kill warrant from the Foundation for World Harmony. It had me listed.

"What the fuck?" I asked. "A frigging kill order! They only give those to terrorists and cop killers!"

"And brown people," Revolutionary Girl muttered.

Mimi just nodded.

"Sorry, this is very surprising!" I said. "I mean, sure, I've killed a lot of people, I mean a *lot* of people, but that shouldn't justify that."

"Doesn't it?" Dana asked.

"You have one too," Gary said, checking his phone. "I'm always checking to see if I've been added but Ultragod keeps pardoning me."

"I have a kill order?" Dana asked, shocked. "How? What? I'm not a member of PHANTOM."

"Obviously not, you're still alive," Gary said.

Dana looked petrified.

"I'm not going to kill you!" Gary said. "I mean, who ever heard of a gay Nazi?"

"Ernst Rohm?" Amanda suggested, looking down at her Nightphone.

"Stop helping!" Dana snapped.

"The thing is that a superhero with class-A authorization has to sign off on kill orders," Gary replied. "Which means that both of you have managed to tick off someone very important. I suggest we break into Foundation for World Harmony headquarters and—"

"It's Ultragoddess," Amanda said, lifting her phone.

"Wait, what?" Revolutionary Girl asked.

"You too, now, RG? Is everyone here a teenage girl?" I asked, staring at them. "What's with everyone getting their news off their cellphones."

"Where would you get it?" Gary asked.

"Not the point!" I snapped.

"Why would my mom order the death of my other mom?" Mimi asked.

"That is very uncharacteristic behavior," Gary said.

"Not really," Selena said. "At least lately. She disbanded the Shadow Seven and stopped all attempts to reform supervillains. Plus, she's trying to kill you."

"She's not trying to kill me," Gary said. "I mean, she's incredibly hostile and has tried to capture me numerous times but I figured that was a flirty villain-hero thing, like Doctor Scientist and Red Splotch."

"She's trying to kill me!" I snapped. "Which is worse! Because it's me!"

"Well, she won't be getting us here. At least for now. I've moved the house off to another dimension—" Gary started to say.

"I thought its coordinates were a bit weird," Leia said, tapping the time machine controls.

"That's a thing?" Dana asked. "How did you change the positronic frequency of the house's quantum entanglement axis?"

"Magic," Gary said.

"Oh," Dana said, disappointed.

"Do you think Ultragoddess is the person who pressured the Foundation for World Harmony to fire a missile at us?" Leia asked, looking directly at Revolutionary Girl.

"The Foundation for World Harmony is a bunch of fascists and neo-reactionaries still full of leftovers from President Omega's administration," Revolutionary Girl said, referring to something I wasn't sure had still happened in this timeline or not.

Man, I hated time travel. Except when it benefited me.

"That's not an answer," Leia said, clearly expecting more from the woman she believed to be Ultragoddess.

"I don't know," Revolutionary Girl said, confusing my daughter and me.

I didn't believe Ultragoddess would harm me, let alone her own daughter, but there you could never depend on anything in the superhero world. Clones, alternate universe doppelgangers, brainwashing, demonic possession, and inexplicable reactions to Twinkies. A lot could turn a good hero bad, strange how it never seemed to happen in reverse, and that was something that had to be dealt with.

I didn't want to contemplate the other possibility that she'd just decided to kill me because of plain old human animosity or combat fatigue. Unlike what you saw in comics or movies, superheroes carried the weight of the never-ending war against evil the same way soldiers who kept reenlisting in war did. Sometimes they did become a lot more ruthless and cold-hearted. But, no, I didn't believe that. First because it was *Ultragoddess*, who I had the poster of since I was fourteen and she wasn't much older as American's favorite teen superhero, and second because I never doubted that she loved her daughter.

Okay, *now* I was doubting she loved her daughter because I remembered Gabrielle was keeping her hush-hush, and having other women—plus one dork—raise her. Mimi was her dirty little secret that, gasp, she'd carried on with a supervillain. I didn't like thinking about that, but the thought played through my head.

"You're not part of Cindy's Seven," I said, finally speaking. "However, let's all do a team up to take down Smog and worry about our sudden but inevitable betrayals later."

"Merciless' Five plus Cindy's Seven!" Gary said, cheerfully.

"I was a supervillain when you were an undergrad," Selena said.

"I like it," Clarissa said.

Chapter Seventeen

We Arrive at Doctor No's Lair (or a Reasonable Facsimile)

"That is one big-ass dragon," I muttered, staring out the window to my side of the *Nightplane II*. It was a big bird-shaped vehicle that functioned as both a jet and a turbine-powered vertical takeoff vehicle that had an unintelligent autopilot as well as an interior large enough for a tactical team. Unfortunately, it didn't have a minibar and I was all too unhappy to be sober as my newly twelve-member team waited for our arrival on Dragon Island.

"What dragon?" Gary asked.

"The one around the hotel," I said, finally glad we'd arrived over the island.

"Oh, that one," Gary said, looking out the same window.

I wasn't referring to Smog, who wasn't visible from the sky, but the enormous stone dragon statue that was built around the central skyscraper that compromised Dragon Island Casino. Dragon Island had once been home to dozens of giant monsters perpetually fighting over turf, but Smog had eventually killed them all and had the place converted to one enormous base for his corporate-criminal empire.

I could see the city-sized resort stretched out for a dozen miles in every direction with its own port, shopping malls, jungle preserve, corporate offices, military base, and space launch facility. A sense of just how powerful Smog was could be summarized by the fact there was a Chinese battleship in the harbor. It said everything you needed to know about him that not only did the country not make territorial claims on Dragon Island but was actively defending the Dragon King's own claim.

"It's supposedly a life-sized version of Smog," Gary said, looking back at me. "Smog himself lives either in the oceans around the island or the massive underground caves that he's been hollowing out for decades."

I was still unhappy that Gary had invited himself on this encounter, but I had to admit he was going to make it easier. Maybe I shouldn't have been so hard on the concept of Gary as my partner, in both senses of the worlds, but I'd never seen a functional marriage in the real world. My mother had been a gun moll for The Wolf, and he'd been in prison by the time I was born. Every one of her boyfriends and husbands afterwards had been an abusive scumbag of one sort or another.

There was also the fact that as much as I loved Gary—God I hated that word, love, it was so cheesy. It meant giving of yourself and I hated doing that. What was I saying? Oh yes, as much as I loved Gary, I never quite believed he loved me as much as I loved him. After all, he'd searched Heaven and Earth to try to find a means of restoring Mandy when she was a soulless vampire. He'd also proposed to Ultragoddess when it was clear Mandy didn't want to be considered his wife anymore.

I was the mother of one of Gary's children and kind of hated the fact that sometimes I was jealous of my own daughter. I hated the fact she probably knew that via telepathy too. I'd wanted to be a better mother to her than my own had been to me, low bar as that was to clear, but I had no idea where to begin. Hence Leia had grown up largely raised by Gary's sister Kerri and later Gary himself. That was the one thing I had over Ultragoddess, or at least a tie, in that she, too, had dumped her daughter on others to raise. That was when I noticed they were still talking about the frigging dragon's living accommodations.

"It's an assumption you really shouldn't make," Dana replied. "Shrinking particles, extra-dimensional spaces, and shape changing. Chinese dragons are well-known for their magical powers."

"No, he's a *prehistoric alien* dragon," Gary replied. "He was just mistaken as a Chinese dragon long ago."

"Oh, that makes a difference," Dana said. "Unless he has prehistoric dragon super-science."

"He does!" Gary said. "Though it's indistinguishable from magic."

"Oh, for buck's sake," Jane said. "He's a comic book dragon. He can do whatever he wants to. He's also the size of a skyscraper. Unless we have a nuke, we aren't going to be do much more than scratch him."

"A nuclear weapon would irradiate what we're trying to get," Case pointed out. "Basic *Goldfinger*."

"I love how in this world, that's your primary concern about getting a nuclear weapon," Jane said.

"I mean, I have three back on my world," Case said. "Leia made one with a bunch of glow-in-the-dark stripes from watches."

"I'm never going to live that down, am I?" Leia asked.

"I love how I'm smart enough not to make a nuclear weapon but I'm not the one who people think is smart," Mimi muttered.

"No one thinks you're stupid, Mimi," Mandy said. "Quite the opposite. You're a terrifying supervillain who combines beauty, brawn, and brains. We're all afraid of you taking over the world."

"Thanks, Mom," Mimi said. "I'm genuinely glad that Dad did the Utah thing."

"It is not a Utah thing!" Dana said.

"Marriage is the capitalist function of regulating the sex lives of women and raising of children under a patriarchal figure," Revolutionary Girl said. "Relationships that are free and open benefit the group."

"That's definitely not a Utah thing," Dana said.

"Stop indoctrinating my kids," I replied to Revolutionary Girl. "There's like a limit to these things. You can only have three partners each not counting hookups. There's like a law for this. So, the entirety of the partners would be like, nine, not counting crossover."

Everyone stared at me.

"Oh fine, that makes no sense," I replied. "The point is that unless you're Ultragoddess, you're not part of the group!"

"I am not Ultragoddess," Revolutionary Girl said.

Gary looked embarrassed. So was I. I didn't know what it was about Revolutionary Girl that rubbed me the wrong way.

"Sorry," I muttered. "I don't know what came over me."

"You said you're sorry," Gary said. "It must be serious."

Leia whispered. "Midlife crisis."

"The fuck it is!" I said. "That's also a thing for men! Not immortal ever-young wolfwomen!"

Case started humming "Forever Young" by Alphaville.

"Shut up, you," I replied. "You're a robot, you don't get to complain about old age."

"I'm like a replicant in that I have built-in obsolescence," Case said.

I blinked. "Oh shit, really?"

Case shrugged. "I've cheated death a few times, but immortality is off the table."

"You should work on that," I said. "Gary's like the God of Pocket Lint and Mandy is immortal too."

"I'm not immortal," Mandy said. "Vampires don't age because we're dead."

"Father only lived to be a hundred and each year became a chore for him," Revolutionary Girl said. "Uh, my father who is not Ultragod."

I stared at her. "What an odd distinction."

Leia facepalmed.

"Death has no mystery for me," Amanda said.

"I'm a shaman," Jane responded. "I don't want to become a dirty-dirty vampire drain on life's cycles. No offense, Mandy."

"None taken," Mandy said. "I agree."

"Well, this conversation got really morbid," I said, feeling the *Nightplane II* start to descend. It landed in the water and turned out to be able to float despite the fact it was a humungous piece of prototype military infrastructure. We were, however, next to a dock and could use the metal wing to depart.

There were a huge number of white-uniformed mercenaries with red berets that I recognized as belonging to the White Tiger PMC. I wasn't particularly worried about them, but Dragon Island was something of a center for the Super trafficking network of the world alongside De La Cruz island. I had no doubt the place had a lot of Supers who had been brainwashed and were now serving as the Dragon King's mercs.

"It's not too late to turn back," Gary said. "Every heist is one you might not walk away from. You can't count on resurrection when you're a supervillain either."

"And whose fault is that?" I asked, giving him a sideways glance.

Gary sighed. "Let's get going."

"Just remember I'm in charge," I said.

"No one ever doubted that," Gary said.

"Are you sure this invitation will cover everyone else?" I asked, wanting to double check before we left the *Nightplane II*.

"It will cover only us but apparently entourages are something expected at an Olympian wedding," Gary explained.

"Entourages?" Selena asked. "Please tell me I'm not expected to bow and scrape before Cindy."

"You were saying about no one doubting I was in charge?" I asked.

Gary shrugged.

"If you have to clarify someone is in charge, they're not in charge," Case said. "My recommendation is you execute one of us to demonstrate your power."

"Which one?" I asked, knowing Case was joking. At least I hoped.

Case paused. "Tough call. I'll have to get back to you on that."

"Yeah, we know it's me," Jane said. "Just promise me you'll do it with me standing over a cliff and falling back into the water so I can seek revenge twenty years later."

"Done," I said.

"Are all heists with you guys so full of...banter?" Dana asked.

"You haven't begun to experience this crowd's true snark," Revolutionary Girl said.

"Like you'd know," I muttered. "In any case, our current plan is to get into the place through the wedding and case the joint. From there, we penetrate the Dragon King's vaults and shrink down his fortune before escaping with it. Along the way out, we use the Spear of Saint George to kill him and become international heroes."

Dana blinked. "That's not a plan. You're describing goals."

"*Saints Row IV* already did that joke," I replied. "In my opinion, the best of the series."

"It's not a joke!" Dana said. "You're just describing what we want to happen and not how we're going to do any of it!"

"Isn't it exciting?" Mandy asked, smiling open mouthed to show her fangs.

"No!" Dana said.

"Well too bad," I said. "How many supervillains are on this island anyway?"

"It can't be that many if they're not inviting women," Selena said. "Certainly, I hope at least some of the—"

"About a thousand," Leia said, looking up from her cellphone. "I'm following the social media coverage of this event. Virtually every male supervillain in the world of note is attending. They just brought along their female guests."

"So disappointing," Selena muttered. "Where is the solidarity?"

"Right here," I replied. "It occurs to me that Amanda might get murdered if she steps out of this plane dressed like the Nightwalker."

"*Now* it occurs to you?" Amanda asked.

"I feel the best plans are those made up on the fly," I replied.

"That is the opposite of how plans should work," Dana replied, showing it was probably a mistake to recruit her.

"Tell me, how many supervillain team-ups have you been on?" I asked.

"Dozens," Dana said.

"How many successful ones?" I asked.

"Two," Dana muttered. "Depending on how you define success."

"And on those two successful ones, did everything go to plan?" I asked.

Dana looked guilty. "Err, not really. The first one had everyone betray everyone else and I snuck away with the loot. The second had the Bronze Medalist catch us all but had to leave because demons attacked the local Chuck-E-Cheese."

"I hate when that happens," Gary said. "That's why I outlaw animatronics at Superhero Pizza. You know that they're going to serve as an easy vessel for the forces of Hell."

"Did you even check if the Spear of Saint George is the real one?" Dana asked, gesturing to our weapon that was leaning up against the wall.

"What do you mean?" I asked.

"I mean, if I was a genius space dragon with a trillion dollars, I would have sent supervillains to steal it by now," Dana said. "I mean, send some Ringwraiths after this thing or something."

I blinked. "Yes, I've clearly thought of that."

"You have?" Dana asked, skeptically.

"I confirmed it was the real thing," Selena said, quickly.

I did a double take. "Oh good, yes, I knew you were going to do that."

"Oh God," Dana muttered.

"So back to disguise," I said. "Can we like give Amanda a pair of glasses or something so she can't be recognized?"

"Or a ponytail," Leia said, looking at Revolutionary Girl.

"Yeah, something like that," I replied.

Selena sighed and cracked her knuckles before pressing her fingertips together. "Disguise."

With that, every single person in the *Nightplane II* suddenly was wearing extremely expensive Oscar-quality gowns or suits.

I didn't feel like any of my clothes had changed so it was clearly just an illusion, but it was an effective one. The biggest change was Amanda Douglas was no longer dressed as the Nightwalker but her own secret identity that was, to my surprise, still secret despite my constant sharing it. She even had her hair up in a way that would have required a few hours at the salon.

"Impressive work, Selena," I said. "But is it going to be an issue having a billionaire debutante here as part of our posse?"

"Entourage," Gary corrected.

"Shut up, Gary," I said.

"I haven't been a debutante in a decade," Amanda said. "But the persona of Amanda Douglas is that of a vapid, spoiled, honestly stupid rich girl who raises charities for animals as the height of her contribution to society."

"You act like that's a bad thing," Gary said. "People suck, dogs are awesome."

"Agreed," I replied. I had to wonder, though, what it would do to your psyche to have your regular identity be someone you despised like Amanda here did. Even her marriage to Mister Inventor was a secret and she had to play the role of a single woman in public. Mostly because Galahad Warren was a popular candidate to speculate on Mr. Inventor's identity. He was also one of my exes, which I only now thought might explain Amanda's seeming animosity to me now.

Huh.

Amanda shook her head. "My point is that it wouldn't be strange for me to show up at this party."

"Gotcha," I said, standing up. "So as long as no one recognizes us then we should have no problem."

That was when Diabloman, wearing a nicely tailored red suit, knocked on the window of the *Nightplane II*. Diabloman was less a man than a mountain of muscle empowered with the energy of a thousand demons plus the look of a Mexican wrestler. He was also someone I did *not* want to ever see again.

"*Hola*!" Diabloman said.

"Why did you say that?" Gary asked, looking at me.

"I don't know!" I replied, throwing my hands up.

Chapter Eighteen

The Wedding Party of the Stars (of Villainy)

Diabloman.

Shit.

That was a complicated collection of emotions right there. Diabloman was the former center of Gary and my trio. We'd only been together a short while before things went to hell, but he'd been a fatherly figure to us both. A Satanic luchador, he'd been a big villain in the late Eighties and Nineties before time and black magic had taken its toll on him. Gary had rescued him from obscurity, and he'd guided us through a lot of pitfalls that we'd otherwise had fallen prey to.

Then he'd betrayed us. Mandy had gotten herself turned into a vampire and a soulless killer of evil. Which, you know, wasn't great for me. I mean, I didn't self-identify as evil, but all the murder and robbery could conceivably convince someone I qualified. Diabloman participated in a grand deception where his sister, the former superhero known as Spellbinder, had possessed Mandy's vampire body. For months, maybe years, she'd impersonated Mandy and been a friend as well as lover to us. I felt unclean just thinking about it.

Eventually, it had all come out and Diabloman was lucky that Gary got to him first because I wouldn't have just kicked him out of our home. Unfortunately, Gary had reconciled with him (somehow) and now Diabloman was married to Gary's sister, Kerri. No, I don't know what is with this family and rhyming names. Seriously: Cindy, Mindy, Mandy, Kerri, Gary, it's damn weird. I keep expecting a third lovechild to show up named Mary or Jerry. No, that wasn't a suggestion, God.

Where was I? Oh yes, Diabloman's presence here was decidedly unwelcome. Unfortunately, I wasn't about to cause a scene that might result in us getting thrown off the island before I could kill its owner and rob him blind. Still, Diabloman made me uncomfortable, and I hoped Gary had invited him on this heist or I was going to have to kick both off this team.

"Hello, Diabloman," Gary said, reacting somewhat reserved and without much in the way of friendliness. It was funny that he was wearing a white tux and black bow tie with his black cloak that made him look like he was cosplaying as Sean Connery's Bond. Perhaps I'd overestimated just how much they'd reconciled.

"What the hell are you doing here?" I asked, stepping into the conversation.

"I am attending the wedding of two dear friends," Diabloman replied, opening the hatch to the *Nightplane II*.

"Really? You're friends with Adonis and Achilles?" I asked, lowering my opinion of both men.

"No," Diabloman replied. "I get the impression that I was invited not as a person they genuinely respected but because they wished to avoid giving me slight."

"Ah, the Malificent invitation," I replied, getting that. "You're right. Better to have a supervillain not show up than feel the need to blow up the place. I mean, it would be absolutely crazy to not invite any women, for example, and they curse all of the guests to be transformed into pigs."

"I see you heard about Circe's reaction to the wedding," Diabloman said.

I couldn't help but grin. "It seems everyone's gotten better."

"They hired good magical security," Diabloman said.

"What about Medea?" Selena asked. "The two of us used to have a thing and I'd be interested in how she reacted."

Selena's comment seemed directed less at Diabloman and more at Mandy. They'd broken up almost twenty years ago and hadn't so much as spent an hour alone since then, but I got the impression there were some unresolved feelings there. Mostly negative ones as I understood it since not everyone possessed my fantastic ability to seduce again any man or woman I used to date.

"It is a good thing that neither Achilles nor Adonis have any children," Diabloman said, calmly. "Medea's wrath tends not to fall upon the perpetrator but their loved ones."

"I wouldn't be so sure about Adonis not having any children," I replied. "Given the way Greek gods and heroes cat about without protection, I wouldn't be surprised if half of Hollywood or the fashion industry is related to them."

"When's the ceremony?" Gary asked.

"In a few hours," Diabloman said. "You arrived just in time."

"Is it going to be a problem being here?" I asked. "I have a history of murdering supervillains and so do most of the others here."

"I don't," Dana muttered.

"We can ditch her, but I want to get the vibe here," I replied. Just because I wasn't friends with Diabloman anymore didn't mean I wasn't willing to pump him for information.

"Rule Fifteen of the Rules of Supervillainy: Supervillains don't hold any grudges against those of their kind who murder other ones," Diabloman said.

"We don't?" I asked.

"The majority of our kind are sociopaths who have no loyalty to others of our kind," Diabloman said. "Criminals are more inclined to kill others than police after all. It is only if you attempt to assist the authorities or rat them out that you are forever tarnished."

"Snitches get stitches," I replied, nodding. "Or the morgue."

"Which may be a problem for this group," Diabloman said.

I glared at Amanda. "How could you?"

"Why are you looking at me?" Amanda asked.

"Not her," Diabloman said.

"I knew it was a mistake teaming up with the Human Tank and Black Witch," I said, sighing. "They've been working with Ultragoddess way too much."

"No, Cindy," Diabloman said.

"Gary, I'm so sorry," I said, sighing. "I knew your brief ill-fated attempt at superheroism would screw us over."

Diabloman crossed his arms, staring at me.

"Okay, I'm confused," I said, admitting that I was genuinely lost. "I mean, I'm fully prepared to throw my children under the bus but if the locals here know they're time cops then we have bigger problems than my reputation."

"They're time cops?" Diabloman asked, surprised.

"Goddammit, Mom," Leia said, covering her face with both hands.

"Why am I not surprised," Mimi muttered.

"What?" I asked. "I'm not the one who betrayed their family by working for the law! Shame on you! Will it help if I declare them my archenemies?"

"Mom!" Leia said.

"Give into the Dark Side!" I said, pointing at her. "Don't make me destroy you! Obi-Wan can no longer help you!"

"Oh, for fuck's sake," Leia muttered.

"Gary, lend me your lightsaber, I have to chop off our daughter's hand," I said.

"Mom—" Mimi said.

"I'd chop off yours too but I'm pretty sure the lightsaber would just bounce off," I said. "Believe me, it's not a reflection on my nonexistent maternal feelings. I have a strong big sister energy for you both."

"It's not your daughters, Cindy," Diabloman said. "It's you. You are believed to be informing on other villains to the Foundation for World Harmony."

I stared at him. "That is ridiculous."

Dana took a deep breath and exhaled. "Well, at least no one thinks I'm guilty this time."

"You're a fascist so nobody thinks you'd work for the good guys," I said.

"Argh!" Dana said, balling her fists and shaking them like she was a Peanuts character.

"You're informing for the Foundation? Gasp, I say!" Gary said, putting his hand over his heart. "I'd ask for a divorce if we were married."

"Funny, Gary!" I said, not remotely finding it funny. Turning to Diabloman, I shook my head. "This is a joke, right? The Foundation for World Harmony has put me in the kill list!"

"They believe that is a deliberate feint to distract from your collaboration with the authorities," Diabloman explained. "After all, you haven't done nearly enough to be put on the kill list, so they are overcompensating to hide your actions."

"That makes no sense!" I said, trying to even parse that.

"Most criminals are deeply stupid," Diabloman said. "Those that aren't are prone to conspiracy theories and persecution complex."

"This is all a plot against me!" I snapped. "Everyone is against me and afraid of me pulling off my latest heist!"

"Latest heist?" Diabloman asked.

"Yeah, we're going to—" Leia started to say.

I gave her a death glare. Diabloman was family to my daughters, but I no longer trusted him and didn't want them spilling the beans to him. I didn't think he'd rat us out to the Dragon King but the fact I wasn't sure was a risk I didn't want to take.

"Something I have in the works," I replied. "It's not important now."

Diabloman shrugged. "As you wish. Either way, you are unlikely to receive a warm welcome here on Dragon Island."

I bit my lip then shook my head. "It doesn't matter. I'm going out there no matter what. Then I'm going to find out who the hell is responsible for blackening my name as well as trying to kill me and my daughters. Oh, you too, Mandy. You were in the plane too."

"Yes, I was," Mandy said.

Amanda didn't bother to correct me that she was there too. I mean, it was bad she was almost blown up too, but she wasn't family.

"Someone tried to kill my nieces?" Diabloman asked.

"They are *not* your nieces," I replied.

"We kind of are," Mimi corrected.

"I mean in the sense that he's married to our aunt," Leia said. "Which, you know, is one of two ways you become someone's uncle."

"The honorific can also be applied to close friends of the family," Mimi said. "Such as Aunt Amanda or Aunt Clarissa, also there."

"Aw, you guys are sweet," Clarissa said.

"Stop adding family without my permission!" I snapped. "Don't I get a veto on this?"

Everyone in the *Nightplane II* looked at me strangely.

"Apparently not," I said, fuming. "But what's going to happen is I'm going to attend this wedding and then go get myself some vengeance. I'm going to kill everyone involved in spreading rumors about me and who fired those missiles at me, Foundation Agents or not. Sorry, Mandy, that includes your dad."

Dana shook her head. "I thought this was going to be a heist but it's like I'm stuck in the world's most complicated family drama."

I glared. "Shut up, Elsa Schneider."

"Not a Nazi!" Dana said. "I voted for Ultragod! Twice! Or you know, I would have if not for the fact I had my right to vote stripped away."

"Couldn't care less," I said. "Vengeance!"

"Vengeance is the Lord's," Diabloman said. "Or so the Great Enemy's servants say. It is not a path to undertake lightly."

"I always felt that was a trick because the Lord is all forgiving," Gary said. "The guy chilled out significantly over the years from Sodom and Gomorra."

Gary was an observant Jew, in the extreme loosest sense of the word, while I was areligious. It wasn't that I didn't believe in the supernatural—I was attending the wedding of two Greek demigods after all—it was just I'd never really felt any desire to pray because of it. Gary believed Death, his boss, was an angel and refused to acknowledge he was a god even though channeling the power of a concept was apparently the general definition of one among cosmic beings. If I was a god, I would be building cults left and right with a phone number as well as donation page for every follower.

"I'm more an eye-for-an-eye sort of woman," I replied, stupidly helping this conversation to keep going. "Except all their eyes!"

"That was actually meant to limit vengeance," Gary said. "It was to restrict the revenge from being all consuming versus retributive justice."

"Could not care less," I repeated. "Vengeance!"

I stood up and headed past Diabloman, shoving past the mountain of muscle while muttering various curses to myself. Once I was on the dock, I managed to get a sense of just what was filling the streets of the mammoth resort I'd seen from the sky. It was a carnival-like atmosphere with parades, tents of incredible gourmet meals offered on display, kiosks where everything from fancy cars to gold-plated helicopters were being passed out as party favors, and places for elaborate gifts like extra-dimensional monsters floating in tanks or the gun that shot Lincoln. Humorously, there was a ten-foot-tall pile of ties next to a five-foot-tall pile of gold Rolexes for people who still believed anyone wore watches. A pity no one was crass enough to donate cash because I would have loved to have made off with that present.

"Excuse me," I said, ducking under Dinosaur Girl's pet T-Rex as it gnawed on an enormous brachiosaur bone.

"You're excused," The dinosaur replied in a pleasant continental accent I couldn't quite place. "Oh, watch out for pickpockets."

"They a problem?" I asked, pausing.

"Yes," the T-Rex said. "There's a game to find all fifty to burn them all alive at the mass sacrifice to Kronos."

"Super!" I said, grimacing. "I suppose that's what passes for entertainment around here."

"I know," the T-Rex said. "What a waste of meat."

The ongoing party at Dragon Island was one that was impressive to look at and reminded me just how much money supervillains were willing to spend on their excessive self-aggrandizement. Even when you were successful, and that was a big if, the millions you took from ransoming the moon or emptying the Federal Reserve were often wasted in lavish displays like the one going on before me. Not only were there hundreds of supervillains present but, as Gary had suggested, they had brought their entourages with them.

There were also politicians, terrorist leaders, and corporate bigwigs who helped make up the super-rich. All of them had come with their henchmen, assassins, eye candy, and more than a few lawyers since some of these people couldn't decide without consulting six different degrees of intermediary. As for Supervillains, there was everyone from the Juggernuke to the King of Crime and Samhain.

"Well, so far no one is recognizing me," I said, frowning. "I'm kind of annoyed."

It occurred to me it was a terrible idea just wandering off from the rest of my group but if I didn't sign in for anything, the only people I had to worry about were those villains I directly knew as well as any magic that could overcome the charms I wore against recognition as anything other than Red Riding Hood.

I could see the Temple of Aphrodite that had been set up in front of Dragon Casino where Achilles and Adonis were holding court in separate thrones. A long line of supervillains was presenting their gifts and/or tribute.

A part of me wondered why the Dragon King had allowed so many supervillains onto his island, especially when he was going to be moving his fortune to a new location. Selena and Clarissa had talked about planning to stop the Dragon King from some evil plan, but I hadn't bothered to investigate. I mean, archvillains were always doing evil plans. Why would this one matter versus any other time? It occurred to me that I might have been illustrating why I hadn't taken the lead on previous endeavors despite my PHD and general savviness in all things. I had rushed headlong into this and browbeat any attempts to rein me in or come up with a plan better than, "It will work because I say it will work, goddammit."

"Is it me?" I asked aloud. "Am I a crappy criminal mastermind?"

"Yes, Cindy, yes you are," a voice spoke behind me.

One I recognized intimately.

Ultragoddess.

Chapter Nineteen

Superhero Shenanigans I Don't Need

My reaction to Ultragoddess' appearance was perhaps not the one you'd expect from someone who had just found out she'd signed off on my death warrant less than twenty-four hours prior. I wrapped my arms around her and gave her a huge hug before kissing her on the lips with both hands behind her head. A Bugs Bunny-esque power move.

"Wassup!" I said, cheerfully.

Ultragoddess, who looked identical to Revolutionary Girl without a ponytail, was wearing a Foundation for World Harmony white general's uniform that made her look like an unusually hot Third World Dictator.

Ultragoddess blinked, looking horrified. "Get off me!"

I shrugged. "Who pissed in your cheerios?"

Gabrielle Anders and I had been pretty close friends for a time back when her father was dead (long story), and she was trying to redeem supervillains as part of the Shadow Seven. I'd also nursed an enormous crush on her for years. Her and Justin Timberlake but I'd gotten them both out of my system.

Mostly.

Gabrielle stared at me. "You are an enemy of all that is good and right in the world, Cyndi Lauper Wakowski."

"Shhh," I said, making a quiet gesture. "I'm trying to get it changed to Cinderella Wakowski. Your kid gave me the idea."

Gabrielle narrowed her eyes. "I have no children."

I narrowed my eyes and cocked my head sideways. "Are you okay, Gabby?"

"Listen you—"

"Oh," I said, breathing a sigh of relief. "I get it now. We're in public. You don't have any children. It would ruin your branding as the sweet innocent, forty-year-old who dresses like a teenage superheroine that would never randomly hook up with a married supervillain to have his lovechild."

Gabrielle blinked.

"I mean, Mandy was dead when you hooked up, so I don't think it counts but they're still both Jon Snow-esque bastards," I replied. "But here's the thing, we don't live in Westeros. No one cares except inbred people living in Bumfuck, Nowhere. You're more likely to get crap for the fact it's an interracial—"

"Be silent," Gabrielle interrupted. "I am here to destroy you and purge this island of evil."

"O-kay," I said, drawing out the word. "So, I take it you really were the woman who signed off on my execution order?"

"Indeed," Gabrielle said, a lot stiffer and more formal than I remembered her. "You are a boil on the face of the Earth. You, your husband—"

"Not my husband," I added.

"Your boyfriend," Gabrielle said. "You make supervillainy look cool and edgy."

"Because it is," I said, crossing my arms.

"You have committed countless murders, thefts, and acts of mayhem. Worse, you haven't been punished for any of them.

You act with utter impunity and people still love you," Gabrielle said, unable to hide her disgust.

"You make it sound like it was a bad thing," I said, honestly offended. "After all, we're the people who make being bad look good!"

"Exactly!" Gabrielle said, her eyes glazing over with unchecked rage. "You must be destroyed to show the world just what happens to evil-doers."

"Yeah, because capital punishment deters criminals in real life," I said, sarcastically. "That never works because a fundamental element of criminal psychology is the belief that you're different from other criminals. Punishment as deterrence never works because no one ever thinks they're going to get caught."

There was something seriously wrong with Gabrielle and I had no idea how to react. Honestly, she'd always been a bit of a hardass, but she'd been one of the more morally flexible heroes. Someone who recognized there were shades of gray and the law didn't always equate with justice.

"Is this like a midlife crisis thing?" I asked. "I hate to ask because I know you have way more motivations than this and I'm feeling like I'm being stereotypical, but did you and Gary have a nasty breakup?"

Gabrielle's eyes started crackling with the Ultra-Force. "Enjoy your remaining time on this planet, Red Riding Hood. It will not be long."

With that, a cape appeared behind her, and she zoomed into the sky with a blast of energy. It drew only passing attention from the other villains around me. I watched her depart until she was unable to be seen even by my enhanced eyesight and looked back down to see Gary and Revolutionary Girl were standing there, apparently having followed me of the *Nightplane II*.

"Oh wow, guys, Gabrielle Anders is evil now," I said. "Well, lawful-lawful, which is worse than evil if you think about it."

"Wouldn't that be lawful neutral?" Gary asked.

"Alignments are an outdated concept," Jane replied.

"Bullshit," I said, distracted from my purpose. "The nine alignments are a fundamental of *Dungeons and Dragons* and I will fight anyone who says otherwise. What's next? Orcs and drow not being always chaotic evil?"

That was when Gabby removed her ponytail and the spell protecting her identity fell away.

"Shiver me timbers!" I gasped. "You're Ultragoddess too!"

Gabby rolled her eyes. "Thank you, Cindy, I don't think they heard you in Russia."

I shrugged. "What's with pretending to be mean to me and flying away? Did you do the superspeed thing to protect your identity?"

"It's not like that," Gary said, sighing.

I pointed at him. "You don't get to talk. I am appalled. The woman you're sleeping with is the mother of your children! That's against all the laws of God and marriage. You should be sleeping with women half her age and no emotional attachment. Age-appropriate mistresses. Ugh. What is this, France?"

Gary stared at me. "I literally could not follow that insane trail of illogic and I am usually pretty good at that."

"I'm not Ultragoddess," Gabby said. "That is a different Gabrielle Anders."

"Oh God, is it another evil you from an alternate dimension?" I asked. "We already did that with your dad. Also, Gary. Also, now that I think about it, multiple other people. Good Cindy really freaked me out."

She was an, ugh, pediatrician. Banishing her back to the dimension she sprang from hadn't come a minute too soon.

"No," Gabby said. "I'm not from an alternate dimension."

"Were you split in half by a transporter? One good, one evil?" I asked. "That happened to both Kirk and Commander Riker."

"The Riker clone wasn't evil," Gary said. "Just kind of a dick."

"Shut up, Gary," I said. "You're not the one your ex, sort of ex, not ex wants to kill."

"I'm not so sure about that," Gabby said. "The other Gabrielle Anders seems pretty focused on destroying this family."

"Yeah, I got that when she promised to destroy us," I said. "Who the hell is she? Future you? Because we have evil versions from the future and past too."

"Your life is very complicated," Dana said, coming up behind me. She was wearing a canary yellow dress and looked less like she was attending a wedding than a Prom.

"Actually, this is pretty typical at the level we operate," I replied. "Still, having the world's most famous superhero wanting me dead while her communist doppelganger—"

"Not a communist," Gabby said.

"—is right in front of me is something worth exploring," I said. "So, what's the reason?"

"It's complicated," Gabby said, looking down.

"No shit it's complicated!" I said. "You're violating the laws of physics here. The Law of Conservation of Matter says there should be only one of you."

"I never liked that law," Dana said. "Newtonian physics are an outdated relic of the Enlightenment."

"Shut up," I said, making a hush gesture. "So, spill, Revolutionary Girl, if that is your real codename!"

Gabby blinked. "Why would it not be my real—"

"Don't try," Gary said. "People try and decipher my ramblings, only to be wacked in the head when they're trying to figure out what the hell I've said."

"It's literally the only reason Gary is still alive," I said. "But the student of saying idiotic drivel has become the master."

"Is that something to be proud of?" Dana asked.

"I said shut up!" I snapped.

Dana did, looking uncomfortable as an intergalactic warlord and his pet cyborg passed by. I was annoyed Syni-Star was invited here. I figured that after you committed galactic genocide, you should be ostracized from polite society.

"Black ultranite," Gabby replied.

"What now?" I asked, wondering what the hell black ultranite was. I knew that white ultranite was about the only substance that could kill Ultragod.

"Ultranite is raw magic concentrated into ore leftover from the Big Bang," Gabby explained. "White ultranite is toxic to Ultra-Force wielders but makes people gain superpowers. Black ultranite causes crazy things like people splitting in two, wild personality changes, and turning into a gorilla."

"What was that last one?" I asked.

"The Silver Age was a weird time," Gabby said. "The Dragon King arranged for a sample of black ultranite to be delivered to me when I was delivering toys for Santa."

Dana blinked then opened her mouth to speak before shutting it.

"How is that jolly old elf?" I asked. "Oh, and you can tell him to blank himself for never delivering any blanking toys to me for Christmas!"

"We're Jewish," Gary pointed out. "Also, blanking?"

"Even I have some standards about cussing out Santa," I said. "And yes, I know the guy has all the good Gentile boys and girls to deliver to, but he could make an exception for the poor girls of Falconcrest City."

"So," Gabby said, taking a deep breath. "I was split between two people."

"One being a radical revolutionary girl and the other being an enormous blank-a-saurus," I replied. "Insert the insult you're thinking of there."

"Sort of," Gabby said. "I seem to be composed of the radical sides of Gabrielle Anders' personality and her emotional attachments. The woman currently flying around pretending to be Ultragoddess is far more ruthless and law-abiding. She also has all of my superpowers."

"Wow, you got the crap end of the stick," I replied. "Is this going to wear off?"

"I don't know," Gabby replied. "It's been months so far and nothing has changed. Usually, the effects of black ultranite end after a few hours."

"Just enough for the end of the issue," I muttered, shaking my head, and leaning on the fourth wall of a nearby kiosk.

"No offense but shouldn't your dad be involved in all this?" I asked. "He's the President of the United States and having his daughter split seems like something he should be concerned about."

"He knows," Gabby said, putting her ponytail back up.

"Gasp!" I said. "Where did you go?"

Gabby stared.

"Yeah, the spell is broken," I replied, shrugging. "I know how this works. My point still stands."

"My father is a great man, but he also has his blind spots," Gabby replied. "Such as the fact he's deeply gullible. He thinks I'm just a copy created in a lab somewhere like all the other Ultragoddess clones."

Dana looked confused.

"Oh yeah, there have been like fifty," I explained to Dana. "They all speak like cavewomen and look like jigsaw puzzles."

"Huh," Dana said.

"Ultragoddess is mostly behaving within the confines of the law," Gary said. "We are criminals after all. She has a lot of protection. So, I'm looking for a way to cure her without harming her."

"Never mind that she's planning on killing us all," I replied, staring at Gary.

"Never mind," Gary muttered, admitting that he had an absurd attachment to people. He hadn't been able to let Mandy go after she died either and was still brooding over his brother's death thirty years ago. Could you imagine what it would be like to have a superhero or villain obsessed with losing family from their childhood while never getting over it? Jeez, that person would have to be utterly bats. Eh, I needed to get off this wall.

"Well, she's just claimed she's going to destroy the island and I'm not going to discount that she can since she once pushed the moon back in place," I replied. "Is there anything more that I should need to know?"

"Agent G put a worm in the Foundation for World Harmony to monitor chatter about us," Gabby said. "Colonel Colton has requested assignment to monitor the situation on Dragon Island. The backup he's requested consists of some of the most zealous ruthless soldiers in the organization. I wouldn't be surprised if they tried something extreme."

"How extreme is extreme? Extreme wearing J Lo's barely there Grammy dress or extreme killing everyone?" I asked.

"The latter," Gabby said. "Imagine if he snuck a nuke on this island."

"Case already explained that would ruin the loot," I replied. "But I suppose from the rest of the world's perspective, it would be a good thing. A nuclear weapon going off here would wipe out majority of the world's evil doers."

"Not all of them," Gary pointed out. "Some would survive, including the Dragon King. Japan nuked him once or twice when he was still in his city wrecking phase. It didn't work. He became a radioactive giant murder lizard."

"Well, there goes plan B," I muttered. "Anything else you see I should be aware about? This is looking like Mardi Gras for supervillains."

"You forgot to bring a present," Cthulhuoid said behind me.

I paused and turned around to see him standing next to a very much alive Crowbar King. The two of them were dressed in badly fitting tuxes that made them look even more out of place than they would have if they had just been wearing their supervillain costumes.

"Oh, for fuck's sake," I said, staring at those two. "How are you two not dead?"

"No force in the universe can destroy the eldritch horror that is the Prophet of the Sleeper Below!" Cthulhuoid AKA Goddamn Jerry said.

Clearly, I needed to hit him harder next time.

"My crowbar's magic allowed me to recover from being *eaten*," said Crowbar King AKA Frigging Liam, sounding very offended.

"Let's not quibble over who ate who," I said. "Also, you were a bit sweet. You might want to see a doctor about possible diabetes."

Dana stared at that then mouthed. "You ate him?"

"Oh, I've eaten plenty of guys," I said. "One of the least enjoyable examples."

Gabby snorted at that.

Jerry narrowed his four eyes. "The vengeance of the greatest Old One will be brought down upon you."

"Okay, first of all, *Cthulhu isn't real,*" I pointed out. "At least in this dimension. So, you come across as even lamer as a guy who decided to make himself a squamous horror for superpowers. I mean, you really limited your dating options there."

"You'd be surprised," Jerry said. "You think you can defeat me—"

"Gary, kill this guy," I said. "I already tried and am dressed too classy to deal with him again."

"Sure," Gary said, conjuring a fireball in his hands.

That was when a spotlight was shined on all of us from above. A booming but melodious voice spoke over a microphone. "Ladies and gentlemen, we have traitors among us."

Chapter Twenty

Well, This Sucks

I became painfully aware of the spotlight that was now illuminating Gary, Dana, Gabby, and me in the enormous horde of supervillains around us. Adonis was holding a microphone on stage where he'd been accepting tribute for himself and his bored-looking groom. He was the source of the decidedly unwelcome revelation that we were considered traitors.

Though I wasn't sure exactly who we were supposed to be traitors to. This wasn't Westeros and I hadn't sworn allegiance to any throne that I remembered. Hell, the last house I'd belonged to was Hufflepuff after I'd taken one of those online tests, following which I was certain they were all rigged.

I did a double take. "Is he talking about us?"

"I do believe he is," Gary said, making the fireball in his hands disappear.

"No, I do believe he has to be talking about Jerry and Crowbar King," I replied, gesturing to the wannabe Cthulhu and guy who should have known better to stay digested. Seriously, I'd had royal heartburn thanks to him.

"We refer, of course, to Red Riding Hood and Merciless: The Supervillain without Mercy™," Adonis said, pointing directly at me. He included the trademark at the end, and I had to admit that had been Gary's best idea in supervillain branding. There were plenty of Destroyers, Exterminators, Dark Lords, and more, but very few who were smart enough get proper licensing agreements. You had no idea how much trouble I had trying to get a cut of people's bootleg Red Riding Hood merchandise.

"I knew I shouldn't have gone with a public domain name," I replied. "You think the instant recognition is going to help you at start but then you realize everyone else can use your stuff. It's like Diabloman said, you can't copyright being a hot redhead in a corset."

Personally, I was glad for the massive crowd of bad guys between myself and Adonis on stage. It meant I could speak a huge amount with my crew and almost no one would hear us unless we shouted at the top of our lungs. Which gave us a small chance to come up with a plan. I had no idea what this plan was going to be, but it gave us a chance to do so. For once, I was glad Gary was here as he was very good at pulling plans out of his ass.

"Well, I'm stumped," Gary said. "Got any ideas, Cindy?"

Sigh. Of course.

"I don't know these people!" Dana pointed at both of us simultaneously. "They've kidnapped me and forced me to be their henchwoman!"

"We also have the filthy henchwoman of Tom Terror, Damselfly," Adonis said, focusing the spotlight specifically on her. "The worst of our admittedly heinous group of ne'er do wells."

A chorus of boos filled the audience, all directed at her rather than us. I admit, that brought a smile to my face.

"Oh, come on!" Dana said. "Really?"

Gary shook his head and pointed at her. "I agree, she's not with us!"

Gabby couldn't help but chuckle. "We're going to die but at least it's going to be entertaining when it happens."

"You've discovered the secret to dating Gary," I replied. "Personally, I'm reconsidering the alure of a long but boring life."

Crowbar King grinned and Cthulhu made a face which I couldn't really decipher past all of the tentacles. I had no idea how these individuals pulled it off, but they'd managed to turn the entire crowd against us.

"You are enemies of the supervillain nation," Adonis said, working the crowd. "Ones that have walked to your doom through the front door!"

"We were invited!" Gary said, sounding genuinely offended.

"I don't think guest right applies here," I replied, shaking my head. Mind you, my response wasn't perhaps the best one, but I was buying for time. Shouting at the top of my lungs, I shook a fist at our host. "What the hell did we do? How are we traitors to supervillainy?"

Unfortunately, Adonis had a rebuttal. "For years, we have watched you two skirt the edges of the superhero and supervillain world. You have killed, maimed, and destroyed countless members of our kind while acting with kids gloves towards heroes."

"We've killed some heroes too!" I snapped back.

"The bad ones," Gary muttered behind me.

"Stop helping Gary," I said through clenched teeth. "They still count, goddammit."

We'd fought the Extreme! multiple times and Gary was responsible for the death of Shoot-Em-Up, our erstwhile gun-toting ephebophile (look it up) mutual object of loathing. Gary was also responsible for killing Ultragod once. Albeit that was an alternate universe version of him and thus probably didn't count. Also, Ultragod had come back from the dead, so his loss was something only cosmic watchers and comic book nerds cared about. Damn, we *were* looking like antiheroes, weren't we?

"Tom Terror, the Ice Scream Man, Big Ben, the Nightmistress, Dracula, and many others have fallen to you!" Adonis said, reciting the names of villains killed by our group. A list that caused the crowd to get increasingly agitated, which wasn't great since they were already a bunch of ornery and half-drunk supervillains.

I was left painfully aware that even on my best day, I couldn't even run away from half of these guys. Some of them had superspeed, others could teleport, and not a few of them had instant death abilities. I'd always kept a reasonably friendly relationship to Falconcrest City's Underworld, but the accent was on the word reasonably.

"Wait, you killed Dracula?" Dana asked.

"Everyone has killed Dracula," I replied. "It's like a Halloween thing among super people."

"Also, why do they care about killing Tom Terror but the fact I was his henchman has them hating me?" Dana asked, just as confused as she was back at Omega Tower.

"Because it's a man's world, honey. Don't ever think otherwise," I replied then shouted. "Listen, I swear, we did it for the money! There was no motivation of good or idealism behind all of it! It was just a territory thing!"

Poaching a supervillain's territory was punishable by death or at least a fight in an abandoned warehouse or rooftop. What had happened with Jerry and the Crowbar King was typical of how supervillains interacted—we weren't one big happy family. Hell, the only reason supervillains hadn't taken over the world despite outnumbering superheroes forty-to-one was the fact none of us were willing to work together for more than a handful of jobs.

Adonis scoffed at my defense, actually scoffed. I didn't think people did that outside of books set in 1920s England. "There is no defending what you have done because you have shown your true colors! You saved the world! Multiple times! The true mark of a superhero!"

I stared at him, opened my mouth, cocked my head to one side then did a double take. "Is he actually complaining we saved the world?"

"Yes, I believe he is," Gabby said. "I mean, he's not wrong."

"It's where we keep our stuff!" I paraphrased the Tick. "We use it too!"

I'd always felt that was the one downside of the various supervillains plotting to take over the world and/or kill all the world's superheroes. If you took over the world, then you had to take over all the duties of defending the planet from everything from alien invasions to rodents of unusual size. Getting rid of the world's superheroes might make things easier for you to avoid getting overthrown once you took over, too, but that also meant that you'd gotten rid of all the world's specialists in kaiju slaying or demon hunting. I mean, really, who wanted all that work?

"Kill them all!" the Typewriter (II), daughter of the original Typewriter shouted. She was quickly joined by a chorus of other supervillains proclaiming similar sentiments. Honestly, we were less popular than New Coke, a reference that would probably go over the heads of everyone my daughters' age.

Speaking of which, at least the rest of the group was free and away from this situation. I didn't know what I would do if my daughters, Mandy, Jane, Case, and my frenemies were also taken hostage. That was, of course, when the crowd parted enough to shove my daughters, Mandy, Amanda, the Human Tank, and the Black Witch up against us.

"Goddammit," I muttered. "Wait, where the hell is Case?"

"Case got away," Jane said. "He is a spy."

"Yeah, like a James Bond incredibly overt spy who announces his name at the table then gets surprised when they kill his companions," I replied. He was probably off at the baccarat table getting into Tara Al-Set or Madame Phantom's pants.

"Silence!" Adonis shouted, clearly not happy at having the full undivided attention of his prisoners. "Our dear friends, Cthulhuoid and the Crowbar Kings have revealed these infiltrators into our wedding!"

"You don't even know these guys!" I shouted back. "Also, we were invited!"

"An oversight I intend to correct!" Adonis said, not missing a beat. Raising his hands in the air, he acted halfway between a televangelist and a ringmaster. "For the sake of all your previous supervillain victims, I sentence you to dea—"

"Parley!" Leia shouted.

"What now?" I asked, turning to my daughter. I was noticing she was slowly developing into a blonde version of me and that was a terrible waste. I mean, who could possibly deal with being a slightly less attractive version of their mother?

"This isn't *Pirates of the Caribbean*, Leia," Gary said, looking sympathetic but unimpressed. "Even if I was runner up to Johnny Depp for Sexiest Man Alive that year."

"And how much did that cost?" Mandy asked, under her breath.

"Clearly more than I paid," Gary snapped back.

Leia pulled out her pad and waved it in the air. "According to the rules of supervillainy, as laid down by Diabloman who is the most successful supervillain of all time, supervillains in dispute have the option of resolving their issues via trial by combat."

"That is not in there," I muttered to my daughter.

"Shut up, Mom," Leia said, under her breath.

"It's okay, Dad, I'll protect you!" Mimi said, punching her fist against her hand and crackling with Ultra-Force energy.

I glared at her.

"You're implied to be protected, too," Mimi said.

Adonis stared down. "Do you think I want—"

"Gladiator fight!" Achilles shouted, looking more than a little drunk.

"Really?" Adonis looked to his groom.

"Gladiator fight!" Achilles said. "It's not going to be a proper Olympian wedding without one."

"I thought that was a Roman thing," I said.

"They branched out," Gabby replied. "Besides, it's all the rage everywhere but Earth. You can't visit an alien planet without having death duels."

Adonis and Achilles started to have a heated conversation that I couldn't hear since they were smart enough to talk away from the microphone. Say what you will about werewolf hearing, but it wasn't like I could tune out all the chatter going on around us as well as Gloria Estefan's "Conga" being played by the DJ in the background. You'd think they'd have turned that off while Adonis was speaking but I suppose they got paid by the hour.

Jerry and Crowbar King exchanged glances that I could tell were them realizing they'd made a huge mistake. Even if I had to squint a bit to read Jerry's four eyes. The two had clearly thought that tattling to the other supervillains about our presence would be enough to get us killed. Which, honestly, was better than ninety percent of supervillain plans.

"I volunteer as tribute!" I said, holding my fingers out in the Boy Scout salute. I could do that since I'd been a Girl Scout. I'd made a small fortune selling pot to go along with my cookies.

"Aren't you a little old to be Katniss?" Leia asked.

I shot her a glare. "In the words of my dearly departed bitch mother, your grandmother, shut the hell up, kid."

Achilles and Adonis finished their argument with the latter clearing his throat. "Well, in honor of my groom's request, I submit that you do have the right to trial by combat. Because why the hell not. I shall select two champions from your ranks and your fates shall be determined by battle to the death!"

I wasn't going to let Leia and Mandy get chosen to fight their champions. Even if Leia was an incredibly powerful psychic who could order them not to breathe and Mandy was stronger than all of us put together.

"That was a really stupid decision, Mom," Leia said, telepathically.

"In retrospect, probably. Thankfully, we have two champions, and we just must choose anyone but Gary to be my partner," I thought back.

"Your partner shall be Merciless!" Adonis proclaimed.

"Are you feeding him lines from my brain?" I thought back. *"Be honest."*

"Well, that's not good," Gary replied.

"Why? You've beaten much bigger threats than these morons," I said. "I'm assuming it's Jerry and Crowbar King."

"Why?" Gary asked.

"Yes, why?" Jerry asked.

"Law of conservation of detail," I replied. "There's already too many Cindy's Seven members. You're not going to introduce a bunch of new characters and further confuse the audience."

Gary stared at me. "Is this what I sound like to other people?"

"Yes," Gabby said. "Exactly."

"I'm so sorry," Gary apologized. "I had no idea."

"Watch me be right," I said, staring at him.

"You shall face our champions: Cthulhuoid and Crowbar King!" Adonis shouted across the crowd to their delight.

Well, everyone's except Jerry and Crowbar King.

"Shouldn't we have a say in this?" Crowbar King asked.

"You don't want to kill them?" Jerry asked.

"Of course, I do," Crowbar King said, putting a hand over his heart. "It's just I died the last time I fought Cindy."

"Red Riding Hood," I corrected.

"Whatever," Crowbar King said, still having not learned his lesson in humility.

"I was really hoping we could get a bunch of these other villains to kill them for us," Crowbar King said. "I mean, I was eaten. Do you know what it's like being eaten? It's terrible."

"You ate a supervillain?" Gabby asked.

"Oh, now you're judging," I said, looking back at her. "I feel judged. This is why no one likes you."

"Wait, what?" Gabby asked.

"I like you, Mom," Mimi said. "Which, when did you get here?"

Leia stared at Mimi.

"What?" Mimi asked.

"It is a simple matter," Adonis said. "Merciless and Red Riding Hood will face Cthulhuoid and Crowbar King in the ring of fire. Whoever emerges victorious will be showered with riches and whoever fails will die. Furthermore, all of their companions will be imprisoned then sold as slaves to the highest bidder.'

"Gee, thanks, Cindy," Jane said, looking at me. "I'm so glad you brought me on this trip."

I rolled my eyes. "You weren't saying no to a working vacation on a tropical island. Do not blame me for this."

"We should be the ones to fight," Selena said.

"Why?" I asked.

"Because I'm one of the most powerful witches on Earth," Selena said, "and Clarissa is a Space Marine."

"Also, I've lost my powers," Gary said.

I did a double take. "Wait, what?"

Chapter Twenty-One

Trial by Combat Is Stupid

"You don't have your powers?" I asked, wondering why this was only coming up now.

"It didn't come up!" Gary said, spreading his hands out.

"Didn't come up!? We had a fight with the Foundation with World Harmony!" I said, disgusted.

"Well, I have my Dungeon magic," Gary said, pulling out an ebony wand with a vampire hair core. Gee, I wonder where he got that from. "Just not my Primal Orb magic. I had the Primal Orbs of Death and Chaos but lost them when the universe was rebooted. The second time."

I rolled my eyes. "You're telling me that you can't do your big awesome magic because you've lost your balls?"

"I wouldn't put it that way," Gary said, displaying the usual male ego regarding these things. "But no, I don't have my super-duper magic. Just the basic level one to nine spells."

"Level nine spells include *Wish*!" I said, remembering my gamer days. "Wish them dead!"

"That never works," Gary said, snorting. "*Wish* is just a license for the Dungeon Master to screw with you."

Jane sniffed, looking on the verge of tears. It was a bizarre reaction.

"What?" Gary asked, looking at her.

"I'm just happy to be among my people," Jane said.

That was when Mimi handed me a letter. "What's this?"

"I was given it by the Black Witch," Mimi said. "She and the others are gone."

"What do you mean gone?" I opened the envelope, ignoring the crowd of confused supervillains around me. "*Dear Cindy, Clearly, you have everything under control. Amanda, Clarissa, Mandy, and I are forming our own supervillain team. We'll be robbing Smog ahead of you. Smell you later.*"

"Really?" Gabby asked.

"Oh, those bitches!" I snapped, crumbling up the latter and throwing it on the ground. "And I *can* use that word."

"Can I join their team?" Dana asked, looking up.

"No!" I snapped. "I can't believe Mandy would join. The others? Yes. But Mandy?"

"Maybe she felt overshadowed," Gary said.

"You shut up too!" I said.

"Ahem," Adonis said into his microphone. "I'm feeling a little ignored here."

"Hush, Mr. Universe, I'm having a labor crisis here," I said, looking up at him. "Is it okay if I substitute someone else? Dana here?"

"No!" Dana said.

"Or Revolutionary Girl?" I asked. "She doesn't have powers, but I wouldn't be bothered by her death."

"Et tu, Cindy?" Gabby asked.

"Sorry, you're just like eighty percent less hot without any powers," I replied. "It turns out flying women is my ultranite. Also, weirdly, handsome geeks."

"Is that why you made me act like Matt Smith's Doctor last Thursday?" Gary asked.

"Way too much information, Dad," Mimi said.

"Try living it every day," Leia said, shuddering. "There's a reason I've been put off sex forever. I mean the reason is I'm ace but it certainly hasn't—"

"Silence!" Adonis shouted, his voice thundering through the island. "There will be no substitutions and the fight to the death will happen now!"

Crap.

That was when Johnny Cash's "Ring of Fire" started to play as a circle of flame encircled Gary, me, and our opponents before spreading outward. The ring drove back both friend and foe while leaving us ample room to fight. Cthulhuoid and Crowbar King seemed every bit as surprised as the event happened while the rest of the villains laughed.

"So, we meet again, Jerry Dabrowski," Gary said, cracking his knuckles. "My old college rival."

Jerry narrowed his alien eyes. "For years, people kept mistaking me for you because of our weirdly similar names. I swear I would have won the H.P. Lovecraft fanfic competition for the Tri-State area if not for the fact people mistook a post by you about how we needed more minorities in fiction to be mine. I lost the entire Alt-Right sci-fi vote."

Gary stared. "You were worse! My Red Sonja vs. Cthulhu fanfic was about to win when you said it was plagiarized!"

"You know each other?" I asked, doing a double take. "God, is there nothing you won't steal from me, Gary? Even my archenemies?"

"It was a small college campus!" Gary said. "There's was bound to be some crossover!"

"A likely story," I said, growing my claws. "Also, that above statement makes me regret ever being involved in fanfic. I'd like to clarify that yes, I did write some erotic Harry Potter fiction about a bisexual Goth and am considering republishing it to get some of that *Fifty Shades of Gray* money."

"Seriously, Cindy?" Gary asked, assuming a fighting position. He looked ridiculous with his wand out, waving it everywhere, and for once that wasn't innuendo.

"Yeah, *Fifty Shades of Grey* used to be *Twilight* fanfic," I replied, slowly assuming my war form. "I figure the adventures of Satanica Ravenclaw would make a mint. We just need to get Rowling to stop trashing the brand."

"Get to killing!" Leia shouted, only to be elbowed by her sister.

I really wondered where I'd gone wrong with Leia. Then, almost immediately, I dismissed any responsibility for my daughter's boorish behavior. After all, I couldn't be responsible for any of her problems as a parent since I'd never been there for her.

Jerry assumed a fighting stance like a sumo wrestler, one foot at a time. "I have been waiting a long time for this, Cindy."

"No, you haven't," I pointed out. "You tried to kill me this week."

"Shut up!" Jerry said. "God, does everything have to be about you?"

"Yes! Absolutely!" I replied with no irony. "Besides, if you were going to kill me, maybe you should think better about trying to do so with a moron like Crowbar King and after already getting your ass kicked once!"

"I find those remarks very offensive," Crowbar King said, lifting his crowbar. "I'll just have to cope with percussive therapy."

Okay, that was clever. "Bring it, asshole."

I'm sure when my biography is published by the Cindy worshiping cults of the year 4050 AD, they will speak in legendary whispers of my triumph here. How Gary was disabled quickly by a sneak lightning attack by Cthulhoid, only to reveal both had been empowered by Adonis' Olympian magic ahead of time. How they double-teamed me, but I was inspired by my love of my daughters to tap into the primordial power of my bloodline to raise holy hell upon them both, rising above their corpses with two decapitated heads. One in each hand.

Yeah, that's not what happened.

No sooner did the four of us start preparing for a long-overdue battle then my enhanced werewolf hearing picked up the sound of something unpleasant coming. Turning to Gary, I shouted, "If you've got some protection magic then now is the time to cast it!"

"*Bubble*!" Gary shouted as a glowing bubble appeared around us, cutting between the fire and our children, Jane, Dana, and Revolutionary Girl.

"Bubble, really?" I asked.

That was when the sky rained hell. I'm speaking figuratively since it occurs to me that with my life the skies raining demons wouldn't be entirely out of the realm of possibility. No, I mean the kind of someone sending some Foundation for World Harmony vertical lift-off jets to drop fricking bombs on us. Yes, someone in the wonderful world of government had realized that the chance to wipe out a huge chunk of the world's supervillains had arrived, and Smog the Dragon was leaving with all of his riches so why bother placating him? We were getting extrajudicially executed.

Crap.

Now as a supervillain, I had seen some seriously messed up stuff in my time. I mean, let's face it, we started this adventure with me eating a man alive and not in the fun way. Well for him, at least. However, watching the entirety of my surroundings go up in flames was damn traumatic. Jerry and Crowbar King disintegrated in front of me and while I wouldn't miss either, it made me aware of everyone around them that died in the resulting conflagration.

After all, this wasn't just supervillains being killed in the sneak attack. The DJs, waiters, waitresses, valets, and poor bastards who'd just picked the absolute worst time in the world to book a Dragon Island vacation met their horrific ends among the worst scum of the universe. Like Leia and Mimi, the Colonel (or Ultragoddess or whoever oversaw this) had no issues executing innocents if it meant they got their target.

Worst of all, it wouldn't even work. Yeah, I know, randomly bombing people doesn't make the world a safer place. Crazy I know. I could already see the most powerful and dangerous of the supervillains moving through the smoldering ruins, looking pissed. If Gary and I could survive this with magic, you can sure as hell bet there were others who'd managed to cover themselves in magical barriers or force fields in time. There were also beings here that anything short of a nuclear bomb wouldn't touch and maybe not even them.

No, the people killed here were the guys in funny costumes that probably had a death ray or ice beam. You know, people regular bombs and guns *could* kill. It wasn't going to do a damn thing to reduce the number of supervillains on the planet since all this did was open a bunch of themes for other criminals to steal. I'd seen the Fifty-Two Pick Up Gang among the dead. That just meant playing card outfits were going to get a boost in sales. God, they hadn't even been murderers, just a clan of jewel thieves from Vegas. There wasn't even fifty-two of them. What was the *point*?

Also, was I on fire? Shit! I was on fire! Smelling the burning cloth of my cloak, I immediately spun around and tried to out my Red Riding Hood costume. The illusion from earlier was shattered and we are looked like supervillains again. Pity. Behind me, I could tell there was still a magical blaze burning brightly between me and the rest of my group.

"Gary, put out the goddamn fire!" I said, smelling the flames and smoke burning inside the bubble with us!

Idiot!

"I'm trying to maintain the bubble while we're in the middle of a bombing!" Gary shouted, keeping his hands raised as they glowed.

"Hey, don't worry about it," Mimi said, walking through the fire and back. "It's not even bothering me. I'm immune to flames!"

"I'm not!" Leia said, leaning up against the back of the bubble and coughing.

"Are you immune to smoke inhalation, Mimi?" I said, staring at the flames.

"Water!" Jane said, lifting her hands and causing a spout of H_20 to shoot out like a fire hose from her right hand. The results weren't pretty, and it was still smokey as well as hot inside, but the results were that we had at least a little more oxygen left.

"Water?" I asked, looking at her. "Where the hell did you learn magic?"

"Gary," Jane said. "I opted into his Merciless Magical Operating System or MMOS. I have moderator privileges and the status of a sixteenth level Druid."

I stared at her. "Never mention that to me again. If this series turns into a Lit-RPG, I will find the guy who writes our biographies and kill him."

The flames and tight nature of the bubble meant there wasn't much left in the way of oxygen even if there wasn't anything actively burning anymore. Unfortunately, as much as I hated to admit it, Gary was right, and our surroundings weren't terribly conducive to survive. We were surrounded by flames, wreckage, and death with the possibility of a double tap by the Foundation almost a certainty.

That was, if you didn't get it from context, when they dropped a second round of bombs just to make sure everyone who could be dead from the first round was really dead. It also was prone to annihilating people who moved in to try to help survivors of strikes like this. You know, just in case you still thought this was a good idea.

Dana, meanwhile, had shrunk back to Tinkerbell size and was fluttering in the air above my head with a terrified look on her face. "Can I please leave your gang now?"

"No!" I snapped. "Shrink us down!"

"What?" Dana asked. "But you wanted me to shrink your dragon—"

"Do it!" I said. "That way, we won't consume as much air!"

"I don't think that's how science works," Leia said. "In fact, there's a lot of questions about how size and mass relate to shrinking regarding oxygen consumption—"

"Do it!" I snapped.

Much to my surprise, Dana did it and we found ourselves shrinking down to six inches tall, making Gary's bubble far, far vaster. Gary dropped the bubble and started casting another spell. I didn't understand what he was saying but even with the exaggerated distance from the flames and destruction that came from being smaller, it was still the equivalent of being in a twisted hellscape.

It was a strange sensation being shrunk down to Smurf size, but I couldn't say it was the weirdest thing that had ever happened to me. To explain the weirdest, I'd probably break several international indecency laws. Still, it was one of those things that gave you a new perspective on life and scale. One minute you were surrounded by a vast inferno and the next minute, well I was still surrounded by a vast inferno, but it was far away. Okay, maybe this would have been cooler if I was some place like my house. I wasn't really getting the full effect here, though I could see the burned-out skeletons of people the size of houses nearby. That was cool in a terrifying, nightmare-inducing sort of way.

"Yeah, Mom, I gotta tell you that you've brought us on the most wonderful family vacation!" Leia said, shouting over to me. She sounded like a chipmunk due to the fact our vocal cords had been affected by the transformation. I didn't know why that didn't seem to effect Dana in her reduced state but maybe she was used to it.

"It's a working vacation, dear!" I shouted back. "If you want to be a supervillain, you have to roll with the insanity."

"I'm not a supervillain," Gabby said. She, too, sounded like a chipmunk.

"You shut up!" I pointed at her. "This is all your fault."

"My fault?" Gabby asked, confused.

"Yes! You!" I pointed at her. "Other you! The evil Ultragoddess who is dropping bombs on her own child!"

"I'd survive it," Mimi said. "I'm kind of awesome that way. It's why I'm going to be the best thief ever."

"Can we talk about that?" Gabby asked, looking concerned. "I'm not sure you becoming a supervillain is a great idea."

"Oh, *now* you want to be my mother?" Mimi asked, staring at her. "Where the hell was this the entirety of my life until now?"

Gabby blanched. "Listen, that's complicated—"

"Cindy is more my mother than you!" Mimi said, putting her hands on her tiny hips. "Do you know how awful of a mother you have to be for that to be true?"

"Hey!" I snapped before pausing. "Okay, fair cop. Also, don't insult your absentee superstar world-famous mother."

"Hey!" Gabby said.

"I'm on your side in this!" I snapped. "Except not. Listen, Jane and Kerri have raised these kids way more than I have."

"This is true," Jane paused before blinking. "Holy crap, it *is* true. I'm a mother and I'm like in my twenties. What am I doing with my life?"

"Yes, we should really be paying you as a nanny," I replied. "Wait, are we paying you? I thought you were kind of paid in room and board which doesn't make you a slave but—"

"I'm going to fly away now," Dana said.

"You better not!" I snapped. "You have to unshrink us!"

"It'll wear off in an hour. Please don't ever contact me again," Dana said.

That was when we disappeared in a flash of magical light. Gary had done a teleportation spell. It made me wonder just how complicated it had to be given that required words and calculations unlike everything else where he just shouted a word. Also, where was he taking us? I probably should have bothered to check ahead of time. Oh well, it wasn't possible that it could be worse than where we were leaving.

And why did I say that?

Idiot!

Chapter Twenty-Two

Gold, Gold, Gold!

My eyes adjusted to the flash of light and greeted with me with the most beautiful sight in the world: mountains and mountains of gold. The sight caused me to blink multiple times, my brain refusing to take in the enormous stadium-sized pile of treasure that surrounded me. It was like the cave in Aladdin, Smaug's Hoard and the Federal Reserve all in one. We'd returned to normal size, but the sight was still overwhelming.

We were in a cavern of some kind, huge to the point you might as well call it a section of the Underdark. There were stalactites and stalagmites interspersed between millions of gold coins, boxes of diamonds, paintings, and stacks of fat bills formed into blocks the size of an apartment. There was even alien currency, with Tsavong drucets that looked like marbles, and star-shaped Thran credits. There were objects radiating magic to my enhanced senses everywhere, which sent waves of greed through my body.

"I think I just came," I said, breathing out a sigh of satisfaction.

"Merciful Moses, Mom," Leia said, disgusted.

"Hush you," I said, breathing in the scent around me. "I'm having a Scrooge McDuck moment."

"A what now?" Leia asked.

I ran up and threw myself on top of the gold pile before rolling around on it like a dog. You couldn't really swim in piles of gold, but you could press it up against your skin with your tongue hanging out.

"Cindy, stop being stereotypical," Gary said, sighing.

"Gold!" I said, laughing and waving around my arms. "Gold! Gold! Gold!"

"Wow, dragons really do keep hoards in your world," Jane said, looking around with a stunned look on her face.

"They don't on yours?" Gary asked.

"The one I'm dating keeps a bank account," Jane replied.

"You're still dating him back on your world, huh?" Gary asked, no hint of disapproval but curiosity.

"I thought you were dating Uncle Case!" Mimi said, offended on his behalf.

"Listen, I date Lucien on my world and Case here," Jane said, frowning. "It's complicated."

"It's called an affair, Jane," I said, putting on a tiara and a bunch of diamond necklaces while holding a scepter. "There's nothing complicated about it."

Jane looked ashamed, which I hadn't intended.

"You should be honest," Gabby said, looking to Jane. "Don't lead either of them on."

"Oh, don't you dare!" I snapped at Gabby. "You started sniffing around Gary when he was still monogamous with Mandy."

"We were engaged," Gabby said, glaring.

"And you mind-wiped him!" I snapped.

"Can I leave now?" Dana asked, now back to normal size. "I know I keep asking but I think I was driven insane a few hours ago."

"How did you know to teleport us down to Smog's hoard?" Leia asked Gary, clearly uninterested in becoming involved in this story.

"I didn't," Gary admitted. "I just combined two spells to transport us someplace safe. Apparently, that is Smog's hoard. Certainly, it's protected from the bombardment going on above."

"Do you think Grandpa Colton is responsible?" Mimi asked.

"I mean, probably?" I said, not feeling much respect for Mandy's dad at this point. "Apparently, he doesn't have an issue with killing kids. Especially when they're not blood related to him. Mind you, Gabrielle—the evil Gabrielle I mean—also threatened me upstairs. I wouldn't be surprised if she was marking the spot for annihilation."

Gabby lowered her gaze. "If my other half is responsible for what happened above, the situation is worse than I imagined. If she has no regard for collateral damage, then there's no way she should have the power of the Ultra-Force."

"Collateral damage," I said, sarcastically. "Nice word for mass murder."

"Indeed," Gary said. "Ultragoddess going antihero, especially with the government's backing, could be a disaster beyond imagination."

Above our heads, I could hear tiny tinklings of sound that told me the government was continuing its second round of bombing. The others probably couldn't hear a thing, but I couldn't help but worry about the others. I had a good feeling they could survive all this, Selena Darkchylde's magic was a great equalizer after all, but it wasn't a guarantee. They were also doomed if Ultragoddess decided to finish them off personally. None of them had the heavy-hitting power to deal with an Ultra Family member gone rogue.

"I hate antiheroes," Gary muttered under his breath.

"Me too, Gary, me too," I muttered.

There had been a dark time in the Nineties called the Dark Age of Superheroes, just as the Silver Age had been the relatively most peaceful. That had been when superheroes—at least some of them, called antiheroes—had taken the kid gloves off and started carrying out extrajudicial killings, often with the full support of the public.

The worst one of them all had been Shoot-Em-Up and I still had nightmares about that psychotic piece of shit. Gary liked to think he had the deepest hatred for antiheroes among us due to his brother being killed, but he hadn't been sold by his mother to one in exchange for killing her pimp. Shoot-Em-Up had wanted to re-enact *The Professional* with me as his fourteen-year-old understudy: the European version. If that horrifies you beyond training a kid in the arts of murder, I applaud your knowledge of cinema. If Gary hadn't killed him, I would have slit his throat that night when we first met.

I paused. "I hope you didn't pick that up, Leia."

"I did," Leia said, sighing. "I know you cope with your dark and troubled past by numbing yourself with meaningless pleasures."

"Hardly meaningless," I said. I decided to lighten the mood. "Gary, I need you to have sex with me on this pile of money."

"No, Cindy," Gary said, rolling his eyes.

"What? Don't kink shame!" I snapped. "I'd invite Mandy but she's not here because she's a stupid traitor. There's room for three. I'd say four but I don't even know what you'd do with that many and it's just a crowd. Though gimme a minute and I might come up with something."

"Oh my God," Leia said, feeling her head. "Kill me now."

"You get used to it," Mimi said.

"I will not!" Leia said.

"Well, obviously you'd leave," I said, making a shoo gesture.

"No, Cindy," Gary said, more forcibly.

"Are you having problems?" I asked. "No, wait, you were fine yesterday. Did I do something wrong? I mean aside from all the things I've done wrong. I mean particularly so. Like that time I betrayed you and Princess Zelda to Gannon to try and hook up with Link."

Gary cleared his throat. "We're in a dragon's lair, Cindy. Perhaps we should keep out on the lookout for the dragon."

I blinked. "Huh. You know, you're right. Maybe I underestimated you. You should totally be my sidekick."

"Sure," Gary said. "We should survey the place and begin taking stock—"

"Of how to steal all this shit!" I said, throwing up my hands.

"I mean, just that chest of diamonds would—" Dana started to say.

"All of it!" I corrected her.

Dana sighed. "Yes, boss."

"Thank you!" I said, getting up. "I declare this hoard officially stolen by Cindy's Seven. Which we qualify as if we're counting me. Your loyalty is appreciated, except for Dana who we know is being forced to work for me."

Dana grimaced.

"Oh, you're still getting paid," I said, shrugging and putting my necklaces, tiara, and scepter in my various pockets across my costume. They were all extra-dimensionally enhanced like a thieves' bag of holding and while I couldn't fit near what was around me, it was nice to make sure I was at least partially covered.

"Let's find an exit and see if the dragon is here," Gary responded.

"You just teleported us here," Jane said, confused.

"Yeah, but I can only use teleport once per day," Gary replied. "Otherwise, you have to memorize the spell again."

Jane stared. "You gave yourself the stupid weakness for wizards from *Dungeons and Dragons* too? *What the hell is wrong with you?*"

"The possibilities are endless," I said. "Anyway, you raise a good point. We should go kill the dragon so we can take its stuff. Also, see if our friends and loved ones, by which I mean Mandy and Case are dead. Amanda I can touch and go on."

"What about Diabloman?" Mimi asked.

"What about him?" I asked, honestly kind of hoping he'd gone up with the baddies upstairs. He'd been my friend and mentor once. Accent on once. There were some things you just didn't forgive, and he'd done a lot of them. I just never thought he'd do them to me or Gary. He sure fooled us.

"We'll see," Gary said. "I'll take the girls. You take Jane and Dana. Gabby, would you mind going it alone? You're the most experienced heroine."

"Hey!" I snapped at Gary. "I'm in charge here."

Gary paused and nodded.

I sighed. "So, yeah, we're going with that."

"Good luck, Cindy," Gabby said.

"Good luck, Mom," Leia said.

"If the dragon comes and kills you, I will punch it to death," Mimi replied.

I pointed at her. "You do that."

To be honest, I *was* worried about the conspicuous absence of Smog. There was also the fact this cave absolutely couldn't fit Smog if he was as large as the stories proclaimed. I mean, a dragon could move around here but we were talking the difference between a Winnebago and a skyscraper.

Could Smog shapeshift? This seems like something I should have found out before going on this quest, but it had been half-assed and ill-considered from the beginning. I'd just figured I could coast through it on charisma and force of will. We'd gotten pretty far but having half of my crew ditch me, getting saved by my daughters and boyfriend from certain doom multiple times, plus no way to transport any of this? Well, it didn't speak much to my leadership capacity. Was it possible I wasn't meant to be a criminal mastermind? Hmm. Nope. Clearly, it is everyone else who was at fault. Glad we got that settled.

"Do I have to go with Cindy?" Jane asked.

"Hey!" Cindy snapped. "We should have solidarity as fellow shifters. You're a deer and I'm the animal that eats you."

"I should point out werewolves aren't cannibals on my world," Jane said. "Also, you aren't a shifter of my race but someone who magically altered themselves. Third, you're kind of awful."

"That hurts, Jane," I said, pounding my heart with my fist. "It gets me right here."

"Yes," Gary said, staring at her.

"Gary is not in charge!" I said, pointing out that she shouldn't be asking him anything. "I am!"

Jane looked at me. "As Tywin Lannister said, anyone who has to point out they're the king isn't the king."

"And we're taking lessons from old crossbow in the privy now?" I asked.

Jane rolled her eyes.

I stomped off, annoyed that apparently everyone did prefer Gary to me as leader. The only person following me was Dana, once again becoming a tiny buzzing wasp woman next to me.

Perhaps that was the key to leadership, intimidating everyone into following you.

"Stupid Jane," I muttered. "It's not cannibalism. I'm not human anymore. It'd be cannibalism if I ate other werewolves, which I wouldn't, because wolves are awesome."

Nothing could cheer me up now, not even the massive piles of gold and treasure around me. Well, that wasn't true. I started looking around for particularly nice pieces and stuffing them in my pockets while singing "It's Gold" from *Austin Powers in Goldmember*.

"You need to get to shrinking all this, Dana," I said, rummaging through a treasure chest for gemstones.

"I'm not sure that's possible," Dana said. "My experiment was packed on the *Nightplane II*."

I stopped rummaging. "Are you frigging serious?"

"Sorry!" Dana said, embarrassed. "I didn't know I was supposed to carry it at all times."

I banged my head against the top of the open treasure chest's box. "Can anything go right on this trip?"

"You survived so far," Dana said, trying to cheer me up. "That has to count for something, right?"

It made me more depressed the reluctant henchwoman was trying to be friendly. "No, not really."

That was when I heard a voice speak through the air, ethereal and echoing. "Cindy, Cindy, I come to speak with you."

I turned around and saw a large ornate broadsword sticking out of a stack of coins. It was possibly the most magical thing here and that was saying something. It was resting next to a glass case containing the ultranite gun that had killed Ultragod, which was impressive since that had been erased from existing following the universal reboot. I also saw the Head of Vecna, a D&D artifact of great infamy.

"You talking to me, sword?" I asked.

"Excuse me?" Dana asked. "Are you talking to someone? Something?"

"Shhh," I told my henchwoman. "Magical thing is happening."

A glowing spectral figure appeared behind the sword of a statuesque redheaded woman wearing utterly impractical armor that, nevertheless, was incredibly flattering. There was a certain resemblance between us, but she still towered over me.

"Brigitte Nielsen?" I asked, squinting. "Oh my God, I loved you in *Red Sonja*! I mean, yes, the movie is crap but it's entertaining crap! It taught me at a young age that we ginger women can kick ass just as much as the men!"

The woman ignored my misassumption about her identity. "I am Red Sindi, She-Wolf of the Steppes, Scourge of Hyboria, and Slayer of the Atlantean Merrow and Stygian Pharaohs. Daughter of Bloody Mary the War Goddess of Cimmeria and a Shem assassin. I am your ancestor and precarnation."

I stared at her. "My what now? Also, Red Sindi? I know we must work around copyright but that's a bit on the nose even for us, isn't it?"

"Do you believe in reincarnation?" Red Sindi asked.

"You can shove that bullcrap," I said. "I'm not a great believer in the afterlife."

Yes, I believed in gods but not an afterlife. Why? Because any sufficiently advanced alien or powerful wizard could declare themselves a god. Q was a god. Cthulhu was a god. All those computers Captain Kirk talked into killing themselves were worshiped as gods. It's not a name with a lot of cachet to me. David Bowie? Okay, he was a genuine god and there were still even odds he was my grandfather.

"You have seen and fought ghosts," Red Sindi said. "Your husband is the God of Death. Well, one of them."

"I've also watched *Scooby Doo* and fooling the mind is a helluva lot easier than constructing an immortal energy being inside every living thing," I replied. "Besides, if you know who my boyfriend is, you know he's a lunatic. I love him but, God bless him, he's the guy who believes in the overall decency of people. Probably why he's the worst supervillain of all time."

"You don't, descendant?" Red Sindi asked.

"I'd laugh at that joke but it's not very funny," I replied. "Fuck no! Every man, woman, and child are out for themselves. We just pretend otherwise because it's fun being selfish together rather than selfish alone."

"Who are you talking to?" Dana asked, fluttering beside me and begging for a smack.

"Brigitte Nielsen," I responded.

"*Rocky IV*'s Brigitte Nielsen?" Dana asked, looking at me confused.

"Yes. The only woman who can compare Arnold and Stallone where it counts," I replied. "Apparently, she's a ghost tied to a magic sword now."

"I am here to offer you unlimited power," Red Sindi said.

I blinked then imitated Sam Jackson's voice. "Shit, Shiska! That's all ya had to say."

Chapter Twenty-Three

The Dragon is Revealed

"If you're offering me unlimited power, I'm all for it," I said. "Lay it on me, Brigitte."

"I am not Brigitte Nielsen, I am Red Sindi," Red Sindi said.

"I'd be in denial too after marrying Flavor Flav and showing it to the world," I replied. "Reality TV removes all dignity. Believe me, I'm speaking from experience."

"Who are you talking to?" Dana asked.

"My precarnation—even though I don't believe in reincarnation—and ancestor," I replied. "Red Sindi."

"The legendary sword and sorcery warrior?" Dana asked. "You're related to her?"

"You've heard of her?" I asked.

"You haven't?" Dana asked. "We did a whole week of my anthropology course on her."

"Why can't she see you?" I asked, looking at Red Sindi.

"Only my descendants can," Red Sindi replied.

"And I'm the only one left?" I asked. "I mean, excluding Leia. Wow, I can't believe I forgot my own daughter. You'd think I'd remember giving birth but thankfully, there's a thing called drugs and a cesarian."

"You are not the only one left," Red Sindi said. "The Hyborian Age was about ten thousand years ago so I have a few more descendants running around.

"How many?" I asked.

"Well, uh," Red Sindi paused. "Let's just say those who burn with the fire hair I was famous for are almost all certainly related to me. That would allow them to see me and channel the power of the Wolf Sword."

"So, any ginger in the world could wield you?" I asked, unimpressed. "Ranging from Nicole Kidman to Ed Sheeran."

"Theoretically," Red Sindi admitted. "That shouldn't make you less proud of our lineage."

"My biological daughter is blonde, is she out?" I asked. "Are we ginger supremacists? If so, I approve. Let all lesser hair colors bow before us."

Red Sindi facepalmed. "I can't have been this much of an ass in life."

"Oh, sure you could have been," I replied. "We're both pretty and powerful. We can behave however we want and get away with it. The recipe for assholes since time memorial."

Red Sindi replied. "Please take the sword in hand. We do not have much time."

"Much time for what?" I asked.

"Time before the dragon Smogothranorax returns to slay you and your family before unleashing its horror upon the world," Red Sindi said.

"Can we just call him Smog?" I asked. "What's your beef with our Tokyo-smashing, terrorism-financing friend?"

"It was I who buried him under a mountain in the last years before the oceans drank Atlantis and the rise of the Sons of Aras," Red Sindi said. "I journeyed across Khitai with—"

"Are we going to get in trouble for this?" I asked. "Seriously, I'm not sure what's copyright protected or not with Robert E. Howard."

"Cindy, shut the hells up and listen," Red Sindi said, putting her hands on her hips. Her voice had the roar of a wolf pack and her eyes blazed with the fire of an age undreamed of. "For once in your gods damned life."

I raised my hand in surrender. "Wow, you are me."

Red Sindi frowned. "As I was saying, it was not long after we'd destroyed the vampire queen Lamia and cast the *Book of Midnight* into the void that my husband, Garee, and wife Mandina—"

"Okay, this is just silly," I interrupted.

Red Sindi sighed. "Short version: we buried the dragon under an exploding mountain. It wasn't enough to kill him, though, and he was imprisoned until the atomic bomb freed him. That left him weakened, though, and it would be years until he rebuilt his power base as well as the technology to achieve what he'd hoped to do so long ago."

"Which was?" I asked.

"To transform our world back into a paradise for his kind when they ruled over it sixty-five million years ago," Red Sindi said.

I stared at her. "So now we're putting 'the dinosaurs were dragons' in this story? Okay. Smog better have feathers, that's all I'm saying."

"I have bonded with this sword and slept for millennia waiting for the time that he might return," Red Sindi replied, her voice ethereal and haunting. "Dreaming of things to come and the actions of my descendants. The blood of the Red Goddess, Bloody Mary, runs through our veins—"

"Again, Ed Sheeran is one of our relatives," I replied. "You're not going to impress me with how badass we are."

Red Sindi frowned. "Fine. You need to take me to slay the dragon. Otherwise, he's going to take his treasures and destroy the world on his way out."

"I was going to slay the dragon anyway!" I said, appalled at the fact my ancestor/past self was wasting time like this. "For a more important reason than saving the world: money!"

"Wow, you are me," Red Sindi said. "Understand, this blade is the only thing that can slay him."

"Except it didn't twelve thousand years ago and we've come a long way since," I said, crossing my arms. "We've got the Spear of Saint George to kill him instead."

"No, you don't," Red Sindi pointed out.

"Eh?" I asked, surprised.

"What's wrong?" Dana asked, having carefully sorted the most valuable pieces and putting them in a pile that she shrunk down with what little in the way of her shrinking particles remained.

"She says we don't have the spear!" I said, shocked. "Which we don't but that's because Mandy had it!"

"The Spear of Saint George was an ordinary iron spear that the Byzantine knight killed the dragon with," Red Sindi said. "However, Smog created a powerful fake spear to entice would be slayers of his kind to wield instead. They worked fantastically but are useless against him. Indeed, this treasure hall is full of hundreds of such items as he has gathered the most powerful mystical weapons in the world while substituting fakes that he could use to betray his hosts throughout time as well as space. Most of these items have some terrible curse applied to them, driving men to reckless abandon or death. Such is why so many superheroes who draw their powers from such have met terrible ends or switched to villainy for seemingly no reason."

Huh, I always thought superheroes switched to supervillainy and vice versa because our world was inherently insane. There were only so many times you could deal with clones, alternate dimensions, gods, magic, super-science, time travel, and so on before your mind snapped like a twig. In my medical opinion, most superheroes and villains both were carrying around low-grade PTSD.

Worse, while there were a few doctors who specialized in the treatment of Supers, they couldn't really deal with the fact it was the very rare hero who could ever stop. They always deluded themselves with the idea that they were needed or more innocents would die if they didn't go out to fight. By the end, those who didn't have access to the Society of Superheroes healing magics or nanotech ended up crippled or shells of their former selves. Even those who did have such healing resources inevitably ended up consigning themselves to grandiose deaths on the battlefield or a never-ending series of ever-escalating battles.

It was why I was a villain and did my best not to think about the fact our struggles ended the exact same way with either jail, crippling, or death. After all, I didn't need the money and yet was still robbing jewelry stores. Trying to slay a frigging dragon. Maybe the She-Wolf of Hyrkania was right and I did carry around some ancient inner barbarian princess because I sure as hell wasn't suited for the regular civilized world.

"Cindy?" Dana asked, apparently noticing I'd been silent for a while.

I stared at Red Sindi, thinking back to what she said about Smog substituting fake magical artifacts for the real thing. "So not only is Smog Godzilla, he's also frigging Sauron? He's doing the whole *The Last Crusade* thing with the fake chalices?"

"Yes," Red Sindi said. "Your friends, if they try to slay Smog with the item you retrieved, will only meet their doom."

I reached over and grabbed the sword by the hilt, raising it up. "By the power of Grayskull!"

Nothing happened.

"I've been welched!" I said, stunned.

"That's a racist term against the Welsh," Dana asked. "My great grandmother—"

"Shut the hell up," I snapped. "Where's the unlimited power?"

"I may have overstated the unlimited nature of the power inside the Wolf Sword," Red Sindi said.

I stared at her. "Well played, me. Well played."

"The Wolf Sword will give you great strength, speed, and is capable of cutting through the hardest of substances," Red Sindi said.

"I have that now," I replied, rolling my eyes.

"And what price did you pay for that?" Red Sindi asked, clearly knowing the origins of my lycanthropy.

I'd hidden it from Gary and Mandy both for months, revealing it only in the Hollow Earth where I figured I could pass it off as one of those random things that happened to superheroes. You know, like when one of them is a vampire, has a kid from the future show up, or splits in two. Huh, all of those literally happened to our group. But no, the source of my werewolf powers was far darker. I'd gotten them from Other Gary AKA Merciful: The Superhero with Mercy™.

Merciful was, in a roundabout way, Gary's archnemesis. Which made sense given he was always his own worst enemy. Merciful had helped President Omega rise to power, killed Ultragod, imprisoned Gary and Mandy in an underground suburban dungeon, destroyed the Earth a couple of times, and even made Falconcrest City into a crime-free utopia. It was the last that pissed me off the most.

Gary had managed to beat Merciful in a wizard duel or something at the sacrifice of his best friend, Cloak. Gary had left Merciful within inches of his resurrected family before shooting him in the head. Neither of them realized I'd been pulled along for the ride. I could have finished off Merciful then and there or left him to die but instead I'd dragged him to a hospital where I'd treated his injuries. It turned out removing the magic bullet in his head was all that was needed.

"Thank you, Cindy," Merciful had said, looking at me from his hospital bed. "I don't know how I can repay you."

"You can give me powers," I said.

"Pardon?" Merciful said, blinking.

"I'm tired of being everyone's Girl Friday," I replied. "You and Gary just exchanged lightning bolts like Zeus and Thor while I was stuck on the sidelines. I wasn't born to be anyone's gun moll. I deserve more."

Merciful nodded. "Do you have any preferences?"

I stared at him. "Something in theme with Red Riding Hood. I've already got a good thing going with my merchandise, charitable foundations, reality show—"

"Please, it's on TLC, the Lousy Crap Channel," Merciful said.

He had me there. "Just something that works with it, okay."

Merciful waved his hand. "Then let me awaken that which was in you all the time. I hope you like your steaks rare."

It hadn't been as bad as that implied. I'd spent the next couple of months learning to control my transformations while Gary and Mandy had been trying to get their lives back in order. The power of being a werewolf had restored a lot of the confidence I'd had shaken by events: watching Falconcrest City get overrun by zombies, watching Mandy be killed by a dragon, watching Gary resurrect her, and watching her become a monster wholly unlike her previous self. Throw in giving birth—something I don't recommend—and I'd needed the sense of power that came with becoming a predator.

"What cost?" I asked, hesitating for just a moment as I awakened from my remembrances. "It seems like I got a pretty sweet deal out of it."

"The cost of having to beg for power instead of seizing it for yourself," Red Sindi said.

I stared at her. "Alright."

"The Wolf Sword will also work with the blood in your veins," Red Sindi said. "The blood of the wolf was once strong on our world but has been driven to extinction. Merciful's magic only awakened what was already there."

"Ha!" I said, snapping. "I knew I was a werewolf! Suck it, Jane! I bet you were wrong about werewolves not eating people too!"

"No, werewolves don't eat people," Red Sindi said.

I blinked. "Oh, just me, huh? Well, screw you all. I don't like eating people!"

"Uh," Dana started to speak before thinking better of it.

"Hush you," I snapped. "Well, it's a magic sword and I'm going to be happy wielding it. Thanks, ancestor. I have only one question left."

"Which is?" Red Sindi asked.

"What is with the chainmail bikini?" I asked, genuinely confused. "I mean, doesn't that chafe? It doesn't provide much protection either."

"There's a cloth underlining," Red Sindi said. "Also, it's enchanted to provide more protection than actual armor."

I stared at her. "How did that come about?"

"Wizards are very often horny, lonely men," Red Sindi said. "Particularly my husband."

"Gary being somehow responsible for this is something that can probably answer most of the world's problems," I replied, blinking. "Anyway, thanks for the sword. Where's the chain mail bikini?"

"Are you serious?" Dana asked, starting to gather all of the shrunken goodies she'd collected into a cloth bag that had previously contained fat stacks of cash.

"I'm just going to try it on!" I replied. "Maybe it defends against dragonfire! Also, fetch the ultranite gun," I said, pointing to the weapon on the ground.

"What, why?" Dana asked.

I frowned, wondering why I had to explain everything. "To kill Ultragoddess. Duh."

"Why do you want to kill Ultragoddess?" Dana asked, appalled. Apparently, she hadn't been paying attention.

"As long as she's separated from her…I dunno, communist half—"

"Not a communist!" a voice shouted from down the treasure hall.

"—then she might be a threat," I said, realizing I'd lost the element of surprise there. "Man, I thought I had super-hearing. No superpowers my ass. So, where's the damn outfit?"

"The chainmail raiment I wore is here in the hoard somewhere, but I cannot say where," Red Sindi said. "So, I suggest you focus instead on slaying the evil dragon before you start dressing like your ancestor."

"Hey, I can work it! I have the body of a twenty-year-old!" I said, extremely proud of what science and magic had accomplished. Once you knew the right alchemists, you could eat like a trucker and still star in a major sitcom. It was what the diet industry didn't want you to know according to the internet.

Dana opened her mouth.

I stared back at her and growled, letting some fang peak through and my eyes turn an inhuman color.

"You and Jennifer Lopez look exactly like you did at twenty!" Dana said, squeaking in terror.

"Damn straight," I muttered. "Remember, you're only my henchwench for life."

"Life?" Dana asked, appalled. Clearly, she wasn't yet as enthusiastic about being my minion forever as she ought to be. I'd have to turn up the pressure.

"You should be honored to fight and die for me," I replied, "Or I'll kill you."

"Yes, I can't imagine why you're having difficulty leading people," Red Sindi said.

"You have to abuse them and terrify them until they become dependent on you for praise," I replied. "Induce Stockholm Syndrome."

"They actually proved Stockholm Syndrome didn't exist," Dana said. "It was created by the psychologist there to explain why the women in the bank didn't defer to his authority."

I stared at her. "Goddammit, there goes my whole strategy for controlling you."

"Oh joy," Dana said sarcastically, developing some of the snark she needed to survive in this business.

With that, I heard an immense echoing roar that sent a gust of hot wind down the treasure chamber, causing my hair to fly out of its pigtails into a long frizzy collection that would take hours of magical charms to get back into place.

"I think the dragon is awake," Dana said.

"No shit, Sherlock," I said, sighing. "Carry that bag of loot over your shoulder and follow me. It's time for me to get in touch with my inner barbarian princess."

"Not a princess," Red Sindi corrected.

"Shut the hell up, Casper. I've got dragons to slay," I said, marching toward the monster and certain doom.

Chapter Twenty-Four

Oh, Not These Guys Again

"Are we actually going toward the dragon?" Dana asked, looking from side to side as we headed to the source of the roar that had accompanied a literal wind.

"Yes, Dana, given we are dragon slayers, that is exactly what we are going to do," I said, dryly. "It's kind of the point of this mission."

"I thought it was to rob the dragon's hoard, not kill him," Dana said.

"It's to do both," I replied. "If we slay Smog then we can remove the treasure at will. If we just stole the loot, then we'd be subject to reprisals later."

"You seem weirdly obsessed with this," Dana said.

I did a double take. "How in the world am I obsessed?"

"Well, you're already rich and a terrifying supervillain," Dana said.

"Really? You think I'm terrifying?" I asked, touched by her description.

Dana blinked. "Well, I'm scared of you. Yes. You're a werewolf who eats people."

"Thank you," I said, sighing. "Because that's what this is about rather than the money. The respect. I don't want to be anyone's sidekick or sidepiece."

"That's an excellent motive for murder," Dana said, nodding.

"Isn't it?" I asked.

"No!" Dana said, appalled. "This is utterly insane! Who wants to be a famous supervillain?"

"Everybody!" I snapped. "You seem to be missing the point, Dana."

"Apparently!" Dana said.

I shook my head and waved my sword a bit. "We need some music. Play something."

"What are you doing?" Dana asked.

"Magical items are always intelligent if they're older than a few years," I replied. "It comes with the package. We need some music and I figure a sword has a decent playlist."

Dana stared at me. "That is the stupidest thing—"

That was when the sword glowed and began playing a song with a big barbarian choir:

Cindy
The Barbarian
Cindy
Woman of bravery
She's more dangerous than any man
Her awesomeness is on demand
Come and see
Cindy, the most badass warrior ever!

I stared at the sword. "Okay, but it's a little Saturday Morning cartoon. You know, back when we had cartoons on Saturday morning."

Dana frowned, clearly hearing the song, opened her mouth then closed it before shaking her head. "I do not understand you, this place, or the insane rules everything seems to follow."

"Welcome to Wonderland, toots," I replied. "We're all mad here."

I was starting to get nervous because there was no sign of the dragon so far among the epic piles of gold, jewels, silver, and bronze around us. If Smog was really as powerful as they said, then there was no way that he should be hiding from us. The fact he'd let us know he was around but was staying out of sight told me this was a game. I'd say a game of cat and mouse, but dragon and human/werewolf/mutated scientist was fine as an analogy.

There was also the fact I didn't see any sign of Gary, Leia, Mandy, Jane, or Revolutionary Girl. The other members of my much-reduced Cindy's Seven were not the sort of people who kept silent. I even made a howl out into the air for Gabby but, unlike before, she didn't answer. That was not a good sign.

"Yeah, this isn't good," I muttered.

The Wolf Sword started playing an ominous creepy chant reminiscent of Basil Poledouris.

"Could we turn that thing off?" Dana asked.

"Why?" I asked.

That was when I heard something past the song of my singing sword. It was the faintest sound of moaning and...sparking? It was not a pleasant sound and I immediately turned into a wolf to bound after it. Much to my surprise, my sword changed with me and accompanied my fuzzy form as I navigated through the vastness of Smog's hoard. I also left Dana behind me, which wasn't something I would have done if I had given the matter a moment's thought.

Much to my surprise, I saw Case strung up by his arms by chains from two poles in a room. The sight was illuminated by torches. He looked like he'd had the shit utterly beaten out of him, which was impressive to do to a guy with a metal skeleton. I could see little metal bits left and right as well as one optical sensor where his outer eye had been destroyed.

I transformed back into a human being with my sword in hand. It occurred to me I should probably steal a scabbard from somewhere. Otherwise, I was going to be dragging this thing everywhere. "Merciful Moses, Case, you look like you went ten rounds with Sarah Connor and not in a good way."

"Cindy..." Case said, his voice raspy and wavering like someone had put a magnet on his hard drive.

"Mmm, Linda Hamilton," I said, walking up to him. "If it's a choice between her and Sigourney Weaver, I can't make it. There's no wrong answer unlike with male action stars. By which I have the secret confession of Michael Keaton. Yes, Tim Burton's Nightwalker. Not the obvious choice but the fact he's playing a real person helps."

"Cindy..." Case said, trying to say something but not able to get it out.

I cut him down with my magic sword, causing a spark with each blow as the chains fell off. The manacles were still around his wrists, but I figured he could move a lot better this way. I lifted him up by one arm and decided to help him walk. "I just want you to know that I have like five people in the world I wouldn't abandon to be killed here. You're on the very short list of people I consider friends. One of whom had to be gestated in my body like the creature from *Alien*. Which, if you didn't get is a reference, Leia. Gary will never be able to repay me for that."

"Cindy, this is a trap," Case finally said, coughing up some blue-white fluid on the ground. I wondered what that was and decided it was more an issue for a mechanic than a doctor.

"Of course, it is," I muttered, dropping Case on the floor. "You could have mentioned that earlier, Threepio."

All around me, I saw figures decloak. They were wearing optical camouflage and I silently cursed myself because my sniffer could have picked them up if I'd been looking for them. Instead, I'd let the smell of machinery and transmission fluid—what the hell else was I going to call it?—distract me. These figures were recognizable by their distinctive helmets and armor as well as the patches on their shoulders: the SES or Super Elimination Squad.

The SES was a product of the late Omega Administration that somehow never got retconned out of existence when non-supervillains took over the United States. Blame the fact that once you expand an office and its powers, it's damn hard to get rid of them. It was one of the nastiest branches of the Foundation for World Harmony, its soldiers enhanced with cyborg augmentations as well as combat drugs. They were currently pointing a bunch of high-tech looking assault rifles at me with laser sights. It was a good thing I wasn't a cat shifter because those things would be damn distracting. Were they better than KNIGHTS? No, but they were much more likely to shoot first and ask questions never.

"Hey, CC," I said, annoyed more than threatened. I had no doubt that it was Colt Colton holding the SES squad's leash.

"A good guess," Colonel Colton said, deactivating his optical camouflage, which looked like a tracksuit with a sci-fi belt.

"Not really," I said, staring at him. "I figured it was you who killed all those innocent people up on the surface."

"Criminals," Colonel Colton said, snarling. "Terrorists."

"Yes, I'm sure the baristas and the DJs were an existential threat to the United States," I said, dryly. "Congratulations, you have undoubtedly pissed off the demigod who is so arrogant that he died looking at his own reflection."

"That was Narcissus not Adonis," Colonel Colton said.

"Who gives a shit!" I snapped. "You also beat up my pet robot and that really pisses me off. He's not nearly as handsome as he used to be. We're going to have to get him reupholstered and everything."

"Not a pet," Case grunted.

"Yeah, yeah, I'll blow you to make up for that," I said.

"I have no response for that," Case said.

"By the way, Jane wants to break up with you," I replied. "She's in love with her boyfriend back on Urban Fantasy World. Sorry."

"What the fuck, Cindy," Case said, looking up.

"I'm just trying to help," I said.

"You're failing," Case said.

"Shut up!" Colonel Colton shouted. "This is a singular moment in the history of the Foundation for World Harmony. For years, the United States and other governments have been forced to rely on so-called superheroes to handle the majority of law enforcement against Supers. Tonight, we strike a blow against superhuman crime and terrorism that will be felt for decades to come."

I stuck out my tongue and blew him a raspberry. "Colonel, they're not going to remember this next week, let alone for decades. All you managed to do was kill the tiny fish and you've successfully pissed off several people who have gods on speed dial if they aren't gods themselves. This is like fishing with dynamite and just as destructive to the dynamite. Let me ask a question, did you come up with this or did Gabrielle?"

Colonel Colton didn't respond, instead narrowing his eyes. "You're going to surrender, Mrs. Karkofsky—"

"Not married," I replied. "Also, we should be like Japan where Gary can take my name. I mean, seriously, Wakowski is a much less ridiculous name."

"You're going to surrender, Ms. Wakowski, and help us round up the rest of your crime family," Colonel Colton said. "If you cooperate then I won't dismantle your pet robot—"

"Not a pet," Case said, clearly pissed off.

"—And maybe you'll see your kids again," Colonel Colton finished.

I blinked. "Is that supposed to be a threat? Really, they'd be better off."

"No, they wouldn't," Case said, finally getting up and looking only slightly better than Darth Vader after his face full of the Emperor's lightning.

"You're sweet, Case, dumb but sweet," I said down to my pet robot.

"I guess we'll just have to ensure their cooperation by delivering your bullet ridden pelt," Colonel Colton said. "Shoot them both until dead. We'll cut off their heads to be sure."

"Never bring a gun to a super fight," I said, lifting my sword. "Bring it, Daddy-in-Law."

"I'm not your in-law!" He shouted. "Fire!"

"I'll save you, Cindy!" Dana shouted, charging in our direction in her damselfly form and blasting away with her tiny energy gauntlets.

It was adorable really.

Still, it gave me the distraction I needed to strike out against the attackers with my sword. I should have assumed my war form but there was something about the blade that channeled that energy into speed and strength. Instead of shifting, I had a glowing wolf-shaped animus appear around me and it seemed bulletproof since one of the soldiers unloaded into it and the rounds bounced against the energy shield.

Sweet!

I could describe what happened when my sword met cyborg super soldier flesh, but it wasn't pretty. Some supervillains had an issue killing government agents, but given they'd just dropped a bunch of bombs above my head and beat the shit out of Case, I wasn't in a forgiving mood. Besides, it would only get me in trouble if there were survivors.

Limbs were chopped off, blood spewed, and heads rolled. The Wolf Sword continued to provide dramatic music—I think it was Blind Guardian's "Time Stands Still (At the Iron Hill)" —and I felt a bit guilty that all my murdering had a soundtrack. I quickly got over that feeling when one of the SES soldiers hit me in the face with a rifle butt then tried to stab me with a silver bowie knife. That was when I redoubled my efforts at swinging and was very glad that a broadsword didn't require much skill when you had the strength of six adult men who pumped iron.

Dana stopped her attack due to the bloodshed and gore I doubted she was used to. That, unfortunately, meant the last two of the SES group tossed aside their weapons to just start wailing on me with their super-strength. Well, unfortunately, that seemed like a better strategy than shooting me since I felt every one of those blows.

"Mighty thews!" I shouted, swinging around my sword one last time with every bit of strength in my arms to slice both in half. It left me on my knees and my face badly busted up even as my lycanthropic blood was already healing it.

That was when I searched for Colonel Colton and saw him holding a gun to Case's head. Case had his hands in the air, but I could tell he was ready to snap the old soldier's neck. Even in his diminished state, one of them was superhuman and the other wasn't. "Don't move another step you murdering terrorist."

Blood soaked and pissed off, I stared at him. "I'm riding the blood rage here man and that normally means something very different for a woman. You do not want to piss me off further."

Colonel Colton stared. "Throw the sword down. And Damselfly, resume your normal size. I should have known you'd end up working together. Fascists stick together."

I'd dealt with some morons in the US government ranging from the woman at the DMV who absolutely insists that I can't renew my license without three forms of ID to the former President who was a time traveling Nazi. However, Mandy's father was proving to be the single most obstipant and foolhardy one of the lot. It was hard to believe this guy had fought in World War Two and been America's premiere spymaster.

"Alright, alright," Dana said, assuming her human sized form. "I'm powering down too."

God, she was a complete amateur at this.

"I'm going to really have to apologize to Mandy for killing you," I said, keeping my gaze focused on Colton.

Colonel Colton reacted to my mentioning his daughter's name by turning his pistol on me, only for Case to effortlessly grab it and throw the man over his shoulder. Colton attempted to react further but, even at his worse, Case managed to get him in a stranglehold.

"Don't kill him," Mandy's voice spoke up as I saw her emerge from the shadows. I don't mean that in the sense she'd been hiding. I mean in the sense that she literally came out of the shadows like she'd been inside them.

"Where the hell have you been?" I asked, looking at her. Dana

"Trying to stop Smog," Mandy said. "We've got a problem, though."

"Which is?" I asked, wondering if she meant the fact we were going to have to drag around her asshat of a dad.

"Everyone else has been captured," Mandy replied. "Smog has them all. Including the children."

"Goddammit."

Chapter Twenty-Five

Preparing for the Epic Battle of Epicness

"What the hell do you mean, everyone's been captured?" I asked, resting my sword on my shoulder, flat first obviously. I really needed to get myself a scabbard.

"It's—" Mandy started to speak.

"Also," I interrupted, pointing my sword at her. "Traitor!"

Mandy closed her eyes. "Cindy, we don't have time for this."

"There's apparently time for treason, though!" I said. "You deserted my army! Mutiny! You are a mutineer! If we had a plank, I'd make you walk it!"

"Are we pirates now?" Dana asked.

"Shut it!" I said. "Also, can you like shrink down Mandy's father to action figure size?"

"What?" Dana asked.

"What?" Mandy repeated.

"I mean, I don't know if that will make him more manageable, I just think it would be hilarious," I said, glaring at him then back at Mandy. "Because someone prevented me from killing him."

"My father is under a spell," Mandy said.

I did a double take between her and him. "Really? Is that why he was willing to kill you and your kinda-adopted children?"

"No, he would have done that anyway," Mandy said. "He's a rotten son of a bitch either way but he's not someone who would have allowed himself to get captured so easily. If he planned those attacks in his right mind, we'd all be dead."

"Real piece of work you've got there as a daddy," Case said. "Are you sure you don't want to kill him?"

"I won't kill my family," Mandy said. "No matter how estranged."

"Really? Because I totally would kill my mom," I replied.

"I *did* kill my dad," Case said.

"Really?" I asked, looking at Case.

He nodded, his one laser eye blinking on and off.

"Kinslayer buddies!" I said, offering him a fist bump. "You, me, Oedipus, Elektra, and Tyrion!"

Colonel Colton struggled in Case's grip to no avail. Even if he was working at a fraction of his strength, I'd seen him break necks effortlessly with the slightest bit of pressure. "I'm not fist bumping that, Cindy."

"Spoilsport," I replied. "I bet Dana would kill her parents."

"No!" Dana said. "I would not!"

"Search your feelings, you know it to be true," I said, putting on my best Vader voice.

"We don't have time for your *Star Wars* nonsense," Mandy said.

"No, Gary is *Star Wars*, I'm *Lord of the Rings*," I replied, directly contradicting the fact I'd just quoted the movie. I needed to slow down the conversation until I had full stock of the situation. That was something that people underestimated the value of banter for: giving yourself breathing room with rambling nonsense. "Never the twain shall meet."

Mandy fell for it. "God, I know. Gary is addicted to that series."

"He was inconsolable for a month after *The Rise of Skywalker*," I replied. "I think the only time he was ever that depressed was when you died."

Mandy frowned.

"Too soon?" I asked.

Mandy's frown deepened.

Colonel Colton stopped struggling as if the memory of his daughter's death was enough to break through whatever juju had been worked on him.

I shrugged. "I had to pay for *The Mandalorian* series to be made to cheer him up. I mean, the last time I had to get him out of a funk, I had Leia and I sure as shit wasn't going to do that again."

"You're going to give our daughter a complex if you keep talking like that," Mandy said, unhappily.

"She knows what I mean," I replied. "Also, I literally do not know how to be a mother and every female I know, as well as some men, do a better job at it. Case included."

Case slacked his grip on Colonel Colton a bit. The Colonel didn't move, probably because he was understanding now that the only person who wanted to keep him alive was the vampire he considered to be impersonating his daughter. Which made him the only person who was a worse parent than me on this island.

"Don't constantly bring up what a miserable experience motherhood is," Case said. "You could start with that."

"See!" I gestured to Case. "I'm doing my best here but the only instruction manuals in the bookstore are from crazy religious fundamentalists and weird psychologists who talk in nothing but jargon."

"You're doing fine, Cindy," Mandy said. "Against all the laws of God and man as well as common sense. Both Leia and Mimi are happy, well-adjusted teenagers."

"I know! What the hell are they planning? They're up to something," I replied. "I just can't figure out what."

"Right now, I suspect they're trying to figure out how to escape Smog's magical prison," Mandy said, dryly.

I blinked. "Oh right! Yeah, the whole thing about them being captured. Sorry, I didn't mean to interrupt."

"You totally did," Case said.

"Quiet Arnie," I replied, giving him an evaluation. "You're looking like he did at the end of *Terminator 2*, and I could probably take you down by breathing hard. I can't believe those SES yokels managed to do so much damage to you."

"They're the best soldiers in the Foundation and you killed them," Colonel Colton said.

"Exactly," I said, showing no sympathy or remorse for the goons I'd killed. "Case shouldn't have had an issue. I mean, I am way more awesome than him but he's basically cyborg John Wick so he could have handled them."

"They didn't, I was in a fight with the Juggernuke," Case said.

"Why the hell would you do that?" I asked, once more distracted. "That guy was created by a nuclear bomb going off. I mean, normally, that would kill you, but science is weird and inconsistent when it comes to the Super gene."

The Juggernuke was one of those supervillains who was going to shrug off being bombed like raindrops. He was the kind of guy that idiot bruisers like Crowbar King and Cthulhuoid dreamed of being. If Case had gotten into a fistfight with him, it was a wonder he didn't look more like a beer can crushed against someone's forehead. Still, it explained what he'd been doing when he disappeared, and I could take him off my "Traitors to Queen Cindy" list. A list that was constantly being updated and would determine who lived or died when the revolution came.

"I saw Adonis and Achilles had prepared a bunch of prisoners for human sacrifice," Case said. "Apparently, they had a little Carthage in their Greece. I figured I might save some of my tattered silicon soul if I rescued them."

I glared at him. "That was very selfish of you."

"Cindy—" Mandy said.

"Did you save them?" I asked, grudgingly admitting it was the right thing to do.

"No," Case replied. "Someone dropped a bunch of bombs on us, and they all died."

"Bummer," I replied.

Dana opened her mouth then closed it.

"Yeah, well he'd thrown me into the lagoon before the explosions, so it all worked out," Case replied, looking down at Colonel Colton.

Colonel Colton's expression was unreadable, but I hoped he was feeling guilt. I mean, I never felt it, but I understood it to be very unpleasant. Okay, that's a lie. I felt guilt. Sometimes. Once in a blue moon, particularly when I was mean to Leia. There was something biological there. Stupid evolutionary brain wiring.

"Okay," I said, taking a deep breath. "What was this about my kids being kidnapped? We need to resolve that."

"You don't say," Mandy said.

"Yeah," I replied. "You, me, the kids, Gary, and Jane need to get off this island. Everyone else can go fuck themselves."

Dana rolled her eyes, clearly looking for a way to escape. Given she was able to fly and shrink both, I didn't know what was stopping her. Probably the fact she knew I'd hunt her down and kill her.

Case just gave me a sideways glare.

"Oh, not you," I said, slapping Case on the shoulder and causing him to grimace. "Right, there's a big hole there with exposed neural circuitry. Sorry."

"Selena and Clarissa explained to me that Smog is actually working against the entire world by evacuating it," Mandy explained. "The dragon is moving his hoard off world so he can enact a virus that will eradicate most of humankind as well as turn a selected portion into subservient serpent men. The rest of the planet will be terraformed into a primeval Cretaceous Era-esque state. Smog will then populate the world with members of his own race."

I stared at her. "And?"

"What do you mean and?" Mandy asked.

"We were going to kill him anyway!" I said, throwing out my hands. "So, he's a supervillain who wants to kill everyone by turning us into lizards. That's a day ending with Y! Blofeld is always trying to nuke the Earth or start World War Three."

"Blofeld isn't real," Colonel Colton said.

"You shut up," I said, pointing at him. "Your plan was stupid, and you should feel bad for trying to blow up children. You probably *did* blow up some children upstairs. I mean, I don't know what families brought their kids to Dragon Island for their vacation but I'm not discounting it was possible. The vacation packages I saw online were pretty sweet."

Colonel Colton blinked.

"Anyway," Mandy said, struggling to not look at me like I was a lunatic—Believe me, it was a look I knew well— "Selena and Clarissa argued we should take advantage of the distraction you were making in order to try to infiltrate the underground in secret."

"Distraction? What distraction?" I asked.

"You picking a fight in front of everyone with Cthulhuoid and Crowbar King," Mandy said.

"Oh, that thing," I said. "I barely remember that now."

"You should see a doctor, seriously," Mandy said.

I shrugged. "So, you all betrayed me and are now traitors. How did you all get captured in what is ultimately karma?"

Mandy ignored me. "We ended up finding the secret entrance to Smog's lair before the bombs dropped."

"How?" I asked, staring at her. "There was like ten minutes total."

Mandy shrugged. "Okay, maybe it was marked DO NOT ENTER - UNDERGROUND LAIR but not everything has to be complicated."

"Mmm hmm," I said. "So, we've found out how you betrayed me. How did you get taken down? All of you are pretty tough cookies."

"And why didn't you invite me?" Dana interrupted.

I swatted her in the arm.

"Ultragoddess," Mandy said, frowning. "Somehow she's fallen under Smog's spell as well."

"Huh," I replied, dryly. "The dragon archvillain is behind all our problems. Who could have possibly predicted this lazy bit of storytelling?"

"We're not fictional characters," Mandy said. "We're real people."

"Are we?" I asked. "Or are we the product of some deranged being's imagination that enjoys torturing us for his or her own amusement? Seriously, ever since I got this kickass sword, I've been revaluating religion."

The sword started playing Feuerschwanz's cover of "Warriors of the World United", and I bopped my head along to it.

"I'm so glad your sword-shaped Omega-pod is a religious experience," Mandy replied, clearly sick of having this conversation. "However, I'm fairly sure that Ultragoddess used her powers to disable Gary, Mimi, Leia, and her doppelganger too."

"Why not just kill them?" I asked the obvious question. "Hell, why not just kill us all? Ultragoddess is vulnerable to magic, but Selena and Gary together would need to hit first, which is hard when she moves faster than the speed of sound. Gary once beat Gabrielle during the tournament but that was because she was mind-controlled and not bringing her A-game."

"I don't know," Mandy admitted. "I don't even know how I escaped. I can't believe it was because Gabrielle felt any sympathy for me. Even if I still believed she felt anything, she's always hated me."

"That's because Gary will always choose you over everyone else," I replied, my voice containing no bitterness. Nope. No sir. No bitterness at all.

Mandy looked sad. "I don't think that's the case anymore, Cindy. Love isn't finite and I think you've come to mean more to him than the memory of a dead woman."

"Aw, you're sweet," I said, stretching out my arms.

"Oh God," Colonel Colton muttered. "What a disgusting display."

I looked at Mandy. "I swear, please, just let me break his legs."

"No!" Mandy said.

"A finger, anything!" I shouted. "You lost your soul, surely you can afford me that."

"I'm past my angry adolescence stage of vampiredom. Two hundred years in the future will do that," Mandy replied.

I blinked. "I love that we live in a world where statements like that can just fly by."

"I don't," Mandy said. "Now we need to go rescue everyone and get the Society of Superheroes to help."

"We're slaying the dragon ourselves," I said, firmly. "We do not need to be bailed out by those nincompoops."

"Are you willing to bet Leia's life on that?" Mandy asked. "Mimi's?"

I didn't answer for a moment before sighing. "No."

"See, you are a good mother," Mandy reassured me.

"Please never say that again," I said, looking at her. "Okay, let's focus on getting the kids back and getting the duck out of Fodge."

I had every confidence that the kids could take care of themselves, but I was responsible for them despite my best efforts not to be. I wasn't abandoning Gary or Jane, either. It surprised me how much I cared about what happened to them. There had been a time when the only person that I did care about was myself—and that wasn't a time I wanted to return to.

"Can we keep what we've stolen already?" Dana asked.

"Of course, we're keeping what we've already stolen!" I stared at her. "God, whoever taught you how to be a supervillain should be ashamed."

"I was mostly kidnapped by Tom Terror and forced to do his bidding at death ray point," Dana asked.

"And Gary killed Tom, so you owe him," I said.

Dana sighed. "Sure."

I looked up at the ceiling and held up my sword. "Death, I have never prayed to you before—"

"Oh Christ," Dana muttered.

"Just go with it," Case said.

"I have no tongue for it. No one, not even you, will give a crap if we were heroes or villains. What we did or how we died.

No, all that matters is we looked badass doing it! That's what's important. Battle pleases you, Death, so something-something revenge. And if you do not listen…then the hell with you!"

"Cindy the Barbarian continues her copyright infringement spree," Dana muttered.

"It doesn't count if it's a parody," I replied.

Nothing happened.

Not that I expected anything to.

That was when the entire chamber shook, and a secret doorway opened up in the side of the wall.

Huh.

Maybe I should reevaluate going to synagogue with Gary and the girls.

Nah.

Chapter Twenty-Six

The Temple of Smog

Sometimes I believed myself to be a fool, other times I believed myself to be a genius. Obviously, the latter was true as I can tell the difference between a preganglionic fiber and a post-ganglionic nerve. Something only non-medically trained people and Doctor Julian Bashir wouldn't get. However, I have figured out that my brain is on a five second delay.

What do I mean by my brain operating on a five second delay? Basically, I make decisions and then come up with an awareness of the consequences just a wee bit later. You could call this being impulsive, but I thought of it as being outright deranged. After all, I only thought it might be a bad idea heading deeper into a dragon's lair because a door opened after I'd already gone through it.

The interior of the chamber was a temple, and I don't mean a nice little church with stained glassed windows or pews, I mean a full-on fantasy villain temple. There was an enormous twenty-foot dragon statue in the center, blood-stained altar, pit of bones, and shackles on the wall. There were a few burning braziers scattered around the place and the smells of incense and charred meat. If you ever wanted to know what an evil temple smelled like, it was a mix of potpourri and a barbecue. Mmm, barbecue.

The others had followed in behind me, giving pay to the statement "Who is the more foolish, the fool or the fool who follows them," by that great scholar Obi-Wan Kenobi. Hell, Mandy's evil dad was accompanying us even though he didn't look like he could fight again. He also had optical camouflage if he wanted to try to make a break for it and put us on the kill on sight list. Oh wait, he already had.

Asshole.

"It looks like the Temple of Doom," I said, surveying Smog's inner sanctum.

"It certainly isn't Temple Beth Israel," Dana said.

I looked at her funny. "What an odd comparison."

"*Spaceballs,*" Dana said. "Everyone else was doing movie references. I thought I'd join in. You know, it's the *Star Wars* parody with John Candy as a dogman? No?"

"Sorry, I don't watch Mel Brooks movies," I replied.

Now Mandy and Case looked at *me* funny.

"Any more Jewish humor in my life and I'd be forced to invade Canaan," I said. "Seriously, I have an upper limit thanks to Gary. No Mel Brooks."

"Not even *Blazing Saddles*?" Case asked.

"Zip it!" I said, making the gesture across my mouth. "Okay, I haven't gotten any sign of Gary or the girls yet."

"Plus, everyone else we're here to rescue," Dana said.

"Them too," I said.

"If I may make a suggestion," Colonel Colton said.

"No, you may not," I replied. "You are a prisoner who actively tried to kill me and also tried to kill my children. Beings I am biologically wired to care about and plan to totally mooch off if I ever get old and poor."

"Ahem," Colonel Colton said, gesturing up to the ceiling with his chin.

I looked up and saw a dozen or more people suspended from their arms on chains with gags around their mouth and power-suppressing collars on their necks. The collars were covered in magical runes. The real magic kind of runes, not the Gary sorcery kind. Oh, and Gary was up there! The girls too! Jane and Gabby! Oh, and stupid Amanda with the other traitors!

"Oh well, that was convenient," I said. "This isn't a set up for things to go horribly wrong."

"You're getting way too meta, Cindy," Mandy said.

"Genre savviness is the only reason we're still alive, Mandy," I replied. "So, how do we get them down?"

Mandy went over to a nearby contraption that consisted of wheels and chains. "This should probably work."

"Yeah, probably should have noticed that," I said. "I promise I will never dismiss you as just a pretty face again."

Mandy blinked. "What?"

I shrugged. "Mandy, I'm saying looks aren't everything. I don't stare in the mirror all day."

"Wait, you're saying I do?" Mandy asked, offended.

"No, of course not. You don't have a reflection," I said.

"Too much Jewish humor, huh?" Case asked.

"Shut up, sexy R2-D2," I replied. "We'll discuss your attachments later."

Dana looked at Colonel Colton. "So, if I were to rescue you, could I maybe get a pardon?"

"I promise you'll spend the rest of your life behind bars if you're not killed," Colonel Colton said, not even looking at her.

"Right," Dana said, sighing. "So, I guess I'm stuck with the She-Wolf of Illinois."

"Don't you know it," I replied, shaking my sword. "Play some more music."

The Wolf Sword started playing Lee Aaron's "Metal Queen" as Gary was lowered down like literal bait on a hook. I had no idea why my sword had an extensive knowledge of fantasy themed heavy metal to go along with Saturday morning cartoon jingles and movie scores, but I wasn't going to complain.

"It can't be this easy," Case said, looking over his shoulder for what I presumed he thought would be a building-sized dragon sneaking up behind us.

"Don't knock our good fortune," I said, lifting my sword up when Gary hit the ground with his hands still suspended upward.

"Mmmph!" Gary said, clearly not happy I was taking a swing at him.

"Relax!" I said, swinging.

Much to my surprise—and Gary's—I managed to cut off the magical collar around his neck before Mandy removed his gag.

"Wow, that was a great shot," Gary said.

I frowned. "Not really, I was aiming for the gag."

Gary's eyes widened.

"What?" I asked, shrugging. "I only started using a sword today. Though I think I have some racial memory from being a barbarian princess."

"You're a descendant of Red Sindi, hot sword lady from the Hyborian Age?" Gary asked.

"How did you know?" I asked, surprised.

"Lucky guess," Gary said, being his usual insufferable self. "That and I found her magical chainmail swimwear and used *Identify* on it."

"Ooo, gimme!" I said, ecstatic.

"First, we have to rescue the others," Mandy said. "We'll need all the help we can get to get off this island, let alone stop Smog."

"You get on that," I said, tapping Gary's chains with my magic sword and severing them with a spark. "I still say we can stop Smog ourselves. I'm a newly badass berserker, you're a vampire queen, Case is fucked up, and Dana useless—"

"Hey!" Dana said. "I saved your life."

"No, you didn't," I said, calmly. "But Gary is a twentieth level wizard."

"I'm actually not twentieth level," Gary muttered, embarrassed.

"What?" I asked.

Gary shrugged, stepping away from where he'd been imprisoned. "I figured that would be twinkish."

"You explicitly have the power of D&D wizardry and you decided *not* to have your level maxed out?" I asked, staring at him.

"That seemed like it would be exploiting the rules," Gary said, guilty.

"*You* make the goddamn rules!" I said, wanting to strangle him. "*Dungeons and Dragons* magic only exists because you used phenomenal cosmic power to alter reality! Forget world peace or curing cancer, a fifteen-year-old in Muncie, Indiana needs to be able to throw fireballs."

"I've gotten a lot of lot of praise from the Red Cross for the fact people now cast *Cure Light Wounds*," Gary replied. "Mind you, that's led to some religious difficulties but—"

"What is your level?" I asked, staring at him.

"Fifteenth," Gary said, breathing heavily.

I took a deep breath. Gary had scared me there for a bit. "Okay, fifteenth isn't bad. It isn't perfect but it sure as hell isn't bad. Being a fifteenth level Wizard, I can work with that."

Gary coughed.

"Gary…" I struggled to control my anger. "What aren't you telling me?"

"I have a couple of levels in Rogue and Fighter," Gary said.

I stared at him in stunned shock, opened my mouth, then closed it. "Gary, you're a Wizard, Rogue, and Fighter?"

"Yeah," Gary admitted.

"Do you play a musical instrument?" I said, narrowing my eyes.

"Well, you know I can do damn well on the keytar and hurdy gurdy," Gary said, unreasonably proud.

"Then you are a bard!" I snapped at him. "A frigging fifteenth level Spoony Bard!"

"Technically, Bards are more like Sorcerers—" Dana started to say.

"Shut up!" I snapped. "I swear Gary, sometimes I think the only reason I like you is because I was a *Dragonlance* fangirl."

"Excuse me?" Gary asked.

"Raistlin Majere, Wizard of the Black Robes," I said, sighing. "So dreamy. I used to spend all my extra money from drug dealing and petty theft on used copies of that series."

After Gary killed Shoot-Em-Up when we were both fourteen, I hadn't a home to return to as there was no way I was going back to my mother or pimp. Gary's family helped me by letting me live in the spare room above their garage until I was eighteen and my dad in prison paid for my own apartment as well as college.

It was amazing what writing a hitman in prison with verifiable DNA test results could accomplish. I still remember going with the Karkofskys every Friday to the Book N Cheap. By the way, if you think that means Gary and I were foster siblings, no, and screw you.

"Raistlin Majere was an archetypical insufferable genius who thought his problems all stemmed from being too smart versus being an ass," Gary said, once again showing he knew enough about fantasy to get all my references but not enough to get it.

"I'm just saying you should be grateful that my fetish was evil wizards and not vampires. Ten more years and I'd have been brooding over Edward Cullen."

"Never say that again, Cindy. Please," Mandy said. "That offends me on so many levels."

"Shut up, Pattinson is the Nightwalker now," I replied.

"Either way, this is a trap," Gary said, taking a deep breath.

"You don't think you should have led with that?" I asked, staring at him. "I love my rambling on about classic Eighties fantasy—"

"I wouldn't know if I'd call *Dragonlance* classic," Dana muttered. "I mean, it's no Shanarra Chronicles."

"Do not even!" I said, pointing back at her with my sword.

"This is all part of Smog's attempt to complete his collection," Gary said. "The hoard and prisoners were just the bait. He's watching our every step and waiting to pounce like a cat on a mouse."

"Well Smog can kiss my furry behind," I paused. "Which is only furry when I'm a wolf or in werewolf form. I feel the need to clarify that. My lycanthropy doesn't affect my human side. This is one hundred percent true and not me making it up."

"Yeah, we know that Cindy," Case said. "I don't know anyone else who buys Nair by the gallon but I'm sure you have your reasons."

Mandy struggled and failed to not grin, Gary just averted his face so I didn't have to see him laughing. "In any case, we're postponing my epic dragon slaying deeds of awesomeness. We're going to call—hock, spit—backup."

"I see you also captured Mandy's dad," Gary said, looking over at him.

"Yes, he's mind-controlled and apparently that's a cure all for everything," I said. "We can't let him go because he'll target the family, so I think we should build a giant glass prison for him with wood chips and a hamster wheel."

Mandy went over to the contraption that lowered Gary and started working on doing the same for the girls. Notably she didn't object to my plan to put her father in an aquarium. Probably because she didn't need to dignify it with a response, but I hoped, in my heart, she saw the practicality of it. Personally, I was hoping I could get Daddy Dearest to remove that kill on sight order for me. That could prove inconvenient if I wanted to resume stalking Keanu Reeves or attend the Cannes Film Festival.

"You people are utterly insane," Dana said, shaking her head.

"Took you long enough," I replied. "Either way, when do you think the dragon will spring the trap?"

Nothing happened.

I cleared my throat. "Ahem. I said, WHEN DO YOU THINK THE DRAGON WILL SPRING THE TRAP?"

"Really, Cindy?" Gary asked.

"I thought our plan was going to go for backup," Dana asked.

"I am altering the plan," I replied. "Pray I don't alter it any further."

"Ugh," Dana said.

"I'm getting kind of sick of waiting around," I said, shrugging. "Seriously, there's only so long you can keep the audience waiting."

"What audience?" Case asked, confused.

"And since when have you ever waited for anything?" Mandy asked.

"Hey, that's a fair cop but..." I paused. "Okay, I thought I had something there but no."

"I confess, I have had more fun watching you run around like rats in a maze more than I have any other fools in decades," a dark, accented, feminine voice spoke that was distinctly un-dragon like.

I turned around. "Finally, I was getting tired of waiting."

I probably should have waited longer because two figures greeted me rather than the single one, dragon or not, than expected. The first of them was Ultragoddess, Gabrielle Anders, now sporting a decidedly black fetish-wear looking version of her uniform. Her eyes were glowing, and it was like she'd hung a big sign around her neck that said EVIL NOW. Even her Ultra-Force aura, usually glowing a beautiful bright sun-like nimbus, had turned to an ominous red.

Yeah, that wasn't good. Even if we had the whole party here, stopping Ultragoddess wasn't something that we were prepared for. We'd assembled out team for the purposes of taking out a dragon and I'd already been informed the Spear of Saint George (which wasn't exactly around) was a fake. Stopping Ultragoddess was something we had a weapon to use but I rather hoped that would be a last resort.

The other individual was someone dressed like a slutty B-movie evil sorceress. Note this is me calling her slutty, which means I heartily approved of the outfit. She was a woman of Asian descent, albeit probably predating any current ethnicity by a few thousand years, with bronzed skin and piercing yellow reptilian eyes. She had a wrap around her breasts that barely held them together as well as a loincloth that didn't do much to hide the fact she wasn't wearing underwear.

Comic book artists tended to exaggerate just how stacked superheroines were and illusion magic was used to make us look our best but, uh, this was just straight up wish fulfillment. Also, kind of tacky, like they weren't quite aware of how human aesthetics or proportions worked. The evil sorceress also had a staff in hand with a skull topping it and she was wearing necklace of long sharpened teeth above her ridiculous bust.

"And who are you, Ms. Porn Star Witch?" I asked, looking at her.

Behind me, Mimi, Jane, Gabby, and Leia had been lowered down. I wish they'd lowered down Serena as she would have been a lot more useful here. Even if she was a dirty-dirty traitor who wanted to save the world rather than get awesome amounts of treasure.

"Who the hell are you?" I asked.

"It's Smog," Gary replied.

"I thought Smog was a man," I said, blinking.

"It's whatever it wants to be," Gary said.

I sighed and closed my eyes. "I walked right into that *Ghostbusters* reference."

"When someone asks if I'm a god, I can say yes," Gary said.

"Stop stealing my scene!" I snapped back at my lover.

"Sorry!" Gary said, holding his hands up in the air.

Mandy was desperately trying to get everyone else free but couldn't do much about the collars until Smog lifted her staff up and all of them fell off.

Uh oh.

"Uh, thanks," I said. "Why do that?"

"Because I have what I've been searching for this entire time," Smog said, staring at me. "This was all designed to get you, Cindy Wakowski."

I blinked. Somehow finally getting the respect I've always wanted wasn't the great moment of joy I'd imagined it to be.

Chapter Twenty-Seven

A Hero Falls and It's Not My Fault

This is all about me?" I asked, staring at Smog. Well, trying to stare at Smog. She looked like a live action version of a Rob Liefield drawing and it was freaking me the fuck out. Seriously, she looked like a porn star with spinal problems. A porn star with spinal problems who was doing a bad fantasy movie.

"You know I'm telepathic, right?" Smog asked.

"No, I did not!" I said, holding my sword on my right shoulder. "Please carry on with your evil gloating."

"Thank you," Smog said, not missing a beat. "For millennia, I was imprisoned by your ancestor, and I waited and plotted for the time I would be free again. To bring back the Age of Dragons that was destroyed by the gods of men. Which I shall do tonight."

"The Society of Superheroes will stop you," Gabby said, balling her fists. Apparently, Mandy had decided the woman with no superpowers was one of the ones to save.

I gave her a sideways glance.

"Sorry, it's obligatory," Gabby replied.

"Yeah, yeah," I said, ignoring her. "Carry on, Puff."

"But destroying the Earth's human infestation is harder than it sounds," Smog replied. "You are a race with countless powerful abominations and the protection of powerful gods. So, for that, I needed the help of the most arrogant, self-absorbed, and petty villain in the world."

Everyone in the room, I swear, looked at me.

"Really, guys?" I asked.

"If the shoe fits," Dana replied.

"I knew you were a threat," Colonel Colton said.

"Haha!" Smog chuckled, turning to him. "You were yet another part of my plans. Your arrogance and desire to prove humanity could stand on its own allowed me to reach into your mind and corrupt your inclinations. Vast amounts of resources were diverted from the Foundation for World Harmonies real goals to chasing down Ms. Wakowski here and blinding you to my actual movements."

"Cindy lives in Falconcrest City," Jane said. "In a big giant mansion. That's like trying to track down Doctor Doom and not thinking to look in Latveria. Oh, I know, let's go see if Spider-Man is in New York or Lex Luthor in Metropolis!"

I made a mental note to look up who those people were. "I'm not seeing how blinding the Foundation for World Disharmony is going to do crap about the Society of Superheroes. Those guys give the keystone cops a bad name."

"You murdered good men today," Colonel Colton hissed at me.

"World's smallest violin, Chief," I said, putting a hand over my heart. "If you don't want to be killed, don't point guns at the she-wolf with a sword."

"Yes, well, it worked," Smog said. "Which crippled the Society of Superheroes."

"How?" I asked. "I don't even know any of those guys unlike SOME PEOPLE who like to hang around them."

I glared at Mandy and Gary.

"The Society of Superheroes gets its information from the Foundation for World Harmony," Gabby explained.

"They get their information from the government?" I asked. "Merciful Moses, it's a wonder the world hasn't been destroyed six times over."

"Cindy, please," Mandy said.

"It was simplicity to set it up so the Society of Superheroes would be off world during my plot. They are even now engaged in battle with Thran pirates and mercenaries led by Khanlor the Warlord. A perfect way to distract them that the real threat is on Earth," Smog replied, displaying all the flaws of the talking killer. Then again, maybe she got a pass since she was older than Babylon and Assyria put together.

"So where does the wedding of two hot Greek men fit into this?" I asked. "Because I'd rather think about that than your spine problems."

"People assume the reason the world has not fallen under the sway of supervillains is due to the efforts of heroes," Smog said, chuckling. "The truth is far more depressing and far more realistic. The reason no supervillain's plans go unthwarted is the heroes are always led to them or their equipment is sabotaged by other villains. Many times, they clashed in secret as well, destroying one another in secret wars hidden from the public by the Foundation. There can be only one ruler of the world after all."

"That is ridiculous!" Gabby said, offended on behalf of superheroes everywhere. "Supervillains are not part of some ecosystem balance! Superheroes are the people who stop evil!"

"Ahem," Mandy said, coughing into her fist.

"Yes, my second favorite abomination against life and goodness?" Gabby asked.

Mandy narrowed her eyes.

"She means that affectionately!" Gary defended.

Mandy glared at him too.

"We're a bunch of supervillains right now opposing another supervillain," Mandy pointed out.

Gabby grimaced at that unfortunate dose of reality. "Yes, well—"

"Good, bad, I'm the gal with the sword," I said, looking at Smog. "And if I have to sacrifice every one of my companions to defeat you, I will!"

Everyone glared at me.

"I thought it was obvious I was kidding," I said. "I'd totally not sacrifice the kids. That'd make me look bad. Gary I'm pretty sure has a get out of jail free card in Hell."

"It's true," Gary said.

"Release all of my prisoners. No one can save you," Smog said, laughed. Her voice filling the chamber like she'd had it modified for supervillainy acoustics. "The heroes are distracted, and the best of the world's villains are dead. Ultragoddess is now my helpless tool, her soul split to render her strength separate from her willpower—"

"So, *you* did that, huh?" I asked, not surprised that Smog had some crazy-colored ultranite laying around. I already had the stuff in the pistol.

"You fiend!" Gabby said, pointing.

"This is my show here, Gabby," I said. "Don't steal my thunder."

"The Queen of the Vampires will burn beneath my flame," Smog said, gesturing at Mandy.

"When did you become queen of the vampires?" I asked Mandy.

"When Dracula died," Mandy said, shrugging. "It's not a big deal. There's like fifty vampires world-wide. It's not like Jane's world where they're everywhere."

"Still, you can open shopping malls and avoid the consequences for your actions like the British Royal Family," I said.

Smog ignored us. "Foolish barbarian, Not even your marriage to Gary the Pink can save you."

Gary stared in horror and made a slashing gesture across his throat.

I did a double take before lifting up a hand. "Hold up."

"Goddammit," Gary said, lowering his head in shame.

Jane and the others had all been lowered down, completing the original group. This included Selena and Clarissa, who were looking embarrassed. I would have been embarrassed to if I'd gotten taken down as easily as they had. Unfortunately, even with the full complement of my henchpeople, we were far from a full *World of Warcraft* Raid Boss team. Smog might have been small right now, but I suspected she could easily become full size and that would probably squash us in these caverns before we hurt her.

"You need to unpack that," I said, both focused on distracting the dragon from straight up murdering us and figuring out what the hell they meant by Gary the Pink.

"Yes, yes," Smog said, rolling her eyes. "You are not married. I know."

"No, what? Gary the Pink?" I asked.

Gary facepalmed behind me while Jane sniggered. "Please, don't ask."

"Well now I have to!" I said.

Smog chuckled. "Oh, he didn't tell you? All the greatest and most powerful wizards of the Earth are granted a color to signify their standing."

I was glad Smog was the chatty sort. "Yeah, I get that. Gandalf the Gray, Radagast the Brown, but what does that have to do with Gary?"

"Thanks, Cindy," Gary said, sarcastically. "Really."

"You're welcome," I said, smirking. I also was trying to figure out a way to disable Ultragoddess and get all of us free but was coming up with a blank.

"In acknowledgement of his accomplishments in spreading magic to the masses," Smog said, spitting to one side as if the very idea of democratizing magic was offensive (and it was—I didn't trust the average man with a car let alone phenomenal cosmic power). "The High Council of Witches and Wizards declared him to be a color mage."

"There's a High Council of Witches and Wizards?" I asked, confused.

"Apparently," Gary said, shrugging. "I was as surprised as anyone when their letter arrived by owl."

I wanted to comment on that but didn't want to bury the lead. "And they gave you the color pink. PINK?"

"More a lightish red," Gary said, burning red with embarrassment—or maybe pink.

"Which we have a name for: pink," I said, stealing a joke from *Red vs. Blue*. "Were there no other colors available?"

"Plaid but I'm not Scottish," Gary replied. "The wizard after me got neon, though. Which is not a color."

"The Neon Wizard?" I asked. "That sounds badass. Who is that?"

Leia lifted her hand, having been lowered down and freed but not ungagged. A thing that Mandy promptly fixed.

"You're a mad scientist, not a wizard!" I said, appalled. "Is everyone in my family crossing their streams? God dammit, now I'm doing *Ghostbusters* references."

"Science becomes much easier when you can ignore the laws of physics!" Leia said, not helping her case. "If you can be a werewolf barbarian princess thief, I can be a mage-scientist!"

"That is completely—" I started to say.

"As I was saying," Smog said, clearing her throat. "Not even your marriage to Gary the Pink, Minor God of Death—"

"Hold up, Gary does not get to be a god and an archmage! He is not Vecna!" I shouted. I mean, I knew Gary was a god, but I didn't think anyone else outside the family took it seriously.

"Yeah, I have both my eyes and hands," Gary said, chuckling and waving his hands.

"Not for long if you don't shut up," I said. "Fifteenth level bards do not get to be both!"

"I am not a bard," Gary said. "I admit I may have been using some online content to pad my resume."

"Pick one!" I snapped. "God or wizard!"

"Gandalf was a god and a wizard," Gary said. "Depending on how you define Tolkien's Istari through his Catholicism."

"You are not Gandalf!" I snapped, trying not to be turned on by his knowledge of the Silmarillion. "I'd like to see you solo a Balrog!"

"I could! I totally could!" Gary said, crossing his arms. "I just don't want to."

Jane stared at me and then Gary. "I suddenly realize these are going to be my last moments on Earth: a GenCon road trip that led to my grizzly death."

"At least you died the way you lived," Case said to Jane. "Also, I'm breaking up with you."

"Wait, what?" Jane asked, clearly not having ever experienced the joys of an "I know you're going to break up with me so I'm going to break up with you first" move. Which I have never had happen to me because, seriously, who the hell would ever break up with me? I mean, aside from the guys and girls who feared for their lives. Not naming names. Linda! Steve!

Jerks.

Smog clapped in amusement. It was surreal, like we were children performing a grade school play. "More, jesters, more! Oh, I haven't had this much fun since I last stomped Tokyo!"

"I am never going to look at Godzilla movies the same way," Jane muttered.

"Me either," I replied. "I mean, seriously, I knew she was a she because she laid eggs in that godawful Matthew Broderick movie but with that fashion sense. I'm not even sure that's a bra. I think it's more like a belt."

Smog smiled. "The only thing dragons love more than gold is bloodshed. I have savored the meal of my plan so far but now it is time to feast. You will all perish in flame and ruin before I make sport of your deaths."

"You know, it's kind of refreshing to have someone engaging in the kind of the unambiguous villain cruelty and bravado that Smog is right now," I said.

"Really?" Jane asked.

"No," I said.

I hefted my sword in front of me at the dragon. "Well, dragon lady—"

I paused.

"What are you doing?" Mandy asked.

"I just realized she's Asian and I called her a dragon lady," I said. "Now, I feel kind of racist."

Mandy stared at me.

"What?" I asked.

Mandy blinked then closed her eyes as if smothering the desire to rip my throat out. "Speaking as a woman of Asian descent, Cindy, shut the hell up and kill the dragon!"

"Right!" I said, staring. "Prepare to die, fiend. Man, I always wanted to say something like that."

"Hahaha," Smog laughed again, this time sounding like she'd just heard the funniest thing ever.

"Is that a good sign?" Gary asked.

"Given what I know about dragons, which is a lot," Jane said. "No."

"I bet," Case muttered.

"Shut it!" Jane said. "You don't get to complain about my other boyfriend when you stop being one."

"Not the best defense in a relationship," I replied. "Mind you, monogamy is extremely overrated. Science says—"

"I'm not going to fight you," Smog said. "My slaves are."

Gabrielle's demonic eyes glowed even brighter as the barest hint of a smile dotted her face. That was when I realized the full depth of Smog's depravity—which is another sentence I always wanted to say—Smog was letting us all get our powers back because she wanted to watch us wail on Gabrielle and possibly kill her before finishing us off. Also, to force Mandy to kill her father or vice versa. That dragon was a damned nasty piece of work.

Colonel Colton fell on his knees. "I can't…think…straight. I… have to kill…supervillains."

"Fight it, Father," Mandy said. "You may think of me as a monster and you're right. I am an abomination to everything I believed in life. The Goddess has turned her back on me and I feel only a shadow of what I felt before. Only my love for those I cared for in life remains and even that is but a memory. Yet, I still treasure you even with all your flaws. Do not become what she wants you to be."

Colonel Colton surprisingly collapsed on the ground, shaking his head. "I am not your trained monkey, dragon. A dragon killed my daughter and a dark wizard brought her back, but I will do the bidding of neither."

"I don't even like you when Mandy was alive, dipshit," Gary said. "Let alone want you to do my bidding. You called me an annoying nerd and sociopath at our wedding. I mean, fair, but no one wants you here."

"I do," Mandy said.

Colonel Colton looked up. Whatever magic had been clouding his mind before was gone now. "Mandy, I—"

That was when the mind-controlled Gabrielle stepped forth and jabbed her hand through the back of his chest and ripped out his heart.

"Ah crap," I said.

Mandy screamed and attacked Gabrielle, while Smog laughed at the display.

Chapter Twenty-Eight

A Choice is Made

Now, a lot of people believe I'm a heartless bitch.

I mean, I am.

I take pride in it.

I wear it on t-shirts.

If my skin still managed to maintain ink rather than simply healing over all body art, I would have it tattooed on my arm. However, as heartless of a female woof-woof as I am, it would have taken a complete monster not to feel something for poor Mandy as she witnessed her father being murdered in front of her.

Mandy was going to get herself killed and look like a fool doing it. One of the things comic books and video games got wrong about Supers is the fact they acted like every one of them was evenly matched. That, under the right circumstances, you could have Splotch beat the Juggernuke. It's more dramatic that way as well as horseshit. In reality, Supers are divided along tiers the same way boxers are. Except, like, much-much more so. Generally, if you fight outside your weight class, you lose. A human gets in a fist fight with a vampire, the human dies. A vampire gets in a fist fight with an Ultra Family member? The vampire dies. It's like a bug on a windshield or Godzilla versus Bambi.

Indeed, the fact I've been a part of the few upset victories where some comic book nerds managed to pull off upset victories against people far out of our league, well, that's the case of it not making any goddamned rational sense. The universe bent itself to that hypothetical Terry Pratchett "million to one shot" where a lone bard managed to kill dragon with a single black arrow.

And we were all out of black arrows.

Predictably, in fact, Gabrielle caught Mandy by the throat and held her up like a cat that was misbehaving only with more strangulation.

"Pathetic," Gabrielle said, speaking with a voice that sounded straight from Hell. "Erasing you from the world will be a blessing."

Seeing Mandy getting her throat crushed, I did the only thing any rational person would do in such a situation: I decided to attack Gabrielle as well. Yes, that was incredibly dumb of me, you don't have to point that out. Indeed, the biggest thing I learned about myself during this trip was that on my other arm, I should have "poor impulse control" tattooed. Instead, it would make a pretty good epitaph.

"Get away from her, you bitch!" I shouted, doing my best Sigourney Weaver impersonation. Which would have been cooler had I been trying to rescue Leia or Mandy, but both of my kids had the problem of being way too competent to need rescuing. Also, does anyone else think what happened to Newt in *Alien 3* was bullshit? You want to retcon movies, Hollywood, retcon that one.

Anyway, I swung down my sword against the back of Gabrielle and fully expected a clash of epic Hyborian Age magic against her sci-fi space god powers. Instead, the sword bounced off her aura with such a reverberation that I shook like a cartoon character. Gabrielle turned around and chuckled, staring at me with those demonic eyes. Whatever mind control juju Smog had worked on Ultragoddess after splitting her in half hadn't made her a mindless puppet. Instead, it had apparently brought out the sadistic bullying side of Gabrielle—which anyone who beat up criminals for a living had even if it was badly suppressed.

"You really thought that would work?" Gabrielle asked.

"Kinda, yeah," I said. "Isn't Ultragod vulnerable to magic?"

"We made that up," Gabrielle said, throwing Mandy over my shoulder and against the side of the cavern wall where she struck with a sickening crunch. Having every bone in your body broken wouldn't kill a vampire, being already dead certainly helped with that, but…

Dammit.

Well, if they did make it up, that didn't stop Selena, Jane, and Gary from unloading their own sorcery on Gabrielle. I had to wonder what Selena thought of throwing *Fireball* and *Call Lightning* spells when she had presumably spent decades learning how to do real magic through complicated relationships with gods or study. I felt it was probably the same relationship I, as a trained surgeon, had with guys who sold crystals at the mall and creek water as a health remedy. Looking at you Gwyneth Paltrow.

The blasts of magic against Gabrielle's aura were like raindrops. Clarissa pulled out something that looked like a gauntlet hidden in a pocket-dimension purse and put it on her hand, firing repeatedly blasts that Gabrielle shrugged off like she was Hulk Hogan, getting her second wind. Yes, I watch wrestling, shut up. Case pulled out a gun he must have pocketed from the Foundation soldiers as it shot laser beams, which he smartly aimed at Smog rather than Gabrielle. Sadly, they hit an invisible shield and reflected into the ceiling.

Amanda whispered a prayer to Death and started conjuring globes of darkness in her hands that she hurled like baseballs. Even Dana joined in the fight, turning into her tiny damselfly form, and blasting away. Leia and Mimi hung back, seemingly discussing something which made me immediately concerned. The only person not contributing was Revolutionary Girl, who was seemingly unable to bring herself to harm her doppelganger—or she just couldn't so jack or shit. Pretty sure Jack left town too, to quote the great Bruce Campbell.

Gabrielle responded by clasping her hands together and shooting a powerful blast of Ultra-Force energy that would have annihilated the entire group at once. Instead, Mimi leapt ahead and caught it, soaking it all up, but doing so forced her to one knee. It also destroyed her cute little Carmen Sandiego outfit and left only her one-piece bathing suit underneath. Gary and I were smart enough to get it made from the same material they made the capes of angels from—don't ask where we got it and if Michael asks where it went, you don't know me.

"Pitiful villains," Gabrielle said, still sounding like she was an Eighties cartoon villain. "Do you not know what you face? I am imbued with the power of a thousand-thousand dragon souls. Smog has summoned us from the realm of Tiamat, and we will live again in the world she has building. Man will serve us or burn!"

"Wait, *Tiamat is real*?" Jane asked.

"Yeah, she's the Babylonian goddess Marduk AKA Bahamut slew to create humanity," Gary said, throwing every spell he had at Gabrielle. "She lives in Hell now. I don't like her."

"Is she a five headed dragon?" Jane asked.

Gary paused. "I mean, she could be."

"Shut it, Gary!" Amanda said. "You can fight this, Gabrielle! You're stronger than all the evil inside you right now!"

"It's not me," Gabrielle said, shaking her head. "Smog took out everything that made me care about others and put it into a pitiful human shell."

"Can we recombine you?" Amanda asked, showing why she was the heir to the Nightwalker and not, well, the rest of us.

"I can try," Selena said. "However, it's a complicated ritual and still might not give you the strength to cast out the dragon souls."

"Do it!" Gabby said.

Selena began chanting before Gabrielle charged at them with her superspeed, only to be intercepted by her daughter. Mimi started taking a pounding from one of the few people on Earth who could hurt her, and I hated myself for the fact that I couldn't do anything about it. I looked to Leia, and she was assembling some kind of cosmic ray gun on a tripod and seemed unconcerned her sister was getting the shit kicked out of her by her demonically—draconically? I'm not sure what term to use when someone is possessed by undead hell dragons—infused mother.

Gary, meanwhile, started casting a bunch of protection spells. I didn't know how much good a *Protection from Evil* spell would do right now, but it was clear everything we were doing so far was having no effect. Maybe he could create enough barriers to keep Gabrielle away long enough to be fused with Gabby. Jane helped matters by casting healing spells on Mimi and actually gave her a fighting chance. The others kept shooting at Gabrielle for simple lack of anything else better to do. I admit, it was starting to feel like we were *World of Warcraft* gamers going after a raid boss and we were about forty or fifty players short.

"Keep fighting," I said, turning around to face Smog. "This is between you and me, Dragonslut. My ancestor buried you alive and I'm going to do her one better."

Smog didn't seem overly impressed. "Gabrielle, do be a dear and kill her before her children. Make it slow."

"Ah crap," I said.

Gabrielle punched me in the gut with enough force that if I wasn't capable of regenerating organs, I'd have been condemned to a slow lingering death right then and there. Next, she hit me in the face and shattered my jaw. I tried to lift my sword but the blow I attempted to strike just bounced once more again against her aura.

The funny thing was that as she grabbed my wrist and broke it, forcing my sword out of my hands, I knew the aura of protection the sword provided was working just fine. If not for it, I probably would have been liquified before I could even respond. It was proof positive that I wasn't in the same league as Ultragoddess. Hell, it was proof I wasn't even playing in the same sport.

"Stop it!" Dana said, charging and blasting only to be smacked out of the air with a glowing backhand that sent her flying. She landed on the ground with a series of thumps, spilling out the contents of her bag of holding.

"Any last words?" Gabrielle said, grabbing my throat and holding me tight. "Before I tear your head clean off?"

Yeah, that would kill me alright. A part of me, a little part, wished someone would come to my rescue but I hated that part of me. If I was going to go down, then I was going down defiantly. I stared up into her eyes, shifted them yellow, and then snarled at her with exposed canines. "Rowrr, grrr, rowwr!"

Wait, crap! I'd become too werewolfy to make a proper comeback. Also, the whole broken jaw thing. Now everyone was going to remember me spitting and growling as my last act. Which wasn't dignified at all. Dammit! I mean, yeah, I would have preferred not to die at all but at least it should be operatic.

It was like finding out the Nightwalker crapped his pants after dying of a heart attack. Speaking as a doctor, yeah, it probably happened but you don't want to know those details.

"Goodbye," Gabrielle said, laughing before there was a gunshot. Gabrielle blinked and looked confused for a second before staring down at her chest to reveal red blood spreading out through her uniform. "Aw, dangit."

While it amused me that Ultragoddess was so committed to her wholesome family-friendly image that she didn't swear even when having been shot, especially when she was carrying on an affair with a married supervillain that had produced a superpowered lovechild, I was more concerned about who exactly had taken the moment to put a round in the world's greatest heroine. Well, unless you voted Guinevere but let's face it, no one voted Guinevere since that time she released a CrimeTube video of her singing "Imagine."

I first looked upon Mimi and the results weren't pretty. Her enhanced biology meant she was already covered in bruises and one of her eyes was swollen shut. Gabrielle's beating made her look like she'd just been through a car wreck. I wanted to rush over to her and give her a hug but figured it would be better to call over Jane to cast some more healing magic, assuming she hadn't already burned through her stash.

It was the first and hopefully last time I also wished I was religious since I would have gladly taken some cleric levels to treat my daughter from another mother. Because apparently Gary was happy to pass out sorcery to people who believed in invisible sky people and entirely fictious deities but not people who'd studied the genuine healing arts. Maybe I needed to make a compact with Mystra or Takhisis.

That only took a second of time to note, though, because the rest of the group was stunned silent. You could have heard a pin drop where once everyone had been shooting, blasting, and casting. Selena had stopped her spell cold, and everyone was looking at Gary holding the ultranite gun. Gabby, much to my surprise, wasn't rushing to the side of her daughter but staring at her lover with a look of complete betrayal. Gary was holding the pistol with both hands and looking, not ashamed, but grimly resigned to the consequences of his actions.

Shoving my jaw back into place and feeling my body begin the painful process of regeneration, I looked back at Gabrielle on the ground and noticed the woman carrying a million dragon souls was now deader than a doornail. Which is one of those expressions you had to wonder about the origins of. Her eyes were wide open and staring into the ceiling with no sign of life behind them.

Gabrielle Anders, Ultragoddess, was dead.

Gabby Anders, nonpowered political activist, was alive.

Never again would the two be one.

Whoops.

"Not that I don't appreciate the assist, but I had her right where I wanted her," I replied to Gary.

Gabby let out a primal scream of rage and frustration. I wasn't sure if it was because her (former) fiancé had killed her alternate self, the fact her alternate self was her, the very likely permanent loss of her powers, or the fact Gary had done it to save me. Then it occurred to me that it was probably all of those things and the fact that with Ultragoddess reunited, we might have had a chance to survive this but without her, Smog was going to kill us all.

Goddammit, Gary.

"Gary, what have you done?" Gabby asked, horrified.

"Saved our asses, *Mom*," Mimi said, collapsed on one knee. The sarcasm there was terrible.

"Yeah, I wouldn't be too sure about that," I said, looking back at Smog.

Unsurprisingly, Smog looked furious. The badly proportioned pin-up model sorceress smoldered with a barely contained rage and I could see her clutch her staff tightly. The dragon gradually began to shift, which was a lot more horrific to look upon than you might think with the skin ripping, tearing, and sloshing off like plastic wrap. Underneath was a hideous, scaly, black thing that looked like it had been compressed into a tightly packed pose in their human skin wrapping. The creature *stretched* outward and spread its wings and limbs before starting to grow.

"This is going to suck," Dana said, getting up and feeling her head.

"No kidding," I said, watching the entire nightmarish process with a kind of perverse fascination.

"Everyone get together!" Gary shouted. "*Now!*"

I hated deferring leadership, but it occurred to me I didn't have any ideas. Besides, leadership turned out to be a lot more responsibility than perks, which was what I was in this for. Turning into a wolf and grabbing Mandy's broken form as she struggled to regenerate, I grabbed her by the coat with my jaws and dragged her back.

Smog was already as large as the cavern by the time we were all huddled together as the mages in our group started shouting mumbo-jumbo together while waving their hands around like it was a rave. Commenting on how silly magic looked in real life wasn't what I was concerned about, though, versus the fact that Smog was starting to smash through the roof of her temple. Which, if you needed it spelled out, was about to bury us all alive.

A magical bubble encircled us and somehow managed to hold against the collapse of the ceiling, leaving only the magic of a weredeer druid, the world's most ridiculous sorcerer, and the Black Witch to stand between us and annihilation.

Thankfully, we also had Amanda and she had the power to turn the bubble insubstantial as well as levitate it up. She stretched out her hands and we began to rise through the stone around us like it was mist. It was, in its own way, a rather staggering example of just what teamwork could accomplish. If I were a kindergarten teacher, I would have given everyone a cookie for their efforts.

Rising to the surface, the bubble popped, and we were in the hellish ruins of the Dragon Island Hotel. Most of the fires had died out but we were still surrounded by carnage and death, with a few other supervillains picking through the ruins. Having emerged from the ground below was Smog in her full-sized kaiju form. Standing on her hind legs, half-a-kilometer tall with her wings stretched out, and breathing fire in the air, she was the embodiment of draconic glory. We were like ants to her.

Turning back into a human and picking up my sword, I looked up at the sight greeting me. My ribs still hurt from being punched but I'd fully healed from my beating due to shapeshifting, which was a useful trick to remember for the future. Assuming I had any.

Taking a deep breath, I summarized our situation as I debated making a run for the *Nightplane II*.

"I think I'm going to need a bigger sword."

Chapter Twenty-Nine

Dragonslaying for Fun and Profit

"You know, I never wanted to be the punchy girl," Mimi said, sighing, looking up at the six-hundred-foot-tall monster in front of us. "I wanted to be a dainty, clever, stylish, fashion-conscious superheroine who relied on her wits rather than fists. But no, I had to be Ultragoddess' daughter, and everyone expects me to look like an Amazon bodybuilder who punches things. Now there's a giant monster and it's going to be up to me to hit it a lot. I'm never going to recover from this. History will remember me, yes, as Punchy Girl and not the stylish Ms. Terri."

I patted her on the shoulder. "If it's any consolation, Mimi, you'll always be Mystery to me."

"Ms. Terri! Two words!" Mimi snapped back. She still looked like she'd gone ten rounds with Mike Tyson and wasn't in any shape to keep fighting. Still, I felt this was a bonding experience for us as I now realized my adopted daughter had an entire inner life that I wasn't privy too. Too bad it had to come right before we were all going to die horribly.

"Insects! Fools! You thought you could slay me, steal my treasure, and thwart my plans! I am older than your species! Older than any filthy mammalian race! I am the heir to a dynasty of sixty million years in age!" Smog spoke, her voice echoing downward. If she'd been speaking right next to us, we probably would have been rendered deaf. As such, I was probably the only one who wasn't straining to hear her. Or was it him? No, Smog was still a her as I couldn't see any lizard junk and figured it'd be visible at this size.

"Is she going to be ranting for a while?" Mimi asked.

"Yes," I said. "Villains do that. If I ever start doing that, just slap me. Also, don't take off my head doing it."

Mimi glared at me.

"Listen kid," I said, taking a deep breath. "I want you to take your sister and start leapfrogging across the ocean. Try to make it to Australia. Take in the sights, meet the Crocodile Hunter's daughter, form a superhero team. Gary and I will cover your escape."

"You're sacrificing yourself?" Mimi asked.

"Fuck no!" I spoke. "I'm going to get the hell out of here whenever I can. Try to rescue my friends and loved ones too. Sorry Dana."

Dana sighed beside me.

"We're never going to get another chance at this," Amanda said, looking up at Smog. I was less than impressed with her suddenly taking a leadership role given she'd apparently gotten her entire team captured. Also, if I had to guess at who had persuaded the others to ditch me and go on a stupid all-woman quest to kill a dragon to save the world versus robbing it then the second Nightwalker was my number one draft pick.

"No kidding," I said.

"Whole nations have quaked beneath my feet! I have burned cities and destroyed armies!" Smog continued.

"Still ranting," I replied, dryly. "The problem with the fact that we won't have another chance at this is the fact that we don't have *any* chance period."

"Working on it," Leia called, almost done with her weird ray gun.

"I'm loath to ask you this, especially given the whole point of this mission, but you got any miracles in your pockets, Gary?" I asked. "This is the sort of eleventh hour bullshit you specialize in."

Gary stretched out his hands helplessly. "I admit to being all out of miracles. It turns out not possessing a magical cloak of ultimate power or godlike orbs makes it harder to beat unbeatable opponents."

"It's okay, we'll try again in half an hour," I replied, making a faux reassuring gesture. "In the meantime, as long as no one does anything stupid—"

I should have realized that last sentence was begging for trouble.

"If none of you will stand against this evil, I will!" Gabby shouted, lifting the Spear of Saint George that I'd almost forgotten about since my precarnation had declared it not only a fake but actively a tool of Smog's to deceive the public.

"Uh, Gabby, I know you weren't there, but I figured if you could hear me talking smack about you then—" I started to say before she started charging at Smog's nearest toe like a Spartan in *300*.

Gabby leapt into the air and drove the spear down against Smog's scales like she expected it to be a killing blow. Which, given she had the memories of a woman who regularly beat up kaiju alongside her father, was perhaps not as insane an idea as it sounded. However, this wasn't her story and the sight that greeted me as I watched like a slow-motion car crash was her being shocked like a rat chewing through a power cable.

Not only did the Spear of Saint George not pierce Smog's flesh, but it sent a wave of black electricity coursing up through the spear into Gabby's body. Revolutionary Girl was sent flying backward and landed at the foot of our group. Gary initially moved to help her, but she hissed at him, showing she wasn't dead at least. It was, however, not the crowning moment of glory she expected.

"Hahaha!" Smog laughed triumphantly, her voice mocking and triumphant. "I haven't had so much fun since I put a spell of oblivion on a door in my treasure room! Thousands of adventurers walked to their doom without their companions ever realizing it."

I stared up at her. "You didn't come up with that trap! Gary Gygax did!"

"We're retreating now?" Mimi asked, looking up. She looked a little better already, which indicated she'd inherited faster-than-normal healing if not outright regeneration. At least she looked like she could see out of both eyes now.

I cracked my back into place and was pretty sure my kidneys had healed. No dialysis or stolen black market implants for me. "Yep. Sorry, kid. There's no one to blame for this clustersuck but me."

"I'm sure you'll find someone," Mimi said, smirking. My adopted daughter knew me so well.

"DO RAY EGON!" Leia shouted before firing her energy ray gun and covering all six hundred feet of Smog in glowing fuchsia, blue, and yellow particle beams. It was a beautiful sight but even more beautiful was the fact it had a noticeable effect on Smog.

Smog shrank.

I stared in a kind of stunned awe. It was like a miracle from heaven, witnessing the dragon god go from being six hundred feet to five hundred feet then two hundred. Eventually, she was a mere hundred feet long from nose to tail before the tripod mounted ray gun caught fire and exploded.

"What have you done?" Smog shouted, her voice radiating in my ears and causing a rush of wind to wash over me. Smog was now only a sixth of her previous size but that was still pretty damn huge, and her voice was far closer than it was before.

"That's…impossible," Dana said, staring at the sight before us. "I wasn't going to be able to achieve nearly that."

"Oh, I saw your machinery and improved on it," Leia said, cheerfully. "It's very clever. It took me a whole day to figure out the principles then take them to the next level."

Dana looked back at my daughter with a mixture of appalled disbelief and professional jealousy. I didn't want to comment on the fact my daughter was quite possibly the smartest person who ever lived, combining telepathy with essentially Neo's power to learn kung fu in fifty seconds. Except, in her case, it was advanced science.

Unfortunately, Smog wasn't having any of it and aimed her mouth towards us, unleashing a breath weapon consisting less of fire than Cretaceous-period radioactive napalm. No, don't ask the biology of that, I stopped trying to figure this sort of thing out well before I graduated medical school.

We all didn't die in a horrific blaze of atomic fire due to Amanda and Gary finally not proving worthless by the former using her ice powers in conjunction with the latter whipping out his wand (hehe) to join its power with her. As such, the magical ice froze the attack before it reached us, which probably only worked because neither attack was entirely of this world.

"Reverse this and I will make your deaths quick!" Smog shouted.

"Not happening, chief," I said, staring at her. "You may still be thicc and make all the boys come to the yard with those majestic wings, but I suddenly like my chances of killing you a lot better now!"

Okay, that wasn't one of my better taunts, but she really was a thicc-looking dragon with majestic wings.

Smog growled and swung out her tail that I and everyone else in the group ducked as best we could to avoid being decapitated or knocked into next week. Smog unfurled her wings and started batting us all with massive amounts of wind that was close to being in a hurricane. This started to push her tons of muscle into the air. I didn't question the physics on that because, hey, magic.

Much to my surprise and delight, Mandy appeared on the back of the monster, claws out, and started tearing into Smog's thick, leathery left wing. She shredded it like a knife through sails, tearing and rending like a rabid wolverine. She screamed as she did so, her voice a mantra of madness and fury. "I hate dragons! I hate dragons! I hate dragons!"

Which, given a dragon was the creature that originally killed her and necessitated her unholy resurrection via the *Book of Midnight*, made perfect sense. Case fired at the other wing, the energy blasts penetrating this time as he'd seemingly put his little gun on maximum now. Jane entangled the dragon in a bunch of thick giant branches from beneath the ground before Amanda threw a bolt of lightning that would have fried Mandy if not for the fact as a vampire, she was immune to being electrocuted. The wizards in our group started throwing up whatever protective spells they could, which was good because Smog attempted to tear through us with her teeth and little T-Rex arms. Even Dana had joined the fight, zipping behind the dragon to continually fire at her backside.

The only people who weren't participating were Leia who was futilely trying to put her machine back together, Gabby who looked shellshocked on the ground from her dual humiliations, and Mimi who was ready to charge despite still being barely able to stand.

I put my hand on her shoulder. "You've done enough, dear."

"I can do more!" Mimi said.

I shook her head. "Go by your sister, Ms. Terri. This last bit's on me."

Mimi looked at me then nodded. "Okay, Mom."

Mimi looked back at her mother on the ground. Gabby, who hadn't been much of a mother to her at all. I didn't blame Gabby for that, some women just weren't meant for motherhood, and it was better that she'd stayed away than tried. Still, it was heartbreaking to see Mimi grab her and drag her off the battlefield to safety. Ultragoddess had done so much good that seeing her suffer a breakdown like this was appalling.

But it was Cindy time now.

Hefting up my sword, I stared right at the dragon who had managed to knock down a good half of the party before throwing Mandy to the ground as well. She was also ready to do another blast of Three Mile Island at us.

Running forward, I unleashed every bit of inner fury and resentment inside me combined with the violent animal savagery from my lycanthropy. "BARBARIAN PRINCESS RAGE!"

What followed was impossible for me to describe and I mean that in the literal sense because I have literally no idea what happened. The adrenaline and noradrenaline kicked in before everything went red. The sword bit into the scales and tore them off, biting into hard muscle and drawing blood. I couldn't even hear the sound of my sword's music that I think, in retrospect, was playing Gloryhammer's "Hootsforce."

I brought the sword down again and again, stabbing then pulling back with each thrust. It was difficult to say what was motivating me most: my hatred of Smog, my humiliation at being considered a second-tier villain when I wasn't relegated to being a henchwench, my family being threatened, the fury inside my blood, my ancestor briefly possessing me, or the simple fact that a part of me loved bloodshed. A big part in fact.

Either way, the aura around me protected me from Smog's claws and bites even as a slash through her throat opened Smog's neck to drip radioactive napalm down around me. Yeah, it was a good thing I wasn't planning on having any more children after this. I was also glad Dana had come up with a cure for cancer because I was probably going to need it.

I cannot be destroyed! Smog spoke in my mind, revealing the dragon to be telepathic. *If you slay this body, I will seek out another one and continue my immortal existence as the rest of my people did in the Astral Plane. We will eventually return and consume this world in fire and blood.*

"Only the Targaryens get to use those words!" I shouted, snapping out of my insanity long enough to leap upward and swing my blade with both hands to chop into the neck wound that I'd already created. "And I have *had enough* with you!"

I chopped.

Chopped.

And chopped again.

Much to my surprise, Smog's head came clean off as the radioactive fire from her now-headless body burst forth and burned me on the side of my arms and shoulders despite the power of the sword keeping me from the worst effect. The body kept thrashing too, sending me toppling to the ground. Only Mimi rushing in to grab me before the headless body of Smog rolled over me kept me from being crushed.

The decapitated dragon took almost a minute to die, her severed head screaming and choking with angry eyes but unable to speak. I briefly worried about Smog's claims she would return but I noted that Amanda walked over and claimed a glowing orb from Smog's head when she finally stopped moving. It helped to have psychopomps on your side when you wanted to make sure something absolutely stayed dead. And dead Smog was. The Dragon King that had menaced the world for literally thousands of years, the last survivor of a race of evolved dinosaurs destroyed by a meteor strike, and Chief Financier for PHANTOM was no more.

Huh.

We really did it.

I hefted my sword in the air before letting out a bellow roar of triumph. "Woot! Whose house? Cindy's house!"

Then I passed out.

Possibly died.

I'm not sure if I was clinically dead there for a few minutes or not. I do recall Amanda using her lightning powers as a defibrillator, though. Which, really, she shouldn't have been doing without proper medical training. This wasn't the movies. Anything else, well, after all that, I had no idea. At least for a while. Personally, I think I earned a break.

Epilogue

Still Alive and the Cake is a Lie

"Ughhhh," I said, waking up with a splitting headache. My vision was blurry, and I couldn't quite make out my surroundings.

"Can I get you anything?" Gary's voice spoke in my ear.

"Liquor," I muttered. "The harder the better. Oddly, I have a hankering for mead like a Viking."

Much to my surprise, I felt a wineskin handed to me. An honest to God wineskin that had probably come from someone's LARP.

"Here ya go," Gary said.

I drank it anyway. Having never had mead before, I didn't know if that was it, but any alcohol was welcome right now. "Ah, that's the stuff. When I pillage Falconcrest City, you'll be spared."

"I should hope so," Gary said.

Gradually, my vision cleared, and I saw I had an IV crudely attached to my arm as I was in the burnt out remains of what looked like a clinic. We were still on Dragon Island and in what was one of the buildings that had missed most of the bombing.

"Please tell me we're not marooned here on what was supposed to be a three-hour tour," I replied, sitting up.

"At least until tomorrow," Gary said. "I have to rememorize *Teleport without Error*."

"Of course you do," I muttered. "How's everyone?"

"Waiting to get off here and picking through the ruins," Gary said. "Leia had to cannibalize her own teleportation tech to make the shrink ray so that's down for now. Apparently, Amazon doesn't overnight here."

"That's genuinely surprising," I said. "Case?"

"In rest mode," Gary said. "I had to keep Leia from stealing parts or experimenting. I'm pretty sure if we let her operate on him, he'd end up like Inspector Gadget."

"I'm more concerned about letting a teenage girl play around with our anatomically correct robot," I replied. "That could give her ideas. Gray ace or not."

"I'll try to get that image out of my brain," Gary said, pausing. "Preferably with bleach."

"I don't suppose we've got access to Smog's enormous hoard?" I asked.

Gary grimaced. "Sorry, no."

"How bad?" I asked.

"Well, the entirety of Smog's hoard was buried underneath thousands of tons of rock," Gary said. "What wasn't destroyed can be retrieved but will probably be by the Chinese government when they send thousands of workers here in the ensuing months."

"Ah," I replied. "I don't suppose we can get the Juggernuke to help? I mean, I'm not happy the guy beat up Case, but I figured a few billion dollars would make everyone feel better."

"The Juggernuke and the other surviving villains left on Adonis' submarine. Diabloman managed to organize the survivors and get at least some of their henchmen to safety in a shelter so there were more than expected," Gary replied. "Not that any of them are grateful. This entire island excursion was a wash. Apparently, Achilles and Adonis are already seeking an annulment due to the fact the former ended up cheating on the latter with Medea an hour into things."

"Huh, I would have thought that would be an open marriage," I replied.

"Achilles didn't invite Adonis," Gary said.

"Ah," I replied. "Celebrity marriages. So, my super-duper epic heist was a complete failure," I said, sighing. "A trillion dollars in loot buried beneath the Earth and no way to get at it."

"Smog is dead," Gary pointed out.

"A small victory," I said, realizing no one on Earth was going to believe I hacked the dragon to death with my plus five sword of dragonslaying. "At least no one important died. Civilians and Mandy's dad aside."

"That's a bit like asking Mrs. Lincoln, 'Aside from that how was the play?'," Gary pointed out.

I was trying not to think of all those kids and families killed in the explosions. The death of Mandy's father was also something I didn't want to emotionally deal with. So, I didn't. It was really that simple.

"We got through it alright," I pointed out. I really didn't want to feel worse about all this.

"Ultragoddess also lost her powers," Gary pointed out.

I snorted. "Like that's going to last. Listen, Gary, one thing I've learned as a supervillain is everything eventually returns to its status quo. No one stays dead permanently, no one is permanently underpowered, and the jails are made of cardboard."

Gary gave a sad look. "If only that were true."

I looked at him sideways. "Gabby will forgive you for shooting her."

"I don't think so," Gary said. "But I'm surprisingly okay with that. In the end, I am aware of what's most important in my life."

"Do you mean me, Mandy, or the kids?" I asked, looking for my sword. It was right by the bed, and I put it over my lap. "Or do you mean supervillainy? Because we all love supervillainy."

"Yes," Gary said. "It wouldn't be nearly as fun without you all at my side forever."

"If you're going to ask me to marry you, you can fuck off," I replied. "I hate being anyone's third choice, even though killing your second for me was weirdly romantic."

"Please don't phrase it that way," Gary said, raising his hands in surrender. "Also, you've never been anyone's third choice or second."

"Liar. It's okay, I'm familiar with you making horrific mistakes." I wrapped my arm around him and gave him a hug. It accidentally tore out the IV, which was only momentarily a problem since the injury healed up almost immediately.

"If it's any consolation, I did snag some goodies before Smog's cavern collapsed," Gary said, not continuing that awkward line of conversation.

"Ooo, gimme!" I said, clapping my hands. "Please tell me you got a Silmaril. Suck it, Feanor!"

"Close," Gary said, pulling out his bag of holding. He pulled out a broken sword hilt first. "Narsil!"

I stared at him. "Narsil was reforged, Gary."

"Oh," Gary said. "Maybe I got from before it was reforged."

"Then we should probably return it or all of Middle Earth will be plunged into darkness," I replied. "Anything else?"

Gary slowly pulled out a ten-foot-long pole with a spear tip and an elaborate dragon-headed handle. "Dragonlance."

I took it. "A bit unwieldy as I don't have a dragon to mount it on and doubt Jane wants to share hers, but it definitely is worth mounting on a wall somewhere."

"Harper Pin," Gary said, lifting a glowing mithril pin in the shape of a harp. "From the world of Toril."

I smiled. "Where we fucked our first elf. Was it a man or a woman?"

"Doesn't matter with an elf," Gary said.

"True." I grinned. "You know, we've visited every *Dungeons & Dragons* setting but *Ravenloft*."

"Yeah, that place is a tourist trap," Gary replied. "Besides, if we want vampires and werewolves then we have those at our house."

"You and your vampire hair wand," I said, smiling.

"It's a werewolf hair," Gary said, smiling.

I stared at him. "As romantic as you think that is, all it's doing is making me think you're pulling stuff out of our shower drain."

"Ah," Gary said, grimacing. "There is that."

A bit of fridge logic—that status when you're visiting the fridge in the middle of the night and realize something you'd missed during the day— kicked in. "Wait, Gary, you mean you had a frigging dragon-slaying magical weapon, and you *didn't use it?*"

Gary looked at the dragonlance. "Yes, for reasons I will think of later."

I snorted. "Anything else?"

Gary pulled out a scale-mail halter top and hoplite skirt. It was made of dragon scales and a lot more covering than traditional depictions of Red Sindi were. "I knew I had to get this for you the moment I saw it."

"Oh, Gary, you know me so well," I said, grabbing the magical outfit and immediately started putting it on.

"We should probably get something for the girls," Gary said, looking around the ruins.

"They've been paid in exposure," I replied. "Everyone on Earth is going to know who they are after this. Mimi and Leia, the Dragonslaying Sisters."

"Mimi wants to be a thief," Gary said.

"Yeah, well, we don't always get what we want," I replied, now happy to fully look like the barbarian princess I was. "But yeah, let's go by Paris and steal the Eiffel Tower like she's always wanted to. Maybe leave some geography-based clues."

Gary smiled. "Thanks. You're finally getting this mother thing."

"Don't insult me," I said, smiling. "In any case, I think I need to reevaluate what I want from supervillainy. I'm going to have to take a few lessons in sword swinging if I really want to get into this new archetype."

"We could respec you," Gary said.

"Excuse me?" I asked.

"Respec. You know, change around your stats." Gary pulled out a scroll and unfurled it. It contained my character sheet. "One of the benefits of the Merciless Magical Operating—"

"Just call it Dungeon magic," I replied. "It sounds cooler, and you already referred to it as such once."

"Fine," Gary said. "At least since the Weave is copyrighted. One benefit of the Dungeon magic is that people hooked up to it are able to have their stats altered."

I stared at Gary and decided I did need to find and kill my author. "Bullshit."

"What? I told you my stats," Gary said. "Yours are listed here."

I grabbed the scroll and looked at it. It listed me as having a mix of Henchwoman, Thief, and Fighter levels. Level Sixteen, so at least I didn't have to deal with the humiliation of being lower level than Gary. There were some definite errors here, though. "Chaotic *Good*? When the hell did this happen?"

"Literally just this week," Gary said. "You shifted from Chaotic Evil to Chaotic Neutral then gradually over to your current state. It's okay, I went through something similar. Albeit, it says I'm Neutral Good now so that's just bullshit."

"It's the fact you're a bard," I said, continuing to peruse the document. The ink glowed and the figures moved around on it, giving a sense of ethereal majesty despite being little more than a glorified gaming supplement. "Wait, it says I have a Charisma stat of thirteen? What the hell? I am hot as fuck!"

"I think that's incorporating personality so it..." Gary paused midsentence, correctly realizing that was not an argument he wanted to start. "Yeah, let's up that to sixteen."

"Thank you!" I snapped. "Wait, Wisdom of eight!? Who wrote this?"

"It's the same wisdom I used to..." Gary started to speak before I glared at him. "Yes, absolutely, we need to fix that."

"Put all my Henchwoman levels in Barbarian Princess," I said, rolling up the scroll and slapping it against his chest.

"I don't think that's a real—" Gary started to say.

"Barbarian Princess!" I snapped. "Min max the crap out of me."

Gary pulled out a quill and started adjusting the figures on the scroll. Oddly, I felt different and not just in an emotional mood sort of way. I started to realize getting people to like you might involve not insulting them so much as trying to see their side of things. Thankfully, I could just ignore this voice. I also suddenly gained a deep knowledge of swordsmanship, survival, and horseback riding. Oh, and a couple of extra language slots that made me able to understand Hebrew and Elvish. "You realize the philosophical implications of this, right? If you're able to respec people, then we're all just magical ink waiting to be changed according to the whims of an all-powerful Dungeon Master."

"Yep!" Gary said, finishing his work and rolling the scroll up.

"Okay!" I responded, thinking about how my life would be without Gary. I realized, in that moment, I really couldn't see it anymore. That no longer scared me. "Okay, I'm not going to marry you, but I feel like I should make some sort of grand symbolic gesture to show that I do love you."

"You don't have to—" Gary started to say.

"Let's do sorta-monogamy," I replied.

"Sorta monogamy," Gary said, clearly not knowing what the hell that was.

"Yeah, obviously Mandy doesn't count," I replied. "Or Nightshade. You know Robyn's kid looks like you."

"He's a plant," Gary said, dismissing the idea he had another kid. Which, given he did know how to use protection, was probably very unlikely. "No mammalian biological material whatsoever."

I started rattling off the other names on my list. "Keanu Reeves, a certain tomb raider, Daniel Craig's James Bond, Daniel Craig, Dinah Meyer—"

"Is this going to take a while?" Gary asked. "Because I didn't get to eat at the wedding, and I was thinking Chinese."

"The entire cast of Netflix's *The Witcher*, Case, Princess Alusair of Cormyr, Drizzt Do'Urden, the *Dragon Age* girls, and Space Cadet Vance Turbo," I finished. I had a bunch of other names but figured those could be negotiated latter.

"Is that all?" Gary asked.

"I'm seriously cutting down, Gary, meet me halfway," I replied. "The thing is that I want to be with you most of all and that means something to me."

Gary took my hand. "Thank you, Cindy. I will always lov—"

"Eh, eh, eh," I interrupted. "Let's avoid using the l word. I said it and you said but it doesn't need to be said a lot. Let's save it for special occasions."

"Sure," Gary said, sighing.

"Glory of Love" by Peter Cetera started playing on my sword. I lifted it up and shook it a bit. "No *Karate Kid* anthems, please."

The sword stopped.

"Thank you," I replied. "We need to keep everyone involved in our crazy relationship. Especially since Mandy is watching from the bushes with her broody glowing eyes," I said, pointing out the shattered windows of the clinic to a pair of glowing eyes in the bushes.

"Does she do that a lot?" Gary asked, clearly uncomfortable. The two still loved each other but would probably never be as close as they were before she became undead. Which was a shame because they were both genuinely good people. They also loved the whole concept of family while I was still figuring it out. However, Mandy hated herself for being a monster and Gary blamed himself for getting her killed. It was all too Young Adult fiction for my tastes.

"Yes," I replied. "I thought the whole tortured brooding vampire thing was over, but no one sent her the memo."

"The living should be with the living," Mandy said from the bushes. "The dead can only be a curse on those who remain. You two—"

"Zip it," I said, making the hand gesture. "Mandy, you lost your dad and I'm sorry. But we're here for you. That includes getting him back from the dead."

"No, Cindy," Mandy said.

"But—" I started to say.

Gary made a throat slitting gesture with his hand. Death's Chosen and demigod of final repose was apparently not supposed to be doing resurrections after he cut them off. I could have told him that rule wasn't going to last.

"Okay, fine," I said. "We're there for you if you need us, though. Which is a weird experience for me. Plus, your family, which I hope will come to accept you as the soulless abomination we know and love."

"You are my family," Mandy said. "The one I chose. Nothing else matters."

"Clearly your medical degree is not in psychology," Gary said.

"Yes, because I have a real medical degree," I said. "But that's neither here nor there. But you're right, Mandyvira, Mistress of the Dark. We have a family now and it's one I don't want to horribly torture and murder. Thank you for that, both of you."

That was when I heard a very familiar voice. "You thought you'd gotten rid of me, Cindy Wakowski but I am as immortal as Great Cthulhu himself."

I turned to see, much to my surprise, that Barry had survived and was crawling out of the rubble next to the clinic He looked ready for round three. Clearly some people didn't understand the definition of insanity was doing the same thing repeatedly expecting different results.

I lifted my sword. "If you'll excuse me, guys, I'm going to figure out if cutting my ex's head off will kill him."

"Have fun!" Gary said, waving.

Bonus Short Story

A *Damselfly* short story

By Michael Suttkus

"Get in there, prisoner."

And with that line, Ironhyde Maximum Security Correctional Facility welcomed me with open arms. Well, burly, angry, shoving arms, anyway. I stumbled forward ungracefully, and the door slammed shut dramatically. I wonder if they paid extra to make them CLANG like that. Some Hollywood sound effects guy has it on his resume.

I picked myself up as spritely as I could. I glanced around my home for the immediate future, taking in my auburn-haired cellmate and the rather intense lack of comfortable furnishings. "In, I am," I said. "Thanks!"

The guard, who clearly considered it her duty to eradicate all cheeriness from the inmate population, if not the entire planet, glared at me. It was a glare that said, "We don't take kindly to smart mouths around here." Clearly, she was someone who glared professionally. She was good at it.

Sadly, I was good at being a smart mouth. They weren't going to take kindly to me around here.

"Do what you're told, don't make trouble, and don't talk back, and you might survive until you get released," the guard said.

Not bloody likely. Leptonics Industries, I mean, the impartial United States Justice System entirely uninfluenced by corporate interests, had piled charges on me to where I'd be 129 before I was eligible for parole. I don't care how good the local health care center is, that wasn't happening.

"That's too bad," I said. "Gives me about a week."

The guard glared harder, which was impressive in its own way. I could tell she was thinking I'd badly overestimated my probable lifespan. "The most important rule: Every night you plug your collar into the charger. If you don't, we know about it, then we come in here and plug it in for you and *you won't like that.*"

"I believe you!" I said, reaching up and felt the lump of iron they'd affixed to my neck. I could feel the Leptonics logo with my fingers. Yeah, I was being depowered with the technology I developed. Ironic, no?

The guard tried to find a way to read my sentence as being, in any way, back-talk. I could have just read her nametag, I supposed, and stopped thinking of her as 'the guard', but that might lead to thinking of them as humans rather than interchangeable guard-o-matics. Then, with one last extremely well-directed glare, the guard walked off.

I took a deep breath and turned to the stranger I was now living with. "Hi, come here often?"

My cellmate was taller than me (but most people were) with olive skin and brown hair that hinted at a Mediterranean ancestry. She looked me over carefully. There was something vaguely familiar about her, but that was probably because I liked to keep track of nearby supervillains. You never knew when you were going to run into someone else trying to steal the same stuff you were, and it was important to know who you could team up with to fight off any passing heroes, and who you were safer just running from on general principle. There were villains and then there were *villains*. Some of us were positively anti-social.

"Only when I'm not busy elsewhere," brown-hair said. "Got a name?"

"Dana Vandergast. No h."

"Does Dana normally have an h?"

"No, but Vanderghast does. Mine doesn't. 'Cause I'm special."

"Got another name?" she asked.

Well, it was a supervillain prison. "Damselfly."

"The terrorist?" Brown-hair asked, suddenly looking more interested.

"Well, there's a difference of opinions on that. I say no, but the jury said yes."

"Juries are funny that way. Tiara Wallace. Arachnegirl."

She said the last with more than a hint of embarrassment.

"Not fond of the moniker?" I asked.

"I didn't come up with it! Always have a name ready before going on a crime spree! If you don't, the media will saddle you with something awful!"

"To be fair to them, there are already a billion people with spider-powers using all the good names. It's always best to meet with an image consultant before beginning a supervillain career."

"I'll keep it in mind next time, but it was rather thrust upon me before. Top bunk is yours. Hope you don't mind heights."

"I hope not, too. Flying is my main thing."

And… that's when I remembered where I knew her from.

Two years ago, before I was Damselfly, feared international terrorist and arch-supervillain supreme, I was Dana Vandergast, Ph.D., a respected particle physicist working for Leptonics Industries. We mostly worked on studying superhumans to figure out how their powers worked so we could duplicate and/or suppress them. Either way was worth good money. I was the one who figured out how shrinking powers worked. I got a Primpton Prize for that one. Things were good.

Until I found out my boss was selling my research to Tom Terror, you know, the international actual mad scientist/terrorist who holds the records for both Most Nearly Successful Attempts to Rule the World and Most Superheroes Murdered. So, yeah, I objected. I tried to report him to his bosses at Leptonics, but, well, they were all in on it.

The whole company was just something Terror had set up to support his world-domination and killing-lots-of-people efforts. I tried to destroy all my research and flee, but they were ready for that and the labs were all rigged with knockout gas. I had wondered what those vents were for.

I'd awakened in a tube, surrounded by what I can only call goop, dressed in what I initially mistook for a red jumpsuit. Numerous hoses were attached to the jumpsuit, which was a kind of full-body hypodermic needle, designed to make sure every inch of me was injected with whatever random chemicals were in those tubes all at once. I felt sick to my stomach.

I handled this with calm rationality, if you ignore all the thrashing and panicking. Thankfully, that was interrupted when the tube opened and dumped me on the floor at the feet of a madman.

"Hello!" said the weirdly cheery Tom Terror. "How do you feel, Dana? May I call you Dana?" He's a lot smaller than he looks when he interrupts all the world's television broadcasts to tell us we must all obey him or die horribly. That doesn't make him less frightening, though. He might sound cheery, but there's no trace of emotion in his eyes at all.

Sure, Tom looked thin and frail, but the knowledge that he was surrounded by enough protective tech to give the world's strongest heroes pause kept me from imagining I was in any position to take him out.

So, what do you say when a homicidal supervillain asks you something like that? "Um… sure. A little queasy."

"Good, good, I've just infused your body with DNA based on a damselfly!"

"What?" I asked, feeling like I must have misheard.

"It's like a dainty dragonfly. Quite pretty, but still a ferocious predator at its own scale. I was going to go with a dung beetle, but I needed something with a theme of being small so I can force you to do repairs on some microcircuitry I'm having trouble with."

There had to be some way out of here. The place looked like a hybrid of a 1940's Hollywood serial's idea of what a mad scientist's lab should look like and store that sells overstocked electronic parts from the past few decades. It looked fairly simple to get out of.

"Now, I'm sure you'll want a demonstration of your powers, so…"

Terror pushed a button and a panel opened beside me. A pile of rattlesnakes started spilling out toward me. I screamed because that's what human beings do in that circumstance. Instinctively, I shrunk down to about three inches tall. Four delicate gossamer wings popped out of my back. I flew backward away from the snakes.

"See? I AM A GENIUS! I even infused you with the instincts to use your powers!"

I had had enough of this. I flapped my new little wings as fast as I could toward the air vent in the wall.

Moments later, I woke up on the floor, with scorch marks on my ugly red jumpsuit.

"I should mention that I have protected the air vents with infrared lasers." He still sounded cheery. Nothing that happened seemed to change his tone. "Now, in addition to your flight form, you have an exoskeleton form, that will offer you some physical protection, and compound eyes giving you nearly 360º vision. You should also find you have a powerful bite. I also gave you the ability to shrink other objects, so you can make miniature equipment for you to use in my service. You'll be quite useful to me." He reached down and picked me up in one hand. "Or you can die horribly. Your choice!"

I sat there between his fingers, trying to absorb all of this. He'd screwed with my body. I knew from my research that most of the people used in these experiments just ended up transformed into a pile of cancerous goo, so…

"I SAID YOUR CHOICE!" Tom Terror said, demonstrating his habit of suddenly shouting in the middle of conversations.

"Right, Mr. Terror, sir, serving you, sounds great, with the not dying and stuff."

"Excellent!" Tom replied without a trace of irony. Then again, there wasn't much ironic about him telling me to join him or die. It was just sad.

I ended up working for him for months. I didn't have any choice! I mostly helped him come up with particle-physics analogs for powers, the same kind of work I was doing before, but for no money and considerably more existential horror. So, yeah, I helped design the power-grafting experiments he did on innocent civilians he'd kidnapped. Tiara Williams was one of them. I don't think she saw me, I tried to avoid interacting with the prisoners as much as possible. Being reminded that my work was torturing people made it hard to remember I didn't have any real choice, you know.

Eventually, the superheroes showed up, smashed everything, stopped whatever Terror's plan of the moment was, and apparently killed him, but of course he came back later. In the outside world, Leptonics Industries had already spread the word that I had been working with Terror willingly, so the heroes were gunning for me, too. I managed to escape with most of my skin intact.

After that, well, it's hard to get a job when your name is on several of the world's Most Wanted Criminals lists. So… yeah, if I wanted to survive, my only choice was to be what they thought I was. I sold my tech, powers and brains to any supervillain team that wanted me. Well, the ones that weren't murderous psychopaths. I have standards. Mostly. Look, a girl gets hungry.

Yeah.

So, look, my moral code wasn't really the best when I started out. I was working for corporate America after all. But after plunging into the supervillain world, it became more of a list of moral suggestions rather than rules. "If it's convenient, try not to get people killed." That sort of thing. I'm not evil-evil. I'm still a decent enough person. I hope.

Decent enough, at least, to still feel guilty for what I did Ms. Wallace and the others like her. Sure, I could say I didn't have any real choice and I shouldn't feel guilty, but guilt isn't a great respecter of rationalizations. I owed Tiara Wallace.

I was just going to have to take her with me when I got out of here.

"You're planning to escape?" Tiara asked with the weary voice of someone who had heard that once or twice before. Maybe it was just the Louisiana sun beating down on her.

"That's the idea," I said, as we walked through the outdoor recreation area the next day. It was hot, muggy, and the air was filled with mosquitoes, but at least it was outdoors. Inside, it was hot, muggy, and the air was filled with mosquitoes, and, also, there were cockroaches. See? Much better out here.

"Everyone here has a plan," Tiara said. "But the smart plan is, just wait for the next big villain to break down the wall and try recruiting grunts for his next scheme, then escape through the hole in the confusion after he's gone."

"Yeah, that happens once or twice a year, but not for us." I kept my voice down. No point in letting everyone in the yard hear what we were talking about. Mind you, most of them seemed to be wrapped up in a basketball game.

"Why not?" Tiara asked.

"Sexism. The villains looking for henchmen want men. They break down the walls while the yard is filled with testosterone and we're baking in the women's wing."

Tiara looked at me strangely, then let out a bitter little laugh. "So, it's not bad luck that I keep missing them. I should have seen that. Wait, how do you know that?"

"Well, I am a professional supervillain. That I might end up in prison wasn't exactly hard to guess."

"Because you're bad at it?" Tiara asked, grinning.

"Oh, I'm good at my job. But so's the opposition. You have to be to fight assholes like Skullbreaker and Slaughterman. At least, if you survive to do it twice."

"Most villains just assume they'll be free forever," she said, clearly starting to take me a little seriously.

"So, yeah, I've been studying prisons, prison breakouts, and the general cycle of the revolving door that keeps supervillains coming back to get beat up by the heroes over and over again. And I decided it was best to make some preparations."

"How?" Tiara asked cautiously. I had her intrigued if nothing else.

I stopped walking by a very specific corner in the yard. "Well, the first thing to understand is that there isn't any general power-dampening technology. These collars have to be designed for each of us specifically, at least, for whatever class of powers we have. Some of them just detect power usage and run large voltages of electricity through you to encourage you to stop. But some, like mine, actually produce a field that disrupts the shrinking field my powers produce."

"So, you can't shrink as long as you're locked in that collar," Tiara astutely observed.

"Correct. But, more importantly for the current discussion, my collar disrupts any shrinking field that I come into contact with. So, if, say, someone was clever enough to have been sending packages to this prison, smuggling in nanobots with useful shrunken equipment, for the past two years, all I'd have to do is touch the right place..." I bent down as if I was tying my shoe, and rested my hand against the corner, and a small electronic tool seemed to materialize beneath my hand. I quickly palmed it and hid it in my sleeve.

Tiara's eyes were as wide as if she'd escaped from some anime into the real world (though the rest of her was far too realistically proportioned for that).

"Close your mouth," I said. "No point in swallowing a mosquito."

"You're seriously prepared to escape?" Tiara asked.

"Are you in or out?" I asked. "If you're up for parole in a month or something, I'll hold off so I don't screw things up for you. But otherwise, I'm getting out of here in a few weeks and I've got room for two."

"I'm in," she said. "I'm so very in."

There was one small, tiny problem. I was lying about the plan having room for two. My plan had been for me and me alone. So, now I was going to have to make some minor adjustments. Good thing I'm a genius, right? I'd just have to come up with a whole new plan. Simplicity itself.

Okay, this is what the plan had been, that is, plan that I had had before I decided I had to save Arachnegirl and thus had to scrap my extremely simple plan. First part, check my special corner every week. My little microrobots are… micro. So, it took them a while to move things around, but they'd keep the schedule! Each week, like clockwork, I could unshrink another useful tool.

Of course, unshrunk tools are just the sorts of things that cops search cells for. It's like they don't trust us prisoners! They treat us like a bunch of criminals. So, the first tool I grew is an invisible pocket! I can slip it into my mattress, where it will hide itself and my tools from prying eyes. The cops would have to get incredibly lucky to find it. No, that is *not* something I said right before I got caught.

Once I collected a few tools, I'd be able to take off this damned collar, and once I could shrink to the size of an action figure, there wouldn't be much this prison could do to hold me. Sure, the alarms would go off the instant I removed my least favorite necklace, but there's no way they could find me at that size. Also, not something I said right before I got caught.

So, how was I going to get Tiara out with me? There were two problems with shrinking her. First, other people's bodies aren't made for shrinking the way mine is. Shrinking her would leave her unconscious at best, conscious and in considerable pain at worst. In either case, I'd have to carry her out, which I can't do while flying. Okay, I could shrink her down to convenient fun-size, and I could shrink myself down to only a foot or so tall, then I'd be strong enough to carry her and fly, but I'd be big enough to give the cops a decent chance of catching me. So, I was going to need more plan. Good thing I'm a genius.

Okay, yes, that's what I said right before I got caught.

"So, I hear you and the spider are getting out of here."

Dozens of random muscles in my body all contracted at once. Isn't it lovely when a secret you're trying to keep just gets blurted out from a random direction? I turned around to look at the speaker. She had short blonde hair that seemed to have missed the last few monthly brushings, but her most noticeable feature was her overly large eyes, ears, and nose. She was Christine Bainbridge, the Owlet, and all her senses were enhanced to ridiculous degrees. That might not seem like the most threatening powers ever, but like I said, I was trying to keep a secret here.

I felt stupid right now for a supposed genius. Of course there were people with superhearing in prison! I hadn't bothered checking the profiles of the prisoners for hearing powers because I hadn't been planning on talking to anyone about my plans! But the mere act of talking about it to Tiara had opened another hole in my carefully laid schemes. Yes, when you go supervillain, you start using the word "schemes" a lot.

I stood up and leaned against the yard wall trying to look casual. No point in drawing even more unwanted attention. "I suppose there's no point in playing dumb," I said. "What do you want?"

"I want in," Owlet said.

"On getting out?" I asked.

"Yeah, in on out." Owlet narrowed her eyes a little as if trying to decide if I'd set her up to say that.

"Okay," I said.

"Just like that? You're not gonna fight me?" Owlet asked.

"Sorry, I didn't realize it was required. Fine, I say, no way. You threaten to tell the cops, or worse, just announce it to the yard. I realize I'm caught over a barrel and grudgingly agree."

"You don't have to be sarcastic," Owlet said.

Oh, you don't know me at all. How the hell was I going to get two people out of here with me?

"When?" Owlet asked.

"I don't know yet. A couple weeks at least. I have to gather up my equipment, as you undoubtedly heard, and then I have to figure out how to get a third person out." I was still working on the second.

"Yeah, well, if you try and leave without me, I'll hear it, and I'll have this whole place down on you."

"I had, in fact, already figured that part out for myself."

I had such a simple plan.

"The Owlet?" Tiara asked. "Bug-Ugly hears everything around here."

We were back in our cell that evening, and I'd explained our new partner. "Which means she's probably listening to you insult her now," I said.

"Doesn't change the fact that she got screwed in the superpowers lottery. Most of us got better looking when we got powers."

She's not exactly wrong. My time with Tom Terror had confirmed things I'd long suspected. A lot of "random" superpowers were the result of viruses Terror and other mad scientists had released in their experiments. Since most of them had the maturity of 12-year-old boys, sticking in some genetics to turn infected women into potential lingerie models was just to be expected. Probably while dreaming of trapping hot superheroines in slow moving, bondage-themed deathtraps. Not that I was going to explain that out loud. I didn't really want Tiara associating me with the man who did experiments on her.

"Look at it from her point of view. She got powers that made her unattractive in a world where women are judged massively on their looks. I can understand her wanting to blow up a few frat houses is what I'm saying."

"So, you think you can get her out, too?"

"Sure," I said. "Simplicity itself."

I hoped Owlet's senses didn't extend to detecting lies.

My cohorts and I spent the next few weeks gathering information on what resources we had available. Volunteering for work details in the laundry or kitchen could provide access to interesting chemicals, but the guards would probably object to me trying to carry out a carton of ammonia.

Everything we might gather incurred risks. If we got caught before I was ready, well, all it would really take is the cops changing out my mattress and my plans would be royally screwed. I only had one copy of each of my tools waiting for me to unshrink and pick up. That was, increasingly, starting to seem like poor planning on my part.

This was especially true now that I had unshrunk my security key for these damned collars. There were advantages to having helped design the collar-tech. With the key, I could have all three of us free of the collars in 30 seconds, but the alarms would go off, and I still needed a way to get the others to freedom. Worse, 30 seconds is actually a surprisingly long time. If I got my collar off and one of the others, the cop on the monitoring board might realize that two lights going off meant it was time to trigger the mass-shock feature, knocking everyone out. That would end a lot of plans right there.

I had briefly considered making a meat-doll out of the cafeteria food. I could have undone my own collar and then thrown the doll at the electrified fence that kept us in. If the police mistook it for me fried to a crisp trying to escape, it would have given me considerable freedom to operate inside the prison until I could arrange an escape for the others.

But it would depend on the police not actually examining it forensically and, well, betting the opposition is going to be as stupid as you wanted them to be was how most supervillains ended up in prison in the first place. It only took one actually competent person to screw you over.

Of course, a lot of this would get easier if we could get these collars off without the alarms triggering. And on that thought, things started falling into place.

"I need wire," I said.

"I'll run right out to Radio Shack to get it," Tiara said. "Oh, wait, they all closed up a few years back. You're on your own."

"Cute," I said. "We can get some from the dryers. I'll show you how to pull some out of the vent-clog sensors so it won't disrupt their normal operation. Nobody will notice for years, if ever."

"They'll notice if they see me opening up the dryer and pulling at the innards," Tiara said.

"Yes, we'll need a distraction," I said. "There's always the classics; I could start a fight with someone."

"Won't work the way you think," Tiara said. "Around here, only the newbies gather around to watch people fighting."

It took me a moment to understand why. "Of course, because nobody wants to be within radius when the guards use a mass-shock on the collars to stop the fight. How big is the radius on that?"

"I've seen them do it so it got everyone within about ten feet. But it's common sense they can hit much wider bunches if they need crowd control," Tiara said.

"Yeah, I'll work on that... can you get me some D batteries?" I asked.

"I think some of the emergency flashlights in the kitchen have D cells," Tiara replied. "But they might be C, I've never properly checked."

"Any kind of alkaline battery will do, but the larger the better. Get a few of those and some kitchen gloves. Clean ones. And some foil. I'll get some stamps from the stationery supply."

"You've got something in mind, don't you?" Tiara asked.

I grinned wickedly and explained the plan.

You know what my biggest problem is with these plans? Whenever I'm trying to pull one off, I had to fight the urge to start humming the *Mission Impossible* theme loudly. DUN DUN DUNDUN... seriously, greatest TV theme song ever.

So, there I am, in the laundry room, with a rubber kitchen glove full of purloined ingredients, carefully mixed and ready to act as a catalyst, hidden in my hideous orange jumpsuit. No, I'm not going to be more detailed. I passed doctoral-level chemistry with an A; if you didn't, don't mess with the stuff inside batteries. Seriously, just don't. I just had to get it into one of the bottles of ammonia the guards were supposed to be watching carefully.

Luckily, they sucked at doing their jobs. I can't blame them, watching us do laundry had to be one of the most boring jobs on the planet. So, I just waited until someone raised their voice on the other side of the room and drew everyone's attention and making sure I wasn't where a camera could see me, I slipped some of my carefully mixed chemicals into a bottle of ammonia and slid it under a table. Slowly, at first, but then more rapidly, it started to bubble.

Now comes the hard part, waiting. And the not humming. The laundry room had pretty good ventilation, with big open barred windows to let the mosquitoes in. I was sure the nitrous oxide, laughing gas if you must, being produced wouldn't build up to toxic levels in here, the question was, was it too well-ventilated?

It was entirely possible I'd put in a bunch of work that would have no effect at all. This is how plans went when you were making things up as you went along. You put the pieces in place and hoped for the best. The effects started slowly. Prisoners started to get a bit sillier, a little more rambunctious than normal. The guards got curious and came in closer, and before long, everyone was telling dad jokes and horsing around a little. I stayed far enough away to keep from being affected. I hoped.

Everything worked like a charm. (A phrase I hate since charms don't work!) Half the room was laughing and getting sillier, and the other half of the room was crowding in to see what all the fuss was about. As soon as all the attention was directed toward the washer side of the room, Tiara and I made short work of pulling wires out of the dryers. My heart was racing. That was the moment where getting caught would have really screwed us over. But, several excruciatingly long seconds later, we were done, and several pieces of short wire were hidden in our waistbands.

Of course, the guards did eventually clue into what was going on. Then we were herded out while the laundry room was searched. I can only assume they found the bottle but there wasn't much to be found from it. Those things had fingerprints on them from hundreds of convicts, and I'd been smart enough not to leave mine on top and avoid the cameras.

Several of the more rambunctious prisoners had gotten themselves put in solitary because the guards felt SOMEONE had to be seen to be punished, even if they couldn't figure out who was guilty. I felt a little bad for anyone in solitary, really. Threats were issued, and privileges were revoked for everyone in the room for a month.

It had gone perfectly.

So, obviously, karma was waiting around a corner somewhere to kick me in the shins.

"Uurlf," I said, because that, apparently, is the sound I make when someone picks me up by my throat and shoves me into a meal-room wall. I had not previously known this.

Physical powers were among the hardest to neutralize, so most of the control collars didn't bother trying. They just worked on the principle of indirectly detecting someone abusing their powers and sending spikes of electricity through the necks of the people doing it. So, say a prisoner had superstrength, a frighteningly common power. They had to wear wrist and ankle cuffs in addition to their collars. The cuffs had motion and force sensors that would detect particularly egregious uses of force and the collar would go off.

Apparently, they weren't tuned well-enough to detect someone being picked up by the throat and shoved painfully into a wall so hard that the air rushes out of their lungs. Someone was going to have to work on that.

Omegapunch, the owner of the hand clamped vice-like around my neck, glared at me angrily. She looked basically exactly how you expect a woman strong enough to bench-press a rhinoceros would. She was at least three feet taller than I was, and it probably wouldn't be good for my health to compare our weights. I had no idea what her real name was. Don't look at me like that. I can't memorize everything! And she was the last person in here that I'd willingly include in my plans.

Notably, nobody else in the room was reacting to this like it was in anyway unusual. Smart people.

"Er, can I help you?" I asked. Well, what I asked wasn't quite that clearly enunciated, because of the sudden difficulty I was having getting air to and from my lungs.

"You're the one who made the gas bomb go off!" she growled.

"Who? Me? I had noth…" I said, followed by some more indistinct grunting. It had been a week since the Great Laundry Room Caper, and I had been beginning to think I'd gotten away with it cleanly.

"I have proof!"

Oh, crap.

"One!" Omegapunch continued. "You're a supergenius."

"No, just a regular genius and…"

The large brown-haired woman lowered me a little bit, just so that I'd be at eye-level with her. "Su-per-gene-yus."

There's a certain stereotype, of the big-strong person who is also dumb as a rock. It exists so that heroes in stories can show how smart they are by getting around someone who is physically superior to them. It's a dumb and unfair stereotype. A dumb and unfair stereotype that Omegapunch more than lived up to. I mean, just because it's a stereotype doesn't mean they don't exist at all.

I didn't feel like arguing that point any further, so Omegapunch continued, "Two! You're a scientist, so you know chemistry!"

"Actually, scientists specialize in different fields and I'm a particle physi-ooooof."

She thumped me into the wall again, apparently disliking my efforts to correct her logic.

"Third! You were the only supergenius in the room!"

"What about Jane Myers? She ran rings around Ultragod for years with her brains! She was right there!"

"She doesn't count! She's boring! Doesn't even have a codename!"

It may have been the lack of oxygen to my brain, but this wasn't making a lot of sense to me. "If I admit guilt, will you let me breathe?"

Omegapunch glared at me again, and then let go. I fell at least two feet to the ground. It felt longer. My feet hurt from the impact, but I was too busy gulping down air to care.

"Okay, look, I see that you're upset…"

She leaned in, pinning me against the wall with her two massive arms. "I'm not getting dessert for a month!"

"We get dessert?"

"I GET DESSERT!"

I would later learn that the powers that be here felt that a happy Omegapunch was much less trouble than a surly one and that she, and apparently, she alone, got pudding cups with her regular meals of slop and glop. Why those got cut off when she was clearly not even possibly responsible for the laughing gas incident was beyond me. Maybe it was about punishing the rest of us?

"I can say, with complete sincerity, that I am very sorry you are not getting dessert."

She leaned back, just a little, then crouched down to whisper conspiratorially, "You're planning to escape."

The way this woman's leaps of illogic kept coming to completely correct conclusions was extremely frustrating. "In the interest of not having my back pulverized again, let's say I agree. What do you intend to do?"

"You're going to take me with you!"

"Of course!" I said, smiling brightly to show my sincerity. "The more the merrier. I just have to set things up. We'll get out in a month. And remember, don't tell anyone."

Of course, unlike Owlet, we could escape under Omegapunch's nose and she'd be none the wiser until after we were gone. So, it was an easy promise to make, but one I would suffer no consequences for breaking.

No consequences at all.

We were leaving the yard the next day when Owlet tapped me on the shoulder and whispered, "Did you know Omegapunch is telling everyone you're engineering a mass breakout in a month?"

"Everyone?" I asked, feeling the strength drain out of my limbs.

"If the cops haven't heard about it yet, they will soon."

I was going to have to invent some new swear words to express my frustration, the existing ones just weren't harsh enough. "Great, now we have to go tonight."

"Are you ready?"

"Doesn't matter, does it?"

"And I have to ask, a mass breakout?"

"Oh, hell no," I said. "Some of these people are criminals!"

"We're all criminals!"

"Yeah, but there's a difference between letting you and Tiara out and releasing Bloodslaughter. I don't need any dead innocents on my conscience."

"Weren't you a terrorist?"

I sighed. "I have to hire a PR firm. Just be ready tonight."

"Ready for what?"

"I'll think of something."

Well, I had successfully invented a complicated electronic device that would let me defeat the alarms on these damned collars. That is to say, I had used postage stamps to attach some pieces of wire to pieces of foil.

"That's all it takes?" Tiara asked. "You'd think people would be taking these collars off left and right."

"No, this just keeps the electrons flowing through the alarm circuit. Taking the collar off still requires a security key, which most people don't have. Are you ready?" I was sitting on Tiara's bunk in our cell for what I hoped would be the last time.

"Ready as I'll ever be," she said.

"Good, now slip the first piece of foil into the joint on the collar, no, more towards the edge. Push it in with the paperclip until you feel the nubbin, then push the foil around the nubbin."

"Okay," Tiara said. And after maybe 20 seconds of work, she added, "I think I got it."

"Good," I said again. "Now do the same thing but towards the inside edge."

There was another twenty seconds of pushing. "Okay, moment of truth time," she said.

I put my smuggled security key into the slot for it and turned. There was a click that stopped both of our hearts. Then I carefully pulled the collar apart at the join.

Only silence. No screaming alarms. No one was coming to beat the hell out of us… yet. We both exhaled simultaneously.

"Now do me," Tiara said.

This really wasn't the time for my usual brand of humor, so I swallowed the urge to jump at that opportunity for a witticism. A minute later and her collar joined mine on the cot.

She rubbed her neck, exposed to the air for the first time in a year. I just immediately shrank to my bug-girl form. GODS, it had been so long! Not being able to use your powers was like having a limb you didn't dare move. Just unnatural!

"Okay, what next?" Tiara asked.

"I slip out through the door," I said. The door conveniently came with holes big enough for hands so the cops could handcuff us before moving us around. "Then I get to the security room and open some doors. When the doors open, you and Owlet make your way to the laundry. I'll meet you there."

"Are you sure you're not going to just skip out on us?" she asked.

"I could have done that two weeks ago," I said. "You're the only reason I'm still here."

She smiled uncomfortably, then nodded. "Hurry up."

It occurred to me that I was starting to feel close to poor Tiara. I would have to sort out those feelings later, though. Now was a time to focus. I nodded back, and then flew out the door.

I was down to my smallest size, about three inches tall. It's small enough to help me avoid notice, but not so small that I can guarantee I won't be noticed. I flew up to the ceiling so I wouldn't be spotted by any prisoners looking out their doors and flew down the hall.

I felt alive in a way I hadn't since I was caught. My heart was throbbing, and I could feel the blood in my veins pulsing with energy. Not literally; that would be unhealthy.

The door at the end of the hall didn't have the nice handcuff holes so I had to drop to the floor and crawl under it. It was a tight squeeze, but I made it. Scuffed up my precious orange jumpsuit, though. I don't think it's in mint condition anymore. That's okay, I don't think I was going to find many opportunities to wear it once I left this fine Correctional Institution. Which is a weird name to call a prison. Makes us sound like a bunch of copyeditors. Get a day off your sentence for every error corrected!

Just past the door was one of the security offices I remembered from when I was brought in. It was manned by one of the guards I still refused to learn the names of, but one of the more assholish ones. Good. Because this was going to hurt.

I expanded to full size and enjoyed the shocked look registering on her face before blasting her with my shrinking effect. I could modulate the ray so that it hurt less, but I didn't, just let it be its naturally spikey self. The guard yelped as she was reduced to the size of an action figure. She staggered around on top of the chair she'd been sitting in moments before. It took about twenty seconds for my shrink-attack to recharge, so I had to keep the mini-guard from escaping the chair for that long before I could blast her again, which I did by spinning the chair around so the guard got dizzy. I couldn't shrink her any further, but the second shot was enough energy to knock her out.

It would be very satisfying to do that with every stupid, sadistic guard here, but I didn't have that kind of time. I took the miniature unconscious body and headed for a nearby janitor's closet. Once inside, I started taking off the guard's clothes. It wasn't quite like undressing a barbie doll, since the guard was a lot floppier than your average plastic supermodel. I had to shrink myself to handle the buttons. Once I'd stripped her to her underwear, I took her miniature uniform and stuffed it into an air vent. Then I was out the door and heading back down the hall, leaving the door just a bit ajar, so they'd be sure to notice it later.

It had taken me a while to find the blueprints for this place while I had been preparing for my possible imprisonment. Luckily, there weren't a lot of prisons in the US rated for holding supervillains, so I'd been pretty sure where I'd be sent if I was caught. All that planning had felt like overkill, but it was totally worth it now.

A left turn, a right. These endless beige corridors seemed almost like a normal office building here. I wonder if that was to lull people into not thinking about the miseries found in the other portions of the building. Another turn and I was to the main door to the main security room for the women's wing. This was where the cameras were monitored, and the doors and collars all controlled. It was always manned by two guards, and this was the place where things could go the most horribly wrong.

Who am I kidding? They could go horribly wrong everywhere.

Getting under the door here was a much tighter squeeze than before, but I just managed it, tearing my top a little on the way. Definitely not mint condition now.

Two guards. Deep breath. Let's do this.

I expanded to full size, catching them both off-guard (sorry). I shrunk the guard closer to the door. The second one dove for the alarm bell, but I caught her arm and pulled it away. The guard surged up from her chair, shoving me back against the wall of the small room. She started to shout for help, but I headbutted her in her chin. The guard returned the favor by kneeing me in the groin and slamming me against the door so that the doorknob impacted my spine. It was all I could do to keep from shouting in pain myself, but by that time my attack had recharged and I blasted her with my shrink ray.

The first miniaturized guard had been thrown off the chair and to the floor in the fight and was now trying to scramble under the door. Luckily, she wasn't nearly as svelte as I was, and I grabbed her before she'd even gotten halfway. I grabbed the other guard for good measure and put them both in a lunch bag someone had brought. It didn't have any effective way of locking it, but I hung it up from a peg along the back wall. If they tried to escape that before they returned to full size, they'd be facing the equivalent of a four-story fall.

"Sit tight, ladies," I said. "This will all be over soon enough."

And now I controlled every door and collar in the woman's wing. That I wasn't cackling with glee showed you I really wasn't a natural supervillain and didn't really deserve to be here. Okay, maybe I cackled a little.

It was tempting to start a mass prison break. I mean, that would certainly keep the guards busy. But, like I said, there were people in here who I couldn't stomach letting out, and I didn't have time to look up every collar number on the control board with every prisoner's name in the book and release people individually. So, I found the doors to my cell and Owlet's and unlocked them, as well as shutting off Owlet's collar. They both heard the click of their doors and I saw them on the hallway cameras sneaking out the doors and heading for the laundry room. Good, everything was going according to plan. I unlocked the other doors they needed to reach their destination.

I waited two minutes to give them a head start, then I undid Omegapunch's collar and door and hit the alarm. Then I opened the security room door, shrank, and flew as fast as I could while all hell broke loose.

In my experience of several supposedly well-planned criminal heists, there comes a point in every plan when, despite all your precautions, things descend into pure chaos. It's best to plan for this and be ready for it.

For several minutes, the chaos was as pure as it could be as the guards tried to determine just why the alarms were ringing. It wouldn't take them long to figure out who was missing, even with Omegapunch providing some distraction back in the cellblock. After all, there aren't many inmates who can leave shrunken guards around.

But, for a while, they didn't know what they were looking for, especially when they found that the security room was apparently unmanned. They started looking everywhere. They looked left, they looked right. The one place they didn't look, the place humans never look, is up. It's true, most people live in a resolutely two-dimensional worldview. I flew over the heads of several of the cops as I made my way to the laundry room.

When I reached the room, it was already being searched. I had been hoping it would have taken the guards longer, but the plans weren't screwed yet. If necessary, I could return to full size and distract the searchers before they got to the pile of clothing I knew my two allies were hiding in.

Luckily, I didn't have to. A voice came over the police radios announcing, "We found Laurie knocked out and shrunk in a closet! They stole her uniform and are pretending to be officers!"

"That means they're heading out through the front!" one of the searchers said, and they immediately ran out of the room.

Well, that had worked better than I could have hoped. That's my best supervillain advice right there: always leave the heroes clues to things you aren't actually doing. It's wonderfully confusing.

"Coast is clear, ladies," I said. "Let's blow this joint."

"You've got plans to get out of the building?" Owlet asked.

"This is the closest room to the outside you could easily reach. From here, there's just some window bars and a bit of fence between us and freedom, nothing I can't shrink in under a minute, and all the cops are looking elsewhere."

"Brilliant," Owlet said.

"Yes," I said, entirely too smugly. "Let's go."

And go we did.

And, at long last, we were free. Okay, it had only been a month or so inside for me, but still! It was a very long month without a bit of decent food. The Louisiana swamps around the prison weren't exactly the best terrain to escape quickly through for my two earthbound companions, but we rapidly gained the use of a small boat by throwing some drunk frat boys out of it.

"Where are we going?" Tiara asked.

"I've stashed some clothes and cash at a rest stop on US 90," I said, steering the boat through the swamps in the dark. "The clothes are sized for me, but they should fit you two well-enough. We just need to keep out of sight until we get there."

"Just how much preparation did you do for this?" Owlet asked.

"Plan for the worst and hope for the best, I always say."

"You're a lot shorter than I am," Tiara said. "Anything that fits you is going to look miniature on me."

"You might have a bare midriff that makes it look like you think you're still in high school," I said. "But it will be fine." I was finally starting to relax.

I probably shouldn't have.

I was completely unprepared when something sticky attached itself to my back. I had barely registered what had happened when I found myself yanked out of the boat. Or, more precisely, the boat kept moving and I had suddenly stopped when the length of industrial-strength webbing attaching me to a nearby tree pulled taut. I flopped gracelessly into the water. Swamp water. Yuck.

A moment later, I'd used a shrink blast on a bit of the web, causing it to snap, and I was flying after the boat, trying to decide if I should be angry or just confused.

Apparently, so was Owlet. As I got back within earshot, the supervillain was saying, "What they hell was that about, Arachnegirl?"

"She works for Tom Terror!" Tiara said. "He wants me back in his lab and she was sent to collect me!"

"Are… are you sure?" Owlet asked.

"It's not true!" I said, landing back in the boat at full size. "This is just a…"

I couldn't finish before I got a faceful of webbing. Arachnegirl kicked me in the stomach and webbed me to the back of the boat. That ended my speech rather completely.

"She was working for him when he experimented on me and gave me these powers!" Tiara was saying. "I knew it was no coincidence when she just happened to be assigned to my cell! And she pretended she didn't recognize me! But I knew her! She didn't like being where her victims could see her, but I saw her often enough to remember her face! I remember what they did to me!"

Bound and helpless, I couldn't even speak in my own defense, and, honestly, I wasn't sure I would have. I could feel the pain Tiara had been holding back, the silent rage she'd been keeping in reserve. What had I been expecting? That if I got her out of prison, I could tell her the truth and she'd forgive me for being part of ruining her life? I slumped in the back of the boat, suddenly too weak to bother fighting against her webs.

Arachnegirl brought the boat to a stop by a bit of land a bit more solid than most of the swamp. "You need to get out now, Owlet," she said.

"What are you going to do?" Owlet asked.

"See the bridge over the swamp up ahead in the distance? I'm going to dump gasoline all over her and crash the boat into the of the pylons."

Okay, back to fighting against the webbing.

Owlet looked between Tiara and me, then got out of the boat and started running. I couldn't blame her. Tiara, true to her word, upended a can of fuel over me, then turned back to the steering wheel and started the boat towards the bridge. She was breathing heavily, and I couldn't tell if she intended to jump out at the last minute or still be in the boat when we crashed. I wasn't sure she'd survive either way, given how fast this boat was moving. She'd be hitting the water pretty hard, and her speed might smash her into one of the pylons anyway.

What I could tell was that the gasoline was starting to dissolve the webbing. That probably hadn't been part of her plan. I couldn't be sure if the boat would hit before they'd dissolved enough to free me. I had to act now. I couldn't move my hands forward to attack her, but I could hit the bottom of the boat. I shrunk part of the plastic floor and the strain of the molecules pulling against each other caused the area to crack open. Instant hole! Water started flowing into the boat, and we started to slow a little. Not enough though. Another might help.

The water sloshing at her feet got Arachnegirl's attention, and she turned around to see what I was doing. She grew angrier, if that's possible, and stepped back before delivering a kick to my stomach, followed quickly by another. A few more of those might have killed me without the need for an explosion, but the webs finally fell apart and I surged forward, trying to grapple her. We both fell into the increasingly waterlogged bottom of the boat.

The boat continued its path forward, though without someone at the helm, it had started to drift to the side. I barely had time to register that bit of good news, before realizing we were just heading toward a different pylon. What had I done to deserve this kind of luck? Oh, right.

Grappling with Tiara was not going to go in my favor. She was stronger and larger than I was. Strength just isn't a damselfly power. With no hope of this ending in my favor, I did what I always do when things go south, and I shrunk myself. That ran the risk of being small and vulnerable, but also made me fast enough to get out from under her before she could crush me.

"Get out!" I screamed at her.

She shot a webline up at the bridge and let herself be pulled upward, out of the boat. The boat crashed into a pylon and sank into the swamp, too wet to properly explode like action movie rules demanded.

She hung there under the bridge, and I flew a short distance away. "Tiara, I can explain…"

She fired another webline at me. It tangled my wings, and I started falling. I didn't have to worry about hitting the water, though, as she was reeling me in, glaring murderous intent at me. I grabbed the line myself, grateful that only the ends of these things were sticky, and bit down on it, snapping it. (Told you damselflies had strong bites.) I immediately started trying to fly away, but my wings were still gummed up with webbing, and I crashed into the water. Luckily, at that size, I didn't weigh much, and the impact was minimal. I started being carried downstream by the current, while she screamed that she was going to find and kill me until I was finally out of earshot.

It was almost dawn before I found the box of gear I'd stashed by the rest stop. I was soggy, exhausted, and worn to the bone. I had to dig a bit to get the box out, leaving my fingernails with so much dirt under them that no amount of washing at the rest stop bathroom could get them clean. Oh, well. Time would fix that.

There was a bus station not too far down the road, and I had enough cash to buy a ticket to anywhere. It might be risky, though, if the police search for us, for me, reached this far. It probably did.

I sighed and started walking. Alone.

About the Author

C. T. Phipps is a lifelong student of horror, science fiction, and fantasy. An avid tabletop gamer, he discovered this passion led him to write and turned him into a lifelong geek. He is a regular blogger and also a reviewer for The Bookie Monster.

Bibliography

<u>**Novels**</u>

The Rules of Supervillainy (Supervillainy Saga #1)
The Games of Supervillainy (Supervillainy Saga #2)
The Secrets of Supervillainy (Supervillainy Saga #3)
The Kingdom of Supervillainy (Supervillainy Saga #4)
The Tournament of Supervillainy (Supervillainy Saga #5)
The Future of Supervillainy (Supervillainy Saga #6)
The Horror of Supervillainy (Supervillainy Saga #7)

Tales of Supervillainy: Cindy's Seven (Supervillainy Saga #7)

I Was a Teenage Weredeer (The Bright Falls Mysteries, Book 1)
An American Weredeer in Michigan (The Bright Falls Mysteries, Book 2)
A Nightmare on Elk Street (The Bright Falls Mysteries, Book 3)

Esoterrorism (Red Room, Vol. 1)
Eldritch Ops (Red Room, Vol. 2)
The Fall of the House (Red Room, Vol. 3)

Agent G: Infiltrator (Agent G, Vol. 1)
Agent G: Saboteur (Agent G, Vol. 2)
Agent G: Assassin (Agent G, Vol. 3)

Cthulhu Armageddon (Cthulhu Armageddon, Vol. 1)
The Tower of Zhaal (Cthulhu Armageddon, Vol. 2)

Lucifer's Star (Lucifer's Star, Vol. 1)
Lucifer's Nebula (Lucifer's Star, Vol. 2)

Straight Outta Fangton (Straight Outta Fangton, Vol. 1)
100 Miles and Vampin' (Straight Outta Fangton, Vol. 2)
Vampiraz4Life (Straight Outta Fangton, Vol. 3)

Wraith Knight (Wraith Knight, Vol. 1)
Wraith Lord (Wraith Knight, Vol. 2)
Wraith King (Wraith Knight, Vol. 3)

Predestiny (Predestiny, Vol. 1)
Lost Future (Predestiny, Vol. 2)

Brightblade (The Morgan Detective Agency, Book 1)

Space Academy Dropouts (The Space Academy Series, Book 1)
Space Academy Rejects (The Space Academy Series, Book 2)
Space Academy Washouts (The Space Academy Series, Book 3)

Psycho Killers in Love

Anthologies (as editor)

Blackest Knights
Blackest Spells
Tales of Capes and Cowls
Tales of the Al-Azif
Tales of Yog-Sothoth

CROSSROAD
PRESS